Michael Hetzer

simon & schuster

The Forbidden Zone

a novel

 SIMON & SCHUSTER
Rockefeller Center
1230 Avenue of the Americas
New York, NY 10020

SIMON & SCHUSTER and colophon are registered trademarks
of Simon & Schuster Inc.

Designed by Karolina Harris

Manufactured in the United States of America

10 9 8 7 6 5 4 3 2 1

Library of Congress Cataloging-in-Publication Data
Hetzer, Michael.
    The forbidden zone : a novel / Michael Hetzer.
       p.   cm.
    I. Title.
PS3558.E7992F67   1999
813'.54 — dc21   98-37107
                                                      CIP

ISBN 0-684-85408-2

"Courage" by Anna Akhmatova and "We're no good at saying good-bye" by Anna Akhmatova, from *The Portable Twentieth Century Russian Reader*, ed. by Clarence Brown, copyright © 1985 by Viking Penguin, Inc. Used by permission of Viking Penguin, a division of Penguin Putnam Inc.

Acknowledgments

The earliest draft of this novel was written at Dom Tvorchestva, *House of Creativity*, a writer's colony outside Moscow operated by the writer's union of Russia. I am deeply indebted to the Russian novelists, journalists and poets who took such an interest in the first novel of an *amerikanyets* writing on a subject many of them would like to forget. Their passionate arguments shaped my first draft in ways I will never fully know.

I also wish to thank:

Alexander Podrabinek for his insights into Soviet psychiatric hospitals, and for the loan of his many books on the subject.

(Ret.) KGB General Oleg Kalugin, for his tantalizing glimpse into the shadowy world of the Komitet Gosudarstvennoy Bezopasnosti, the KGB.

The Amsterdam-based group, International Association on the Political Use of Psychiatry, for its invaluable publications and trove of verbatim transcripts of patient interviews.

All my talented and dedicated colleagues at *The Moscow Times*, but in particular Derk Sauer and Meg Bortin, who supported my year "on the road" in Russia without which this book would have turned out very differently. And to Doug Greene and Taylor Maxwell, who accepted my decision to write this book with a great deal more grace than I had a right to expect.

My circle of readers—Janice, Anne, Walter, Steven, Conrad, Bob, Larry, Joe and Jana.

Marysue Rucci, my editor at Simon & Schuster, who made the final stretch of the journey the best part.

Victoria Sanders, my agent. In a perfect world, every writer would have such an agent.

And finally, my wife, Tamara. We made this journey together, and her light illuminates every page.

To the world, "sputnik" is a proper noun, the world's first artificial satellite, harbinger of the space age. But in Russian, the word is ancient and means "traveling companion."

And so I dedicate this novel to the sputnik of my life, Tamara, my wife.

The U.S.S.R. in 1983

Laptev Sea

Yenisey

River

Lena River

S.   R.

Russia

Lena   River

Ust-Nera .

Oimyakon •

Yakutsk .

Stepan's Cabin ▪

• **Novosibirsk**

Lake Baikal

M O N G O L I A

C H I N A

©1998 Jeffrey L. Ward

Sea of
Japan

N. KOREA

S. KOREA

JAPAN

part i

The Vow

1

April 3, 1983
Oimyakon Province, Eastern Siberia

. . . and beside our cabin a stream rushes over the icy rocks and brave weeds five miles down Suntar Ridge before emptying into the headwaters of the Upper Tunga River. But on that stretch of river before the junction, where it passes by our cabin, it has never been named. So I would propose to call it Nadia's River, after my wife. And because "nadia" is short for nadezhda, *which means "hope," the name also comes out River of Hope. Oh, what irony! And perhaps all my misery could be justified if only there were to appear on Soviet maps, in the midst of this long-suffering, hope-starved land, a river bearing such a name.*

In the dim candlelight of the tiny cabin, the man with the stub nose put down his pencil and rubbed his old eyes. He had no desire to write this, to second-guess fate. What was the point? To live was to suffer. The only surprise was that any light at all should shine in the darkness.

But he wasn't doing this for himself. It was for Nadia.

Stepan Bragin looked up from his manuscript and surveyed his cabin. It was built in the style of a Mongolian yurt—a hexagonal room with timber walls and no windows (which was why he worked by candlelight, though the sun shone outside). Furniture ringed the walls creating areas that passed for a bedroom, a kitchen and a den. In the center, an iron stove crackled pleasantly, filling the air with the scent of pine. The cabin was little more than a hunter's hut, but in Siberia the supreme luxury was warmth, and in this respect the little yurt might as well have been a palace.

Stepan went on with his work. It was excruciating. He wrote in English, so each word had to be exhumed from the cemetery of his mind. It had been decades since his thoughts had spoken to him in his native tongue, and now, to face the strangeness of those foreign words was to gaze back across a tundra of lost years to someone he barely knew, to a man he used to be.

After several hours, he could write no more, and he put down his pencil. He looked toward his wife.

Nadia lay on the pine bed he had built for her in a desperate bid to improve her comfort now that she was bedridden. Her eyes were open, and she was watching him.

He smiled. "You're awake."

"I didn't want to disturb you," she said. "You were so intent."

"Yes, well . . ." he said and slammed closed the book. He didn't finish the thought. Instead he stretched his arms and yawned noisily.

Nadia wasn't fooled. "What were you doing?"

Stepan knew where the question was leading, and he changed the subject. He pointed at the bed. "We never made love on this bed."

Nadia smiled wearily. "Some other time, dear."

Stepan blinked at that, and he looked at her as though for the first time. Her skin, pale from her long illness, was still as brown as milk chocolate. She had a round, dinner-plate face, and coal-black eyes that were oriental in shape. She was not a beautiful woman; her face was puffy and her eyes were too far apart. Her build, invisible beneath the blankets, was squat, like a large dwarf. But she would always be Stepan's Mongolian angel, and looking at her then, as always, brought a lump to his throat.

Stepan went to her and sat down on the edge of the bed. He straightened the blanket over her chest. "Are you cold?"

"Stepan, I want to talk about what I said last night."

He grimaced. "All right. But first, let me get some wood for the stove."

"Don't be long."

He jumped to his feet and hurried out.

It was late morning on Suntar Ridge, and the sunlight danced on the snow. Stepan was relieved to be outdoors, away from the cloud of death that hung within the cabin. He had spent his life watching men die, yet his spirit had never wholly hardened to the pitiless brutality of that last desperate struggle, though sometime after his twentieth mass grave it did get easier. Leave it to Nadia to make him feel the pain all over again.

The thought shamed him. It was a grim business, this, but grief was the price he had to pay for his return to the world of men. He had always known there would be a price. In a few minutes, Nadia would ask an even greater price of him, and he couldn't think of how to refuse. It terrified him.

Stepan crunched over the snow to the wood pile, where he spent several minutes picking through the logs for just the right mix, as though choosing well could somehow make everything right again. To his left, a small stream ran, the starting point for the melting snow's violent, thousand-mile journey to the Arctic

Sea. Stepan thought about what he had written that morning and realized he was pleased with the portion about naming the river after Nadia. Of course, it was too much to hope that such a thing would ever come to pass, but what an idea! He smiled at his audacity.

He looked at the stream. It had begun to flow briskly with spring runoff. It occurred to him suddenly that he had lived through another Siberian winter. The thought brought him no comfort.

He filled his arms and went back into the cabin. He set the wood beside the stove and then pushed two logs into the hearth. He latched the grate and stood up to stretch his back.

He turned toward Nadia, and his blood went cold. Her eyes were squeezed shut and her face was contorted in pain.

"Nadia!" he cried and ran to her side.

"Oh, god," she said and arched forward into a sitting position.

Stepan took her hand. Her grip tightened like a vise. She gasped and fought the pain as though it were an enemy trying to possess her body. Stepan sat helplessly beside her willing her sickness to pass through her hand into his body. But it would not, and the invisible enemy remained hidden within her.

He cursed the cruelty of his fate. Here he sat, sixty years old and as healthy as a Siberian buffalo, while his young bride withered away before his eyes.

The spasm passed, and Nadia fell panting back onto the bed. Stepan took a cloth from the bedside table and dabbed her forehead.

"They're getting worse," he said.

Nadia nodded.

"Perhaps I could get the doctor to come out and see —"

"He won't come."

He knew she was right. Their cabin rested in one of the most remote places on earth, the Oimyakon province of Yakutia in eastern Siberia. There were only two ways to reach them — by helicopter or jeep. No one was going to pay for a helicopter, and the eight-hour jeep ride . . . well, it wasn't going to happen. Not for a terminal cancer patient.

For the moment at least, Nadia was at peace. She looked at Stepan, and he braced himself for what was coming.

"Have you thought about what I asked?" she said.

Stepan dropped his eyes. He had thought of little else.

"Oh, Nadia," he said. "I'm so old."

"Stepan, look at me."

He raised his head.

"I'm not dying," she said.

Stepan stared blankly at her.

"It looks that way, I'll grant you," she said with a thin smile. "But that's just our narrow point of view. What we call death is part of a migration, like a reindeer going to the taiga in winter."

This last analogy seemed to please her. Nadia was an Urguma Eskimo, a nomadic people who lived by herding reindeer across the tundra.

Stepan smiled too. He loved it when she talked like this, even if he didn't understand half of what she was saying. She had a reassuring voice that rose and fell like notes in a melody. Her pronunciation was strangely clipped, which betrayed that she was not a native Russian speaker. But then, neither was he.

"We're all gods making a great journey," she said.

"To where?"

"Heaven."

Stepan sighed. He wished he could believe that with one-tenth of Nadia's conviction. Like all her people, Nadia was animistic. Gods moved everything: the snow, the sun, the grass and the sky. Her Soviet education, with its foundation of atheism, had failed to dislodge this faith. And how could it? Nadia didn't just *believe* in this world of the gods of the lower case, she *inhabited* it. Stepan, on the other hand, had lived his life among men, and he had seen little there that could be called magical. Men were animals. They lived like animals; they treated each other like animals; and they died like animals.

A gust rattled the door, but inside the cabin it remained warm. Stepan could hear the logs cracking in the hearth, logs he had split last summer, back when Nadia's illness first began to reveal itself, back when there was still hope . . .

"Maybe you're right," he said.

"So you'll do it?"

He could, of course, say "yes," and then not carry through. Who would fault him for a merciful lie made to appease a superstitious, dying woman? Anyone could see that her request was unreasonable. Stepan was not even a free man. The land his wife loved, the land of her gods, was the land of his exile. Siberia was Stepan's prison. Its severe climate, isolation and unfathomable immensity kept him locked away behind walls more insurmountable than anything men could have built.

But could he betray Nadia, even with a lie of mercy? She had loved him, *him!*, the man with the stub nose, the man whose nose had fallen away from frostbite.

What had she seen in him? He had often pondered that mystery. After all those years in the prison camps he had hardened into something that was only barely a man. He was like a piece of fruit whose pit had grown and grown until there was no fruit left at all, just the hard pit nobody wanted. But she had wanted him. She had married him and given him four years of happiness. After the misery of his life, *there* was a miracle.

So the question of her extracting a promise had never really been in doubt.

He would give her his word, and what's more, the vow would be kept. That's what the manuscript was all about. It was his insurance.

Nadia believed that in order for Stepan's soul to ascend to heaven, his earthly body had to be buried in the land of his birth. For Stepan, that meant a long journey to a place he had nearly forgotten, to a land where they spoke a different language, and where he was known by another name.

Stepan smiled bravely and patted Nadia's hand. "We swore eternity, my love."

Nadia closed her eyes and sighed. "Thank you."

And then from somewhere far, far away, she said, "The spirits have kept you alive for a purpose, Stepan. Perhaps in this quest you will at last find it."

Nadia fell asleep, and Stepan went back to his papers.

That evening, she awoke feeling better. She sipped some reindeer broth and then told Stepan stories about her life as a child in an Urguma tribe. She laughed when she talked about her soft-hearted father, Yulan, and how awkwardly he carried the stiff-lipped banner of tribal chief. Gradually, her voice weakened, until at last she fell asleep. Stepan sat beside her a long time watching her chest rise and fall with increasing unevenness. The end was near. He held her hand and waited. As the night wore on, her breathing grew more and more labored.

Suddenly, the howl of a faraway wolf echoed over the mountain, and Nadia stirred. Stepan searched her face, thinking she was about to open her eyes. Instead, she gasped once and then never breathed again.

Nadia was dead.

Stepan laid his head on her chest, and, for the first time in longer than he could remember, he wept.

Dawn came slowly to Siberia, and the sun hid below the horizon like a shy child. In the gray light of predawn, Stepan carried Nadia's body onto the mountainside and set it on the ice beside the stream. He dug until he reached frozen ground. Then he built a small fire to melt the soil. After the fire died to cinders, he dug with a pickax beneath the ash. He repeated the process four more times, sweating with the effort, but refusing to rest. His grief had given him a rare clarity, and from that he drew strength.

After an hour, he had a rectangular hole about three feet deep — deep enough to keep away the wolves. He lowered Nadia's body over the edge and placed it at his feet. The ground still steamed from the scars made by his ax. He climbed out of the grave and began to fill it up. Finally, he gathered rocks from the stream and piled them atop the mound in the traditional way of the Urguma people.

He stood back to look at his work.

Suddenly, a gust of wind swirled over the grave, lifting snow high into the sky. His eye followed it up, and that made him think about what Nadia had said the previous night. She was on her way to heaven, for her body rested in the land of her birth. The thought made him feel better. Then something occurred to him that made him smile. There might have been another reason he agreed to make the long trip to his own birthplace:

What if she were right?

He raised his head from the grave and looked up into the pale sky.

"Bon voyage, my love," he said.

F o r the next five months, the man with the stub nose traveled west. His route was a bit unorthodox, but it got him past the KGB checkpoints. It amused him to think of the mystery his escape from Oimyakon would present to someone in Moscow.

Just ten miles east of the Norwegian border on the Kolsky Peninsula, 130 miles north of the Arctic Circle, Stepan Bragin came at last to a stop. He had been pushing through the swamps—an unfamiliar hazard—when he fell into quick-sand and nearly drowned. Though he was maddeningly near to his objective, he decided to camp beside a stream until the weather turned cold and the marshes froze. If nothing else, Siberia had taught Stepan patience and a respect for nature's dispassionate regard for the frailty of man.

He speared trout and snared rabbits, cooking them over low fires he built at night. Helicopter patrols passed over several times a day, but the slicing *thumpa-thumpa* of their rotors gave Stepan plenty of warning to take cover in the rocks. One morning, after a month, he awoke to find the ground covered by a thin layer of snow. He was once again on terrain he knew well. He moved on.

He reached the border with Norway two days later. The forest suddenly ended, and he found himself looking across a man-made clearing about twenty yards wide. He frowned at what he saw: two barbed-wire fences, ten feet apart, and, between them, a *zapretnaya zona*, a forbidden zone. It was just like in the camps; any man caught in the forbidden zone would be shot immediately. He had seen many men commit suicide that way. There was dignity in the death certificate that read, "Shot while trying to escape." But there was no guard tower here, just a frozen road running along the outside of the first fence. The fences were each twelve feet high with long-needled barbed wire woven into the chain links like a pattern in a sweater. At the top and bottom, barbed-wire strands spiraled like thistled springs.

He waited all day and night for sight of a border-guard patrol, but except for the helicopters, none came. Then he understood. The border guards were count-ing on nature to do their work for them. They hadn't counted on Stepan Bragin.

Stepan snapped a birch branch from a tree and, sweeping the snow to cover his tracks, walked to the base of the fence. He took a rabbit from his pouch and tossed it against the wire. He turned and retreated quickly to the forest, again covering his tracks with the branch. The trail faded almost immediately as the wind polished the surface of the snow. Stepan began to count.

Five minutes later, a jeep crested the rise in the north and sped along the road to the point where the rabbit lay. Two soldiers in gray uniforms armed with Kalashnikov machine guns got out. One man spotted the rabbit and rolled it over with his foot. From his hiding place at the edge of the forest, Stepan could hear their voices. They looked around. Their eyes fell on the foliage surrounding Stepan. He held his breath. They looked away. One of them picked up the rabbit and threw it in the jeep. They got in, did a U-turn, and sped back north. A minute later, the jeep disappeared over the hill. All was again quiet.

Stepan lay there and thought. So the fence had impact sensors. That gave him five minutes to climb the two fences. Was it enough time?

Oh, Nadia. I'm so old.

He shook his head. A young man might have been able to scale the fences, but Stepan would never make it—one fence maybe, but not two, not in five minutes. He had to find another way. How? He gazed at the fence a long time, weighing options, calculating. The ground was too frozen for a tunnel. He didn't have the tools to cut through the wire, and even if he had, five minutes was not much time. Suddenly, he remembered a prison break he had heard about many years ago. Yes, he decided, it might work.

Stepan began to gather small logs, roughly the diameter of his forearm, until he had several dozen in a neat pile. He got his reindeer-bone hatchet from his backpack and went to work notching the wood. He worked until nightfall, then ate some of his cooked rabbit meat and went to sleep. In the morning, he returned to work.

One of the skills he had learned in the camps was carpentry. Four times during his long confinement in the gulag, he had been forced to construct new camps out of the bare forest. That meant building barracks, bunks, towers, fences, furniture—you name it, Stepan had built it using tools not much better than his little hatchet.

It took him four days to complete his task. And as he chipped and fitted the wood joints, he was free to look back over the long, tortuous road that had led him there.

Prague, 1944. Moscow, 1945. Siberia, 1946.

Nearly forty years.

He thought of his first seven years in Siberia. They had been the worst; he had spent them in solitary confinement in that cell with the green bed and the dirt floor so cold—like frozen beef—he was forced to stay in his bed. When he thought about it, he could still smell the acid mustiness of the clay. Once, during those long years, he had forgotten his name. He had gone to bed that night praying he would remember it when he awoke. Mercifully, he had. He had been tempted then to write his name on the wall, lest he forget it again, but he didn't dare; his true identity was the curse of his life.

That cell had burned down in 1953.

The things he had seen! He had watched a nineteen-year-old guard beat his best friend to death with a shovel. He had endured strip searches in temperatures of sixty degrees below zero. He had watched once-vital men lie down in the snow and refuse to get up no matter how much the guards beat them. He had once seen a man driven to such despair he had committed suicide by stabbing himself in the stomach over and over again with a piece of rusted sheet metal.

True, there had been instances of kindness. A physician who had been treating Stepan for pneumonia had risked becoming a prisoner himself by smuggling in two potatoes and a piece of pork. It was this, not the hospital bed, that had saved Stepan. But such moments were like the yellow taiga flowers that pushed up through the ice. Stepan had never seen a prisoner who didn't grind them beneath his boot.

At the end of the fourth day, Stepan finished his work and stepped back to inspect the result. Before him were two fourteen-foot-high ladders—one self-standing, the other a simple stepladder. He tested them in the forest, bouncing with all his weight on the rungs. They held. He practiced carrying the straight ladder on his back as he climbed the standing ladder. It was clumsy, but after a few tries he mastered it. From the top of the ladder he looked down and winced as he thought of how his ankles would fare in the fall. He thought of Nadia, and his resolve was restored.

Night descended like a velvet curtain, and he crawled under his blanket. He looked up at the stars a long time going over in his mind his plan for the next day. When at last he fell asleep, he dreamed of Nadia. She came to him dressed in her traditional Urguma costume of reindeer hide. She floated six inches over the snow like a brown-skinned angel of the north.

"Come, Stepan," she called out.

He tried to reach her but a barbed-wire fence separated them. The mesh of the wire was so tight he couldn't even drive a finger through it.

"I can't," he said. "I'm too old."

She spoke to him again, but this time she didn't call him "Stepan." With a shock, he realized she was using his other name.

Donald . . . Donald.

He screamed. He sat up straight and listened as his own cry echoed through the forest. He was terrified—from the dream as well as the thought that he had given himself away to the border guards. He sat a long time panting and waiting for the sound of a jeep or helicopter. But the forest remained silent. He looked around and realized with a start that dawn had come.

It was time.

Snow fell lightly as Stepan carried his ladders to the base of the fence. He didn't bother to cover his tracks. He set up the stepladder and then snaked his arms through the rungs of the straight ladder, using it for balance like a tightrope-walker's pole. He began to climb. At the top he looked out over the swirling barbed wire. He flung the straight ladder over the fence into the forbidden zone. It landed silently in the snow. He counted to three and flung himself over the fence. As he pushed off, his stepladder fell backward. He sailed out into space.

He landed hard and rolled. His left ankle exploded in pain.

Ahhh!

He clutched the ankle. It was as crooked as a dog's hind leg. Broken. Damn. He lay there a while panting. He didn't worry about the border guards: he had not tripped the impact sensors, so he had time for a short rest. Then he would drag himself and his straight ladder across the forbidden zone to the next fence. The second ladder, of course, would trip the sensors, but he would have five minutes before the border guards arrived. By then, he and his broken ankle would be in Norway.

He lay there a while catching his breath, massaging his ankle. He rolled over and looked back through the fence. He gasped.

The stepladder was leaning *against the fence*. He understood at once what had happened. When he had pushed off to jump, the stepladder had rocked and then fallen *forward*.

The impact sensors! The border guards were already on their way!

How long had he lain there?

He got to his feet and gingerly put weight on the broken ankle. It buckled, and he nearly fell. He tried again. It was no use; the ankle was worthless.

And he had to hurry.

He hopped to the ladder, which lay on the snow where it had fallen. He wedged his broken ankle between the rungs and took a deep breath. He closed his eyes.

"Nadia," he whispered, and then threw his body hard to his right. His ankle, caught between the rungs, twisted sharply. The pain nearly caused him to pass out.

He tried the ankle. Still, it buckled.

They're coming!

He put his foot back in the ladder and tried again, this time twisting even harder.

The ankle popped, and he dropped to the ground. He probed it with his frozen fingers. The joint was back in place. He got to his feet and tried it out. It could take weight now, though every step was agony.

He picked up the ladder and began to limp toward the second fence. Through the net of barbed wire he could see minute details on the snow — ice patches, dirt, bits of sand.

Norwegian sand.

The thought gave him strength. He reached the fence and raised the ladder against it. He began to climb.

Halfway up, he heard the distant whine of a jeep engine. His heart raced.

He got to the top of the ladder and swung his right foot onto the fence. He stood a moment atop the crossbar and then jumped.

He landed, and this time the pain in his ankle was something unbelievable. Tears clouded his eyes and then promptly froze in his lashes.

He pulled himself into a sitting position against the fence. He felt like a corpse who had risen from his grave and was now relaxing against his headstone. It occurred to him that's how the world would see him: a man returning from the dead.

You made it!

He tipped back his head and let a snowflake drop on his tongue. He turned his head and gazed east through the fences toward the Soviet Union. At that moment, he could feel no bitterness. His enemies were all dead. Hitler was dead. Stalin was dead. The men who had replaced Stalin were dead. The guards who beat him, who drove him like an animal, who starved and humiliated him — they were dead too. He had outlived them all. There was no one left to hate.

There's still one.

No, he wouldn't think about him now. The time had come for the man with the stub nose to say good-bye to Stepan Bragin. It was time to rediscover the identity he had buried so long ago in that cell with the green bed and the frozen floor. But now he found himself strangely reluctant. After all, if he hadn't become Stepan Bragin he wouldn't have met Nadia.

He raised his head and shouted, *"Ya yeshcho chelovek!"* Then, just for the thrill of it, he repeated the phrase in English, savoring the alien, near-forgotten sounds as they escaped his throat. "I am still a man!"

He paused, half-expecting a response.

Then a voice cried out in Russian, "Get out of there, you fool! They're coming!"

He flinched. *What? A voice here?*

A jeep crested the hill and sped along the access road on the far side of the two fences.

Stepan got slowly to his feet, balancing on his good leg. Through the barbed-wire he watched, confused, as the jeep bore down on him.

"Halt!" one of the border guards cried.

But he was safe, wasn't he? They were in the U.S.S.R. and he was in Norway—

Thwing. The first bullet whistled by him like a bottle rocket.

My god! They're shooting across the border!

He turned to flee, but his ankle buckled under him and he went down. The pain shot up his leg all the way to his hip. He scrambled back to his feet and began to hobble away. He took four agonizing steps and then something hit him in his shoulder blade. It felt like a punch. Another blow struck the arch of his back. He fell.

He must have passed out, because the next thing he knew he was being rolled onto his back. He opened his eyes. A young man with a black beard and shining, deep-set eyes knelt over him. He wore civilian clothes.

"You're still alive," said the stranger.

"Bastards shot me," Stepan groaned.

"I saw."

A snowflake fell into Stepan's eye, and he blinked. As his vision cleared, a strange clarity washed over him. He lay on the snow, yet his body was warm. He could feel where the bullets had pierced him, but he felt no pain. Even his ankle had stopped throbbing.

"Who are you?" Stepan asked. His voice gurgled.

"That doesn't matter," said the stranger.

Stepan grabbed the stranger's wrist. "Answer me!"

"I'm like you," said the stranger. "A border dasher."

"How . . ."

"From the forest—I was watching you. I used your ladders to follow you over."

The stranger glanced anxiously to the north. "They'll be back in a few minutes. They had to circle up the road to the gate at A-1, about a mile. We have to get you out of here!"

"I don't understand," said Stepan. "Isn't this Norway?"

"This is the Soviet Union. You're in the forbidden zone."

"I thought—"

"There's another fence, further west."

"A third fence," said Stepan. "Damn."

The stranger frowned. "Can I move you?"

"It doesn't matter."

"Of course it matters!"

"No," said Stepan. The alertness held, but he couldn't know for how long. He had to do something. Stepan asked, "Can you make it to Norway now?"

The stranger looked west, calculating. He shook his head. "It's too far. There isn't time."

"Can you go back?"

"I think so."

"Good, you can try again later," said Stepan. "Right?"

"I guess."

"Right?" Stepan demanded, his voice rising to a wheeze.

"Yes, right. I'll try again tomorrow."

"Good. Now, do you want to help me?"

"Sure, but—"

"How much time do we have?"

"A few minutes . . . maybe."

"Okay. Listen."

For the next three minutes, Stepan gave his testimony to the bearded stranger. The man listened carefully. He had intelligent, trustworthy eyes. Stepan began to wonder if he hadn't been lucky, after all. Perhaps this was how it was meant to be.

Stepan finished and pressed a small pouch into the stranger's palm.

The stranger looked at it. "What's this?"

"Something that is of no use to me. Now go!"

"I can't just leave—"

"Go!" he said, and, in the distance, an engine raced. "They're coming!"

The stranger stood up.

"Your name?" asked Stepan. "What is your name?"

"Anton Perov."

"Anton Perov," he repeated. "May the gods be with us both, Anton Perov."

Anton took a last look at Stepan and darted back east to the fence. Stepan watched as the stranger scaled the fence. Clever boy. He wore heavy gloves and several layers of clothing to protect him from the barbs. He had powerful arms that lifted him up the fence like a spider in a web. Ah, to be young. Anton reached the top, swung his legs over and scampered down. He dropped the last few feet to the ground and gazed back through the fence at Stepan.

The sound of the jeep grew louder.

"Go!" cried Stepan.

With a last look back, Anton darted for the eastern fence. Stepan shut his eyes. The jeep drew nearer. Minutes passed. He heard men's voices.

"Over here!" a voice said excitedly.

Stepan looked up into the falling snow. Slowly, out of the dance of falling flakes, the figure of his wife appeared floating over him. She looked afraid.

"Don't despair, Nadia," he whispered. "There is still hope."

She nodded. Then her figure faded and coalesced into a man looking down at him. He wore a gray uniform and held a machine gun.

"We got him," he said.

2

Six months later
April 15, 1984

T h e pilot spoke in Russian. The announcement was short, and when he finished an icy hush fell over the plane.

In her seat, Katherine Sears flipped through the pages of her Russian-English dictionary trying to translate what had been said. It was hopeless. She might have let the matter pass but for the reaction of the passengers, which couldn't have been more chilling if the pilot had just informed them that an engine had failed.

Katherine gave up and turned to the Russian man beside her. "Excuse me, what did he say?"

The man removed the plastic headphones from his ears and raised his eyebrows. "You *do* talk," he said in accented English. "I sit here whole flight from London — four hours! — and you not say anything. I think, 'I must talk with this pretty lady.' But then I think, 'Don't embarrass her; maybe she's a mute.'"

"I'm sorry. Is there a problem with the plane? I mean, the captain's announcement . . ."

"Everything — A-okay," the man grinned. "The captain said: 'Now we enter Soviet airspace.'"

"Oh." Katherine felt a moment of relief, and then her stomach twisted into a knot. In less than an hour she would be in Moscow. She wondered for the millionth time if she was really up to this.

He frowned at her. "You don't like to fly?"

"Why do you say that?"

He pointed at the napkin on the tray in front of her. It was shredded to confetti. She smiled thinly and brushed the paper into her empty drink cup. She raised the tray and put the cup neatly in the pocket.

The man watched her. "You are American?"

"Yes," she said.

"You don't speak Russian?"

"Not really. I know a bit from my father."

"He's an immigrant?"

"No. An academic, a sovietologist."

"Really? I'm an economist with the Institute of the U.S.A. and Canada."

Katherine's heart sank. Christ! The man was a KGB informant, if not an outright spy! Now she was in a bind. Katherine remembered what they had told her in Amsterdam: Never volunteer information. God, she was such a fool. What was she doing here? She was an astronomer, not a spy. Had a more poorly prepared agent ever been sent into the fray of the Cold War? If so, Katherine pitied the poor bastard. She braced herself for the inevitable next question. The man obliged immediately.

"What's his name?" the man asked.

She tried to act nonchalant. "Sears."

"*Jack* Sears!" he exclaimed.

Katherine nodded.

"Lord!" the man said and then began to mumble to himself in Russian. He made no further attempt to talk to her.

Katherine turned and looked out the window. Thirty thousand feet below, the muddy, untended fields of Belorussia slid past. The lifeless sight did nothing to lift her spirits.

A p r i l is Moscow's ugliest month. Snow retreats to reveal four months of uncollected garbage, carcasses of animals, excrement and a layer of grime that clings to everything like paint. Trees, mostly bony poplars, are still a month from their first bud. The only birds are Soviet ravens, large gray-black scavengers that screech like crows and present a threat to small cats. The world is devoid of color; all is either the featureless gray of the overcast sky or the chocolate brown of mud. City morgues bustle from suicides.

Katherine Sears's plane touched down at Sheremetyevo-2 Airport on a cloudy afternoon in mid-April. She came through the gate past an official in an olive-green uniform. Their eyes met, and she looked away.

Oh, that was slick. You're already acting suspicious.

A voice called out from a corner. "Katherine!"

She turned. It was Olga, her tour guide.

Olga had met Katherine and the other eleven Americans in her tour group while in London's Heathrow Airport. Olga had taken command at once, ordering them about like privates in her little platoon. Already some members of the tour group were calling her Sergeant Olga. Katherine was depressed to see how vigilant her guide was. Perhaps posing as a tourist had been a bad strategy. But what choice did she have? It was the only way to get a visa. Katherine supposed that if she were a real spy, then the American embassy could have given her a cover as a diplomat or an academic. But as it was she had only a few Dutch radicals to help her. It was Intourist — or nothing.

"Over here!" Olga cried.

Katherine joined the others in the corner, where Olga was assembling the group.

"Did you enjoy your flight, Dr. Sears?" Olga asked. Olga spoke in a nasal falsetto that Katherine found grating. Olga had gone to pains to make herself stylish, but her stumpy frame, poorly bleached hair and heavy makeup undermined the effort. Katherine would have been afraid of her even without Titus Waal's assertion that all Intourist guides worked for the KGB. Thinking of Titus gave Katherine resolve. Of all the men in Amsterdam, only Titus had believed in her. Katherine feared he would have been disappointed with her performance so far.

Katherine smiled at Olga and said, "The flight was nice, thank you."

"Splendid!"

Olga collected their passports and visas, counted heads and then herded her wide-eyed Americans to the security gate.

The passport control officer, a bony-faced boy in an olive-green uniform, scowled at Katherine a long time, comparing her passport photo to her face. Finally, he handed back her passport and visa minus the entry portion. The little gate in front of her clicked, and she pushed through. In front of her, over the baggage claim conveyer, a sign said "Welcome to Moscow." Her stomach tightened again.

After passport control, Olga counted heads again and then moved the group to baggage claim. Once everyone had their bags, Olga counted heads again and took them to customs check-in. Everywhere, special lines opened up before the group, and then vanished when the last of them passed through. Olga worked the airport like an army general, barking orders in Russian at anyone who strayed onto her battlefield. At least Katherine *assumed* Olga was shouting in Russian. Katherine understood little that was said. Growing up, her father's insistence that his daughter learn Russian was one of the few edicts in the Sears household that wasn't taken seriously. But Jack Sears had his revenge. Whenever one of "Dad's Russians" was at the house, her father quizzed her language skills with the guest. Inevitably, it ended in embarrassment. Now, with Katherine's new interest in Russia, she had been pleased to discover that at least some of what she had learned as a girl lingered in her mind.

Not enough.

That accusation had been leveled at her the previous day in London. Koos, Titus's boss, had flown in from Amsterdam to give her the contact codes for her mission to Moscow. It was the first time they had met, and his displeasure had gone even further than her poor Russian. "Look at her!" he had exclaimed. "She's a fucking princess. Moscow will eat her alive. She'll wash up like driftwood on the steps of the American embassy begging for a Big Mac and fries."

Katherine had listened mortified.

Titus was unmoved. He had brought her in, trained her and now he seemed prepared to stand behind her. "This is no time for anti-Americanism, Koos."

"Fuck America, and fuck her," said Koos. "This has nothing to do with that. She'll blow the whole network. She'll get . . ." he lowered his voice, ". . . you-know-who killed."

In the end, Titus had prevailed and Katherine had been given the contacts she needed for the trip. Now she wondered if Koos hadn't been right after all.

At the customs desk Katherine's canvas carry-on bag came up for inspection. A uniformed official unzipped the side pocket and poked around. He took out a Pushkin anthology given to her by Titus. Katherine tensed. But the official didn't flip through the pages, so he didn't find the envelopes tucked there. He nodded, and Katherine picked up her book, closed the bag and moved on.

At length, eleven Americans found themselves standing on the central promenade of Sheremetyevo-2 Airport, surrounded by their bags, waiting like foot soldiers for their next command from Sergeant Olga, who counted heads and then guided them out the front door and onto an idling bus with the word "Intourist" on the side. Olga counted heads again, gave an order to the driver and they were off. It occurred to Katherine, as the bus pulled away from the curb, that in all the hectic business of getting through the airport, she hadn't spoken a word to anyone but Olga.

Is this how Moscow would be?

Katherine rode with her face pressed against the window. She saw featureless housing blocks and, occasionally, store fronts with signs like "Bread," "Sausage," "Tailor," and "Watch Repair." At least she could read the signs. They *did*, after all, speak Russian in Russia.

Her first glimpse of the Worker's Paradise was everything she had expected — gloomy, oppressive and sinister. She had grown up hearing nightmarish stories of the evil empire from her father, one of the staunchest anti-Soviet warriors of the Cold War. Jack Sears had made this trip dozens of times — under the protection of the U.S. Embassy, of course. Katherine had never thought she would see the U.S.S.R. with her own eyes. Now she wished she had paid closer attention to his "sermons," as her mother called them: One thing was certain: If Jack Sears had known where his daughter was and what she was planning to do, he would have dragged her home, and then checked her into a psychiatric clinic. Before she left the States, Katherine had told him only that she would be attending an astronomy symposium in London. If all went well, she would be back in London for the last day of the meeting, and then she would return home on schedule to her teaching post at Cornell University. No one—least of all her father—would ever know about her detour to Moscow.

An hour later, the bus reached the hotel, which was located directly across from Red Square. Katherine got off the bus and, like everyone, gawked at the sight of the mad, swirling onion domes of St. Basil's Cathedral.

"Come on," Olga said impatiently. "We'll see all that tomorrow." She counted heads again and led them into the hotel lobby. On the way, they passed two security guards.

After check-in, Katherine passed another security guard—this one seated at the elevators. The guard got on the elevator and rode with her to the eleventh floor. There Katherine faced an old woman behind a small table. Katherine got out and the elevator guard went back down to the lobby. Everywhere, eyes were upon her, and Katherine began to appreciate Titus's warning that slipping away undetected would be difficult.

Katherine gave the woman a slip of paper she had received downstairs. The woman handed Katherine a key. Katherine went along the dim corridor over a threadbare runner to her room. She unlocked the door and went inside. She put her back against the door and closed her eyes.

She had made it. She was in Moscow. The impatience, the sleepless nights, the endless preparations—they were over at last.

It was time to act.

O l g a gave the group an hour to freshen up for dinner. There were plenty of groans at that, but Olga insisted that the antidote to jet lag was motion.

"You must stay up as late as possible the first night and then sleep no later than nine o'clock the following morning," said Olga. "I'll see to it."

No one doubted she would.

"Time is so little," Olga had said.

Katherine agreed with that. Three short days. She needed to get to work immediately.

In her room, she threw her suitcase on the bed and went downstairs, past the old woman and the security guard, to the reception desk. She had seen pay phones outside the hotel so now she asked what kind of money was needed.

"Oh no, no," said the clerk. "You don't need money. No. You may call from your room."

Titus had warned her against using phones inside the hotel.

"Yes, I realize that. I was just wondering—"

"So. Good day, then." He turned his back on her.

Katherine sighed and looked around the lobby. The hotel offered five-star services like an atrium café, concierge and service desk, but the atrium café was closed, the concierge was absent, and the woman behind the service desk was reading a novel. There was a garden with a broken fountain, and even from twenty feet away Katherine could see that the plants were plastic. Katherine spied three courtesy phones on the wall. It was tempting to use them, but too risky. She would make her call later, she decided. She went back to her room and slept like the dead.

An hour later, Katherine and the rest of the hollow-eyed group were assembled in the lobby. Olga counted heads and told them they would walk to a nearby Georgian restaurant called the Aragvi.

"It was Stalin's favorite," Olga whispered as though she were sharing a state secret. Katherine had read it in her guidebook.

They walked past the security guards onto Gorky Street. It was dusk and long shadows fell over the famous street. The puddles were frozen, and snow clung to the sidewalks around the light poles. Muscovites hurried past them, much like dwellers of any bustling city. The group passed many shops, but Katherine saw none of the infamous, block-spanning queues her father talked about. They might have been there, concealed within, but Katherine really wasn't interested in that. She was busy making a study of the pay phones. The phones were bolted to the walls under signs that read *taksifon*. They had squashed-funnel slots at the top, but no indication of the nature of the coin that would satisfy them. She counted them as she passed. After ten minutes, they passed the eleventh *taksifon*. It hung on a brick wall, around the corner from the entrance to the Aragvi.

The group descended to a basement dining room colorfully painted with mountain scenes of Caucasian peasant life. They were seated at a table choked with little plates of vegetables, potato salads, sausage, tomatoes, lavash, red caviar, black caviar, champagne, wine, cognac and vodka. There was scarcely room to set a glass.

A waiter in a tuxedo opened several bottles of champagne and filled everyone's glass. One of the Americans, a man of about forty, got to his feet and made a toast in Russian, which struck Katherine as ridiculous since Olga was the only other person at the table who could understand him. His name was Vladimir, after his Cossack grandfather. He finished his toast, and Olga clapped her hands together and squealed with delight.

"Such Russian I have not heard since my grandfather died," she said.

Vladimir didn't seem to know what to say to that.

The party went on. Soon the heavy eyelids of the group seemed to lighten. Eyes sparkled under the effects of alcohol. Perhaps Olga had indeed discovered the cure for jet lag.

After an hour, the plates were whisked away and then shish kebab, which was presented as a Georgian dish called *shashlyk*, was set before them along with several spicy sauces. There was a cheese-filled bread called *khachapura* and tiny ravioli, *pelmeni*, which Olga explained were Siberian, not Georgian.

"We're all members of the Soviet family, though," she said happily. Olga was on her fourth glass of champagne and showing the effects.

Katherine was still sipping her first glass of wine when she excused herself to go to the bathroom. Olga flashed a look of concern at one of her flock wandering off, but then she shrugged and returned to her food and drink.

Katherine climbed the stairs to the entrance and told the guard at the door, in her best Russian, that she wanted some fresh air. "Pyani," she said, *drunk*. The man grinned as though they now shared a secret. She walked toward Gorky Street. She wasn't wearing her coat—just a turtleneck and a sweater—and the cold soaked into her skin like water through a sponge. At the corner, she turned and contemplated the mysterious taksifon. A woman walked toward her.

"Excuse me," Katherine said in Russian. The woman passed without slowing. A man approached. "*Izvinite,*" said Katherine. He stopped.

"Taksifon? Money?" she said in Russian and held out her hand like a street beggar. "Please."

He gave her a two-kopeck coin.

"*Spasibo.*"

Katherine put the coin in the slot and dialed the number she had memorized back in Ithaca. She stamped her feet on the cold pavement. The phone rang. At the other end of the line came a *click,* and then the coin fell into the slot.

"*Allo?*"

"Maxim Izmailov?"

"*Da-da.*"

"*Zdravstvuyte,*" said Katherine. "Hello. May I speak English?"

"Yes."

"You don't know me. I'm a friend of Titus Waal. He said I could—"

"Titus!" he cried. He pronounced it like "Tea-toos." "God, how is he?"

"He's fine."

"Still slogging through nineteenth-century poets, is he?"

"He published an anthology of Pushkin last year."

"Pushkin! Good heavens. I certainly hope he didn't do the translation himself. Where are you calling from?"

The man's English was superb, just as Titus had promised. Maxim and Titus had met on an exchange program ten years earlier when they were both language students.

"I'm in Moscow," said Katherine. "I'm calling from a pay phone. I have some books for you from Titus."

"Marvelous. Where are you?"

"I'm with an Intourist group, so I'll have to sneak away."

"Excellent."

Katherine looked across the street. A man under an eave seemed to be watching her. Their eyes met, and he stepped back into the darkness. Katherine turned her back to him.

"There's a favor I'd like to ask of you," said Katherine.

"I'm listening."

"It could be dangerous. I really don't think so, but —"

"If Titus Waal felt it was important enough to give out my phone number then that's good enough for me."

"I need to deliver some letters to someone."

"So drop them in a mailbox."

"These letters must be delivered in person." Katherine took an envelope from her pants pocket. She read off the name — Lena Ryzhkova — and then the Moscow address written on the front.

"I need you to contact this person," she said. "She doesn't know me, but tell her I knew her father. I have some letters from him, written before he died. Then set up a meeting for tomorrow night."

"What time?"

Katherine squeezed the receiver. "I can get away about ten o'clock."

"This address is Strogino," said Maxim. "A new suburb on the extreme west side. It will take an hour to get there by metro."

"Eleven-thirty, then, at her apartment. I will need you to accompany me, as a guide and interpreter."

"Naturally. And where shall we meet?"

"I was hoping you would have a suggestion."

"I do. Listen carefully."

He finished and said, "One more thing."

"Yes?"

"If it's not too much to ask, what is your name?"

T h e surveillance report on the American tourist Katherine Sears was filed by telephone and recorded on two separate devices — the second one was unknown to either of the parties.

". . . Subject went to the Aragvi restaurant with the tour group, as scheduled. Subject left the restaurant, once, alone, at 10:45 and made a three-minute phone call from a taksifon."

"Did you pick it up on the directional microphone?"

"We only have two, comrade-major. They're both broken."

"*Detsky sad*," he groaned. *Kindergarten.*

"We had an agent in the area, but he doesn't speak English so there was no point—"

"Take him off surveillance."

"Of course."

"What about the search of her room?"

"Nothing there."

"Anything else?"

"She speaks some Russian. Not much, but enough to borrow two kopecks from one of our agents."

"*We* paid for the call?"

"I'm afraid so, comrade-major."

The voice snorted. "*Detsky sad.*"

3

Katherine spent the day as an American tourist in Moscow.

She strolled over the cobblestones of Red Square and even took clandestine pictures with an instamatic camera held at her hip. She waited in line an hour to file past the glass coffin that held a waxen Vladimir Ilyich Lenin. She shook her head in bewilderment. By contrast, she was genuinely moved by the solemn eternal flame of Russia's tomb of the unknown soldier in Alexandrovsky Gardens. After lunch, Olga took them on a tour of the Kremlin grounds.

Moscow architecture was big and powerful and not much else. Katherine saw gargoyles and Greek nudes side-by-side on a single facade. The builders certainly weren't concerned about the vagaries of form as they set out to inspire awe in peasants. To make matters worse, there were no outdoor cafés, no quaint coffee shops, no intriguing gift shops. Moscow was the ugliest city Katherine had ever seen.

She returned to her room at five o'clock and changed for dinner and an evening at the Bolshoi Theater. The meal was subdued by the previous day's standards; the seven o'clock showing for *Swan Lake* preempted another eating orgy. The group had third-row seats, and it should have been a memorable night for Katherine, but she barely acknowledged the performance. Her thoughts were on her coming meeting.

The ballet ended at nine o'clock. The group gathered around Olga, submitted to a head count and then went outside to the square in front of the theater. They started to cross the street to the Metropol Hotel where they were to have coffee, when Katherine spoke up.

"I'm exhausted," she said. "I just want to go back to my room."

Olga gasped. Then she began to argue. Katherine simply *couldn't* miss the special Russian coffee. And the atmosphere — *superb!* The hotel was an *historic* monument, the same one used in the film *Dr. Zhivago*.

But Katherine would not be dissuaded. Several members of her group shot her envious glances, but none showed the courage to stand up to Olga. It would have been like joining a mutiny. Finally, Olga relented. But now the question became: How was Katherine to return to the hotel? Katherine insisted on walking alone, a suggestion that horrified Olga. For an instant, Katherine felt sorry for her guide. Olga was like a mother duck whose ducklings were paddling in opposite directions.

"Are you sure you will be all right?" Olga asked doubtfully, and Katherine knew she had won.

Katherine pointed to the Intourist Hotel over the tops of the city buildings.

"I can see it from here," Katherine said. "How could I get lost?"

"Don't forget, we meet tomorrow in the lobby at eight-thirty," said Olga.

"I won't. Good-bye."

Katherine started toward the hotel along Karl Marx Prospekt. It was exciting to be alone on the streets of Moscow, liberated from Olga's anxious gaze. She reached Gorky Street, but instead of turning right, up to the Intourist Hotel, she kept on going along the great asphalt square that had once been Moscow's merchant district. She threaded her way through the hurrying Muscovites, thrilled to be part of the bustle. It was the best part of her day. Ten minutes later she came toward an unpretentious, two-story building with a sign that said, "Library of V.I. Lenin." It was the Lenin Library, the largest library in the world. In front of the building, under a glowing-red letter "M," Katherine spied a medium-built man in a black parka and a bright red "1980 Olympics" ski hat. He paced to the foot of the library's stairs and then turned back to the "M." He looked like a man trying not to look like a man waiting for someone.

"Maxim?"

He looked up. "Katherine!" He kissed her three times, alternating cheeks. "Any problems?"

Katherine shook her head.

"Good. Everything is on. Let's go."

The letter "M," it turned out, stood for "metro." They descended the stairs into the subway, the Moscow Metropolitan of V.I. Lenin, the object of so much praise in Katherine's guidebooks. Maxim pressed a metal token into Katherine's hand, and she dropped it into a gate and passed through.

"Stay close to me," Maxim whispered.

They rode two stops, got off and then wove through the tunnels to another platform. They caught a second train. They rode it nine stops, about twenty minutes, and then stepped onto a platform in a station called Shchukinskaya. They stood a while in the dark (the streetlights didn't work) with several dozen other Muscovites waiting for a tram. No one spoke, and it was strangely quiet. After fifteen minutes, they boarded a tram and were soon rattling their way across a long bridge over the Moscow River. Ahead, a gigantic housing project rose like the emerald suburb. Strogino.

They got off the tram and plunged directly into Strogino. Katherine felt as though a door had closed behind her. In all directions rose monolithic buildings of mind-numbing sameness. All were concrete, obviously prefabricated. There was no landscaping. Grass tried to poke up in a few places, but mostly the ground was covered by alternating splotches of weeds, mud, snow and dirt. Clothes hung frozen on balconies. Though clearly tens of thousands of people lived in these buildings, it was quiet on the street except for the barking of dogs. She could not imagine how Maxim found his way.

And then, just as she was concluding that there was something sinister — even unnatural — about Moscow, she came upon a sight that hinted of something deeper, the way bubbles on the surface of a pond portend life below. She and Maxim were passing through a yard between two low buildings. Outside the building to their right, atop a pile of dirty snow, three men were shouting up to a third-story window. A woman held a baby to the glass. The men began to dance and slap each other on the back. One man was weeping.

"What is going on?" Katherine asked.

Maxim smiled. "Maternity ward. Fathers are banned from delivery rooms for ten days."

Katherine was witnessing a father's first look at his newborn child. At that moment, Moscow became real to her: Like a newly discovered species, it was now a *living* mystery.

They came to a pencil-thin, fifteen-story building like all the others, and Maxim said quietly, "This is it."

They went in and took the elevator to the seventh floor. The smell of urine and garbage was overpowering. Katherine looked at her watch. It was eleven-thirty. Right on time.

Maxim led her to a door at the end of the hall and rang the bell. Inside, a dog barked. Footsteps approached. The lock turned and the door opened.

A woman of roughly Katherine's age gazed out at them. She wore a black evening gown and fresh makeup.

"Lena Ryzhkova?" asked Maxim.

The woman nodded and motioned them to come inside.

Lena Ryzhkova's apartment was more like a large closet. There was a single room, plus a microscopic kitchen at the end of a short hallway. Off the hallway stood two side-by-side doors leading to a toilet room and a wash room. And that was it. A bookcase was turned perpendicular to the living room wall to create a false wall behind which her eight-year-old son slept. The sofa was Lena's bed. The furniture was tacky and didn't match, but it was adequate. There were several nice paintings on the walls, books in the cabinets and, in the corner, a color television set. She did not live well, but she was at least comfortable.

Lena was very pretty. Her dress, perhaps handmade, had a wide collar that was out of fashion by fifteen years. She wore high-heeled shoes and heavy eye makeup. Her hair was freshly styled.

She seated Katherine and Maxim on the sofa. Cookies, chocolates and cheese were laid out on the coffee table with the precision of a magazine photograph. The serving dish was chipped, but was of attractive china. Lena excused herself and rushed to the kitchen to bring tea. She returned a minute later, her best tea set jingling atop a serving tray. Maxim flashed a grin at Katherine. He seemed amused by the girl's desire to be seen by the American as a proper hostess.

Lena Ryzhkova spoke no English, and Katherine was too shy to try her Russian, so Maxim had to translate everything.

"This is all so wonderful!" Katherine exclaimed. "Like a picture!"

Maxim translated, and Lena beamed.

But her smile faded, and she said something to Maxim.

"She asks how well you knew her father," said Maxim.

"Hardly at all," Katherine said. "We met in Helsinki, at the World Astronomy Symposium, the day before he died."

Lena nodded. She spoke again and Maxim said, "You have some letters?"

Katherine opened her purse and pulled out five sealed envelopes. Each was stamped in red ink, "RETURN TO SENDER." Katherine handed them to Lena, who put them on the table beside her.

"She wants to know how you got the letters."

"A month ago, after I decided to make this trip, I went to New York City to talk to your father's colleagues at the New York Institute of Technology. I was hoping to —"

Lena interrupted. Maxim said, "She asks, is that where Vladimir lived? New York City?"

"Of course. She didn't know that?"

Maxim shook his head. "After he defected, they told her nothing."

Katherine frowned. "Anyway, I went there to try to find your address. Nobody knew anything. They let me look through some of his personal effects from the office. That's where I found the returned letters."

Maxim finished his translation and Lena nodded. Then Lena began to talk.

"Father was a dreamer. He used to talk seriously about things like living in outer space or on the far side of the moon. He was like a child. I remember being embarrassed at times to have such a father."

Lena's eyes were misty. She wrung her hands in her lap. "A couple of years ago they appointed a new director at the institute, and things got real difficult for him. 'Politics and science don't mix,' he used to say. But I am a simple girl. I don't know about such things. I have my little boy to think about."

Lena dabbed her eyes with a tissue and took a sip of tea.

Katherine asked, "Why did he defect?"

Lena thought a moment. "I knew he was unhappy, but the actual defection

. . . I think it wasn't planned. He was in Oslo, and I think he just saw the chance and took it. He was like that."

Lena and Maxim spoke a while. Maxim summarized. "It seems that the KGB came to her after the defection and interrogated her. It went on for several weeks. The poor girl didn't know anything. The institute wanted its apartment back, so she was forced to move here about six months ago. She complains that it is far from the center and very small."

Lena said something very softly. Katherine could guess what it was, and Maxim confirmed it. "She wants to know: Why did he kill himself?"

Katherine looked into Lena's puffy eyes, and for the first time Katherine spoke in Russian. "I don't know."

The room was quiet. They all took a sip of tea.

Then Katherine said, "Tell her I'm a scientist — an astronomer. Until six months ago, I was working on a joint Soviet-American star survey."

Maxim translated. Lena nodded and looked at her, waiting.

Katherine said, "The name of my Russian partner was Victor Perov."

Lena smiled. "You know Victor?"

"Victor is the reason I'm here."

They had met five years earlier at the Josef Kepler Cosmology Conference in New York City.

Like hundreds of attendees that year, Katherine had come to meet Victor Perov. The young Russian had just published a ground-breaking paper on the distribution of so-called Dark Matter in the universe, and he was being held up as the Soviet Union's new superstar of the scientific establishment. Using measurements of x-ray emissions from the center of the galaxy, Victor had concluded that the amount of matter trapped inside black holes — Dark Matter — was far greater than anyone had previously estimated. If true, it would have enormous consequences for the future of the universe, virtually guaranteeing its eventual collapse to a single point in an event astronomers called The Big Crunch. Katherine admired his paper enormously: It was the work of a first-rate mind.

It took Katherine three days to summon up the nerve to approach Victor with her idea. In constructing his theory, Victor had used just two data points — not enough to extrapolate with any precision. With a trembling voice, Katherine proposed to Victor a joint Soviet-American survey of the Large Magellanic Cloud — an area ripe for the formation of black holes. As an astronomer at Cornell University, she had access to the large radio telescope at Arecibo in Puerto Rico. Victor, through his institute, could use the dish in Soviet Georgia. By combining the resources of the two countries, she argued, and using the diameter of the earth to magnify the accuracy of their measurements of x-ray emissions, they could accomplish in three years what would otherwise have taken decades.

It was an audacious proposal. The year was 1979, not a good time to be launching a joint Soviet-American project. Relations between the countries were at a low. The year before, the U.S.S.R. had invaded Afghanistan, prompting then president Jimmy Carter to impose a slew of sanctions, including a boycott of the Olympic games in Moscow. Katherine's own father had told her she was wasting her time. She had phoned him one evening at Princeton University, where he was working as a visiting conservative scholar, and he had assured her that Victor would never agree. The Perovs were good communists. His mother was the deputy minister of agriculture. Victor was a beneficiary of all his country's system could provide. He would never risk embarrassing his country by sharing any potential glory with his Cold War enemy.

To everyone's amazement, Victor embraced the idea unreservedly. In fact, from the start he was more enthusiastic about it than she was. If politics caused him concern, then he concealed it well. Jack Sears concluded that Victor was either astonishingly naive, or so supremely confident of his country's superiority that he saw no threat. Later, her father added a third theory: Victor was a spy.

Katherine had laughed at that one, though she really didn't have an explanation for Victor's enthusiasm. So she simply assumed he was what he appeared to be: a scientist so afire with passion for his work that all other concerns receded to insignificance.

As it happened, Victor's Communist party connections were the greatest factor working in favor of the project. In the eyes of the Soviet apparatus, Victor Perov was a citizen above reproach, and even the KGB was unable to find a reason not to give the project a nod. And so, after nearly two years of excruciating negotiations, it began.

For the next two years, Katherine and Victor kept up a weekly correspondence as they worked jointly from opposite sides of the Iron Curtain. Katherine's standing at Cornell University rose dramatically as the astronomical data mounted and evidence grew in support of Victor's theories. A revolution in cosmology was in the making.

"We were so happy," Katherine told Maxim and Lena. "Victor's letters bubbled with excitement. This spring we were supposed to publish our results."

Katherine took a deep breath. "Then, last November, Victor's letters just stopped. No explanation. I tried to contact the SAPO Institute where he works, but they wouldn't take calls. The Soviet Embassy in Washington cited 'reasons of national security' for the dropped contact. The project, they said, had not been canceled. So I kept on working and sending my data through the embassy to Victor. But he never replied. I had no idea if he was even working on it anymore. It was infuriating."

Lena spoke and Maxim translated. "Did you say November was the month he stopped sending his letters?"

"That's right."

"That's when Victor learned that his twin brother had been killed."

Katherine nodded. "Anton."

"How do you know about that?" asked Lena. "I thought you said he stopped all contact."

"That's where your father came in," said Katherine. "Last December, I read in the journals that Victor had won the 1983 Hubble Prize. It's one of the highest honors in theoretical astrophysics, and I knew he would have to attend the conference. The presentation was set for Helsinki on December 21. Here was my chance. I registered for the conference and made the eleven-hour flight to Finland."

"On the plane I read in the newspaper that Yevgenia Perova had been appointed U.S.S.R. minister of agriculture. This made her a member of the Central Committee and a candidate for the Politburo."

"Lord," breathed Maxim. "He's *that* Perov?"

Katherine nodded.

"Did Victor come to Helsinki?" asked Maxim.

"He came, all right, but he was impossible to see," said Katherine. "He was surrounded constantly by KGB and the other members of his delegation. Finally, I got so frantic I ambushed him in the hotel lobby on the way to the banquet where he was to receive his award." Katherine smiled and shook her head. "I yelled out to him over all these people. It was ridiculous. I was like a groupie trying to get the attention of a pop star at a concert. He must have heard me, but he wouldn't even meet my eye. One of the KGB agents actually shoved me. It was unbelievable. But not so unbelievable as what came next."

Lena said, "You mean, when Victor denounced my father."

"Right."

Maxim snapped his fingers. "Now I remember. I saw this on the news."

As the world media would report, Victor Perov turned down the 1983 Hubble Prize. He complained that the award acknowledged the work of his former teacher, Vladimir Ryzhkov, Lena's father. A year earlier, Ryzhkov's defection had embarrassed the Soviet scientific establishment. Now came the payback.

From the lectern, Victor delivered a blistering indictment of Lena's father calling him a "parasite," "an intellectual thief" and a "propaganda puppet under the control of the military-industrial complex of the United States."

"It was so absurd," said Katherine. "I can see now that he had to distance himself from a defector for the sake of his mother. But at the time I was confused. I felt as if I didn't even know him. I was still trying to figure it all out when I discovered a note on the floor by the door of my room. It was from Victor. It asked me to meet him in the children's department of the Stockmann department store the following morning."

"Victor contacted *you?*" Maxim said, astonished.

Katherine nodded. "I was so angry at him I considered not going. He told me to flush the note down the toilet but I just threw it in the trash can."

"What happened?"

"I went, of course, and Victor was there, just like he said, looking at a toy fire engine for his nephew. Somehow, he had managed to be with just one other Russian. The two came over to me, and Victor pretended it was a chance meeting. We spoke for only a few seconds, but in his words he buried a message."

"How did he do that?" asked Maxim.

Katherine closed her eyes. She could see Victor Perov as he had been that morning, his uncombed brown hair lying like a mop atop his head, his engaging grin and his intense blue eyes, which had seemed to Katherine to hold a touch of sadness she had not seen before. Katherine repeated Victor's words exactly — going over them syllable by syllable, as she had so many times since that morning four months ago.

"Katherine!" said Victor. "What a pleasure!"

"Hi, Victor."

"Please make the acquaintance of my dear colleague, Dr. Mikhail Yakovlev. Excuse Mikhail. He speaks only a little English. Pass message for Mr. R. I've been trying to work with Mikhail a bit, but with no success I'm afraid." Victor slapped Mikhail on the shoulder. He smiled awkwardly. "Where is my brother? He doesn't seem to take to languages very well. They're lying to me. Help. Have you enjoyed the symposium, Dr. Sears?"

"Uh, yes."

"Good!" He proclaimed it as though something had been decided. "Well, we must go. It was a pleasure meeting you. Shake Mikhail's hand if you agree to pass the message to our friend. I look forward to your future letters, Dr. Sears."

Katherine opened her eyes and looked at Maxim and Lena.

Maxim said, "That was it?"

Katherine nodded. "It took me a while to figure it out. It was all so weird, so unexpected. I took a long walk through the streets of Helsinki, eventually winding up down at the port beside a ship called the *Estonia*. It reminded me of Victor, so I went into the port authority building and asked about it. The ship, no more than a ferry, made the four-hour trip to the U.S.S.R. three times a week. It struck me how close I was to Victor's homeland — and yet how far. I sat down and went word by word over Victor's message. Gradually, I understood. He was asking for help in finding out what had happened to his brother Anton. For some reason, he doubted the official explanation. He asked me to contact 'Mr. R,' your father. Obviously he couldn't say the name 'Ryzhkov' in the presence of the other Russian."

"You remember all that?" asked Maxim doubtfully.

"I have a photographic memory," Katherine said matter-of-factly. "I see words." Maxim didn't look convinced.

Katherine shrugged. "It's like having my own tape recorder running inside my head. I can play back things I've read and conversations I had. Anyway, I used it with Victor during our first meeting in New York City when I repeated precisely something he had written three years earlier. It came up a few times in our letters, too, so Victor knew about it, and that's why he could be confident I would understand his message that day at the department store."

Katherine breathed deep and went on. "Victor chose me because he had seen your father and me together. We met in the cocktail lounge the first night. Like me, your father was there to meet Victor. But your father, as a defector, was the one man harder for Victor to contact than me. So Victor used me as a courier to get to your father. But then, before I could deliver the message . . ."

Lena finished the thought. "My father killed himself."

"He was so distraught, Lena. He must have missed you and his grandson, Victor. I was probably one of the last people he spoke to—we had dinner together—and all he talked about was the life he left behind in Russia."

Lena put her head in her hands and began to sob.

Katherine waited a moment and said, "There was one other piece of Victor's message. He said it just as I was leaving. Now, a day doesn't go by that I don't wish I could somehow have delivered it to your father."

"What was it?"

" 'Sorry, Vova.' "

Lena smiled. She wiped away a tear.

Katherine said, "I learned later that 'Vova' is a nickname for Vladimir."

Lena began to talk. "Victor didn't need to apologize. Father would have known what the speech was all about. Victor was not just a friend to father, he was a son—only closer because they shared their work. They would get together and argue about nothing. They would get so excited they would wake up the baby. It was unbearable. I would shut the door just to get away from it.

"After father defected, Victor came back from Oslo to give me the news. He has such good connections that the KGB agreed to let him tell me. We held each other and cried and cried. It was like both of us had lost a father. For Victor, it was the second father he lost."

Katherine said, "Your father also defended Victor."

"He did?"

It was at the cocktail party the first night. Victor had made a toast for his Russian colleagues, and Ryzhkov had shouted something across the room, Katherine didn't know what. Victor and Ryzhkov eyed each other and there was a quick exchange in Russian. After Victor spoke, all the Russians cheered and patted him on the back. Ryzhkov went sullenly to the bar and ordered a drink.

Katherine slid in beside him. "Excuse me for prying," she said. "But what was that scene all about?"

Ryzhkov tossed back his shot and signaled the bartender for another. He leaned on the bar and kept his eyes straight ahead. "Politics."

"What?"

Ryzhkov's drink arrived, and he gulped it down. The chatter in the room was back at full volume.

"If you don't mind my asking, what did Victor say?"

Ryzhkov stared straight ahead. "He who sings not with us . . ."

Katherine shook her head helplessly.

"It's Mayakovsky, the poet." He raised his voice, reciting. " 'And he who sings not with us today is against us!' "

Katherine clucked her tongue. "That's completely paranoid."

Ryzhkov turned and looked at her for the first time. "Have you ever been to Russia, Doctor . . . ?"

"Sears. No."

"Do you speak Russian?"

"No."

"Have you ever read Anna Akhmatova?" His tone was sharp now.

"Who?"

Ryzhkov finished his drink and set the glass on the bar. His hand was shaking. "Do you know how many days the siege of Leningrad lasted?" His voice trembled with emotion.

"No."

"I wonder then, Dr. Sears, how you dare presume to stand before me and judge Victor Perov when you don't know even the first thing about Russia?"

He turned and stormed out of the room.

In her living room, Lena smiled at the story. "That sounds like Papa."

A moment passed, and Katherine asked, "Do you ever see Victor?"

"About once a month," said Lena. "He was here two weeks ago. He brought some antibiotics for my son. Vanya had . . ." Maxim interrupted. "I'm sorry. I don't know the word for this disease. It's like a sore throat."

"Strep throat?" offered Katherine.

"Maybe," he shrugged and went on with his translation. "Anyway, none of the pharmacies in Moscow had any antibiotics. It's *defitsit*. But the institute has a well-stocked pharmacy and Victor brought me some. He seemed very sad. Ever since Anton's death, he hasn't been the same. They were twins, and I think part of him died with Anton."

Katherine fidgeted anxiously.

"Victor's grandmother died, and his mother moved out. He's living with some woman and her child now."

"He's living with someone?" Katherine asked, startled.

"That's what he said."

"I have to talk to Victor Perov," said Katherine.

Maxim interrupted. "Katherine, my dear, that's quite impossible. It's one thing to sneak away from your tour group to meet me. But this Victor Perov is a scientist at a mail box—that's what we call a secret lab—and the son of a Central Committee member. He'll never agree to it. It would be suicide."

"He will meet me."

"How do you know?"

"I know."

Maxim paused. "Give the message to me. I'll take it to him."

"I can't let you take that risk. Besides, the people who gave me the message said I must deliver it in person."

"You're scaring me," said Maxim with a frown. "What is this all about?"

"I can't say."

Lena sat puzzled, watching the exchange. Katherine noticed and told Maxim to translate. Maxim did, and Lena asked what Katherine wanted her to do.

"Ask her if she would be willing to call Victor," said Katherine.

"When?" asked Maxim.

"Now."

"His phone may be bugged," said Maxim.

Katherine hadn't thought of that. "Then ask her if she can contact him in person."

Maxim spoke with Lena a minute, and then he said, "She is afraid. She says she is divorced. Her son depends on her."

"I understand. That's why I won't ask her to carry the message, only to contact him to set up a meeting."

Lena listened and sat very still. She looked at the letters on her lap and then raised her eyes to Katherine. "Why are you doing this?"

Katherine considered concealing her hidden motive. But she suspected Lena had already guessed.

"*Ya ego lyublyu,*" said Katherine.

I love him.

A small smile came to Lena's lips. "You can never be with him."

"Perhaps. But that doesn't really change anything, does it?"

The room was quiet. Katherine held her breath. Had she erred in revealing her personal secret? Perhaps Lena had her own feelings for Victor, in which case she might refuse to help, just to keep them apart.

"Why should I believe you?" Lena asked at last.

Maxim began to protest Lena's blunt question, but Katherine stopped him. "It's all right, Maxim. She has a right to ask that."

Katherine twisted a ring off her finger and handed it to Lena. The ring had a large amber stone in a silver setting. It looked like an antique. Lena turned it over in her hand a moment. She frowned, puzzled.

"You know this, don't you?" Katherine said in Russian.

"Where did you get it?" Lena demanded.

"Read the inscription," Katherine said, gaining confidence in her Russian.

Lena peered at the inside of the band.

Maxim said, "What does it say?"

Neither woman answered. They stared at each other a moment, and then Lena handed back the ring. Katherine slipped it on her finger.

Lena turned to Maxim and spoke with him a moment.

Maxim translated. "She has agreed to help. She wants to know what she should say to him."

Katherine breathed deep. "Tell him that Katherine Sears is in Moscow. Tell him I leave the day after tomorrow. Here's a copy of my tour schedule." Katherine handed Lena a paper and went on. "I won't be able to sneak away from the group like this again. Victor will have to make contact with me somewhere along the line. We need two minutes together. That's all."

Maxim translated and Lena replied.

"It's settled," said Maxim. "She'll go to Victor Perov tomorrow morning."

A few minutes later, Katherine and Maxim put on their coats and left. They had been gone five minutes when Lena Ryzhkova heard a knock at the door. She turned the latch thinking that Katherine or Maxim had forgotten something. She pulled open the door and looked into the hard faces of two strange men.

4

It was after midnight at Little Rock Special Psychiatric Hospital, and Inmate 222 had given up trying to sleep. He lay on his back on his regulation three-centimeter mattress and stared up at the red eye.

The eye was in fact a dim light bulb that bathed Cell 34 in an eerie glow, like a photographic darkroom. But to Inmate 222 it was the eye-that-never-blinked.

Sleep was pretty much out of the question. At eight o'clock that evening, orderlies had given him a large dose of haloperidol. Inmate 222 blinked and struggled to focus his eyes. The blinking and the sleeplessness would go on through the night — provided he didn't have a seizure. Doctors called the seizures "hyperkinetic-hypertonic syndrome" and dismissed them as a necessary side effect. All part of the treatment.

There were seven other men in Cell 34. Inmate 222 listened to the sound of their sleep — the steady breathing, the snoring, the occasional shifting of position. He hated them for it. He never used to hate people. He was learning.

Suddenly Igor Kolstov, the lunatic who slept on the bunk below him, began to thrash in his sleep. "Goddamn you. Bastards. Kill. Kill. Stop. No. Yes. Black. Goddamn you. Bastards . . ."

Inmate 222 swung his pillow at Igor and hit him in the head. Bull's-eye. The ranting stopped.

An ammonia smell rose in the room. Igor had wet the bed again.

"Bastard," muttered Inmate 222.

Inmate 222 returned to his vigil, hands behind his head, staring at the red eye.

An hour passed and Inmate 222 climbed down from his bunk. He went to the door. "Orderly!" he called out.

The metal slat in the door slid open and two beady eyes peered in.

"What?"

"I have to piss."

Urinating in the cell was forbidden. In Little Rock prison, called a hospital, inmates, called patients, were expected to get permission from the guards, called orderlies, in order to relieve themselves. It was part of the daily regimen of torture called treatment.

"Hold it," said the orderly and shut the flap.

Inmate 222 turned and looked around the cell. He went over to Igor Kolstov's bed and stood there a moment. He opened the flap in his prison uniform and took out his penis. He held it over Igor's bed. At first, nothing happened. He often had trouble urinating; his bladder had been weakened by repeated drug therapy. But soon urine hissed against the mattress, and the sound of it helped to increase his flow. He stood there a long time emptying his bladder beside Igor. Finally, he shook his penis and put it back in his pajamas. He climbed up to his bunk, put his hands behind his head and stared at the red eye.

A few minutes later, Inmate 222 sniffled.

"Oksana," he whispered.

A tear rolled down his cheek, hit the pillowcase and soaked into the fabric. He sniffled again.

"Victor."

5

The Nightmare comes to Victor Perov in a place between sleep and consciousness.

He is underwater. He is looking for something, but the water is muddy and he can see no more than a few feet. He has been under a long time, too long, and his lungs are straining for air. He needs to rise, to find the surface, to give up this foolish search.

For what?

Even as he dreams he wonders. But he knows he can't quit. He goes deeper.

He is claustrophobic. The weight of all the brown water above him is compressing him, pushing him deeper. The current is strong, and he must fight it too as he swims deeper still.

He is weakening. His lungs are burning now, and he knows with terrible certainty that he can hold out no longer. He must rise. Already, it may be too late to reach the surface. He starts up.

Then, in the depths below him, he sees a shadow . . .

A NTON!''

In bed, Victor Perov sat up straight and screamed.

He opened his eyes. It was dark. Oksana Filipova was beside him.

"Victor, it's all right."

Victor was panting. His body was drenched in sweat.

"It was just another nightmare," said Oksana.

"Jesus."

Oksana pulled him back down to the bed. She wriggled in closer, and her breasts pressed against his side. She laid her head on his chest.

"Was it the same one?" she asked.

Victor swallowed. He was still trying to catch his breath. "Yes."

"Can you remember what you were looking for?"

Victor thought about that. "No."

"You called out, 'Anton.'"

"I did?" Victor knew the dreams were trying to remind him of something, something he had nearly forgotten. They were connected to Anton; they had begun the night he learned about his twin's death.

"He's gone, Victor," said Oksana. "He was killed in Afghanistan."

"Gone. Yes."

"If I can accept it, why can't you? I was his wife. I am raising his son."

Victor didn't answer. They lay quietly a while, and then Oksana lifted her lips to his. At first, he didn't kiss her back, but after a few seconds he found himself pressing against her. Their tongues met, and she let out a tiny gasp. He pulled her closer. They made love slowly, rising and falling to the rhythm of their heartbeats, consoling each other with their bodies.

Afterward, they lay in each other's arms.

"It's not wrong what we're doing, is it?" asked Oksana.

Victor rolled over onto his back and stared up at the ceiling. "Not for the reason you think."

"Why then?"

Victor thought about his inability to save his brother, his ridiculous speech in Helsinki, the suicide of his friend Vladimir Ryzhkov, and his abandonment of his own work at the institute.

"Because I don't deserve you," he said. "I'm nothing."

Oksana's eyes flashed angrily in the dark. "You're not 'nothing'! Grisha needs you." She paused. "We both need you."

" 'Need'?"

"Yes."

"But not 'love.' "

Oksana began to sob.

Victor felt miserable. He longed to take her in his arms, to comfort her, but he could not. He lay on his back staring at the ceiling. Gradually, Oksana's sobs quieted, and her breathing grew steady. Victor listened to her sleep. He searched himself for an answer to Oksana's question. Why *couldn't* he accept Anton's death? But when he looked into his heart he found nothing—no feelings, no thoughts, no passion. Just a hole as deep and dark as the shadow in his dream.

Grisha took the call. It was 7:00 A.M., and Victor was slicing cheese and sausage for breakfast. Oksana was in the shower.

It *had* to be Grisha who answered the call. As master-of-all-matters-relating-to-the-telephone, no one in the household dared pick up the phone without permission from the three-year-old. Once, about two weeks earlier, Victor had made that unfortunate mistake. Grisha had thrown himself to the floor and begun screaming. He had been inconsolable. So Victor had put on his coat and gone outside to a taksifon on the street corner. He called the house. Grisha answered and they talked that way for several minutes. When Victor returned, Grisha was at the kitchen table eating his dinner as though nothing had happened.

Victor cherished the commotion provided by the toddler. It kept his mind off other matters.

He took the phone from his nephew and tensed when he heard the burly voice come over the line. Boris Orlov was head of the KGB for the Special Astrophysics Observatory—SAPO. Though Victor and Boris were well acquainted, Victor could not remember the KGB man ever having called his home. Victor listened for several minutes and then hung up. He stood a moment thinking and then went to the bathroom where Oksana was drying off.

"Can you sneak out for lunch today?" Victor asked. Oksana was a librarian at the newspaper *Izvestiya*, and employees were expected to dine in the staff cafeteria. "I want to take you and Grisha to the skating rink."

Grisha overheard that and let out a *whoop*. Grandfather Frost had given Grisha a pair of double-bladed training skates on New Year's. He was in a perpetual state of readiness to go to the rink.

Oksana wrapped herself in the towel and tucked the end between her breasts. She looked at Victor and a shadow crossed her face. Ever since Anton's death, she had become fearful of news.

"I suppose so," said Oksana. "What's going on?"

"Not now. I'll pick you up at noon. We'll talk then."

The SAPO Institute was located on the west side of Moscow, about fifteen minutes from Victor's flat. Victor had once shared the flat with his mother, but since her appointment to the Central Committee, Yevgenia lived in a four-room palace in the center. Victor had never been invited there. The Iron Perova, as his mother was known, had never been the greatest living companion—after all, she was a woman who didn't even allow her own children to call her "mother." But her departure, coming so soon after Anton's death, had left Victor feeling unbearably lonely. He began spending more time with his brother's family—Oksana and Grisha. After a while, it just seemed silly not to have them move in with him. Sharing a bed with Oksana had not been part of the plan, but it had happened nonetheless. Victor blamed himself. Oksana was beautiful; he was weak.

Victor came through the glass doors of SAPO at eight-thirty that morning. The security guard greeted him with a smile and waved him through. The omission of the security check was a sign of the guard's respect for Victor.

"Good morning, Ivan," said Victor. "How's your daughter?"

"Better, thank you."

Victor took the stairs to the second floor and walked the long corridor to his office. Along the way he passed through the institute's observatory, a circular, two-story room dominated by a thirty-two-inch reflector telescope aimed at a slot in a dome fifty feet overhead. In 1937, the telescope had been one of the biggest in the world, a symbol of Soviet technological might.

What an impression that telescope had made on Victor the first time he saw it, just five years ago! Even then, the telescope had not been of much use for serious science: The city had grown up around it creating smog and a glow of light that obscured the heavens. Still, there were times in the early hours before dawn, when the lights of the suburbs had not yet come up and a steady breeze had swept away the smog, when the telescope hinted at its former glory.

Victor paused to look at her. A voice came from below him.

"She's a fine old girl, yes?"

It was Mitya, the telescope's maintenance man. He stood on the catwalk below, a wrench in his hand. "They want to take her out, you know, to put in some more offices."

"I heard."

"I guess there's not much use for her since . . ." His voice fell away.

"Since what?" asked Victor.

"Since Dr. Ryzhkov left."

Victor smiled. "He sure could make her dance."

Mitya nodded. "Baryshnikov."

Victor went up the hall to his office and opened the door. He hung his coat on the rack, threw his briefcase on the desk and went back out into the hall. Boris had asked to meet Victor first thing that morning. Victor locked his office and started up the hall to the office of the First Department, the KGB.

On the phone that morning, Boris had gotten straight to the point. He knew all about Helsinki. Incredibly, Katherine was in Moscow. She had told Lena Ryzhkova. Lena, under interrogation, had told Boris. Now there would be hell to pay.

Victor shook his head. It had never occurred to him that Katherine Sears would take his request onto her own shoulders. His message was meant for Ryzhkov, and it should have ended with his death. But now Victor saw clearly his error. Katherine was earnest and a little naive, which was to say she was American. Katherine wasn't brilliant, but she was industrious and thorough in the way a good astronomer must be. In this respect, she reminded him of his old friend Vladimir Ryzhkov. Katherine was one of those astronomers who was more at home behind a telescope than in the company of people. For the purposes of their joint survey, Victor couldn't imagine a better partner. Around SAPO, she was known as "The Nun" because of her unflattering clothes and shy manner. There were the inevitable jokes about her being a virgin. The others tried to get him to join in, but Victor just smiled and kept his thoughts to himself.

Victor wasn't sure how Katherine had figured out everything she needed to understand his message in Helsinki, or even if she had. Like most academics she was adept at using a library. She could have figured it out.

But to come to Moscow disguised as a tourist—it would have been laughable if it hadn't been so dangerous. The KGB had picked up her trail right away, before she had even set foot in Moscow. For the last two years, their joint project had been under special KGB scrutiny, cleared at the highest levels. As chief of the First Department at SAPO, Boris Orlov's head was on the chopping block, and he wasn't about to take any chances. Boris had always distrusted the motives of the Soviet-American project. Since he had no interest in science, he viewed it purely as a reckless threat to security. Katherine Sears, in his view, was nothing but a clever spy. So naturally Katherine's name had been on all the usual watch lists—including the U.S.S.R. Department of Registrations and Visas. When she had applied for a tourist visa it had been caught immediately. The visa request should have been turned down. The fact that it wasn't meant that Boris was up to something.

What? Victor had to find out. Victor was no stranger to the brutal rules of Kremlin politics. He had grown up watching his mother suffer in their grip. After a meteoric rise in her early career, the Iron Perova had languished for fifteen years in the Ministry of Agriculture, unable to advance because of an invisible enemy neither she nor her allies could flush out. Her astonishing promotion that winter had at last broken this stalemate. Victor often wondered how Yevgenia had pulled it off. But she never discussed such things, and he hadn't asked. Still, the Iron Perova had powerful enemies, and information about the indiscretions of her son could be valuable ammunition against her. It might even bring her down. Victor couldn't bear to be the cause of that. Her promotion had been one of the few bright spots in the dark winter.

Victor came through the door. Boris's enormous frame was parked behind a large desk. As usual, not a scrap of paper interrupted the desk's mahogany sheen. Victor wondered sardonically where the furniture ended and the man began.

When Victor took a step into the office he saw the frightened young woman in the corner.

Lena Ryzhkova.

"What the hell . . ." said Victor.

"I believe you know my guest," said Boris.

Victor went to her. She wore a pretty blue dress and her makeup was smeared. She got out of her chair and they embraced.

"Lena? Are you okay?"

She nodded.

Victor turned to Boris. "You bastard. If you hurt her I swear I'll have you arrested."

"Come, Victor. This isn't 1937. We merely had a chat. What's more, comrade, you're in no position to dictate anything. You are in a great deal of trouble."

"What have you done with Vanya?" Victor asked.

Lena began to cry.

Boris said, "Little Vanya's just fine. He's at school. One of our agents took him. Now please, both of you sit down. I have a very simple proposition that should settle this matter quite suitably. Lena can go home, and Victor, your indiscretion in Helsinki need never be a part of your record. You may even get a commendation."

"What do you want?" Victor said coldly.

"Sit, please," said Boris.

They sat.

"Katherine Sears is a spy," said Boris.

Victor snorted in disgust. "Nonsense."

"How naive you are. But perhaps I can change your mind. Can you tell me why, Victor, in the last four months Katherine Sears has had daily contact with dozens of different anti-Soviet émigré organizations and so-called 'human rights groups'?"

"How do you know that?"

Boris waved his hand. "It's my job to know. I also know she has made two phone calls to the Moscow bureau of the *New York Times*. We have the recordings. She spoke to Grayson Hines."

Victor frowned. Grayson Hines was well known to him. His name popped up from time to time in the Soviet press as a provocateur and possible CIA spy — the usual accusation leveled against American journalists. But even more significantly, Hines had been one of the few Western correspondents in Helsinki when Victor rejected the Hubble Prize. Had Katherine really gone to him?

Boris went on. "She asked some rather pointed questions about Afghanistan."

"Afghanistan!"

"What has astronomy got to do with Afghanistan?" Boris asked.

"Anton died in Afghanistan. If you really know everything, then you know she was only doing what I asked — finding out about my brother."

"But why is she here now?"

Victor paused. He was wondering that himself. Since Helsinki, Victor had learned the truth about his brother. Anton was dead.

Boris said softly, "I know about the file your mother gave you on Anton's death."

Victor stiffened. The file — its very existence — was a secret he had kept even from Oksana. Boris laughed. "Don't look so surprised. Such an irregular request would have had to have been cleared by me. After your speech in Helsinki, I gave the go-ahead. Think of it as a reward for good behavior."

Victor glared at him.

"So we both know that your brother is really dead," said Boris. "And if that is true, then I ask you once again, 'Why is Dr. Sears here?' "

Victor shrugged, and Boris seemed to take that as a victory. Victor shot a glance at Lena. She sat in the corner with a glazed-over expression. She appeared to be in shock.

Boris went on. "Dr. Sears is here on a mission. She thinks she can trust you, probably because you broke with protocol in Helsinki. She's very clever. She doesn't know about the file, so she is assuming you will think she knows something new about what happened to your brother. She assumes you will meet with her to find out. Then she will reveal the true nature of her mission."

"Katherine Sears is not a spy."

"*Was* not, Victor. Was. You have had no contact with her in how long? Six months—not counting Helsinki, of course. Things change. She could have been recruited."

"No."

"Let her prove it then."

Victor took a deep breath. "How?"

"This is why I have asked you here. We will meet Katherine exactly as she asked, only you will be wearing a wire. When she reveals the true purpose of her trip we will swoop in and arrest her." Boris gazed over Victor's head as though picturing this triumphant moment. "Together, we will catch an American spy. As I said, you may get a commendation out of this."

"And you get a big promotion—colonel, perhaps?"

"That's not my primary consideration."

"Sure it isn't," Victor scoffed. "Does Lubyanka know what you're up to?"

Boris frowned. "It's to your advantage as much as mine that the higher-ups are kept out of this."

"And if I refuse?"

"Oh, Victor, you have a brilliant career ahead of you. You can't help the socialist cause if you're thrown out of the Academy of Sciences. And Lena . . ." He let his voice trail off.

"What about her?"

"I'd hate to see Vanya grow up as an orphan. Victor, think about it. There's not a person in Russia who would come to the defense of the daughter of a defector after she has met with a suspected American spy. I doubt even your mother could save her—assuming she would try. If you want to blame someone for all this, blame Dr. Sears. She started it."

Victor looked at Lena. She had listened to their conversation as though they were two executioners deciding how to kill the prisoner.

He turned to Boris. "What's the plan?"

"Katherine is scheduled to have dinner tonight at the Moskva Restaurant. We will do it there."

W h a t are you going to do?" asked Oksana.

"I don't know. If I go along with Boris, Katherine will be arrested. If I don't, Lena will be arrested."

Victor and Oksana were seated in the bleachers beside the skating rink. A blanket covered their legs and a tray of bread and sausage lay beside them. Lower down on the rink, Grisha pushed himself cautiously forward on his skates.

"Boris is right about one thing," said Oksana. "It's Katherine's fault. No one asked her to come here."

Victor grimaced. "That's not true."

"What?"

Victor told Oksana about Helsinki. When he finished, Oksana said, "And that's why she went to Lena Ryzhkova?"

Victor nodded.

Grisha called out to them from the rink. "Look, Mama!"

"That's good, honey," said Oksana. "Not so fast. No, don't look at me . . . oy!"

Grisha fell. Almost immediately, he was back on his feet. He did a quick spin just to show he was all right.

Oksana laughed. Victor watched her watch her son. Even in her parka and rabbit hat, her cheeks over-red from the cold, Oksana cut a stunning figure. She was like a woman from a Russian fairy tale painted on one of those black lacquer boxes the tourists liked so much. She had a round face with high cheekbones and long blond hair. Her complexion reminded Victor of ice cream. Dimples, high up on her cheeks, appeared magically when she smiled. She had round eyes with long lashes she batted at people when she wanted their attention. It rarely failed.

Oksana turned to him. "Have you considered the possibility that Katherine has some real information about Anton?"

"That's not possible."

"But you had some doubts. The date on Anton's last letter didn't match his location. You said so yourself. That's why you went to her in Helsinki."

"That was before . . ."

"Before what?"

"Before I had Yevgenia look into it."

"Yevgenia!"

In February, after a particularly bad nightmare, Victor confronted his mother in her Kremlin office. She kept him waiting two hours. When he told her what he wanted, she flatly refused.

Victor looked into Oksana's eyes, which had grown hard at the mention of Yevgenia. He said, "I know you think Yevgenia's a monster. But you're wrong. Anton was wrong. She was very upset when she heard about the letter. She turned as white as a bed sheet."

"The Iron Perova?" Oksana scoffed. "I don't believe it."

Victor looked away. "Anyway, she came back two days later with Anton's service file."

"She gave it to you?" Oksana asked, amazed.

Victor opened his briefcase. He pulled out a manila folder and put it on her lap. Across the side in red ink was stamped "Sovershenno Sekretno," *Top Secret.* Oksana gaped down at it as though it might bite her.

"Open it," said Victor. "It explains everything."

Victor looked over Oksana's shoulder as she opened the file.

It began with the death certificate.

> *Perov, Anton Borisovich. Nationality: Russian. Rank: Private. Division: 20th. Entered service: 14 July 1983. Basic training completed: 16 September 1983. Special Considerations: Mother, Yevgenia Perova, Deputy Agricultural Minister of U.S.S.R.*
>
> *Killed in action 14 December 1983 in Mazar-e-Shariff in battle with Ittehad-e-Islami clan. Armored personnel carrier struck by antitank rocket. Body not recovered.*
>
> *Notification of family: Official status "missing in action." Soviet presence in Mazar-e-Shariff sensitive.*

So viet presence in Mazar-e-Shariff sensitive," quoted Victor. "That's why the date on his last letter didn't match the location quoted in the newspaper reports. They were changed by Army intelligence."

Oksana nodded. She turned the page. Next came army records from basic training. Nothing special. The results of a physical. Anton was in good health. Stapled to the report was a passport photo of Anton in his uniform, and Victor's eye went to that. His brother's head and face had been shaved. If Victor hadn't seen the photo before, he wouldn't have recognized Anton; his brother had worn a beard and long hair ever since high school.

Oksana went on reading the report while Victor's mind wandered. He kept looking at the photo. Anton looked younger, not that different from how he had looked on their twelfth birthday. Suddenly Victor was thinking about that day, the day Victor decided to become an astronomer — February 28, 1964.

It was a Saturday and the family had gone to the dacha in Petrovka, an hour outside of Moscow. Yevgenia was at a meeting in the city, as usual, and Papa was drinking, so the twins went out to the gazebo in the backyard to be alone. It was cold, but the sun shone brilliantly. The day felt magical, and the boys were anxious to give each other their presents.

Victor went first. He handed Anton a knapsack. Anton unzipped it. Inside were a half-dozen tubes filled with a complete set of topographical maps of the U.S.S.R. They were military maps, practically impossible to obtain. With Yevgenia's help, Victor had ordered them six months earlier. Anton withdrew one of the maps and contemplated it.

"They're perfect," he said, and he slid the map carefully back into the tube. Anton's eyes sparkled. "Now it's your turn. Are you ready?"

"Ready."

"It's right below us."

"Huh?"

Anton giggled. "Don't just sit there, silly. Look!"

Victor went down the gazebo steps. Under the floorboards he found a rolled-up carpet. He pulled it onto the lawn and unrolled it. There lay the white body tube of a telescope.

"There's more," said Anton, and he dashed to the storage shed. He came back with an armload of parts. He made two more trips for parts. In minutes the telescope was assembled, a three-and-a-half-inch reflector Anton had built himself, from scratch, secretly. He had even ground the lens.

Victor was speechless.

"You'll be able to see the rings of Saturn and the red spot of Jupiter," said Anton.

Victor stroked the lines of the body tube. It was a work of art, complete with a finder scope and counterbalances made from metal pipes and cement. "It's beautiful," he said.

That night, the twins hauled the telescope a half-mile to the clearing on Baron Kerensky's old estate. The equipment was so heavy they invited their neighbor Kostya to help. He was a big boy, a year older than the twins. Victor was impressed that Kostya already had hair under his arms. Kostya agreed immediately to help. The boy had no friends or siblings and could always be found playing by himself down by the railroad tracks. He was overweight, clumsy and serious beyond his years. He was always anxious for the companionship of the Perov twins, so their proposal of a freezing evening behind a telescope sounded like a great adventure to him. The three boys set out at twilight. Kostya carried the cement counterweights, while Victor and Anton juggled the rest.

Despite the subfreezing temperatures, the three boys passed four hours trading places behind the lens. They studied the moon, Mars, the cluster of the Seven Sisters, the rings of Saturn. By midnight they were shaking so badly from the cold they couldn't keep their eye over the lens.

"So you really like it?" asked Anton as they walked along the dirt road back to the dacha.

Victor stopped, set down the telescope and gave his brother a hug. And then, for the first time, they kissed three times on the cheek in the traditional Russian fashion. At that moment, Victor felt very grown up. "It's the best birthday I ever had," he said.

The file went on to the next stage in Anton's life: thirty-seven pages detailing Anton's political activities at Moscow State University, where he was a geography major, from 1978 to 1982. Most of it was known to Victor. Anton was a suspected member of a subversive environmental group called Green Russia. On February 4, 1980, Anton was arrested for planning a proenvironment demonstration intended to disrupt the 1980 Olympic Games. He was released three days later after promising to cease his political activities. He was arrested again in April 1981 for unfolding a banner in Red Square protesting the construction of a paper mill in Karelia. He was released a week after that at the request of the Communist party. This last intervention came from his mother.

Anton and Victor had had a huge fight after that incident. It took place in Anton's dormitory room. By that time, Anton already was refusing to live at home.

"Do you *want* to ruin your life?" Victor had asked.

Anton sat behind a small, pressed-wood desk that sagged under the weight of dozens of books in Russian and English. He sported a shaggy beard that Victor hated. "There are worse things than death, Victor. Living as a coward, for one."

Victor stood between the tightly packed beds of the dormitory and shook his head. His brother was becoming a stranger, and Victor was powerless to stop it.

"And I suppose you think I'm a coward."

"I didn't say that."

"But I'm a Party member. I must be the enemy."

"You're a survivor, Victor. It takes courage to live in a country like ours."

"So you're the coward then."

"Maybe I am."

Victor sighed. "I'm so tired of this nonsense, Anton. It's going nowhere. Can't you just stop it?"

Anton fanned the pages of a textbook. "The funny thing is: I *had* stopped it."

"Really?"

"I've met someone. We're in love. She hates all this as much as you. I was concentrating on my studies."

"So what happened?"

"That paper mill, Victor," said Anton. "It's on Lake Sini."

"I know."

"That's *our* lake," said Anton. "We went there with Papa. Don't you remember how beautiful it was?"

"All I remember is him getting drunk and you fighting with Yevgenia the whole time."

Anton flinched. "Those are my best memories of us as a family."

"Your mind is playing tricks on you."

Anton got out of his chair and took a step toward Victor. His dark eyes flashed. "They will destroy it, Victor. In twenty years the lake will be dead."

"They know what they're doing."

"How can you say that?" asked Anton. "How can you stand by and do nothing while they destroy everything that is good? I won't let someone else fight my battles."

"What battles?" cried Victor. "You're not starving, are you? You're getting a university education, aren't you?"

"I can't hide away in some institute and pretend it isn't happening."

Victor frowned. "Is that what you think I'm doing? Hiding?"

Anton didn't answer.

"I suppose you'd like to emigrate," said Victor.

Anton's eyes narrowed to slits. His jaw slid forward. For a moment, Victor thought his brother was going to strike him. "I'll never leave Russia. But at least I live *in* Russia. You think you can look through a little lens, and that it somehow transports you away from all this. But it doesn't. Your feet are still on the earth, brother. I'm surprised you can see the stars through the barbed wire."

Anton was so close now his words rained saliva on Victor's cheek. Victor wiped it away with the back of his hand. He looked hard into Anton's eyes. "I didn't come here to fight."

"Then why did you come?"

"To talk some sense into you, but now I can see that's not possible."

"I take it back," snapped Anton. "You *are* a coward. You would lie to yourself rather than face the truth. You're as bad as Yevgenia."

"Yevgenia?" Victor cried, his eyes widening. "It's thanks to her that you're not in prison!"

Victor could feel himself losing control. The room had receded, and now he saw only his brother's eyes, wild and hostile. Anton was deliberately provoking him. Why?

Anton took a step closer. The bristles of his hated beard were inches from Victor's chin.

"She only did it to save herself the embarrassment of having a son in prison," Anton sneered.

"Shut up!" said Victor. "She has done her best for you."

"That commie bitch wouldn't do —"

Victor hit him. His fist struck Anton's left cheek, just above the jaw. There was a thump and then a crash as Anton fell against his desk. He collapsed to the floor, and a stack of books rained over him.

Victor looked down over his brother, panting.

Anton massaged the side of his face, which was already turning red.

Victor couldn't think. He just stared down at his twin in disbelief.

Anton struggled to his feet. He walked to Victor and turned his other cheek.

"Go ahead," Anton said. "Hit the other side. One more blow for the Communist party."

Victor turned and left the room.

It was the last time he'd see Anton alive.

In the months following his brother's disappearance, Victor spent many hours with Oksana, trying to understand Anton's self-destructive nature.

"It was the only way he could live," she told him. "To feel he was part of the struggle." Though Oksana was sympathetic to Anton's work, she was too practical to be involved personally in dissident activities. "I told him many times, nothing but pain will ever come of it." Oksana had married Anton a few months after the big fight with Victor in the dormitory room. Two years later, Grisha was born, and Anton became increasingly secretive. "It wasn't that he was sneaking around," said Oksana. "He was protecting us. When the KGB interviewed me — as they did several times — I was able to say truthfully that I knew nothing. They even tried to turn me into an informant against him — my own husband! The sad thing is, I don't doubt there are women in our country who would take such an offer. Imagine! Trading your husband for a larger flat!"

In the files, reports of Anton's environmental activism went on for three more years. This was mostly new information to Victor — rallies, newsletters and not-so-secret meetings. By then Anton was totally cut off from Victor and Yevgenia. Victor didn't even know about Grisha's birth until his nephew was two years old.

In February 1982, Anton was arrested for the last time — this time for editing and distributing an "anti-Soviet" publication called *The Green Gazette*, a monthly report on the Soviet Union's environmental record. Victor had never heard of it. Such journals were passed around in very small circles. Anton's arrest was part of Soviet leader Yuri Andropov's last clean-up operation before his death, as though the rot of the country could be laid at the feet of a few subversives. Once again, Anton was released from prison within a week, but this time the KGB had a new tactic, and it was plainly spelled out in the file.

"Suggest immediate draft into Army. Inform university admissions."

Victor already knew what happened next. Anton, ever a good student, began to fail his courses following his release from prison. He refused to believe the KGB was behind it. He was a husband and a father now, and he was terrified of being separated from his family. He cut himself off from all his political contacts and studied like never before. But the hard work had no effect. Anton received three consecutive failing grades. He became eligible for the draft. His notice arrived by telegram on June 1, 1982.

Because of her position, Yevgenia was informed of the notice, and she told Victor. He tried to speak with Anton about it, but his brother refused to take his calls. It was then, while speaking on the phone with Oksana, that Victor heard the cry of a child in the background and learned he was an uncle.

Anton entered the Army in October. He was sent to Afghanistan in December, and was reported killed in February. The KGB's strategy had worked. An enemy of the people had been eliminated.

Oksana looked up. Her eyes were filled with rage. "They murdered him."

Victor said nothing. He had wanted to spare her this. In a way, he had wanted to spare himself too. He knew that, once again, he would be put in the position of defending the system. He didn't know how to defend this.

Oksana reached the last page in the file. It was a copy of a letter Anton had mailed to Oksana just before he disappeared, a typical letter from a soldier to his girl. He missed her. He missed Grisha. What new words had Grisha added to his vocabulary? He was sorry he hadn't stopped his dissident activities earlier. He was a father now and had new responsibilities. He would make it up to her. He would be careful. He would come back alive. He would live to see Grisha grow up. In this, the unedited version, the dates and the location matched. The mystery was solved. Victor need never have involved Katherine Sears.

"He's gone, Oksana."

Oksana closed the file and handed it back to Victor.

"I want you to do something for me," she said.

"Anything."

"You have to promise."

"Oksana . . ."

Her eyes grew misty with a mixture of sadness and rage. In that moment, Victor was a little scared of her. "Promise!" she said.

"Okay. I promise."

"Meet her."

"What!"

"Meet Katherine."

"I told you. She'll be arrested."

"No. Meet her under her terms. Not Boris's."

"You're forgetting about Lena."

"You'll have to fix that somehow."

"You have a great deal of confidence in me."

"I trust Katherine," said Oksana. "I don't know why, but I do."

Victor stood up and pushed the blanket over Oksana's legs. "This is insanity.

You know I can't get anywhere near Katherine. She's under constant surveillance. Boris will be watching me too."

"You can find a way, if you want to."

"Oksana—"

She began to cry. Victor sat down, and she put her head in his chest. She sobbed, "You can do it, Victor . . . you can . . . you can . . ."

Suddenly, a child's cry rose from the rink. They both looked up. Grisha lay sprawled on the ice screaming. Oksana jumped to her feet and rushed to where he lay. Victor followed. Oksana started to pick up her son.

"No!" he screamed, kicking the ice. "Papa! I want my papa!"

Victor and Oksana exchanged glances. "Uncle Victor is here, Grisha," Victor said and scooped the little boy off the ice. "Uncle Victor."

In the car on the way home, Grisha fell asleep in Oksana's arms.

Victor put both hands on the wheel and squeezed. "I'll explain it to Grisha tomorrow, Oksana. I'm his uncle, not his father."

"He's confused," said Oksana. "It's understandable."

"It's not right. I don't want him thinking—"

"Victor," said Oksana, and she put her hand on his knee. "Anton loved you."

Victor drove on, his mind a jumble. He felt as though he had never woken up from the nightmare that had begun his day; the feeling of drowning was still with him. He considered Oksana's request. It was desperate and foolish.

I don't deserve you. I'm nothing.

He drove on. He arrived at the turn-off for his flat, but at the last minute he took the car into the thru-lane and kept speeding along Kutuzovsky Prospekt toward the center of Moscow.

"Where are we going?" asked Oksana.

"Into the hurricane."

"So you'll do it? You'll meet Katherine?"

"This is crazy."

"What's the plan?"

Victor laughed. "You really think a lot of me, don't you?"

"I do," Oksana said solemnly. "It's all I ever heard from Anton—what a great man his brother was."

Victor stared ahead thoughtfully.

Oksana said, "So? How are you going to do it?"

"I'm going to need the help of an old friend."

Oksana looked nervous. "Who?"

"We'll get to that. First, we have to save Lena. That means going ahead with Boris's plan."

"But Katherine will be labeled a spy, you said so yourself."

"Not if she refuses to meet me."

"Why would she do that? She's come so far."

Through the windshield, the Russian Arch of Triumph came into view. In another quarter-mile they would cross the Moscow River. From there, Victor would take the car a short distance south along the embankment road to the twelfth-century convent of Novodevichy. The former convent was one of the wonders of Moscow; no tourist visit to the Russian capital was complete without a tour of its grounds. Katherine Sears and her tour group were scheduled to arrive there at 3:30 P.M.

Victor squeezed the steering wheel and drove on.

"Someone's going to have to warn her," he said.

6

O l g a was so furious she could barely look at Katherine Sears.

It was eight-thirty the next morning, and the group of American tourists had gathered in the lobby of the Intourist Hotel for the start of the second day of sightseeing.

Vladimir inched closer to Katherine. "What did you do to Sergeant Olga?" he whispered.

Katherine shrugged. "I went for a walk alone last night on Red Square."

He made a face to show he was impressed. "Call me next time. How did she catch you?"

"The guard by the doors reported me when I came in. She got to my room before I did."

Vladimir chuckled. "Is this a hotel or a prison?"

Katherine shrugged.

"Was it worth it?" Vladimir asked.

Katherine didn't answer. She took her tour schedule from her pocket. It was a copy of the document she had given to Lena Ryzhkova the previous night.

Day Two:	8:00	Breakfast, National Hotel
	9:00	Kremlin Armory, Cathedral Square
	12:00	Lunch, Metropol Hotel
	1:30	Tretyakov National Art Gallery
	3:30	Novodevichy Convent
	5:00	Rest, Hotel Intourist
	7:00	Dinner, Boyarski Room of the Hotel Moskva
Day Three:	7:00	Breakfast, Hotel Intourist
	7:30	Bus leaves for Zagorsk
	10:00	Tour begins of twelfth-century Sergei Trinity Monastery
Day Four:	7:00	Breakfast, Hotel Intourist
	7:30	Bus leaves for airport
	10:55	Plane departs for London

Somewhere on this itinerary, Victor would find her. Where? It gave Katherine butterflies to think about it.

She was in good spirits, immune even to the wrath of Olga. The previous day had gone off smoothly. The worst was behind her. She could relax a little now and enjoy her tour. She owed it to herself to try. The trip had cost her three thousand dollars.

S w a n Lake, it turned out, was actually Swan Pond. It wound like an hourglass along the west wall of the medieval Novodevichy Convent. But its diminutive size made it no less worthy of Tchaikovsky's great ballet, for a more idyllic Russian scene Katherine could not imagine. In its glassy surface, the pond reflected the red brick towers, gold onion domes, and Orthodox crosses of the convent as though it had brought them magically to earth. There were no swans to be seen, however, just gray ravens that cawed and demanded handouts.

"Should be 'Raven Lake,' " Vladimir said to Katherine.

Vladimir had taken a liking to Katherine.

Snow fell lightly as the American tour group filed out of the bus. Vladimir and Katherine exchanged cameras and took turns posing.

"Perhaps Olga is afraid you'll wander off on another unscheduled stroll," said Vladimir, as their guide led them around the lake to the entrance of the convent.

Katherine nodded. Olga's gaze had rarely strayed from Katherine all day. She began to wonder how Victor could possibly make contact. So much for relaxing.

Inside the convent itself, there was little to see. They toured a small cemetery set off to one side. A souvenir shop sold crosses and poorly printed post cards. A chapel stood against the east wall, and Olga explained that it was customary to light a candle and place it in the candelabra. While in the chapel, Olga instructed, the men must keep their hands out of their pockets; the women were to cover their heads. Olga passed out white scarves she had brought for the occasion. Vladimir crossed himself three times and bowed before the icon over the door. Then the group went inside.

At first, Katherine was blind in the dimly lit chapel. The exhilarating smell of burning paraffin came to her nose. A voice spoke melodically. Gradually, her eyes adjusted. The chapel was illuminated by three bulbs suspended by cables from the high ceiling. The rest of the light was supplied by hundreds of candles. Icons of rich reds and black-flaked golds flickered in the candlelight. The walls were stained wood, almost black. A bearded priest in black robes stood at the front of the chapel chanting. He had an enormous gold cross around his neck. The scene was solemn and breathtakingly beautiful, the Middle Ages alive and well in the late twentieth century. About a dozen seemingly ordinary Muscovites were also inside the church. Most were old. One pretty young woman with round eyes and a red scarf over her head stood off to the side. She crossed herself and bowed.

Katherine went to the small table beside the door. A middle-aged woman seated behind an offering plate handed her a thin, yellow candle. Katherine dropped ten kopecks onto the plate. Following Vladimir, she carried the candle self-consciously to the front of the chapel. Olga remained at the door. Katherine lit her wick from the flame of one of the dozens of candles already burning in the enormous candelabra. The heat of the candles warmed her face. Katherine was only a few feet from the priest now. Vladimir whispered a prayer, crossed himself and turned away.

The girl with the red scarf slid into the space Vladimir had vacated. Katherine was about to turn and follow him when the girl spoke.

"Victor sent me," she whispered in thickly accented English.

Katherine froze. She stared straight ahead.

"KGB follows you. Lena Ryzhkova arrested. Understand?"

The room whirled, and Katherine thought she might fall. She focused on the priest. He waved a bronze dish on a long chain.

"Yes," Katherine said through her constricted throat.

"Do not contact Victor tonight. No matter what he says. You will be arrested. Understand?"

"Yes."

The priest resumed his chanting.

"What about my message?" asked Katherine.

Katherine turned. The girl was gone.

A c r o s s the convent grounds, beside the souvenir shop, a tourist in a leather cap was taking pictures. He took pictures of the cemetery, the convent towers, the walls and the icons. He took pictures, too, of Katherine Sears as she stepped blinking into the daylight, her scarf still over her head. He watched as she looked around her nervously. She seemed to be searching for something. The man made a mental note of her unusual movements and then turned away. He took more pictures of the grounds.

By the time the group was back on the bus, the man had dozens of pictures of Katherine Sears. She was an attractive spy — if that's what she was — with almond eyes, chestnut-brown hair and a shapely figure he could detect even beneath her gray wool coat. He wondered what it would be like to have her alone in a KGB interrogation room. But the days were over when a KGB agent operated with that kind of immunity. Taking advantage sexually of a suspect would bring reprisals. The Soviet Union, alas, was getting more civilized.

The man left, satisfied that he had documented every inch of her movement, with one exception. There were no pictures *inside* the chapel.

Within the chapel, cameras were forbidden.

W h a t the hell went wrong?" asked Boris Orlov. He looked hard at Victor Perov.

Victor shrugged. "I told you. She's not a spy."

The two men were seated at a linen-covered table in the Moskva Restaurant. A glass wall treated them to a spectacular view of Red Square and an illuminated St. Basil's Cathedral. It was eleven-thirty that evening, and the restaurant was empty except for a few waiters still clearing tables.

Ten minutes earlier, Katherine Sears and the group of American tourists had left the restaurant to go back to the hotel. It had been a long evening for everyone on Boris's team — the agent posing as a waiter and the seven phony diners borrowed from a counterintelligence team at Lubyanka. The buffet had gone on for three hours. The entertainment was tacky and interminable. A Cossack troupe, dressed in smocklike shirts, rope belts and riding boots, danced to the balalaika and accordion. Women in red peasant dresses and tall white hats danced while a violinist played the theme song to *Fiddler on the Roof.*

Victor had made contact with Katherine Sears at the coat check-in. She had just handed over her coat when he slid in beside her. He put his coat on the counter and waited for his check slip. It was exciting to be so close to her, and he knew she felt the same; he could see her hand trembling as she reached for her slip. But she kept her cool and never looked at him.

"In the corridor — 10:40," Victor had whispered in English. He wore a wire, so the recording confirmed the contact to Boris. The bait was laid; the trap was set.

She never came.

Dinner ended, then the show. The group left, along with Katherine. Part of the regular surveillance team went with her, of course. The others went home. That left Victor and Boris alone at the table to ask, "What the hell went wrong?"

"She was spooked," Boris said. "What spooked her, comrade?"

Victor shrugged. "I'm tired. Can I go home?"

Boris narrowed his eyes at Victor.

He suspects something.

Boris nodded. "Of course."

■

Boris watched Victor leave the restaurant. Oleg, Boris's top agent, sat down. "So, what do you think?"

"I think he double-crossed us," said Boris.

"How?"

"I don't know. Victor's always been a good Party man. But since his brother died . . . I don't know. Listen, tomorrow, I want to go over every scrap of surveillance data on both of them — notes, photographs, tapes, everything. Have it on my desk, first thing."

"Yes, Major," said Oleg. "Anything else?"

"Yes. Tell the team to come out of the shadows. The game's up. She knows about us. So let Katherine Sears see our agents. Maybe we can scare her into doing something reckless. And increase the surveillance on Victor."

"You don't think he would try to contact her?" asked Oleg. "He'd have to be crazy and stupid."

Boris lit a cigarette and blew smoke out into the room. "Victor is neither. But he is desperate. A desperate man is a danger to himself and others. We may have to protect him from himself. I want him watched round the clock."

In room 1133 of the Intourist Hotel, Katherine Sears put her head on her pillow and thought: *Was it all for nothing?*

She had seen Victor Perov. She had stood within a few inches of him at the coat check. It was maddening. He had told her where to meet. And she had done nothing. But that was what the girl in the chapel had said to do. And she said Victor had sent her.

Was it over?

Was it all for nothing?

Victor Perov took his car along the Moscow River and then circled Red Square past KGB headquarters on Lubyanka Square. The evening had gone well. A catastrophe had been averted. Lena Ryzhkova was safe at home with Vanya.

Now, he could go ahead with the next part of his plan.

Even before Oksana's promise, Victor had known there was a chance of meeting Katherine. He had realized it in Boris's office that morning when he saw Katherine's itinerary. But it would mean bringing someone else into it, an old friend. Victor hadn't seen him in a decade, yet there was no one in the world he trusted more. The friend's name had once been Kostya, the same Kostya who had spent a magical evening in Baron Kerensky's orchard looking at the stars through

Victor's new telescope. Today, Kostya lived in a world just as magical. In keeping with its mystery, he went by a new name: Father Andrei.

Victor reached the northern border of Moscow and was stopped by a traffic policeman at a permanent checkpoint. Victor submitted to a routine document check, slipped the lonely man a ruble and then continued north. An hour later, fifty miles outside Moscow, Victor passed a sign marking the entrance to the village of Zagorsk.

Victor found Father Andrei asleep in his room at the rectory on the grounds of the monastery. The priest dressed, and they greeted each other with three kisses, alternating cheeks.

In his black robe and heavy Orthodox cross, Father Andrei was a far cry from the chubby boy who had always been the last one picked for soccer. His decision, at age nineteen, to join the church had alienated him from his Communist party family and, of his few friends, only Anton had stood by him.

Priests in the U.S.S.R. were among the loneliest men alive. Many who wore the robes were, in fact, KGB informers, and it was impossible to know whom to trust. True believers like Father Andrei were locked away in monasteries, where they were displayed like actors in the Communist party's Potemkin village of religious tolerance. In the end, each used the other — communists and priests. The communists needed the priests to keep up a front to the outside world, while the priests exploited this weakness to keep the Russian Orthodox Church alive. It was a dangerous game, and the travails had strengthened Kostya, built him into a husky man who looked more like a lumberjack than a priest. The beard hid his face, but his eyes reflected the intelligence and peculiar self-assurance Victor remembered from childhood. But there was a weariness there now that showed in the way the eyes had sunken. They were the eyes of an old soldier who had seen that there were greater things to fear than death.

The two men sat in Father Andrei's study and talked as old friends. Father Andrei complained of the KGB's infiltration of the church, and he fantasized about moving to a place where he would have more freedom to worship.

"Where would you go?" Victor asked.

Father Andrei's eyes glistened. "Perhaps some small village in Siberia without even a proper church. I would go door-to-door like one of these dissidents." He smiled at the impossibility of it. "But alas, sermons were never my strong suit."

Victor laughed. He had nearly forgotten about his friend's offbeat humor.

When the laughter died down, Victor asked if the priest knew about Anton.

Father Andrei nodded. "Such a troubled soul. I was surprised sometimes a mortal body could contain it."

Sunlight crept through the window. Victor told Father Andrei what he needed. The priest didn't hesitate. Yes, he would help.

"I have only one condition," said Father Andrei.

He explained, and Victor laughed. "You never give up, do you?"

But the priest remained serious. "It is your soul at stake, Victor. How could I ever give up?"

"Okay, old friend," said Victor. "You win. I'll do it."

7

At eight o'clock the next morning, Boris Orlov was in his office behind his conference table. Across from him sat Oleg. Between them, in two piles, lay the surveillance reports on Katherine Sears. They both stared a moment at the papers.

"What exactly are we looking for?" asked Oleg.

"Any contact between Sears and Perov," said Boris. He reached for the pile on his right and began.

By ten-fifteen, the neat piles were a clutter of hand-written notes, cassette tapes, typed transcripts and hundreds of photographs. They lay scattered so that not a speck of the tabletop was visible.

Boris was going over the material from Katherine's tour of Novodevichy Convent the previous afternoon. His suspicions had been aroused by a note that said Katherine had appeared nervous after her visit to the chapel. Why would she be nervous? But Boris had twice gone through all of the surveillance pictures. There was nothing suspicious. Now he studied the dozens of ordinary tourist shots the agent had taken to maintain his cover. One of these caught Boris's attention. It showed the archway leading to the monastery grounds. On the right side of the photo, the agent had unintentionally captured an image, slightly blurry, of a woman in a red scarf.

After a minute, Boris slid it across the table to Oleg. "That girl," he said, pointing, "does it mean anything to you?"

Oleg squinted at it. He picked up his magnifying glass and held it over the blurry image.

Oleg dropped the lens and began shuffling through some papers. He found Anton Perov's case file and pulled a picture from it. It was a black-and-white photo of a pretty, blond-haired girl. Oleg set it beside the photo of the woman in the red scarf. He looked at one. Then the other.

"Devil!" he said at last. "That's Oksana Filipova."

Boris took the pictures and studied them.

Oleg said, "She must have warned Katherine to stay away from the meeting. But when? Sears was under constant—"

"In the chapel," said Boris. He fell back into his chair and shook his head.

He had them meet in the church where he knew our agent would not follow."

"Damn clever," said Oleg.

The phone rang and Boris put it on the speaker. It was Pyotr Siminov, director of SAPO.

"Victor Perov just called in," said the director. "Thought you should know. He said he was tired after last night and wanted to stay home."

"You talked to him?"

"Yes. He wouldn't normally call me, but given all that's going on —"

Boris hung up. He and Oleg exchanged glances.

Oleg said, "That makes things awfully easy, doesn't it?"

"Too easy. What's Victor's number?"

Oleg gave it to him and Boris dialed. The phone rang. No one picked up. Boris's stomach grew queasy. "Is Victor's car outside his apartment?"

Oleg was on his feet. "I'll get the surveillance team on the radio to check it out." He dashed from the room.

A few minutes later, he came back to the office wearing an expression that gave Boris the answer.

Boris grabbed his coat and started for the door. "Come on!"

"Where are we going?" Oleg asked.

"Zagorsk."

At the same moment Boris Orlov dashed past his secretary, a red Intourist bus bounced over a railroad crossing north of Moscow. In the back, Katherine Sears was shaken awake. She looked sleepily out the window. A sign on the road said, "Zagorsk — 30 km."

Katherine had slept poorly the previous night, partly because of her bad mood, but mostly because of several not-so-mysterious phone calls she had received at one-hour intervals throughout the night. The caller always hung up, but she had a pretty good idea who was responsible. At least Olga, too, looked tired.

Olga picked up her microphone and blew into it. "Attention," she said in her nasalized English. Katherine closed her eyes. Everything about Olga annoyed her this morning.

Victor Perov had let her down. But she had let herself down too. Katherine had come to Russia utterly unprepared. Her so-called "intensive" Russian language course with Titus Waal had been of little help. What little she remembered from childhood was, as Koos had said in London, "not enough." Even as a tourist, the last two days had been a disappointment. Katherine had seen just enough to hate Russia. She felt bad for Titus, who had invested so much time and faith in her ability. Titus was a young scholar of the U.S.S.R. who had once worked for

Jack Sears. He had been to the house several times, and Katherine came to realize he had a crush on her. So when Katherine needed help, she had shamelessly tracked him down in Amsterdam. He had put her in touch with Koos.

"You're stronger than you know, Katherine," Titus had said. "You can do this."

She had used him. How could she have behaved so terribly?

There was only one answer, and it made her ashamed: Because she needed to see Victor again.

It was such a mess. She didn't understand anything substantial about Russia. Even Victor Perov had become an enigma. Perhaps Vladimir Ryzhkov had been right—as an outsider, Katherine could never know the first thing about Russia.

Thank god her father knew nothing about this.

Olga was speaking into the microphone. "The monastery of Zagorsk has been a place of pilgrimage for centuries . . ."

Katherine tuned out the awful voice. She knew it all anyway from her guide-book.

The monastery had been founded in 1325 by St. Sergei, a monk who advised princes and blessed armies. He had played a critical role in the unification of Russia. His body still lay in the monastery. The monastery appeared repeatedly at important moments in Russian history. If the Kremlin was the heart of Russia then the monastery was its soul.

The bus rattled along for another twenty minutes. They passed through several Russian villages. Katherine smiled at the rickety, wood-plank houses with their brightly painted lattice shutters like puny assaults on a black-and-white world.

The bus came over a hill. Katherine looked ahead and gasped. About a quarter-mile away stood a village. In the center of the village, atop a hill, an oasis of color —blues, golds, oranges, yellows and greens—rose out of a desert of Soviet, cement construction. Surrounded by a high, medieval wall lay a tightly packed clump of perhaps a dozen churches, onion domes and towers. A tangle of Orthodox crosses rose into the sky like television antennas atop a New York City apartment block.

Katherine put aside her gloomy thoughts and took an interest in what lay ahead.

B o r i s Orlov's Volga sedan, its blue lights flashing, sped along Yaroslavsky Shosse like a black bullet. Drivers did not so much pull to the side as avoid being run over. Boris's driver wove the car confidently from the passing lane to the shoulder and back again, even as he spoke into the radio.

Boris and Oleg sat in the back seat, surrounded by curtains that covered the windows. They held tightly to the handgrips above the doors.

"I told you we should never have approved her visa," said Oleg. "If he manages to contact her—"

"Shut up. I'm trying to think."

The driver said, "I've got someone from the surveillance team on the radio."

"Thank god," said Boris, and grabbed the microphone.

"The bus has just pulled into the monastery parking lot," said the agent over the hiss of heavy static. "Everything is under control."

"I'll be there in an hour," said Boris. He looked ahead as his driver swung the car onto the shoulder and whizzed past a truck. "Maybe forty-five minutes."

"Major, that's really not necessary."

"Perov has slipped surveillance," said Boris. "It must be assumed he will try to make contact."

"I thought he was cooperating."

"Negative. Perov is unreliable. I repeat. Unreliable."

The radio crackled a moment, and the voice said, "Understood. But you have nothing to worry about, Major. The place is crawling with agents. There's no way Perov can get within a kilometer of the monastery grounds."

"See that he doesn't. If he gets anywhere near the monastery I want him arrested immediately."

"And the girl?"

Boris looked at Oleg. "Major, we don't have the authorization to arrest a foreign national. That's counterintelligence."

Counterintelligence? Things were getting out of hand, and for the first time since Boris had begun this dangerous power play he felt fear. How had he ever let himself get into such a mess?

"Goddamn it!" Boris threw the microphone onto the front seat. "When I get through with Perov the only experiment he'll be conducting is how much coal a hungry man can mine in a single day."

Katherine stepped through the gate to the Trinity Monastery of St. Sergei and, for the first time on the trip, was truly overwhelmed. The monastery was ablaze in color. The four onion domes of the Cathedral of the Assumption were the first to demand her attention. They were painted sky-blue and covered with ten-point gold stars. A building on her left was a riotous checkerboard of orange and green. Dozens of tiny chapels dotted the grounds, each an independent statement of devotion, each screaming in turn for attention. It was all beautiful, yes, but it was the work of madmen, like a painting by Vincent van Gogh. What passionate fevers had spurred reclusive monks to such daring expression?

Katherine watched three priests shuffle by. They wore black robes, black hoods and six-inch wooden crosses about their necks. One of the members of Katherine's group raised his camera to take a picture. Olga put her hand over the lens.

"As a matter of respect, the priests ask that you do not take their pictures," she said. She made it clear with her tone that she considered such reticence provincial.

The tour began. They took turns taking pictures in a charming open chapel over a well, then stood in line at the solemn Metropolitan's Residence to see the coffin of St. Sergei. The faithful paused to kiss the coffin. Vladimir, trembling with emotion, bowed and pressed his lips to it.

They went to a small museum of Russian icons. Here, Katherine was captivated. At first, the icons all looked the same—paintings of Mary and the infant Jesus on wood. But the more she looked, the more she felt the minute variations between them. Behind every modification in the shape of the eyes and the position of Jesus' hand, Katherine sensed the artist yearning to express himself in a form so severely regulated that a misplaced brush stroke was blasphemy. Spirituality, humanity, repression and rebellion blended into an art form that expressed something Katherine had herself felt from the moment her airplane had touched down in Moscow—a claustrophobia she had been unable to articulate. These icon painters, centuries ago, had put her feelings into their icons.

She looked up and realized she was the last member of her group in the museum. Ahead, she caught sight of a man in a leather cap. Their eyes met, and he did not even bother to look away. Katherine hurried out of the museum to join Olga and the rest of the group.

Throughout the tour, which had gone on for nearly an hour, Olga asked questions from time to time of the priests. She explained that the priests were unpredictable and might close any chapel without notice depending on their own needs and the religious calendar.

"It makes a tour guide's life difficult," Olga sighed.

The group started across the central grounds toward the Cathedral of the Assumption, the same building that had taken Katherine's breath away when she had spotted it from the bus a quarter-mile away. A priest came up to Olga and spoke briefly to her. Like many of the priests, he had a hood pulled over his head. He looked like a druid.

Olga's face lit up, and she clapped her hands together. "We're in luck. The bell tower is open. The view from there is marvelous. I can't remember when it was last open for tourists. We must go up."

She started toward a blue-and-yellow tower on their left. The group shuffled after her. The priest turned to go with them, and just for a second his face came out of the shadow of his hood. His eyes met Katherine's.

It was Victor Perov.

■

B o r i s ' s car sped into the monastery parking lot and came to a skidding stop beside Katherine's tour bus.

Boris leaped out. An agent came toward him. "Major, this is really unnecessary—"

"Where is she?"

"With her group, in the monastery."

"*Where* in the monastery?"

The agent sighed and spoke into his walkie-talkie. A voice crackled over the speaker. "The group has just entered the bell tower."

O l g a and the priest led the group of Americans through a wooden door to the ground floor of the tower. The musty smell of a dirt basement filled Katherine's nose. On the far wall rose a simple stone staircase. The group ascended. The priest walked beside Olga while Katherine hung near the back. Olga pointed out to the group how the stone steps were worn in the center from the passing feet of centuries of monks. The group gathered on the second floor at the base of a narrow, stone spiral staircase that twisted up into the ceiling like a corkscrew. The priest said something to Olga, and she nodded.

"It is four stories to the roof," she said. "We'll go single file. Follow me."

They started up, Olga leading. The priest stood to the side and let the group pass. His face remained concealed by his hood. Katherine held back until only she, Vladimir and the priest remained. Vladimir waved his arm chivalrously for Katherine to go before him, but she smiled and returned the gesture. He shrugged and started up, ducking his head at the low ceiling, which was, in fact, the underside of the steps swirling around above him. Katherine started up behind Vladimir. Only the priest was behind her now; she could hear his feet on the stairs. As the staircase twisted, she saw the top of his hood below her. His face remained hidden.

They reached the first of two overlooks on the way to the roof. The group paused and bunched up to admire the view of the Cathedral of the Assumption. They went on. The second overlook, the last before the roof, was so small that Vladimir, Katherine and the priest were forced to wait on the stairs until space was cleared by the rest of the group as they continued up the staircase to the roof.

Katherine climbed to the tiny platform. Olga and the other members of the group were already out of sight overhead. Vladimir was still in front of her, and she could see a woman in front of him. The woman disappeared around the bend. Vladimir crossed the platform and headed straight to the next level of the staircase. He glanced back at Katherine, smiled and started up. The priest was still behind Katherine, still invisible beneath his robes. Katherine followed Vladimir onto the stairs. She took three steps, and then she felt a hand on her wrist. It pulled her back down the stairs.

Now she stood beside the priest on the cramped platform. The only way on or off the platform was by the spiral staircase. To her left was a railing and a close-up view of the star-flaked onion domes of the Cathedral of the Assumption. To her right hung the ropes that controlled the bells of St. Sergei, presumably suspended above her. The ropes disappeared through holes in the floor and the ceiling.

The priest's face, still concealed by his hood, was turned toward the staircase, where presently Vladimir disappeared around the bend. Overhead, the scuffling feet of the tour group grew fainter, and then faded altogether into silence.

Katherine turned to the priest. He pulled back his hood and his face was revealed.

She and Victor Perov were alone.

8

Victor smiled. It was a warm, confident smile that betrayed no urgency. He might have been on a picnic watching Katherine set out the fried chicken.

He took a step toward her and kissed her three times, alternating cheeks. "Are you all right?" he asked in English.

She nodded. "How are Lena and Maxim?"

"Lena is fine," he said. "Who is Maxim?"

She told him about Titus Waal's friend.

Victor memorized the information. "Maxim Izmailov. Language teacher at the Moscow Pedagogical Institute. Right. I'll find out for you." He shook his head in awe. "You've been very busy, Yekatarina."

"You have no idea," she said.

"We only have a minute," he said. "I believe there was something you wanted to say to me."

Katherine took a breath. "Victor, your brother is alive."

He stared at her. "That's not funny."

"It's true. He's being held in a psychiatric hospital. There is a man —"

"This is nonsense!" Victor said sharply. He turned and took a step away from her. He spun around to face her. "Why do you think it?"

"There is an organization called Soviet Psychiatry Watch," said Katherine.

"I know it," Victor snapped. "A capitalist propaganda tool."

She ignored that. "They have an agent here in Moscow, a Jew. His code name is Sigmund. He knows everything about Anton."

"Why didn't he come to me himself?"

"He's scared. Everyone is. Your mother's position . . . well, he's just scared. But he has agreed to meet with you. He'll explain everything."

"You spoke to this man?"

Katherine hesitated. "No. I spoke with his liaison in Amsterdam who contacted a friend of mine. The whole organization is worried about getting involved. They said the only way they would permit the information to reach you was if I gave it to you in person."

This was thanks to Titus Waal. As a student in Moscow, Titus had once helped

SPW director Koos sneak out of the dorms for a rendezvous with his Russian girlfriend. Now that Katherine needed the contact information on Sigmund, Titus called in that twenty-year-old favor. But even that had not been enough to convince the director of SPW. So Titus told Koos the truth about Katherine's relationship with Victor. It must have been a painful moment for Titus, but his commitment to helping Katherine was absolute. And it worked. Koos was at last persuaded that any information about Sigmund and SPW would go no further than Victor Perov, provided Katherine brought it to him herself.

Victor shook his head. "Yekatarina, I fear you have been . . . how do you say . . . 'duped.' These people are using you to get to me, the son of a Central Committee member. Don't you see? They're trying to discredit my country. It's . . . transparent."

Katherine's eyes flashed angrily. Victor was starting to sound like his speech in Helsinki. "I don't think so," she said. "Anyway, I couldn't risk not believing. How can you?"

The muscles in Victor's jaw clenched. He stared hard at Katherine for several seconds. She felt as though he were trying to read her thoughts. His expression softened. A small smile came to his lips.

"Why did you do it?" he asked.

"Do what?"

"Come to Moscow? Risk everything?"

"They told me what is done in these hospitals, Victor. It's horrible. They use drugs and torture. It's worse than prison. It's like hell —"

"And you believe everything they say?"

"I don't know what to believe," said Katherine. "I have Sigmund's phone number for you. You must memorize it. Are you ready?"

She recited the seven-digit number.

He nodded and smiled. There was a pause. The meeting was over, and they both knew it.

"So, what do you think of Russia, Dr. Sears?"

Katherine, not knowing where the words came from, broke into Russian.

> We'll stop in this church and see
> Someone buried, or christened, or married.
> We'll leave, avoiding each other's eyes.
> Why does nothing work out for us?

Katherine gasped at her presumption. The poem was by Anna Akhmatova, something Katherine had been studying with Titus Waal before she left for Russia. Perhaps inspired by the religious beauty around her or by the knowledge that in a few seconds Victor Perov would be gone forever, the words tumbled out of her.

They came unbroken, not in her usual tortured Russian, but for the first time with a feeling for the beauty of the language.

Victor didn't move. He looked at her as though she were something new, no longer the unattainable *amerikanka*. By invoking words that cut to the very soul of Russian culture, Katherine had taken a step toward him.

How would he respond?

His eyes, his face, his posture revealed nothing. Then, with a sweep of his hand, he drew her against his body and kissed her on the mouth. She fell against him, swallowed up by the kiss. They had only a few more seconds together before Olga or any number of KGB agents discovered them. There was no time for words. Katherine could feel her body communicating her feelings to him. She was powerless to stop it from happening—even if she had wanted to. The way she allowed him to support her weight, the way she met his kiss surely told Victor Perov more about how she felt than she had even admitted to herself.

And then he released her. He smiled and reached forward to brush the hair from her face. She looked up into his eyes, searching.

"I look forward to discussing astronomy with you again someday, Dr. Sears," Victor said, and he turned and disappeared down the staircase. The last thing Katherine saw was his robe flapping behind him. Katherine stood a moment staring at the place where Victor had been. The smell of his skin was still in her nose, and her heart raced as though she had just climbed a flight of stairs. She walked to the railing and looked out over the monastery. The day was gray, but the domes of the churches broke up the gloom like man-made suns.

Katherine leaned on the railing and wet her lips. She soaked in the view. A gust of wind blew against her face, and she closed her eyes and let it wash over her. The air should have chilled her, but, strangely, she snuggled in its touch.

And then the bells of St. Sergei began to ring.

Victor Perov was on the ground floor when the bells sounded. He hurried across the chamber and pulled his hood tightly around his face. He stepped through the bell tower door and nearly collided with a man shouting into a walkie-talkie.

Boris Orlov.

"*Izvinite*," said Victor, keeping his face hidden.

Boris glared at him a moment and turned to his colleague. "Do something about those goddamn bells," Boris said. "Christ Almighty!"

Victor lowered his head and walked on.

A minute later, Victor was back in the rectory. He found Father Andrei in his study.

"Did you meet her?" the priest asked.

Victor nodded. "Thank you, Father."

"Was it worth it?"

"I don't know," Victor frowned. "Anyway, I believe we have a debt to settle."

"Debt?"

"Your condition for helping me. I'm ready."

Father Andrei smiled. "Bless you, Victor. But I'm not going to hold you to that. It means nothing unless you truly want it."

Victor sighed and thought about Katherine Sears. "I think I do."

Father Andrei raised his eyebrows. "Very well then."

He got up from his chair, and Victor followed. He led Victor along a corridor that connected the rectory to the Church of St. Mikhail, a small chapel not much larger than a closet. Father Andrei crossed himself and bowed before the altar. He opened a drawer and pulled out a white-and-gold gown. He slipped it on. He placed a gold sash around the back of his neck so that it fell forward over his shoulders.

"My working clothes," he said with a smile.

They walked together to the altar. Father Andrei crossed himself, and Victor imitated the act clumsily. Father Andrei put his hands on Victor's shoulders and turned him gently to face the door.

The priest dipped his hand into a bronze bowl filled with water. He stirred the water a moment and then brought out three wet fingers. He let three drops fall on Victor's forehead. They rolled down Victor's cheeks like tears.

The priest drew an Orthodox cross on Victor's forehead.

"I baptize you, Victor Borisovich Perov, in the name of the Father, the Son and the Holy Spirit."

Amen.

K a t h e r i n e Sears rejoiced.

"You did it!"

She said it to herself after she rejoined the tour group on the roof of the bell tower. She repeated it as she toured the Cathedral of the Assumption. She whispered it as a private prayer before lunch at the restaurant. She said it again and again during the long bus ride back to Moscow. She said it in the lobby of the Intourist Hotel after Olga reminded the group that the bus left for the airport at seven-thirty the following morning. And Katherine was still saying it when she stepped through the door of her hotel room and saw the two men near the window.

She gasped and took a step backward, but a third man came out of the bathroom into the hall behind her. He was enormous, with a thick coat of dark hair over his face, neck and arms. He looked like a bear. She drew a breath of air to scream. He grabbed her hair and threw her head against the wall. There was a *thump*. The room spun, and then . . . nothing.

part ii

The Man with the Stub Nose

9

T h e midnight summons had been vague, and Yevgenia Perova knew it could not be good news. As she walked the long Alexander Corridor of the Kremlin's Hall of Palaces she tried to imagine what could have gone wrong. She scarcely noticed the doors she passed—doors bearing the nameplates of the members of the Politburo of the Union of Soviet Socialist Republics. She showed no awe at her proximity to the highest power in the land. Her blue eyes were thoughtful, and her head was pushed forward slightly as though she were walking into a strong wind. Her head was too big for her body, which gave her the oversize facial features associated with the Iron Perova—that, and the hair bun that lay on her head like a ball of twine. She reached an exit and went through.

Ahead, a soldier of the elite Kremlin Guard stood beside a metal detector. Beyond him was a second door that led outside. The soldier motioned for Yevgenia to pass. "He's waiting, comrade minister."

Yevgenia went out. The night was cold with a strong, swirling wind that stung her face. On the cobblestones, a Zil limousine idled. A man in an olive uniform pulled open the car door, and she climbed in.

A frail, old man smoking a cigarillo in a long, ivory holder sat in the back seat. The door slammed shut and the car took off at once.

"Where are we going?" she asked.

"Lubyanka," he said.

"What does the KGB have to do with this?"

"There's been a leak. An American. She may have contacted your son."

"Impossible," Yevgenia scoffed. "No one can get anywhere near Anton without—"

"Not Anton. Victor."

Yevgenia stiffened. Her defenses went on alert.

Outwardly, Anatoly Podolok was the Iron Perova's greatest ally. He was the Politburo's Communist party secretary for ideology, one of the most powerful men in the world. It had been his connections that had led to Yevgenia's promotion to minister of agriculture that winter. But their alliance was one of cold convenience. There was no love, not even respect, between them.

Podolok said, "Some bonehead KGB agent over at SAPO decided to—"

"Boris Orlov?"

"You know him?"

Yevgenia nodded. Anton's file.

"Anyway, Orlov was running a rogue operation with your boy." Podolok shook his head and clucked his tongue.

"You said there was a leak," said Yevgenia. "How did Stepan Bra—?"

"SILENCE!"

Podolok's eyes bulged and his body trembled. "NEVER utter that name!" He took several deep breaths.

Yevgenia thought he might be having a heart attack. She smiled faintly.

Podolok caught his breath and went on. "We'll find out everything in a few minutes. General Belov is interrogating Orlov now."

The limousine went through the gate at Lubyanka's eastern entrance. Yevgenia had been here only once before—after Anton was arrested for the third time. She cringed to think of that night. Before using her influence to get him released, she had gazed at her son a moment through the two-way mirror. He had let his hair grow, the way all the young *uligani*, "hooligans," were doing. His beard was spotty and unkempt. He had a bruise on his left cheek, a souvenir of his tussle with the KGB agents in the Red Square. He slouched in the straight-backed chair, arm thrown over the side, and she could see clearly his impudence, his lack of respect for the sacrifices she and so many others in the Party had made. Did he care that her comrades in the Party were beginning to talk? They were snickering that the Iron Perova couldn't control her own son! Getting him released from Lubyanka that night would be another small blow to her power; a new debt against her name on the balance sheet of favors and debts that ruled Party politics. At that moment, Yevgenia could almost hate her son.

She had no idea then how much worse things would get.

The driver parked in an underground garage and jumped out to help Podolok. Yevgenia watched with contempt as the old man labored to get out of the car. At seventy-two years old, time had been no kinder to Podolok than it had been to doddering old Leonid Brezhnev, his life-long friend and protégé. But Brezhnev was dead a year and a half already, replaced by Yuri Andropov, whom Podolok had despised, now two months in his grave. The current Soviet leader, Konstantin Chernenko, was more to Podolok's liking, though Chernenko might as well have been dead for all the life that was left in him. Things had reached such a state that Podolok had personally banned radio stations from playing organ music; one bar of organs could send the whole world into speculation about the death of another Soviet leader.

Podolok got to his feet and leaned heavily on the car as the driver closed the door. Yevgenia shook her head. Time ages men differently, and it was Podolok's fate to wither. Every day, no matter how much he ate, he lost a little more weight. It was as though he were fading away, rising each morning to find himself a little more translucent. There was no telling how long this could go on, but to those who knew him it seemed certain that someday he would disappear completely and all that would be left was one of his brown cigarillos, still burning in an ashtray.

Under Podolok's coat, Yevgenia spied a round medal on a short ribbon pinned to his pocket. It was the Order of Lenin, presented to Podolok by Josef Stalin, after Podolok had returned from Berlin a war hero.

Yevgenia glared at the medal. "I thought I told you to not wear that medal in my presence."

"You forget yourself, comrade," Podolok hissed.

"I know the truth, don't you ever forget it."

"How could I?" Podolok pinched his jaw. "Damn that stub-nose mongrel! Damn him for staying alive all those years! Damn him for bringing the likes of you and General Belov into my life!"

A KGB officer led them to an elevator and inserted a key. They began to descend into the infamous Lubyanka prison. When the door finally opened, General Yuri Belov was there to greet them. He was an enormous man with sagging jowls that prompted some men to call him "the hound," though Belov himself would attribute the nickname to his keen senses. Belov was perpetually drenched in sweat (a gland problem, he once explained), and even in the dim lights of the basement, his face glistened with perspiration.

Belov led them up the new corridor. Dim bulbs cast flickering shadows on the cement floor. Yevgenia's heels echoed loudly. As they moved deeper into the prison, Belov briefed them on Boris Orlov's interrogation, and Yevgenia heard for the first time the extent of her danger—Victor's message to Katherine Sears in Helsinki, Katherine's contact with Lena Ryzhkova in Moscow, the botched meeting in the Moskva Restaurant and Victor's strange disappearance shortly afterward. Yevgenia listened with a mixture of horror and outrage. She kept her eyes straight ahead and allowed herself to betray no emotion. She was a woman in a man's world, and Podolok and Belov would be looking for signs of weakness now. She could show none. Whatever conclusions were to be drawn, whatever actions were to be taken, she had to take the lead.

Belov finished and Yevgenia said, "We must assume the American knows everything."

"I'm glad to hear you say that, comrade," said Podolok.

"Where is she now?" asked Yevgenia.

"In a dacha outside Moscow," said Belov. "It was too dangerous to bring her here."

"Good," said Yevgenia. "The main thing now is containment."

"Absolutely," breathed Podolok.

"Remember, Boris Orlov knows nothing," said Yevgenia. "He thinks Anton died in Afghanistan; he saw the same bogus file I gave Victor. And we've got the American."

"Which leaves Victor," said Podolok.

Belov and Podolok studied her for a reaction. She shrugged.

At that moment, they stopped at a heavy door.

"Shall we go in?" asked Belov.

Podolok nodded and Belov put a key into the lock.

"Comrade secretary, you can't go in there!" said Yevgenia. "He'll—"

"See me?" Podolok sneered. "Let him."

Yevgenia froze. She looked at Belov. His face was stone.

No weakness.

They went in.

Behind a table in the center of a small room sat Boris Orlov. He was dressed in the same suit he had worn that evening at the Moskva Restaurant. His tie was pulled loose and his eyes darted about nervously.

Boris jumped to his feet. "Comrade Perova? You didn't have to—" He saw Podolok and stopped. "What the hell?"

Podolok went to a chair in the corner and sat down. Boris's eyes followed him.

Yevgenia and Belov sat opposite Boris at the table.

"You know my guests?" asked Belov.

Boris swallowed hard and nodded.

Yevgenia said, "General Belov has apprised us of your statement, comrade major. There is one point to which I must return."

"Yes?"

"Did this American . . . Katherine Sears . . . speak to Victor Perov?"

Boris shook his head vigorously. "No."

"You're certain."

"Yes. I mean . . . I don't see how."

"But Victor did send Oksana Filipova to warn the American," said Belov. "They met in the monastery chapel."

"That's my theory, yes," said Boris. He looked miserable. He shot a fearful glance at Podolok. The old man smoked a cigarillo in his ivory holder.

"Victor should be commended for refusing to cooperate with this ill-considered fishing expedition," said Yevgenia.

I only wish he had come to me. But even as she thought it, she knew he could not have done that. Victor was trying to protect her. But he only made matters worse. For a brilliant man, Victor could be incredibly naive about his own country. He was so much his father's son, always accommodating, while Anton had inherited her own headstrong nature. Too bad he couldn't have put it to better use.

"Victor has behaved exactly as I would expect," said Yevgenia. "He felt responsible, and he found a way to save Lena, the American and himself."

"And then he disappeared," Podolok pointed out.

Yevgenia bit her lip. She must not appear to be making a case for her son.

Boris came to her rescue. "That doesn't mean they met. He could be at the dacha in Petrovka. He could be at Oksana Filipova's. Why would he risk everything to meet this woman? It doesn't make sense."

Yevgenia and Podolok exchanged glances. Podolok nodded at Belov.

"That's all for now, comrade," said Belov. "Someone will be along for you shortly."

They went out and locked the door.

"He's useless," said Yevgenia. "Only Victor and Katherine know if they met today."

"You must confront Victor," said Podolok.

"How do I ask about a meeting that may never have taken place?" said Yevgenia. "No. Asking him would only tip him off."

"What do you suggest?" asked Podolok.

"We have Katherine Sears in custody. Let her tell me."

"Tell *you?*"

"Who else?"

Podolok thought about that and nodded. "General Belov will go with you. Take my car. You must leave at once."

Yevgenia understood the need for Belov to accompany her—Podolok didn't trust her. Yevgenia paused to consider the two men who had become her closest allies, and she suffered a rare attack of doubt. Belov was a pig who had spent his life putting men like her son Anton into prison camps. While Yevgenia didn't agree with Anton's actions, she believed the KGB's behavior toward her son— and others like him—was a national paranoia. It was simply unworthy of a great nation like the U.S.S.R. And as for Podolok—he was a rat. And just how *much* of a rat was something only two other living people knew. One of them was with her now. The other . . . she couldn't permit herself to think about him. She had a job to do. Victor's life was at stake.

"Let's go," she said to Belov. "We have no time to lose."

D o w n s t a i r s in the interrogation room, Boris Orlov paced anxiously. How had General Belov found out about Katherine Sears? The answer was obvious: Oleg.

Damn the ungrateful rat. When Boris got out he would . . .

What?

For once in his life, Boris Orlov found himself devoid of plans. To be summoned to Lubyanka like this had been unnerving to say the least. And to see comrade secretary Anatoly Podolok — it made no sense. How was he involved in this?

Boris knew one thing for sure: He was way out of his element. All he wanted now was to get home to his wife and son. Raisa was redecorating the kitchen, and she was counting on him to hang the wallpaper. Next month, Dima would graduate from the university. In the fall, he would start at the KGB Academy. Boris had pulled some strings.

The lock rattled and a guard came in.

"Come with me."

The guard led Boris along a dark corridor. It didn't seem to Boris that it was the same way they had come in. But how could he know? The damn place was a maze.

They went down a flight of stairs.

Down?

"Where are we going?"

The guard pointed to a door. "That way, comrade."

Boris found himself in a narrow, dimly lit room with a concrete wall at one end. It was chipped and pockmarked, and he realized with horror that they were bullet holes. He spun around. The guard was closing the door.

Now Boris understood.

"There must be some mistake," he said. His voice cracked.

The guard raised his pistol. His face was expressionless. "No mistake."

10

Katherine Sears had been trying for a long time to open her eyes when she realized suddenly that her eyes *were* open. The images before her were blurry, and she tried to force them to take shape. The effort only made her nauseated. She shut her eyes.

The room buzzed like a hive of bees. Her head hurt. She tried to raise her hand, and that's when she realized she was seated in a chair with her hands tied behind her.

The recognition shocked her, and she tried again to see. A man's face came into focus — a huge man, the bearlike man from her hotel room. Then it came back to her: the strange men, the big man behind her, him grabbing her hair, her head striking the wall . . .

"Where am I?" she said. Her voice surprised her. It sounded composed.

"*Ona prosnulas,*" said the big man, the bear.

"*Ya pozovu vracha,*" said another voice. She turned. A man left through a doorway.

The language was Russian. Katherine played it back in her head and struggled to translate. The first man had said, "She's awake." The second man had said something about calling the doctor.

A doctor?

Katherine was in what looked like a hunter's cabin. A piece of dirty plywood was nailed over the place where a window should have been. She saw two doors — the one the man had just left through and the exit straight ahead of her. The room reeked of cigarettes and body odor. It was cold, and she could see her breath in front of her. Two electric space heaters offered the only heat. The bear wore a suede coat; she shivered in her blouse.

Two men entered the room to her left. The first was the man she had seen leave a moment earlier. He was of average build, with dark, oriental-shaped eyes. A Tatar, she guessed. The second was short and frail-looking with thick lips and beady eyes that looked anywhere but straight ahead. He came beside her and sat down. He pulled back her eyelids and shone a light into her eyes. He felt her throat and took her pulse.

He nodded and said, *"Ona gotova."*

She's ready.

For what?

The big man said something she didn't understand. The Tatar laughed. The Tatar was the boss, Katherine guessed. She considered speaking to him in Russian, but decided to keep her knowledge of the language, such as it was, a secret.

The doctor opened a small, black bag at his feet and pulled out a syringe and a small medicine bottle. He plunged the needle into a bottle and drew out a clear liquid.

Katherine tugged at the ropes on her wrists. He barked at her in Russian. When she kept struggling, he jabbed the needle roughly into her arm. He rammed his thumb on the plunger and the fluid rushed into Katherine's bloodstream so quickly that her arm froze in that spot. She became still. He pulled out the needle, and she said in English, "Bastards!"

The Tatar slapped her. "Listen to me," he said in English. "We not hurt you. We have for you some questions. We give to you, uh, *narkotika*, to help. Understand?"

Katherine nodded. Something was happening to her. The buzzing in her ears became a ringing.

"Now," he said. "Tell me please, what is your name?"

"Katherine Sears," she said. Strangely, her own voice sounded farther away than the Tatar's. It was as though he had supplanted her will with his own. So be it.

"Why did you come to Moscow?"

"To see Victor Perov."

"Why?"

"To tell him something."

"What?"

So Katherine told him. The drug made her *want* to tell him. She told him about Titus Waal and Koos van der Laan. She told him about Soviet Psychiatry Watch. She told him that Sigmund had learned that Anton Perov was being held in a psychiatric hospital. She even offered Sigmund's telephone number.

Time passed. She dozed off. When she awoke, a hood was over her head. There was a new person in the room; she sensed the presence. The voice spoke in a whisper. The Tatar spoke again.

"Did you tell any of this to Victor Perov?"

"Yes."

"When?"

"In Zagorsk. In the bell tower."

More whispering. "How much did you tell him?"

"All of it."

The whispering went on for a while. Someone picked up a telephone. The Tatar was talking into the phone in Russian. Out of the unintelligible string of Russian rose the word "Sigmund."

They were talking to Sigmund.

The realization chilled her. The drug was wearing off.

Then they were off the telephone. More whispering. She heard the interrogator say, *rechnoy vokzal*, which meant "river station." But that didn't make any sense. God, she wished she knew more Russian!

Then the door opened, and footsteps went outside.

Now she heard only the voices of the doctor and the big man. The Tatar must have left with the others. There was the sound of a match being lit. A few seconds later, the smell of burning tobacco reached her nose beneath the hood.

The men's words came through in maddening lapses of comprehension. "Not enough (the doctor) . . . Usual way (the big man) . . . Where? (the doctor) . . . Not find it (the big man)." The conversation became clipped and then ended. Something had been decided.

Her hood was removed. She blinked up at the big man. He held a double-barreled shotgun at her face. Behind her, the doctor was untying her hands.

"*Vstavay!*" said the big man. When she didn't react, the doctor grabbed her shoulders and lifted her to her feet. Her hands were bound behind her back. Her legs were numb and tingling from being bound, and she started to fall. The doctor caught her.

The big man motioned with the barrel of the gun for her to go toward the front door. The doctor opened the door and stood aside for her to pass. She went outside. It was dark. She wondered if it was the same night. The porch was slippery from the frozen snow, and she nearly fell again. It was difficult to walk with her hands behind her.

The two men talked some more. The doctor disappeared behind the building and returned a few seconds later with a shovel.

"*Poshli!*" the big man said, and poked her back with the butt of his shotgun. They started along a trail that skirted the edge of a large field. It was a clear night, and she had no trouble spotting star Sirius in the east. The Magellanic Clouds were up there somewhere. Perhaps Victor, too, was gazing up at them. The thought came to Katherine as though from a dream.

They walked on through the frozen mud and snow. Katherine's teeth chattered.

The ground rose and then fell. Ahead, a forest created a line of darkness. They were making directly for it. Katherine began to sob.

The men didn't notice. They talked constantly. She understood none of what they said.

Suddenly, the big man said, "*Stoy!*"

She stopped. The men talked some more. She heard the words "back at the hut . . . best. Why not?" They seemed to change their minds about something. The big man circled around her and then pointed for her to go back along the path they had come.

What had just happened?

They went back along their route. The men did not speak at all now. They seemed lost in thought. After fifteen minutes, they got back to the cabin. The big man pushed her across the living room to the back room. She went through the doorway, and before her was a bed. The big man pressed the gun hard into her back, propelling her toward the bed. He growled something at her. She turned and looked at their faces. The doctor was mumbling to himself. His eyes darted about nervously. The big man looked anxious. Excited.

Then Katherine understood.

The big man pushed her onto the bed. She landed on her stomach, so that she was hunched over the bedside. The doctor turned her over and lifted her feet onto the bed. He grabbed her breast. She screamed and kicked him in the side. He groaned, and the big man pushed him away with the end of his gun. They began to argue. Katherine lay on her back, her hands tied behind her. She struggled against the ropes but they were too tight. She gave up and lay still.

She saw it now as if it were on a movie screen in one of those twelve-plex cinema complexes at the mall. These two men would rape her, taking turns until she no longer interested them. Then they would zip up their flies and walk her along the trail to the forest she had seen. At some point, perhaps a designated place where this sort of thing was done, they would stop. The big man would take a step back and raise his shotgun at her face. She would blink at him. He would pull the trigger. A flash and a bang. She would be blown backward by the force of the shot and would fall to the ground. Somewhere far off a dog would bark. The men would stand over her body and remark upon how very dead she was. They would argue over who would do the digging, and then, once the work was underway, they would debate whether the hole was deep enough. The work would take all night, but finally they would roll her corpse over the side of the grave. It would fall like a sack of potatoes and land with a *thud*. Then there would be the filling-up to do, the disguising of their handiwork, don't forget to bury the shell casing . . . so much to think about! Then the long hike back to the cabin. Perhaps for a shot of vodka. Perhaps a bath. Perhaps not.

In the cabin, the big man handed the gun to the doctor. The doctor held it awkwardly, as though it were a snake. He sat in a chair at the end of the bed and let the barrel drop to the wood floor. There was a little *tap* as it touched the floor. The big man looked at her.

Everything was very clear to her now, exaggerated, slowed down. She saw that the big man's one eye was open a fraction more than the other. He had a small tattoo on the back of his hand. His fingernails were chewed down. His eyes were brown with gray flakes. His teeth were yellow, and he had one gold tooth way back in his mouth.

He took off his coat and hung it over the back of a chair. He began to unbutton his shirt, keeping his eye on her. He took off his shirt, then his shoes, then his pants, layer after layer, until he was naked. He was built like a bull, all muscle, none of it defined. The hair on his face crawled down his neck and fanned out over his chest, his back, his ass, his legs, his feet, even his toes. His penis was erect and stood out ridiculously from his body. It was the only thing on him not covered by hair.

He came toward her. His face was deadly serious. He lifted her effortlessly and plunked her in the center of the mattress. She wriggled some more against her bonds. It seemed to excite him. He crawled onto the bed and kneeled beside her. He said something to her, and then, in one movement, ripped open her blouse. Buttons flew like shrapnel. They made *chink-chink* sounds on the wood floor. He grinned at her exposed bra. Another rip. There went her bra. He pulled at her blouse but it would not give up so easily; the ropes binding her wrists were holding it in place. He pulled harder, lifting her body off the mattress. She cried out. It became a battle of bone against fabric. She feared he would dislocate her wrists, but this was a matter of no concern to him as he pulled again and again. There was a *rip*, and the cuffs of her blouse surrendered and slipped free. He tossed the blouse aside.

Something felt different on Katherine's wrists. With a start she realized what it was: His final yank had pulled the ropes partially over her hands. Katherine twisted her right hand behind her. The rope fell away.

Her hands were free beneath her body.

By now, the big man had already removed her jeans and panties. The doctor watched it all from his ringside seat at the end of the bed. He leaned on the barrel of the shotgun and craned his head forward for a better view.

The big man held his stubby hand in front of her and then lifted his index finger, displaying it to her. A moment later, a fat finger penetrated her vagina.

The violation gave Katherine a burst of strength like none she had ever known. She jerked herself to a sitting position and drove two fingernails into the man's eyes. It was a direct hit. There was a popping sound like a grape being squashed on pavement. He screamed and fell backward. With his hands over his eyes, he rolled off the end of the bed directly into the lap of the doctor. Together, the two of them rocked backward in the chair, which promptly collapsed. The gun came loose and fell beside the doctor. The big man landed on the other side of the doctor from the gun, and he was already getting to his hands and knees. He was not as badly wounded as Katherine had hoped. With lightning speed, he dove across the doctor for the gun. Katherine leaped headfirst off the bed. She was closer and fell on the gun as he dove into her side. She curled her fingers around the barrel, pulled it against her body and rolled two times away from him. She got to her feet, but the big man was already coming at her. He was a foot away, hands out, reaching for the barrel of the shotgun. She raised the gun and pulled the trigger. The gun leaped back into her shoulder, and the big man's chest exploded in front of her. It looked as though a bomb had gone off *inside* his body. Blood splattered over Katherine. He fell to the floor on his back, and didn't move. His face wore a look of astonishment. His penis was still erect.

The doctor cowered on the floor at the foot of the bed. She pointed the gun at him, and he began to weep and repeat something over and over in Russian.

Katherine walked to him. The report of the shotgun still rang in her ears, and her shoulder ached from its recoil.

So he expects me to kill him, she thought. There was indeed a second, loaded barrel for the job. She stood over him for a while listening to him whimper. She turned the gun around and raised the butt end as though it were an ax. She swung it onto the doctor's head. There was a tremendous *crunch* and his body went limp. Blood gushed from his wound.

She raised her eyes and found herself looking into a mirror. What she saw caused her to drop the shotgun. In the mirror was a woman, naked, her face and breasts covered with blood. It was like a scene from a B-grade horror film.

She ran to the sink in the kitchen and turned on the water. She found some soap and began to wash. She kept on scrubbing long after the blood was gone. Finally, she turned off the water and went back into the bedroom. The room smelled like rotten fruit. She stepped over the body of the big man and found her clothes. They were in shreds. She remembered that the doctor was about her size and went to where he lay. She began to undress him. Blood continued to ooze from his head wound. She frowned and checked his pulse. He was dead. Damn.

You're on a roll tonight girl. Bang! This one's dead! Whack! That one's dead! Hooray for the good guys! Anyone else care to try his luck against Dr. Death?

Honey, you're hysterical.

Damn right!

She put on the doctor's pants, shirt, sweater and coat. They all fit her snugly. She took his fur hat from the floor and looked in the mirror. A Russian peasant woman looked back at her. She picked up the shotgun from the floor and used a bed sheet to wipe the blood from the stock. She took a last look at the bodies of the men and left the room. She started across the sitting room toward the door. She stopped and thought a minute. She went to a space heater and kicked it over. She did the same to the other one. The red coils hit the wood floor, and smoke began to rise.

She went outside. She stepped off the porch and looked up at the sky. Her gaze fell on Sirius and a jolt of hysteria ran through her like an electric shock. She looked away. She could not allow herself to fall apart. That would come later.

An owl hooted. It alone disturbed the stillness of the night. There were no other houses about, no lights but the stars overhead, just fields and trees stretching like the sea to the horizon. She started up the driveway, sidestepping the frozen puddles. Behind her, the cabin began to glow as flames engulfed it. Her shadow danced eerily before her in the red-yellow light. She didn't look back. She scanned the sky for the North Star. It was on her right.

She was alive. She was heading west.

11

The blackness of Rechnoy Park enveloped Victor Perov like a blanket. He looked anxiously over his shoulder, peering into the darkness to see if he was followed. A deserted asphalt path stretched back a few yards and then disappeared into a thin forest. The night was still except for the distant howl of a dog. He saw no one. That was good. It was 2:00 A.M. in suburban northern Moscow and anyone walking about would have been suspicious.

Ahead a red "M" glowed sinisterly. It marked the metro stop Rechnoy Vokzal —River Station. It was from here that Victor would make the short trek to the river, to his rendezvous with Katherine's contact.

Sigmund.

It was the last place Victor wanted to be, and he wondered if there was still time to turn back. He felt like a man who had boarded the wrong airplane. The only way off was to jump.

The trip back from Zagorsk earlier that day had gone off without a hitch. The KGB agents that had swarmed over the monastery left shortly after Katherine's tour bus pulled away. Victor waited a while longer and then departed himself. He wore the priest's robes out of the monastery walking to a side street to where he had stashed his car. He stripped off the robe, got his license plate from his trunk and put it on the car. He kept to back roads until he reached Moscow's outer ring road. From there, he blended into the great stream of traffic to and from the Soviet capital. He passed three permanent traffic police checkpoints without being stopped.

But he had not gone straight home. He needed to think, so he went to Red Square instead. He called Oksana from a taksifon and told her he was safe. He hadn't spoken to her in two days. She asked when he would be home, but he didn't say. He said nothing about Katherine; it was too dangerous to talk on the phone. Besides, what would he tell her?

Anton—alive?

It came down to this: Who did he believe? His mother? Or Katherine Sears? That was an easy choice. But what reason would Katherine have to lie?

She wasn't lying.

He was sure of that. He had looked into her face. He had heard her astonishing words in Russian. He had held her. They had kissed.

He smiled at the memory of that. It had been a crazy thing to do, but it had seemed oddly right at the time. It had been a long time since Victor had permitted himself that kind of foolish impulse. It felt good.

He scuffed the cobblestones of Red Square with the heel of his boot and kept on wandering through the ancient marketplace.

No, Katherine was not lying. She believed Anton was alive. But that didn't make it true.

With no particular plan in mind, Victor made his way to the river and got on a boat. He got off when he saw the Ferris wheel of Gorky Park. He found a bench beside the carousel and, for an hour, watched the children ride. He smiled at their joy, but it made him strangely sad. He didn't know why.

The park was closing when he made up his mind—he could not ignore Katherine's message. He had to follow through: He owed her that much. He owed Anton that much.

He went to a taksifon by the river and dialed the number Katherine had made him memorize. The phone began to ring.

"Allo?"

"Sigmund?"

There was a short pause. "Da."

Victor's stomach turned over. He had not expected Sigmund to be real. He had an impulse to hang up.

"Do you know who this is?" asked Victor.

"Da."

"Our friend said you would meet me."

"Not my friend," said the voice. It was bitter. And scared. "You are not my friend either."

Victor said, "That's true. I'm not."

"I don't like this."

"So let's not do it."

The line crackled and the voice said, "Do you believe what you were told?"

"I believe my friend believes it."

"Hmm."

Victor looked out over the river. A boat was steaming upstream. "Look, uh, Sigmund—"

"Tonight. Two o'clock. Walk from the Rechnoy Vokzal metro stop to the passenger port, Berth 4-A."

"Wait a minute—"

"I'll make contact. If you're followed, I'll know it. You have one chance, one chance only."

"But—"

Click.

Victor stared at the receiver and thought, what the hell just happened?

The next six hours were an anxious time of more wandering and waiting. But at last he began to make his way to his rendezvous. He flagged a taxi and took it as far as Vodny Stadion Station, about fifteen minutes south of Rechnoy Vokzal. The streets of Moscow were quiet. The taxi driver tried to strike up a conversation, but Victor was buried in his thoughts.

At 1:45 A.M. he got out of the taxi and began to hike north through the dark park. He walked slowly, checking his watch, pacing himself so that he would arrive at the meeting point at exactly two o'clock.

He reached the metro stop and looked around. About a quarter-mile away a housing block rose over the trees. It was a relatively new region and the housing had not yet begun to crowd the boundaries of the metro station. An ambulance was parked beside a shoe store. No one was about. Overhead, he spied Sirius, the Dog Star. The Magellanic Clouds, invisible except with a powerful telescope, were located in that direction. He gazed up as though he could see the star cluster with his unaided eyes. He thought of Katherine. He felt better knowing she was safe. Tomorrow she would be on her way back to the United States, out of reach of the KGB.

Victor shivered. He started northwest toward Berth 4-A of the river port, Rechnoy Vokzal.

B e h i n d the steering wheel of his ambulance, Sigmund watched Victor find the pedestrian underpass for Leningradskoye Shosse, disappear into it and then emerge a minute later on the far side of the highway. Victor followed the asphalt path past the thirty-foot-high gates that led to Moscow's main river port. A few seconds later, Victor was gobbled up by the darkness of the tree-lined drive. Sigmund sat stroking his dark beard for several more minutes searching for signs of surveillance. It would take Victor another fifteen minutes to reach Berth 4-A. No hurry.

Pavel Danilov, alias "Sigmund," was a registered nurse, an ambulance driver and a Soviet Jew. He liked being a nurse and an ambulance driver because he liked helping people. He cared nothing about being a Jew, though others did, which was why he was a nurse and not a doctor. And he certainly was *not* an enthusiastic participant of the kind of spy games he played now.

His work for Soviet Psychiatry Watch was 99 percent clerical. He did interviews with people who had been released from psychiatric hospitals. From these talks, he created databases, meticulously kept in forty-two notebooks concealed behind a loose tile under his bathtub. Another 215 notebooks had already been smuggled out of the Soviet Union to SPW headquarters in Amsterdam through a sympathetic attaché at the Dutch embassy by the name of Koos van der Laan. Danilov had never been to Amsterdam. He hoped to go someday.

Who was he kidding?

Some of Danilov's research was published anonymously in émigré journals in Europe, Israel and the United States. Or so he was told. Most of it, however, remained in the notebooks. The notebooks represented eight years' work.

For this secret occupation, the ambulance provided the perfect cover. He had a state salary, a state-supplied apartment in Moscow, use of a state vehicle and lots of night hours alone. He was as happy as he could imagine being. He was glad to be Russian, and he was honored to be part of Russia's struggle. Often, Danilov was in awe of what he was doing. He considered himself a simple man.

Who was he kidding?

In his interviews with former inmates, he was part prosecutor, part sympathetic ear. Many of the people he met were still suffering from the effects of their antitherapy. When they cried, he handed them a handkerchief; when they trembled, he held their hand; when they had no place to sleep, they spent the night on his floor (provided his wife and four-year-old daughter were at the dacha). But when the business of the interview got underway, Danilov was transformed into a prosecutor. He tolerated no vague answers. Was the nurse's name Chermuka or Chermyuka? Did she dispense fifty milligrams of Sulfazine twice per day or one hundred milligrams once per day? Did the patient say he was from Saratov or Saransk?

He pressed relentlessly for names. Who was your lead physician? Yes, we know him. Your nurse? Yes, we know her. Your night nurse? That's a new one. What can you tell me about her? Was the club they beat you with wooden or rubber? Were you bound with rope or wire? What patients did you meet? No name? Then just the first name. No first name? Then give me a description. Was he younger than twenty or older than eighty? Okay! That's a start!

A detective reconstructs a crime after it is committed. Danilov worked *as* the crime was taking place. And it was a new kind of crime, better understood than it had been when the KGB began to use it widely in the late 1950s, but still mysterious and always changing to fit the times. It wasn't as though you could book a tour of a special psychiatric hospital. It wasn't as though medical students received textbooks with chapters on how to use drug-induced Parkinson's disease to reduce a healthy person to an automaton who needed help walking. Punitive medicine took place behind high walls topped with barbed wire. Those who went in never came out the same.

The chief practitioners of punitive medicine needed to be identified, their crimes documented, so that one day, when the hour came for justice, fingers could be pointed and specific charges brought.

Who was he kidding?

This was the 99 percent. The other 1 percent—the work of an undercover spy—was what concerned Pavel Danilov now. And if he was any good at it he knew he would not be making this contact. The second phone call from Victor Perov had been very peculiar. It was reason enough to cancel the meeting. On the telephone, Perov had seemed confused. He said he wanted to reconfirm the meeting. Why? If Perov hadn't known the proper code word and phone number, Danilov would have thought it was a different person calling.

But Danilov, normally a patient man, was impatient to put this meeting behind him. In all the thousands of cases he had researched, he had never come across one like Inmate 222. The poor man was kept in a cell with the worst mental cases of Little Rock Special Psychiatric Hospital, one of a dozen such hospital-prisons in the Soviet Union. The patient's real name was never used, just the number, 222. His drug regimen was aggressive. In another six months he would be a vegetable, if not dead, which, all things considered, might be the most merciful outcome. Already, 222 would be suffering some memory loss.

Danilov had heard about 222 during a routine interview in February. Later, he convinced a Little Rock orderly with whom he cooperated (on an economic basis) to take the extraordinary risk of copying part of the case file. Danilov was terrified just to possess it. He had hidden it in seven different spots around his apartment. No place seemed good enough.

Now, as Danilov sat in his ambulance watching the shadows around River Station for signs of pursuit, he carried in his breast pocket a document from that file: Inmate 222's admission slip, the only place where the man's name appeared:

Anton Perov.

When Danilov saw the name, he understood why the case was so extraordinary. But when he saw who had approved Perov's commitment order, he wished that he had never heard the name Anton Perov.

To be committed to a special psychiatric hospital, one did not have to stand trial. Indeed, the whole purpose of having such asylums was to incarcerate people for crimes not described in the criminal code—just declare them insane and they were out of the way. That's why these prison-hospitals were kept under the jurisdiction of the KGB, not the Ministry of Health. Admittance required signatures from two people: a KGB agent from the Fifth Directorate and a prosecutor from the Ministry of Justice. But Anton Perov's admittance form bore neither of the required signatures. The first signature was that of Yuri Belov, the number-two man in the Leningrad KGB. That made no sense. The second signature was of the deputy minister of agriculture of the U.S.S.R., and, as it happened, the patient's mother:

Yevgenia Perova.

Danilov read the newspapers. He was aware that the careers of both of these people had taken exceptional turns since signing that admittance form. Belov had been promoted to KGB major general and transferred to the director's personal staff in Moscow. Perova had been elevated to the Central Committee and made a candidate-member of the Politburo.

Danilov was tired of fretting over this. Amsterdam assured him that Victor Perov could be trusted and had even assigned the code name "Sigmund" so that a reliable contact could be established. Tonight Danilov would put this Perov business behind him. He would give the admission slip to Victor Perov. Then he would go back to his beloved notebooks, back to the 99 percent. He would go back to writing his book, the *magnum opus* he would one day publish.

Who was he kidding?

He turned over his engine and started toward his meeting at Berth 4-A.

Victor Perov reached Berth 4-A and stopped. The wharf was deserted. A river cruiser, the *Alexander Blok*, was moored there. A few lights shone from the cabins. Twenty feet below him, the Moscow River, swollen by spring runoff, lapped against the sides of the ship.

Rechnoy Vokzal was Moscow's central port. From here, ships went as far north as Leningrad and south to the Black Sea. Large cruisers like the *Alexander Blok* were moored alongside small ferries, party boats and dozens of knifelike hydrofoils, *rokety*, which carried commuter traffic through the network of rivers, canals and reservoirs formed by the confluence of the Moscow and Oka Rivers. Victor had been to Rechnoy Vokzal many times as a student, traveling with friends to a picnic ground somewhere farther up the river. Those had been happy days of *shashlyk*, vodka, guitar, a little skinny-dipping and then, if all went well, a private stroll in the woods with one of the girls.

Six years earlier, Anton had joined him on one of those summer picnics. It was one of the last meetings between the twins that did not end in an argument. Everyone got drunk and played soccer. As usual, Anton was the best player and scored three goals. Later, with extravagant flair, Anton played the role of master chef for the shish kebabs. When someone suggested that Anton join a particular girl in the woods, Anton smiled coyly. No, he replied. He had his eye on someone at the university, though the girl didn't know it yet. Victor had brooded at the time that his twin could be so over-serious as to remain faithful to a girl who didn't even know of his affection. As it turned out, the girl was Oksana Filipova.

The mooring ropes of the *Alexander Blok* groaned.

On a summer afternoon, Rechnoy Vokzal bustled like an amusement park. But at 2:15 on a freezing morning in April, the port was as spooky as that same amusement park after hours, when the rides are closed and the clowns go about without makeup, nipping vodka from flasks.

Sigmund was not here. Victor shrugged and started back along the path he had come.

On the bank above him, two headlights sliced the darkness. They were moving down the steep road from the station to the river. They grew closer. Victor stood still, waiting. Behind him lay the gigantic stern of the *Alexander Blok*. After a few seconds, Victor was able to identify the vehicle. It was an ambulance.

It came nearer. Quickly. Too quickly.

The ambulance picked up speed down the hill and sped across the wharf straight for the river. Victor leaped to his right just in time to avoid being hit. The ambulance reached the edge of the wharf and sailed off the pavement. Airborne, it glided silently into the darkness over the river. It glanced off the stern of the *Alexander Blok*, twisted and fell to the water, grill up. There was a tremendous splash. Victor ran to the edge and looked down. The ambulance was sinking rear-end-first into a boiling kettle of bubbles. By the light of the *Alexander Blok*, Victor saw the driver through the front windshield. He was a dark-haired man, perhaps thirty years old, with a black beard. He didn't move. Sigmund? Lights came on in cabins all over the *Alexander Blok*.

Victor kicked off his shoes and jumped feet-first into the river. He hit the water and went under. He rose to the surface, gasping from the cold. He located the ambulance and started toward it. It was twisting like a screw on its way down. Someone shouted something from the deck of the *Alexander Blok*.

Victor reached the ambulance, which by now had sunk up to the back of the passenger cabin. The driver was unconscious, seated like a cosmonaut on the launch pad. Victor struck the window with his fist.

"Open the door!" Victor cried.

The man didn't move. Victor tried the door handle, already six inches under water. He pulled, but all he did was draw himself against the side of the vehicle.

"Wake up! You're going to drown!"

Victor tried the door handle again, but by now it was too far underwater. The freezing water was sapping Victor's strength. He sensed he was losing the battle. He beat frantically on the passenger window, but the man did not move.

The flooding water reached the man's back and lifted him off the seat. His limp body turned and Victor gasped. A spot of blood painted the man's forehead.

A bullet hole.

In seconds the cabin filled with water and the ambulance went down in front of Victor. He trod water a minute in disbelief. Bubbles rose around him.

Someone on the deck of the *Alexander Blok* threw Victor a life preserver. It hit the water a few feet away. He swam toward it and grabbed on. He was numb and exhausted.

They pulled him by rope to the side of the ship. As he was dragged, Victor looked back at the spot where the ambulance had gone under. The river no longer boiled. All was calm again. The water lapped against the side of the ship. People shouted somewhere overhead, but he kept looking back at the spot on the river where the ambulance had gone down.

Sigmund was gone. The river had swallowed him up.

12

T h e night began as another exercise in tedium for traffic policeman Konstantin Tarasov. It was after 4:00 A.M., and the northern Moscow suburb that was Tarasov's post was quiet. Tarasov sat in his cold booth reading a cheap thriller about a dedicated KGB agent outsmarting CIA dimwits. Tarasov laughed out loud at the well-dressed, worldly KGB hero who spoke exotic languages and knew all about French wines. Tarasov had never met a KGB agent who drank anything but straight vodka. Who would trust a Russian who drank anything else? Still, Tarasov couldn't read enough of these thrillers; sometimes he raced through two a night. His job gave him lots of time for reading. His chief responsibility was controlling the traffic signal at the intersection of Leningradskoye Shosse and Ulitsa Krasnoy Armii, which meant sitting in his two-story booth and pushing the buttons—red, yellow, green—as traffic demanded. By the time Tarasov came onto his shift at midnight the traffic signal was already set for blinking-yellow. He would pour a cup of coffee from his thermos and pull out one of his novels.

At 4:07 A.M., the radio on his shoulder hissed.

It was the handset, which meant the caller was either Grigori, a half-kilometer south, or Misha, a half-kilometer north.

"Konstantin?" said the voice.

"Go ahead, Grigori."

"We got a bullet. Coming up fast."

"Drunk?" A driver almost had to be drunk to speed at this time of night. He would be passing dozens of bored *gaishniks* like Tarasov who would love nothing more than to break the monotony by stopping a lawbreaker. Sometimes Tarasov got so lonely he pulled over cars just to see who was in them.

"He's weaving pretty bad. I'm going out."

"Understood. Be careful."

Tarasov set down his novel. He pictured the clumsy Georgian making his way down the ladder from his booth and then lumbering out onto the highway. Tarasov climbed down the ladder himself. He peered up the highway. Headlights approached Grigori's post.

Konstantin radioed north to Misha. "Be alert. Grigori's got a bullet."

109 / The Forbidden Zone

"Yeah."

"Get your lazy ass out of that chair!" Konstantin barked.

"Okay. Okay."

In the headlights Konstantin could just make out the silhouette of Grigori. He was on the highway with his baton out. Grigori's voice hissed over the radio.

"Devil, it's a *chlenavoz*."

This was slang for a black Volga. Literally, it meant "member carrier," as in "a-car-that-is-carrying-a-member-of-the-Communist-party." But "member" was also slang for penis. Tarasov winced. On the streets, the expression was common enough, but to hear it over a police radio annoyed Tarasov. Grigori had worked south of him for all of the two years Tarasov had been assigned to traffic, and his comrade's vulgar familiarity was a sign that he had deduced Tarasov's feelings about the Party. It occurred to Tarasov that he had been getting too friendly with his men.

"What's the number?" asked Tarasov. License plates were coded — "K" for KGB, "MOS" for Moscow City Council, and so on. Yellow was foreign mission. Red was diplomatic. The system was supposed to be secret, but every Muscovite knew it.

"Just a minute. I'm trying to see. Damn, why doesn't he dim his lights?"

There was a screech of tires, and the radio crashed.

"Grigori!" Tarasov cried into the radio. "What the hell's going on?"

"I'm down! Son-of-a-bitch swiped me."

Tarasov took off at a full run for his car, which was parked in the median of the divided highway. The Volga was coming fast toward him now. As he ran, Tarasov radioed ahead to Misha. "Grigori's down! Repeat. Grigori's down! Get over there with your car. He may need to go to the hospital."

"SOP is to call an ambulance," said Misha.

Tarasov was still running. "Too slow. He could be hurt."

"I'm not supposed to leave my post—"

"Misha, goddamn it! Get your ass over there. That's an order. I'm going after the car."

"Yes, Inspector."

The Volga sped past just as Tarasov turned over the engine. He flipped on the siren and hit the gas.

On good roads Tarasov's Moskvich was no match for the Volga, but this far from the center the asphalt was a battlefield of potholes. The driver couldn't hit top speed, and Tarasov knew where to weave. After a four-mile chase, he came up behind the Volga, and it pulled over.

The plates were issued by the U.S.S.R. Supreme Soviet.

A real big shot.

Tarasov got out and went to the Volga's open window. The driver was alone in the car. He was about fifty years old with thin gray hair and an expensive watch on his wrist. He wore a tailored suit with a tie that was pulled loose. Tarasov could smell the vodka on the man's breath. Tarasov saluted.

"Good evening, Inspector."

"Get out of the car."

"Now, Inspector, I'm sure we can—"

"I said, get out of the car. Now!" Tarasov boomed.

The man handed Tarasov his red Communist party card. Twenty rubles was stuck in the pages.

Tarasov glared at it. "Are you attempting to bribe me?"

"What the hell are you talking about? That's a week's wages. Take it."

"Get out of the car, comrade."

The man narrowed his eyes. "Do you know who I am?"

Tarasov pulled open the door and snatched the man from his seat.

"You hit an officer of the State Automobile Inspectorate this evening, comrade. You're going to jail."

"I did? I mean, I only saw him at the last minute. It was so dark."

"You are under arrest for suspicion of driving while intoxicated. At this time I will take you to headquarters where you will be given a sobriety test. Depending on the results of that test, charges will be brought against you."

"Charges! Are you insane? I'm a people's deputy of the Supreme Soviet of the U.S.S.R. Let me go now and maybe I won't have you busted in rank."

Tarasov slugged the man hard in the stomach. He doubled over and dropped to his knees. "Garbage," Tarasov muttered.

He put the man in cuffs and led him to his car.

The station was quiet when Tarasov arrived with his prisoner, and he took him directly to the holding area. "Do a sobriety test on this one," he told the duty officer. "Let me know the results right away. I'll be at my desk."

"Yes, comrade inspector."

Tarasov went to his desk and got right to work on the arrest paperwork. Later, he felt someone standing over him. He turned and looked up at Major Karl Rostovsky.

"I thought you'd want to know, Grigori's going to be all right," said Karl.

"Thank god."

"He's in the hospital. His spleen ruptured and they had to take it out."

"Son-of-a-bitch."

Karl sat on the edge of the desk. "You working on the arrest paperwork?"

"Almost finished. I just have to—"

"Forget it. He's free."

"You let him *go?*" Tarasov exclaimed.

"Had to. He never should have been brought in, and you know it."

"He hit Grigori! He could have killed him!"

Karl waved his hand. "Don't even start with me about this."

Tarasov shook his head in disbelief.

"Listen, there's something else I wanted to talk to—"

Tarasov wasn't listening. "This is dog shit, Karl. That guy was as drunk as a Cossack!"

"Will you shut up about it!" Karl said irritably. "Why do you always have to act like the only honest cop around here? I'm sick of it."

Tarasov wadded up the report and tossed it in the trash.

Karl said, "Now, there's something else I want to talk to you about. Something happened tonight, and it's presented me with a problem."

"Really?" Tarasov said with exaggerated interest.

Karl scowled. "We're friends, right? I mean, I got you this job when you needed it. We went to school together."

Tarasov shrugged. "Sure."

"I need some advice." He shot Tarasov a sideways glance. "It's about the KGB."

"You know I have no contact with Lubyanka," said Tarasov. "It's been over two years."

"I know that. It's just that . . . oh, shit, my neck is really in the noose on this one, Konstantin. I just don't want to wind up in the gulag, you know?"

"What's going on?"

"We fished the son of a Central Committee member out of the river tonight."

"Jesus."

"That's not all. We pulled out another man, a Jew. He had a bullet in his head."

Tarasov whistled. "You think the son did it?"

"Maybe. Frankly, I don't care. The KGB has taken over the case. Some general by the name of Yuri Belov."

"Belov!"

"You know him?"

Tarasov pinched his lips. "We've crossed paths."

"I thought you might have. You were pretty high up. I mean, that's what I heard, not that you ever talk about it."

Tarasov shrugged. "And now you've got to figure out how to file your report?"

"Right. I mean, we've got a homicide here. You know this General Belov. What would he want me to do? Bury the report, or play it straight? I can't very well ask him."

"Belov would want you to bury it," said Tarasov. "He'll take credit for keeping the matter quiet and he'll have another chip on a Central Committee member. He's got more chips than a poker player on a good night."

"Bury it," Karl breathed. "Thanks. What a relief."

Tarasov stood up. "If that's it, I'm exhausted. I just want to get out of here."

"Going home?"

"Of course I'm going home! Things aren't that bad."

"How is she?"

"Marina? She's still after me. The usual. Flat's too small. Neighborhood's lousy. She wants some new furniture; we're at the back of the queue."

Tarasov didn't mention the most serious issue — Sasha's coming draft notice.

"We've all been there," said Karl. "A woman marries a *gaishnik*, she's not exactly set for a life of luxury."

"That's the problem — Marina married a KGB-shnik." Tarasov went to the door. "By the way, who was the Central Committee member?"

"Yevgenia Perova."

Tarasov blanched. "The minister of agriculture? You're sure?"

"Of course. It was her son at the scene. The astronomer." Karl frowned thoughtfully at him. "What do you know about it?"

Tarasov shook his head and went out.

Tarasov came through his front door and hung his coat on the peg. He noticed at once that his wife's coat was missing.

"Anybody home?"

No answer. He went to the kitchen. A note lay on the table.

Call me at mother's. — Marina.

A sick feeling came over Tarasov. He went to the bedroom and opened the drawers of Marina's dresser. Empty. Her closet. Empty. He went to Sasha's room. The same.

He picked up the phone and dialed. Marina answered.

"What's going on?" he demanded.

"I'm leaving you," said Marina.

"Just like that? In the middle of the night?"

"I'm sorry. I told you, I can't live like this anymore."

"Like what? Do I drink too much? Do I hit you?"

"You know what I mean. A tiny flat in a factory neighborhood. No car. No status. Queuing for everything. I can't do it."

"Others do."

"I can't. And I have to think about Sasha."

"*I'm* thinking about him all the time. Every minute."

"You weren't thinking about him when you left Lubyanka."

Jesus. Tarasov sat down. "I thought we were getting through all this."

Marina said, "You may as well know. I'm going to marry Vladic."

The room spun. *"Titovo?* No. My god, Marina. The man's an imbecile! You can't be serious!"

"Sasha will be drafted in two years. Our little Sasha. If you had stayed at Lubyanka you could have gotten him into the academy. Now . . . you can't even guarantee he'll get an easy assignment."

"And Vladic can?"

"He's an undersecretary at the Ministry of Foreign Affairs. Of course, he can."

"Since when are you a whore, Marina?"

"Call me names if you like," snapped Marina. "If I ever need a ticket fixed, I hope I can still call. Good-bye."

"Wait! I'm sorry. I didn't mean that. It's just . . . I can't live without my family, Marina. You know that."

"I don't know what to say, Konstantin. I've said it all."

"Say you'll come back."

"I can't."

"You won't."

"All right. I won't."

Tarasov thought hard. "What if I said I could get my old job back at the KGB?"

"I'd say you were crazy. They'd never have you back. Not after what you did."

"What if I said I knew a way? Would you come back then?"

"I'll believe it when I see it."

"Just give me a chance. But I need some time, Marina. A month."

"I've given you the last two *years.*"

"A month, Marina. You owe me that. How much is it worth to you to avoid spending the rest of your life under Vladic Titovo?"

Marina was quiet a moment. "One month. I'll put off Vladic somehow. I'll stay here at mother's. But a month from today, if you're not back at Lubyanka then I'm going to marry Vladic Titovo. I have to get on with my life."

She hung up.

Tarasov got his address book from the drawer and looked up a number. He dialed.

"Allo?"

"Hi, Leo. Kill anybody lately?"

"Konstantin Tarasov? Jesus, I thought you were dead."

"Very funny. Put me through to Shatalin."

Leo laughed. "You're quite a comedian. You still think you can call up the director of the KGB, just like that? I've got a news flash for you: You're a gaishnik. Go give someone a ticket."

"Just put Shatalin on the line."

"He doesn't want to talk to you."

"He does about this."

"Oh yeah? Why's that?"

"Tell him it's about General Yuri Belov. I may have some information for him."

"I'll pass it along."

Leo called back five minutes later. "I'm sending a car over now. And Konstantin—this had better be real."

T h e black Volga took Tarasov to the Moscow City Council Theater, a low-budget acting company that was an argument against state-supported arts. The driver parked at the front door and handed Tarasov a ticket. "Enjoy the show," he said.

The ticket was for Balcony Row X, Seat 14. Tarasov went into the theater and climbed to the balcony. The auditorium was empty and nearly dark. He found his seat and sat down.

A few minutes later, two men appeared—one at each exit. A moment later, a third man came down the aisle toward Tarasov—Oleg Shatalin.

Tarasov had met the KGB director fifteen years earlier, shortly after Tarasov joined the service. Shatalin was then a middle-level agent in Foreign Intelligence. He would become the closest thing Tarasov ever had to a mentor. As an overseas operative, Shatalin had been brilliant. But even more important to his success were his political instincts. He was far more ruthless with his political rivals than he ever had been with the Americans. Shatalin shot up the ladder, always inviting Tarasov to go with him.

Shatalin's last promotion had come just a year earlier, and this was the first time Tarasov had seen his old comrade since he became director. He wore a gray double-breasted suit and fashionable Finnish spectacles, like a Western businessman.

Tarasov rose from his seat.

"Stay as you are," said Shatalin.

Shatalin came beside him and sat down. He did not offer his hand.

"Sorry about the meeting place," said Shatalin. "But you know I can't let you be seen in Lubyanka."

Shatalin took out a silver cigarette case and snapped it open. "Smoke?"

In the dim light, Tarasov saw that they were Winstons.

"As I recall, you developed a taste for American tobacco," said Shatalin.

"I've learned to smoke *papirosy*."

Shatalin wrinkled his nose. "Terrible Russian stuff." He snapped a lighter and held the flame to Tarasov's cigarette. He lit his own.

"So what's this about General Bassett Hound?" Shatalin asked.

Belov had been Shatalin's enemy for twenty years. While Shatalin had been coming up through the Foreign Intelligence route, a more customary path to the top, Belov remained in Moscow cracking down on internal dissent and building powerful allies in the Communist party. They had crossed paths on several occasions, and it had never been pleasant.

Shatalin's promotion to KGB director should have spelled the end of Belov's career. Shatalin couldn't demote him, so he did the next best thing—he assigned him to Leningrad, where he was their number-two man. That assured him such benign duties as border fortifications on the Finnish and Norwegian borders. For an ambitious career man like Yuri Belov, it might as well have been Siberia. Then, in January, Belov returned from political exile and was installed by powerful men in the Party as head of Counterintelligence. Essentially, he was placed on Shatalin's staff. Tarasov had shaken his head when he heard about it. Belov was a spy for the Communist party. The KGB and the Communists spied on each other even more than they did on the Americans.

"I've been following General Belov's remarkable change of fate."

Shatalin snorted. "Is that so?"

"I left the KGB, not the country."

Tarasov took a hit off his cigarette. He'd forgotten how good Virginia tobacco could taste. "My guess is you've been unable to find out how he pulled it off."

"Why do you say that?"

"Because Belov's still there."

Shatalin took a deep breath. "And I suppose you know?"

"I do. Podolok."

Shatalin took a deep hit off his cigarette. "Go on."

Tarasov knew he had the director's attention now. In all the world, there was only one man Shatalin hated more than Belov, and it was Anatoly Podolok.

Tarasov said, "Clearly, Belov has some dirt on Podolok, something so damaging that he was able to blackmail Podolok into rescuing him from exile in Leningrad. Now, if you had that information . . . just think."

"You have some idea about this?"

"I might. You know Yevgenia Perova?"

"The Iron Perova," Shatalin shrugged. "Sure. Hard-working. Earnest. A real goody-goody. I read about her in the papers like everyone else."

"It's very suspicious, don't you think, that both she and Belov were promoted the same week, both with ties to the same man—Podolok."

Shatalin shrugged. "You're reaching."

"Last night at Rechnoy Vokzal the Moscow police found Yevgenia Perova's son at a murder scene. The KGB has taken over the case. Guess who's in charge? General Yuri Belov."

Shatalin sat up straight. "How do you know this?"

"What does that matter? I know it."

Shatalin smoked thoughtfully. "I'm going to tell you something . . . I hadn't made the connection until just now."

"What?"

"An American scientist named Katherine Sears disappeared from the Intourist Hotel last night. She was Victor Perov's partner in some Soviet-American project." He paused. "My men tell me it looks like an abduction."

"Ours or theirs?"

"Ours."

"That's a hell of a coincidence — Victor Perov going in the river on the same night his American partner is abducted."

They both sat quietly smoking and thinking about it.

"Podolok, Belov, Perova," Tarasov said finally. "An interesting triangle."

"The American — she could be the key to breaking it up."

"Right," said Tarasov. "But Belov's got her. Hell, she's probably already in a shallow grave somewhere."

"So where does that leave us?"

"Perhaps there's another way."

Shatalin threw his cigarette on the floor and stamped it out. "What do you want?"

"My old job back, restoration of my rank of colonel."

"Why not *my* job while you're at it?" Shatalin scoffed. "Why do I need you? I could put any number of detectives on this."

"Like Leo Yakunin?"

Shatalin didn't answer.

"You need me because you want to involve as few people as possible, and I'm already involved. Because I'm on the outside, and you don't have to worry about a chain of command. Because you know I can keep a secret. Because I'm desperate and I can't afford to fail. And because I'm the best detective you ever had."

Shatalin's lips turned up in a small smile. "What do you need?"

"First, some kind of official status. Special consultant to the director, or something like that."

"I'll have Leo set it up."

"I assume a task force has been organized to find the American."

Shatalin nodded.

"I'll need to attend the meetings."

"Impossible. I'll get you the transcripts. Good enough?"

"It will have to do," said Tarasov. "I'll also need access to KGB files, records, surveillance reports — that kind of thing."

"Leo will serve as your liaison. I don't want to see you in the halls of Lubyanka, Konstantin."

"Fine. But not Leo. We have a history, and it's not good."

"You mean West Berlin?" Shatalin snorted. "You acted like a fool, Konstantin. You wouldn't believe how many times I have had to explain to the boys in wet-ops why the father of the poison-tipped umbrella is working as a Moscow *gaishnik*." Shatalin shook his head vigorously. "I want to keep this investigation as contained as possible—just like you said. It's Leo, or no deal."

Tarasov sighed. "I'll need a month."

Shatalin put out his hand and smiled. "Welcome back, comrade."

13

O n the docks of Rechnoy Vokzal, it took police only a few minutes to identify Victor Perov as the son of a high-ranking official. They wrapped him in a blanket, gave him hot tea and drove him home.

As they neared his apartment, Victor warmed his hands on his cup and asked: "Aren't you going to even ask me what happened?"

"I'm not on the case," said the officer.

"Who is?"

The officer put his finger to his lips.

Victor understood. The KGB had taken over, which meant he would soon be getting a call from Yevgenia. What would he tell her?

Back home, Victor and Oksana went over and over the events of the past forty-eight hours — the dinner at the Moskva Restaurant, Sigmund at the river, Katherine's message. They talked for hours in the kitchen over coffee about what Victor proposed to do next. By dawn, there was nothing more to say. Victor got to his feet.

"You're sure?" Oksana asked one last time.

Victor had changed out of his wet clothes and was now dressed for work. Oksana was in a robe, her eyes puffy from crying. Even then, she managed to look beautiful.

"It's best this way."

She tried to hug him, but he withdrew.

She put her hand to her mouth. "Oh, god," she sobbed. "How did this happen?"

"I'm so sorry."

She wiped her eyes. "Grisha and I will be moved out when you get back."

"I'll call."

"We're going to miss you."

Victor tried to reply, but his throat clamped shut. He put on his coat and went outside.

■

H e stepped through the doors of the SAPO Institute at 9:15 A.M.

"Feeling better, Victor?" asked the security guard.

Victor had nearly forgotten — he had called in sick yesterday.

"Much better, Ivan."

Victor went to his office and began to dig through the papers in his file cabinet. A voice came from the door.

"Doing a little housecleaning?"

Oleg stood in the doorway.

Victor went back to his work.

"Stop by after you're done," Oleg said cheerfully. "We need to have a chat. I'll be in Boris Orlov's office."

Victor continued paging through his files. "I can't. Sorry, Oleg. Lots to do."

"This is not a request."

Victor looked up. He thought about something Oleg had said. "Why are you in Boris's office?"

"Boris has left SAPO."

"Really?" Victor paused to consider the news. It was odd.

"So I can expect you then?" asked Oleg.

"No, Oleg."

"No?" Oleg was incredulous.

Victor kept on sorting his files.

"This is very strange behavior, comrade." He paused. When Victor still didn't reply he went on. "You should know, your continued participation in the Soviet-American survey is by no means guaranteed."

Victor stopped. He walked around his desk toward Oleg, who still stood in the doorway. Victor swung the door shut. The last thing he saw was a look of wide-eyed astonishment on Oleg's face.

By ten o'clock Victor had assembled a six-inch stack of notebooks and memos. He put them in his briefcase and hurried out of the institute.

He drove toward the center of Moscow along Kutuzovsky Prospekt to a point not far from the river. He parked on the roadside, grabbed his briefcase and got out.

The monstrous Ukraina Hotel, with its gargoyled facade, was behind him. Across the Moscow River it faced the gleaming white marble of the Russian parliament. Ahead rose a tight cluster of yellow brick buildings ringed by a chain-link fence. A single entrance for cars and pedestrians opened directly in front of Victor. A KGB agent, disguised as a policeman, stood in a bare aluminum booth near the entrance. Inside the compound, exotic, foreign cars were visible — BMWs, Mercedes, Chevrolets. All bore yellow or red license plates. This was "Kutuzovsky Seven," the city's largest foreigner ghetto. Like all but a handful of Muscovites, Victor had never been here. But of course he knew about it. Everyone knew about it.

He walked briskly toward the wide gap in the fence. The KGB man came out of his booth.

"Where do you think you're going?" he demanded in Russian.

"I . . . no Russian speak," said Victor in Russian.

The agent frowned and surveyed Victor. By his clothes, his appearance, the Soviet-made briefcase in his hand, Victor was clearly a Russian.

"Wait here a moment," said the man.

Victor smiled and said, "*Spacibo*." He walked straight ahead at the same brisk pace.

"Wait!" the man called. "*Stoy!* Stop!"

But Victor was already on his way. As Victor glanced back the man dashed to his booth and picked up the telephone.

Victor went to the east building on the quad and stopped at a door with an engraved metal plate. It said:

The New York Times

He went inside. A secretary looked up and said in Russian, "Can I help you?"

"I would like to see Grayson Hines," said Victor in English.

Boris Orlov had led Victor to the American correspondent — unintentionally, of course. That day at SAPO, with Lena trembling in the corner, Boris had been trying to convince Victor that Katherine Sears was a spy. "She called *The New York Times*' Moscow bureau," Boris had said. "We have recordings. She spoke to Grayson Hines."

Katherine had been foolish. *The New York Times* bureau was under constant surveillance by the KGB, and her calls had been recorded. Her name was linked to Victor's through the astronomical survey and SAPO. It wouldn't have taken long for those recordings to find their way to Boris Orlov.

Now Victor needed Grayson Hines's help. For what he would do next, Victor had to have someone on the outside. If Katherine trusted Grayson Hines, Victor hoped he could too.

Grayson stood in the doorway smiling. "Victor Perov, how nice to see you. Please, come in."

Grayson wore blue jeans and a sweater. He looked as relaxed as a man on holiday. He led Victor past several doors into the most fascinating office Victor had ever seen. Soviet offices were like theater sets prefabricated to create a single effect: the impression of power. They held obligatory portraits of Lenin alongside the current Soviet leader, the complete works of Lenin in a bookcase, two to seven phones on the desk, and as many chairs as could be squeezed into the space. By contrast, Grayson's office was something totally new. Books in English and Russian lined every wall. Newspapers — *Izvestiya, Pravda, Soviet Russia, Literature Gazette,* even obscure periodicals like *Railroading News* — were piled up on his desk and floor. A coffee-stained mug sat atop one of the piles. But that was not the most astonishing thing. On the wall to Victor's right was a poster of Leonid Brezhnev in a bikini bathing suit. He was at the beach standing ankle-deep in water. His enormous pot belly fell over his swim suit, and he was grinning. Someone had tacked the words "Going for the Gold?" across the top, an obvious reference to Brezhnev's love of medals. Just looking at it made Victor feel treasonous. He had entered another world, a terrifying world. Was this freedom? If so, he had an urge to bolt outside, past the KGB guard, back to the world he understood. He looked away.

"I hope I'm not interrupting," said Victor.

"Not at all," said Grayson, oblivious to Victor's discomfort. He pointed to a chair, and they both sat down.

"In fact, it may be fortunate that you showed up," said Grayson. "Perhaps you can help me with a piece I'm working on."

"I doubt that."

Grayson laughed. "Not for the record. It's about the six-month anniversary of the shooting down of the Korean airliner. I don't expect the government to apologize, of course. So instead I went into the street to interview ordinary Muscovites, looking for signs of compassion, but they were even more rabid than the government. They said things like —" he checked his notes "— 'Serves them right,' and 'Shoot down more of them.' " Grayson shook his head in disbelief. "Two-hundred and sixty-nine people were killed, and I heard not a hint of compassion. Can you explain that?"

Victor gaped at the American. Did he really expect an answer? How could anyone compress into a single thought Russia's cultural short-circuit that precluded compassion for the men, women and children who perished on that plane? Victor himself felt the common man's self-righteous fury, even as he felt shame for his lack of sympathy. This duality — how could anyone explain it to an outsider? Victor quoted in Russian:

> *And courage will never abandon us.*
> *We're not afraid to be shot dead,*
> *Not bitter to be bereft of home.*
> *We will defend you, Russian speech,*
> *Guard you, great Russian tongue.*
> *Free and unsullied we will carry you through,*
> *Save you from bondage, for our children's children.*
> *Forever!*

"Anna Akhmatova," said Grayson.

Victor nodded. "This patriotic anthem was written in 1942, after her husband was executed; after her closest friend was tortured to a point where he tried to commit suicide; after the government had excluded her from publication and labeled her 'a mixture of nun and whore.' "

"So the answer to my question is *patriotism?*" Grayson asked doubtfully. "I don't buy it. Americans are patriotic."

Victor shook his head at the young correspondent from the United States. "You have an impossible job."

"That's what I tell my editors back in New York."

"No, not for the reasons you think." Victor stood up. "Let's take a walk."

Grayson thought about that a moment. Victor could see him weighing the risks. Expulsion was always a risk to foreign correspondents. Finally, Grayson said, "What the hell," and got to his feet.

They retraced Victor's steps out of the compound, past the guard post. The guard scowled at Victor.

"He will report you," said Grayson.

"I know."

They crossed Kutuzovsky Prospekt and skirted the Ukraina Hotel to the river bank. The day was gray and it was hard to tell where the sky ended and the Russian White House began.

Grayson said, "I'm a little surprised to see you. I don't believe I've ever had a person of your background as a visitor."

"I wanted to thank you for what you did to help Katherine Sears."

"What exactly did I do?"

Victor smiled and leaned on the railing. He watched a barge move up the river. It reminded him of Rechnoy Vokzal. Sigmund. Last night. This morning. He suddenly felt very tired.

"Under your desk you will find some notebooks," Victor said. "They're very technical. You'll need an expert to decipher them."

"You put them there?" asked Grayson. He looked nervous.

"Don't worry, they're not military. They're Dr. Vladimir Ryzhkov's notes on our theory of Dark Matter. We were partners. I lied in Helsinki."

"I see."

A man walking a dog passed by. They waited until he turned the corner.

Victor said, "Don't judge me too harshly. It is what I am doing now that will be judged harshly by my comrades."

"What *are* you doing now, Victor?"

Victor laughed. "Stepping over a cliff." He leaned on the railing. "Will you write an article?"

Grayson shrugged. "This is not what I would call 'big news.' I'll file a brief, but what ultimately gets published is not my decision. I have editors who make that call."

Victor frowned. "Surely you can explain to them how important this is?"

Grayson smiled indulgently. "Our system doesn't work like that. I'll do what I can. I promise." He gave Victor a sideways glance. "Actually, there is one thing I could do to almost guarantee that the story gets published."

"What?"

"Reveal my source. Can I use your name?"

"I expected nothing less," said Victor.

A n hour later, Victor was in his mother's Kremlin office.

He told her everything. She listened with patience and said, "You have behaved foolishly, Victor. I expected more from you."

"Are you listening? I'm telling you Anton may be alive."

"Anton is dead," said Yevgenia. "You saw the file."

"The file the KGB gave you. Perhaps they're hiding something."

"Nonsense."

"How can you say that after what I've told you?"

"What have you told me? Some American says Anton is alive because some Jew told her?"

"Who said Sigmund was a Jew?"

Yevgenia's face was like a mask. "I got a call from the KGB about Rechnoy Vokzal. I heard all about your swim in the river."

"What else did they say?"

"Nothing about a bullet wound, if that's what you're asking. This man you call Sigmund is really Pavel Danilov. He drowned after he drove his ambulance off the wharf. He was probably drunk."

Victor got up from his chair and walked to the window. The inside of the Kremlin's red brick wall stared back at him.

"Why won't you hear me?" he asked softly, almost to himself. He turned, frowning. "What are you not telling me?"

"Victor, leave this thing alone."

"There *is* something."

Yevgenia sighed. "Your brother is gone. All you can do now is ruin your career. You've worked so hard—"

"My career?" Victor said incredulously. "What's the matter with you?"

Yevgenia looked away. Her eyes fell on the portrait of Lenin. "I couldn't bear to lose both of you."

Victor stared at her a moment. His face softened. He went around the desk to her.

"Why don't you come around and see Grisha?" he asked. "He's always asking about you."

"I doubt I'd be welcome."

"You mean Oksana? Nonsense. She would love for you to spend some time with your grandson. He's growing up so fast. He's really starting to look like Anton. You should see the way . . . Yevgenia? What's the matter?"

The blood had drained from Yevgenia's face.

She shook her head as though trying to cast away some thought. The color returned to her cheeks, and she was the Iron Perova again.

"I'll try to make it over sometime," she said noncommittally. "But I'm very busy right now."

Victor nodded and went to the door.

"Victor," Yevgenia called after him. "Don't do anything stupid."

"Good-bye, Yevgenia," he said.

T h e door closed and Yevgenia picked up the gray phone on her desk. The line began to ring at once. Anatoly Podolok picked up.

"What is it?"

"I've just spoken to Victor. He confirmed what the American told us. The proof died with the Jew."

"That was fast work sending the Tatar to Rechnoy Vokzal. We nearly had a disaster. But Victor must suspect his brother is alive."

"He suspects."

"Won't he try to find him?"

Yevgenia stared out the window. Her jaw line, normally so pronounced, had vanished.

"Yevgenia?"

"Huh?" She was surprised to find herself still on the telephone.

"What's the matter with you?"

"Nothing. Go ahead."

"I said: Won't Victor hunt for his brother?"

"Let him look," said Yevgenia. "It's a needle in a haystack."

14

From the case file of Patient 222, Little Rock Special Psychiatric Hospital. Interview 19. April 1984. Attending physician, Dr. Yefim Lazda. Also present, Chief Nurse Olga Gusarova.

LAZDA: Why do you think you are here?

PATIENT: I am sick. I would hardly be here if I were well.

LAZDA: That is true. But do you think you are sick?

PATIENT: It hardly seems relevant what I think. I'm not a professional.

LAZDA: I will decide what is relevant. Now answer the question.

PATIENT: What question?

LAZDA: Do you think you are sick?

PATIENT: I must be.

GUSAROVA: He's playing games.

LAZDA: You're playing games with me. That won't help you.

PATIENT: I have been diagnosed as suffering from sluggish schizophrenia by leading Soviet psychiatrists such as yourself. What do you want me to say? Tell me. I'll say it.

GUSAROVA: We only want to hear the truth. Why are you acting this way?

PATIENT: I'm trying to answer your question.

LAZDA: No you're not. You're trying to avoid it. Now answer me: Do you agree with the diagnosis?

PATIENT: I don't understand the question. It's not for me to agree or disagree. I'm just a patient.

LAZDA: Clearly we haven't treated you enough.

GUSAROVA: We're the only ones who can help you. Don't you realize that?

PATIENT: I put my faith in God.

GUSAROVA: Faith in God is absurd. People who believe in God are sick.

PATIENT: Really? But there are billions of Christians —

GUSAROVA: Billions. Trillions. Statistics don't matter. Faith in God is a symptom of mass psychosis. It's in all the medical literature.

PATIENT: I hadn't read that.

GUSAROVA: You don't read the specialized literature.

PATIENT: No, that's true. I don't read the specialized literature. Tell me, nurse, where did you get your medical training.

GUSAROVA: That's enough. I can see your treatments will have to be continued.

LAZDA: Why did you stage that demonstration?

PATIENT: To save Lake Sini. They're building a paper mill. It will destroy the ecosystem.

LAZDA: But the state is building that plant. Don't you trust the state?

GUSAROVA: Answer the question!

PATIENT: I think people make mistakes. The state is made up of people.

GUSAROVA: Ah-ha! Don't you see? This paranoia is a symptom of your schizophrenia.

LAZDA: What do you think of the war in Afghanistan?

PATIENT: Same as you, I suppose.

LAZDA: There you go again. Don't you understand that your whole diagnosis depends on how you answer these questions?

PATIENT: I understand that very well.

LAZDA: Good. So answer the question.

PATIENT: I think more troops should be sent in.

LAZDA: Why do you think that?

PATIENT: The region is mountainous and it's hard to wage war.

GUSAROVA: We're not waging war there. We're a peace force.

PATIENT: Then the peace force will be there for a long time.

LAZDA: What do you think of Andrei Sakharov?

PATIENT: I've never met the man.

GUSAROVA: Sakharov is an enemy who plots to bring down the Soviet state. He is a traitor.

PATIENT: I don't know about such things. Sakharov is an educated man, whereas I never finished college.

LAZDA: Why not?

PATIENT: I flunked out.

GUSAROVA: Did you know that the majority of academics are schizophrenic?

PATIENT: No, I didn't know that. Why aren't you treating them too?

GUSAROVA: They aren't disturbing the peace, so there is no need.

LAZDA: Would you be willing to write a statement recanting your views?

PATIENT: I'm not a good writer.

LAZDA: That's okay. We could help.

PATIENT: I don't know. . . . People might think I'm writing it just because I'm sick.

LAZDA: No one would think that.

PATIENT: What would I write?

LAZDA: Just what you said today. You're sick. Doctors are treating you. Sakharov is a traitor. You support the war. You support the building of that paper mill on Lake Sini.

PATIENT: I didn't say that.

LAZDA: Are you refusing to do it?

PATIENT: That's politics. I'm not political.

LAZDA: Everyone is political.

GUSAROVA: Are you for the state or against it?

PATIENT: I prefer to keep my views to myself.

GUSAROVA: Then you are against it. A citizen has a civic duty to speak his views.

PATIENT: But in our country it is dangerous to speak one's views.

GUSAROVA: I find that statement outrageous. You are indeed an enemy of the people.

PATIENT: I thought we stopped using that phrase in 1953.

GUSAROVA: We use it here.

LAZDA: Such a pity. And I thought you were getting better.

GUSAROVA: He's no better. Just more clever.

LAZDA: I concur. Nurse, I order a continuation of his insulin shock treatments. Also, start him on sodium Amytal—that might make him more cooperative. Comrade, for you the most important thing is to acquire a realistic understanding of Soviet reality.

PATIENT: I'm getting there.

15

Leo Yakunin called Tarasov at home about the fire.

"It was at a KGB safe house near Lubertsi, an hour-and-a-half east of Moscow," said Leo. "Two agents from Leningrad died."

"Leningrad?" Tarasov asked, startled.

"Right. It occurred to me that this may have been where Belov held the American. You want me to check it out?"

"No. You're going to Leningrad."

"Bullshit. You're not my superior officer anymore. You can't just order me around."

Tarasov sighed. It was just like old times.

He had spent the morning reading through the KGB reports on the disappearance of the American. What they knew was this: At ten o'clock, three men entered the Intourist Hotel using counterfeit passes. Minute bloodstains were found on the wall in Sears's room. No other signs of a struggle. Nothing stolen from the room, so far as anyone could tell. Her purse was on the bed with her passport and visa. A cleaning cart was found near the loading dock with some discarded service uniforms. It was pretty clear what had happened. Three men had ambushed Katherine Sears in her hotel room, knocked her unconscious and then concealed her beneath the cart. Disguised as hotel workers, they wheeled her to the service elevator and descended to the basement, where they loaded her into a waiting car.

The conclusion was inescapable.

"It was a KGB job, Leo," said Tarasov.

"Probably."

"The three men had to come from somewhere, and it's a safe bet General Belov wouldn't have wanted to risk Shatalin finding out through Moscow channels. He would have used freelancers from Leningrad."

"Shatalin didn't say anything about me going to Leningrad."

"He said you should cooperate with me," said Tarasov. "Cooperate."

"Devil!"

"You're looking for any connection between Belov and Perova. Belov was working in Leningrad at the time of their promotions. The link must be there somewhere."

"Let me get this straight. You expect me to go poke around the Leningrad KGB? It's not exactly the public library."

"We'll invent a cover. I know people up there. It'll work." Tarasov grinned into the receiver. "I have confidence in you, Leo. You were never a bad researcher. It was always common sense you lacked."

"*Poshol na khui!*" Leo cursed.

Go to your prick.

T h e next morning, Tarasov stood in an open field in Lubertsi kicking at the charred remains of a two-room cabin. Little was left to kick. The walls and roof had collapsed. Only the chimney stood, rising like an obelisk. A local policeman showed Tarasov around the site.

"It was a typical Russian firetrap," he said. "All wood, amateur electrical wiring. We believe a space heater was responsible."

"Where were the bodies found?"

The man pointed to the back of the structure. "It was an intense fire. Nothing left but bones."

At the opposite end of the wreckage Tarasov spotted some pipes and the remains of a sink lying basin-side down. For no particular reason, he picked up the pipe.

"Hey," said the policeman. "Are you sure you should be here?"

Tarasov ignored him. Using the pipe, he flipped over the sink. Beneath it were some jars and rags. They were charred, but less so than everything else. He picked up a burned rag and unwadded it. When he got to the center, he found red blotches. Blood. He slipped the rag into his pocket.

He stepped off the porch and looked around. Fields rose to the horizon in all directions.

"Pretty isolated up here," said Tarasov.

The policeman shrugged.

"Have you had any rain in the last few days?" Tarasov asked.

"No. Listen, maybe you should talk to my captain —"

"Where does this path go?" asked Tarasov, pointing.

"Into town, through the forest over there," he said.

Tarasov started along the path.

"Hey, where are you going?" the policeman called after him. Tarasov didn't answer. His eyes were on the ground. The policeman went back to his car, sat down on the fender and sulked.

After about five minutes, Tarasov reached a low place where a mound of winter snow was melting steadily into a puddle. Tarasov knelt and studied the ground. Footprints. Three sets. Two men — one large, one small. The other set was made by sneakers. A woman's? He couldn't be sure.

Tarasov went back to the house and found the policeman. "I want that forest searched," he said.

"On whose orders?"

"KGB Director Oleg Shatalin."

The policeman stood up straight. "Are you kidding?"

"What do you think?" snapped Tarasov.

"Okay. Sure. What are we looking for?"

"A body," said Tarasov. "A woman."

Tarasov spent the rest of the day in Lubertsi meeting with the police chief and interviewing neighbors. About five kilometers away, he found a cabin that had been broken into. The burglar had entered through a window and apparently taken shelter for several days. Jars of pickled mushrooms and tomatoes had been taken. There was nothing else to steal.

"Happens all the time out here," the policeman assured him.

Late that night, Leo Yakunin called Tarasov from Leningrad.

"Your friends have set me up as an auditor looking for missing capital equipment," said Leo.

Tarasov laughed. "That should keep people from asking questions."

Tarasov told him about the fire.

"You think she's still alive?"

"Maybe. But we can't count on it. Even if she is, Belov will have half of Counterintelligence looking for her. We couldn't get near her. Forget about her. The key is in Leningrad. Remember, two years ago, Belov was powerless to stop his own transfer to Leningrad. Whatever information he acquired on Podolok, he got it *while in Leningrad,* and he got it with the Iron Perova's help. There's a link. Call me when you find it."

16

I f Katherine Sears had looked carefully from the window of her train as she sped through a railroad crossing on her way to Moscow, she might have seen the black Volga sedan that was carrying Major Konstantin Tarasov to the burned-out cabin. As it happened, she did not.

Katherine had spent the four days since her abduction in an empty cabin three hours' walk from the KGB safe house. She found it near a cluster of houses outside the village of Lubertsi. The sun was just coming up as she drove the butt of the shotgun through the window, felt for the latch and lifted the frame. She might have marveled at her audacity, at her improbable survival after her abduction and attempted rape. But she wasn't marveling at much of anything. She moved as though in a strange dream. It might have been shock, or even the lingering effect of the truth serum. Whatever the reason, Katherine climbed into the cabin that morning feeling as though she were outside her body, watching herself lift one leg, then the other over the window sill.

The cabin had two stories, with two rooms on the first floor and one room on the second—much like the cabin she had burned down. She found some blankets in a closet and climbed into bed fully clothed. She no sooner pulled up the blankets than a strange darkness descended around her bed, as though she had donned dark sunglasses. The horror of the previous night swept over her like a wave. She drew herself into a fetal position and began to shake. She lay like that a long time, slipping in and out of consciousness. Dream and reality became indistinguishable. She awoke with her thumb in her mouth. That was Day One.

On Day Two, she got up and began to explore the cabin. In a kitchen cupboard she found a cache of pickled mushrooms and tomatoes. She ate cautiously at first, and then ravenously. She never left the cabin.

At first, she thought no further ahead than the next minute. Food, warmth, sleep and her own recovery were all her mind could handle. But gradually, lucidity returned. It came from deep within her, the untested strength, a determination to survive.

Night fell on Day Two, and she lay down on the cot knowing that the next day she would have to do something; she couldn't live on tomatoes and mushrooms forever. She didn't want to think about that now, though. Her eye wandered the dim room, eventually falling on the amber ring she wore on her left hand. She stared at it awhile and then slipped it off. She read the Russian inscription.

S lyubovyu.

She smiled.

Katherine and Victor worked together three years before their relationship took its unexpected romantic turn. Their passion crept up on them like a cat, and when it finally pounced they were both breathless and stunned. And exhilarated.

The affair was nothing if not unconventional. They had never kissed, much less made love. They had never seen a movie together or sat down to dinner. Nearly all of their communications were monitored by the KGB, which Katherine had come to think of as an organization of professional chaperones.

In the romance department, Katherine Sears was not what people would call "experienced." A bad complexion and a late-blooming figure had left her pretty much out of the hunt for boys during her teens. She buried her head in her books and pretended it didn't matter that she was asked to neither her junior prom nor her senior ball. College was only a little better. Her complexion cleared and her body matured, but by now she was distrustful of men. They were such shallow creatures—intriguing, but shallow. Wasn't she the same person she had been before she had hips and breasts? In her thirty-two years, Katherine had relationships with exactly three different men, and had never once felt even a fraction of the longing she felt when she thought of Victor Perov.

It was all so complicated. She used to shake her head at colleagues who would complain of their "long-distance" relationships. They had no idea. Of course, there was no way they *could* know. It was a secret.

It began with their notes. After the international survey was approved by both governments, Katherine and Victor began to exchange letters daily through their respective embassies.

At first, their correspondence consisted only of work—data on x-ray emmissions, sectors surveyed in the Large Magellanic Cloud, sectors unsurveyed, conclusions and thoughts on how to improve techniques. But as the project wore on, elements of their personal lives slipped in. That first Christmas, when Katherine wrote that she would be spending the holidays alone, Victor asked why. She told him about the death of her mother a few years earlier, her father's quick remarriage, and Katherine's life-long troubled relationship with her brilliant, exacting father. Victor wrote back that he knew about exacting parents, his own mother was known as the Iron Perova. "People express their love in different ways," he wrote. "It may not be the kind of love you would want, but that doesn't make their love any less. Go home for Christmas, Yekaterina." She did.

In the spring, Katherine noticed a lapse in Victor's work and asked about it. He wrote back about the death of his "Baba Raya," who had essentially raised him. Yevgenia was too busy as a rising star in the Communist party to give much thought to rearing her twin sons. "Motherhood is just not in Yevgenia," he wrote. Victor had made peace with this in a way Katherine could not imagine. He went on to describe the hardships Baba Raya had endured, travails typical for a Russian of her generation. Her father, husband and two sons were all killed by the Nazis. She had survived the siege of Leningrad by eating rats snared by her clever eight-year-old daughter — Yevgenia.

Victor said nothing about his father, and Katherine wondered about that.

Katherine called the American embassy in Moscow and asked them to send flowers to Baba Raya's funeral. A few days later, Katherine received a thank-you note from Victor along with a description of the ceremony. She felt as though she had been there.

And so their letters became more personal. She knew the KGB was reading them, but there was nothing she could do about that. Nothing was ever censored. She assumed this was due once again to Victor's connections in the Communist party. Gradually, she came to feel she knew something of her Russian partner. Katherine was hungry to know more, but how could she penetrate the mysteries shrouded by the Iron Curtain? Victor was a communist, a believer, and she sensed whole, dark parts of himself that he kept hidden — questions in her letters that were left unanswered, words carefully chosen on issues of politics and economics.

In the cabin, Katherine thought about Titus. By now, he would know that she had not returned from London. He would be frantic.

What would he do?

She slipped the ring back on her finger and admired it. Her mind went to the moment she had received the gift.

It was a year earlier, during the long-planned summit in Ithaca between the Russian and the American sides. By then, the survey was already two years old and everyone was maneuvering to take credit for its success. Katherine didn't care about any of that. She was going to get to see Victor, and she was a coiled spring of nervous energy.

Victor arrived in New York City with a delegation of seven Russians, including a Russian television correspondent, a writer for a Russian magazine and an oafish man named Boris Orlov. Boris never took his eyes off Victor. When Boris looked at Katherine, he wore a knowing smirk, as though they shared a great secret. In a way, they did; Boris had read their letters.

The summit progressed in a businesslike way through the three days. On the last night a banquet was held with fifty people, including the president of the university, key alumni and a congressman. Victor and Katherine sat at opposite ends of a long table. Katherine was depressed. Victor was leaving the next morning, and they had barely spoken.

Near the end of the meal a middle-aged Russian passed by Katherine and whispered, "Victor requests to meet you at midnight in the science library." The previous day, Victor had asked for—and received—a key to the library. He had explained that he suffered from insomnia and might want to wander the stacks.

Katherine didn't know it then, but the man who had given her the message was Vladimir Ryzhkov, the man whose suicide in Helsinki had sent her on her long journey to Moscow.

The library was quiet and nearly dark when she arrived. Victor was seated at a long reading table.

He went to her and kissed her three times, in Russian fashion.

"Is this safe?" Katherine asked. "Us meeting, I mean?"

"For a while."

He told her to sit down and then sat beside her. "It's good to get you alone, away from the craziness."

Katherine nodded. There was so much she wanted to say.

"I'm afraid we haven't much time," said Victor. "There's something I want to give you."

He handed her a small package wrapped in simple brown paper tied with a string. She envisioned a lens or a Russian trinket.

"Your letters have meant a lot to me," he said.

Katherine swallowed. "Me too."

Victor's blue eyes glowed with a light of their own in the dark library. The eyes smiled, but they were anxious too, nervous.

About what?

She tried to memorize him. Victor Perov wasn't handsome in an obvious way; his face was soft, almost pudgy and lacked those stone-carved features women were supposed to love. He had a face like a priest—kind and solemn, a little sad. Victor's shoulders were broad and he had powerful arms, which Katherine had admired the previous day while he hoisted some heavy equipment into a van. She was amazed and a little embarrassed by how much she desired him.

"Aren't you going to open it?" he laughed.

"Oh yeah," said Katherine. She tore off the paper and lifted the lid on a small felt box. She gasped.

Inside lay an amber ring.

"It was Baba Raya's," he said. "I want you to have it."

"Oh, Victor . . . it's . . . so beautiful."

"I hope you can accept it," he said. "I had it inscribed."

She read the inscription, *S lyubovyu.*

"What does it mean?" she asked.

He was nervous again. "You might not accept it if I told you."

Their eyes met, and he spoke. "It means, 'With love.' "

She slipped the ring on her finger. And then she was crying.

"My darling," he said and opened his arms. She was about to fall against his chest when the front door to the library rattled. They froze.

They were still hidden by the book stacks, but if anyone came in he would find them at once.

"What do I do?" Katherine whispered.

"Stay here."

Victor went around the stacks toward the door. Katherine sat in her chair trying to quiet her own breathing. She heard Boris's raspy voice.

"Victor! There you are!"

The two men talked for a minute and went out. She was alone again.

Katherine hated Boris Orlov for destroying her moment. It was so unfair. But after creeping from the library, every time she looked down at the ring she would think: "There will be other moments." She began studying Russian and fantasizing about helping him to defect.

Victor's inexplicable silence came that fall. After his bizarre behavior in Helsinki, it began to seem that there would be no other moments. She would never see him again. It was unbearable. Titus Waal suggested that she try to forget about Victor, that she "get on with her life," and she slapped his cheek, which only made Katherine more miserable.

When Titus got word from his old friend at Soviet Psychiatry Watch that Anton was alive, it was all the inducement Katherine needed to try to reach Victor on her own. How could she allow him to go on mourning a brother who wasn't really dead? But her mission to Moscow wasn't 100 percent altruistic; she was honest enough with herself to recognize that she was using it as an excuse—she *had* to see Victor, at least one more time.

And she had! Those precious seconds in the bell tower had completed the moment destroyed that night in the library. Now it was time to move on—Titus was right about that. Tomorrow she would begin her long journey home. Somehow.

On her cot in the dark of the unheated cabin in Lubertsi, Katherine Sears fell asleep.

D a y Three began with Katherine thinking about her next move. Without a passport and exit visa, she couldn't leave the Soviet Union. There was always Victor, but she wouldn't know how to go about finding him. And even if she could, what could he do? She decided there was only one place in Moscow that could help her—the American Embassy.

So just after dawn, Katherine Sears picked up her shotgun and started across a field in the direction of the trains she had heard from the cabin. Her cheeks were hollow, and her eyes had the glassy sheen of a drug addict. She still wore the clothes she had stripped from the doctor. She walked until she hit the railroad tracks. Then she turned west, keeping her feet on the ties. She passed through a patch of forest and threw the shotgun into some weeds. After an hour and a half, she reached a station platform. She had no money for a ticket, so when the train came, she just got on. After several stops, an officious, middle-aged woman in a navy-blue hat came into her carriage and began checking tickets. The train pulled into a station, and Katherine got off. She waited on the platform ten minutes for the next train. Then she was on her way again.

And so it happened that at nine-thirty, exactly a week after her arrival in Moscow, Katherine Sears stepped into the central hall of Moscow's Paveletsky Station. A garbled voice on a loudspeaker made an unintelligible announcement. She stood a minute, looking around her like a peasant girl on her first trip to the capital. A group of a dozen men and women came toward her wheeling carts that overflowed with bags. They stopped to rest, using the bags as chairs. She spied a policeman checking documents, and she ducked toward a side exit.

How far could the embassy be? If she could just get inside the gates, onto American soil, she could get a new passport and work through the consular office to get an exit visa. She hoped to be taking a hot shower in an embassy apartment by evening. The thought made her impatient.

She circled the building. Along the edge of a wide stretch of pavement at the main entrance, dozens of taxis were parked. Men with derby caps and cigarettes dangling from their lips stood in groups chatting.

Titus Waal had once said that taxi parks were magnets for black marketeers. Katherine needed a black marketeer. She picked a group of three men and walked toward them, rehearsing her Russian. The men looked her over and went back to their conversation.

"Excuse me," she said in Russian. "You help me?"

"A she-Polack," one of them muttered.

The tall one looked at her over his shoulder and asked, "Where are you going?"

"I sell something."

"This look like a bazaar to you?"

They all laughed and turned their backs on her again.

"Look," she said and held up her right hand. She wriggled the finger that held her amber ring.

The tall man looked at the ring and shrugged. "So?"

"I want selling it," she said.

The tall man whistled at a group of men a short distance away.

"Sergei!" he called.

A man turned. He was about five feet eight inches and stocky. He might have been a wrestler in his youth, but he was well past that now. Katherine estimated his age at forty-five years. Thin brown hair escaped around the edge of a corduroy derby cap. He took a drag from his cigarette, threw it on the pavement and threaded his way toward them through the bustle of the station traffic.

"Yes?"

The men spoke a minute. Sergei lit a cigarette and turned to Katherine. His dark blue eyes glistened as though something amused him.

He clucked and said in Russian, "What can I do for you, girlie?"

"I selling something."

"So I heard." He said something in Russian that she didn't understand. She looked at him helplessly. "Where are you from?"

Katherine said, *"Ya iz Estonii."*

"Estonian, eh?" He said something else, which, again, she didn't understand. Now he squinted at her suspiciously.

Her heart raced, and she considered turning away. But then he smiled warmly.

"Come with me," he said and led her to his taxi. She got in. He slid behind the wheel and they were off.

Katherine had not expected that. "Wait . . ." she began, but she couldn't find the words to ask where he was taking her.

"Don't worry, girlie," he laughed. "I won't rob you. It's dangerous here. Railroad police everywhere."

He drove five minutes to a place along the river beside an old Orthodox chapel. The structure must have been lovely once, with four delicate onion domes rising into the sky, and a fresco over the door. But as Katherine looked at it from the taxi window, grass grew off a spot in the roof and the gold onion domes were as dull as brass. The fresco was an uneven brown, roughly the color of mud.

Sergei swiveled in his seat and asked to see the ring. She gave it to him. He looked at it a minute and shrugged noncommittally. "How much?"

Katherine figured the ring was worth a thousand dollars. "Five hundred rubles," she said. That was about seven hundred dollars at the official exchange rate.

He nodded. "I'll give you a hundred."

She flushed. "Five hundred."

He laughed and said something she didn't understand. She glared back at him. They settled on two hundred rubles. He got out the money and gave it to her. She took one last look at the ring and passed it to him. He slipped it into his pocket. The deal was done.

"Now American embassy," Katherine said.

"I am your servant," he said. He put the car in gear, and they sped away.

He drove ten minutes and then stopped along a busy road near an underpass.

"Where is the embassy?" Katherine asked, alarmed.

He pointed.

And then she saw it. About a quarter-mile ahead the stars and stripes were hanging from the side of a yellow building. A lump swelled in her throat.

"It's better here," said Sergei. "Close, but not too close."

Katherine nodded. He was right, of course. Not too close.

She said good-bye and started along the sidewalk, keeping her eyes fixed on the flag. She was about halfway there when she saw something that took her breath away. Standing on the sidewalk about thirty yards in front of her was the last person on earth she expected to see.

Jack Sears. Her father.

"Dad!" Katherine cried out.

He didn't hear her over the street noise.

She couldn't believe it. Her father! He was even wearing the sweater she had given him for Christmas! He was looking around with a face she recognized at once — disgust. He looked like a man sniffing bad fish.

She dashed toward him. "Dad!"

He turned in her direction. His face was puzzled. He knew the voice, but he couldn't find her on the crowded street. Or perhaps he didn't recognize her. No matter. In about ten seconds she would throw her arms around him . . .

From a driveway on her left, two men appeared. The first locked his arm around Katherine's neck and slapped his hand over her mouth. The other grabbed her legs. She recognized the second man from the cabin: the man with the oriental eyes, the Tatar. In seconds she was swept from the sidewalk into the alley. She kicked and fought but they carried her wriggling deeper into the alley. The street noise faded. The alley opened into a small, gravel courtyard where several cars were parked. The men trotted toward a small, blue Zhiguli. They reached the car, and the Tatar set her feet on the ground while he fumbled with the trunk keys. She fought again, and a hand came free. She used it to pry the second man's hand from her mouth. She screamed. A fist came down hard on her right eye. She collapsed.

They had the trunk open now. They lifted her over the side.

An engine roared behind them. Katherine looked over the side of the trunk. A taxi bore down on them. The driver's door swung open and smashed against the second man. He was thrown ten feet to the ground as the taxi skidded to a stop. Gravel rained over the alley like hail. The Tatar let go of Katherine, and she rolled from the side of the trunk to the ground. The Tatar reached under his coat. The driver of the taxi — Sergei! — sprinted toward the Tatar with a pipe in his hand. He swung it at his head. There was a crunch, and the Tatar collapsed. A gun tumbled onto the gravel.

Sergei helped Katherine to her feet.

"Come on!" he said.

He pushed her into the back seat of his taxi, shut the door and leaped behind the wheel. Beside them, the men were getting to their feet. Sergei rammed the shifter into reverse and pounded on the accelerator. The taxi sped backward toward the alley entrance, nearly hitting a woman pushing a baby in a stroller. Then there was a *pop*, and a bullet hole cracked the windshield just below the rearview mirror. Sergei kept his foot on the accelerator and they raced across the sidewalk. There was a second *pop* followed by a *clank* from the front grill. They came onto the road directly in the path of a car. The driver leaned on his horn and swerved hard to the right. He struck the back of a truck, and his front grill exploded. Glass and plastic flew. Sergei spun the steering wheel to the left, which sent Katherine sprawling across the back seat. He shifted and hit the gas hard. Tires squealed. The car leaped forward up the ramp and back onto the main road. By the time Katherine managed to sit up, they were already past the American embassy. She looked back to where she had seen her father. She thought she glimpsed his figure in the crowd. The embassy fell away behind them. The last thing she saw was the flag. Then they passed under Mayakovsky Square, heading east.

"That was no mugging!" said Sergei. "That man had a gun!"

"They were waiting for me," Katherine said in English.

"Who are you?"

Katherine frowned at Sergei. "How did you know to come for me?" she asked in Russian.

Sergei didn't answer. He looked angry.

"Tell me."

"Curiosity," he said bitterly. "You said you were Estonian. I'm Estonian. And you, girlie, are definitely not. So I followed you."

"Curiosity," Katherine repeated. *Lyubopytstvo*. Yes, she knew that word.

Sergei drove hard, snaking through residential streets, past mile after mile of dreary housing blocks. He braked hard and accelerated harder, pressing ever deeper into the concrete maze. At first, Katherine figured they were heading northeast, but after a while she lost track.

"Where are we going?" she asked.

Sergei only waved his hand. She heard him mumbling to himself. She fell back into her seat. She was too tired to resist. She fell asleep.

When she awoke it was dusk beneath a thick blanket of gray clouds. The landscape had changed from urban-grim to rural-bleak. Untended fields rose to meet the sky in all directions. Mud and dirty snow competed for dominion over the surface. The wind howled indignation at the car, the only thing in sight to slow its progress.

Katherine closed her eyes, not to rest, but to shut out the world. She saw her father's face combing the crowds for his daughter, then the Tatar, the trunk, the gun . . .

It was 4:30 P.M., nearly dark, when Sergei pulled his taxi onto a gravel road that led to a settlement of about a dozen wood cottages. Their lights twinkled invitingly. He pulled up to a cottage, more or less like all the others. Smoke rose out of the house's single smokestack. Sergei turned off the engine, and the croaking of frogs came to her ears. Sergei twisted in his seat and looked at her. He spoke his first words in three hours.

"What is your name?"

"Katherine."

"Not anymore," he said. "You are Yekatarina Yurgina. You are Latvian. You live in Riga. Understand? You are from the countryside, which is why your Russian is poor."

"What is this place?"

"My grandmother's house," said Sergei, speaking very simple Russian. "Understand? You were visiting a friend in Moscow. Understand? I offered to show you the New Yulia Chapel. It's about a half-mile from here. Understand? But then my car broke down. So now you need a place to stay for the night. Understand?"

Katherine nodded throughout, grateful for the breaks in speech that gave her time to translate.

"Don't worry about your Russian," said Sergei. "Baba Krista's is not much better. She's Estonian."

They went inside. The house was cozy and smelled of burning firewood and the rootiness of fresh vegetables. An old woman shuffled up the hall toward them. She was hunched over to about forty-five degrees, and looked at them over her brow. Her head was wrapped in a red scarf tied under her chin. Her eyes were wet and glistened with a light of their own in the dim hallway. They were Sergei's eyes. Her face was carved with such a labyrinth of wrinkles that it seemed the whole murderous history of the twentieth century was etched there. Katherine could have studied that face for days. If she had the courage.

Sergei kissed the old woman's cheeks three times and spoke in Estonian. The old woman replied in a gravelly voice.

They looked at Katherine and spoke for a minute. Katherine smiled uncertainly back at them.

"Meet Baba Krista," said Sergei.

"Pleased to meet you," said Katherine in Russian, offering her hand. The old woman looked at it, puzzled. Just as Katherine was about to pull it back, Baba

Krista took it limply, as though it were the first time she had ever shaken a hand. Her skin was as coarse as asphalt.

They went into a cramped kitchen and sat on stools behind a small table. The wooden floor was uneven and everything rocked in its place: the chairs, the table, even the refrigerator from which Baba Krista retrieved a plate of butter. An orange cat jumped onto Katherine's lap. It circled twice and then lay down to sleep. Katherine thought about her cat, Niels Bohr, in a kennel in Ithaca. Poor Niels. He hated the kennel.

"The cat's name is Pushkin," said Baba Krista.

She began to lay out plates and silverware on the table.

Katherine leaned close to Sergei, "I should help her, yes?" she asked.

"Only if you want to insult her."

They sat quietly and watched Baba Krista prepare their meal. Soon fried eggs, fried bacon and fried potatoes lay on plates before them. They began to eat. The smell of grease upset Katherine's stomach, but she cleaned her plate anyway. Sergei poured vodka into an ordinary water glass and was about to drink when Baba Krista growled something at him. He pursed his lips and got up from the table. He opened the back door and splashed several drops on a pile of snow near the door. He sat down again and drank.

Katherine closed her eyes. She decided to give up trying to make sense out of this bombardment of images.

After dinner, they went into the front room and sat down. Baba Krista and Sergei spoke Estonian while Katherine stroked a purring Pushkin. After fifteen minutes, Sergei rose and came beside Katherine.

"You will be safe here," he said and went out of the room. She heard him clanking in the kitchen.

Baba Krista sat in a chair across from Katherine and knitted, a feat Katherine would not have thought possible, having felt the coarseness of those ancient hands.

After about ten minutes, the cottage became quiet. A clock on the wall ticked pleasantly and the fire crackled inside the wrought-iron stove beside Baba Krista. Katherine asked where Sergei had gone.

"He left."

Katherine almost jumped out of her seat. Only Pushkin kept her where she was. "Left? Where?"

"Moscow. He said something about replacing a *peredneye*."

"A what?"

"The front window."

Of course. The bullet hole in the windshield.

Katherine felt defeated. She had lost all control of what was happening to her. She was a child who could not speak the language of adults, and who did not know the dangers that might befall her. She closed her eyes. Perhaps Sergei was going to bring the police. She didn't care anymore.

"You want to sleep?" asked Baba Krista, who had watched Katherine shut her eyes.

Katherine nodded. The old woman led Katherine to a tiny bathroom. A single faucet swiveled between the sink and the bathtub. Baba Krista gave her a hand towel and pointed out the toilet room and Katherine's bedroom.

Katherine closed the door and looked in the mirror. Her right eye was underscored by a purplish-black arc like a crescent moon lying dead on its back.

She washed and went into the bedroom. The heat from the stove did not reach her room, and she could see her breath in the air. She turned off the light. She stripped naked (she still had no underwear) and crawled under the half-dozen layers of mismatched blankets and afghans. Their weight was a comfort. A sliver of light slipped over the top of the door and fell on an icon of St. George and the Dragon beside a single red candle high on a shelf, almost to the ceiling. They seemed to glow. She remembered reading about the Russian Orthodox tradition of the Red Corner. It had been theoretical then, back in Ithaca, an example of Russian provincialism. Quaint. Far, far away. Now, here it was. She stared at it a long time through the mists of her own breath. She felt herself drifting off to sleep.

Katherine didn't dream that night. She slept the sound, healing sleep of a soldier who, after weeks at the front, finds himself on a soft bunk far from the war, in a place where no shell may fall.

She woke the next morning to cat whiskers tickling her nose. She swept Pushkin off the bed and looked around. The bedroom door was slightly ajar. Light shone brightly through a single window. It felt late. The house smelled of strong coffee and fried potatoes. She heard voices in the kitchen.

She got up and found clean clothes hanging over a chair. She put on the underwear and scooped up the rest. She crossed the hall to the bathroom and looked in the mirror. Her black eye had faded slightly. She washed with a bar of rock-hard soap then found some shampoo and washed her hair. She found a tube of toothpaste and brushed her teeth with her index finger. She slipped on her new clothes: a polyester dress with a blue, floral pattern, like cheap kitchen wallpaper. It wasn't bad. She looked almost human. She felt almost human. She went out to the kitchen.

Sergei sat on the same chair he had occupied the previous night. Baba Krista was behind the stove, stirring potatoes in a skillet. She smiled at Katherine and went back to work. Sergei surveyed her appearance, and his eyes glowed with approval.

"Good day," he said in Russian.

"Day? What time is it?"

"Two-thirty."

Katherine pulled at the hem of her dress. "Thanks for the clothes."

"They're my wife's."

Katherine sat down beside Sergei and whispered, "We need to talk."

"Later."

Baba Krista served the food. Katherine devoured it so ravenously that afterward, she felt obliged to apologize.

Sergei shrugged and nodded at Baba. "She approves."

Katherine sipped politely at a cup of Russian coffee, an espressolike drink with the grounds still muddy in the bottom. Sergei drank vodka — after splashing several drops on the snow. Katherine asked about that.

"First drop to the snow god," he said.

They finished and put on coats and went outside. They strolled along a grass-and-mud tractor path that was, Katherine quickly realized, Ivanovka's main street. Katherine listened as Sergei told her about the village.

Ivanovka was an ancient Russian settlement that Sergei assured her could be found on sixteenth-century maps. For centuries, the village's population had hovered around two hundred. At present, it was eleven. Its trouble began with the formation of the collective farm, White Dacha, two miles away. That was 1937, the year the communists came to Ivanovka, twenty years after the Bolsheviks took power in Moscow.

"It took communism an extra twenty years to get to Ivanovka," Sergei said.

It happened one sunny day in June. A so-called Revolutionary Worker's Brigade of four men came into Ivanovka and rounded up the villagers. They shot the priest on the main street and sent the church elders off to Siberia. They left behind a revolutionary council that organized White Dacha. After that, Ivanovka's old church was used to store manure. For years, young communists took target practice at the icons. It burned down in 1964. Meanwhile, everyone was expected to move to the new village, Bolshevichka. Gradually, they did. In 1974, Ivanovka was eliminated as a train stop. In 1978, the bus stop was torn down.

"Only the old people are left," said Sergei.

His mother had lived in the cottage until the bus route disappeared. Then she moved to Moscow where she now shared Sergei's one-room apartment with his wife and three daughters, an unusually large family for a Muscovite. After a long battle, Baba Krista agreed to move from Tallinn to Ivanovka, close enough that Sergei could drive up several times a week to look after her, an extravagance she considered preposterous even though every morsel of food in the cupboard was supplied by those trips.

All this information came to Katherine in the laborious process of communicating in Russian, which involved lots of hand signals and pleas to "use a different word."

Sergei grew quiet now. They reached the edge of the field.

"You're American, yes?" asked Sergei.

She nodded.

"I thought so," he said.

"Thanks for rescuing me," said Katherine. "And for bringing me here."

Sergei nodded. After a pause, he asked, "Are you a spy?"

"No."

Katherine waited for him to ask more, but he just stared out at the field. After a while, she realized he wasn't going to ask.

"I need to call Moscow," she said.

"Baba Krista doesn't have long-distance service," said Sergei. "There's a private phone at the collective farm."

They went back to the cottage, got in his taxi and drove five minutes into a small village, much like those Katherine had seen that day on the tour bus to Zagorsk. It was Bolshevichka. They stopped at a cottage. Sergei went inside. He came out a minute later waving a key.

"Do you know everybody?" Katherine asked.

"Better a hundred friends than a hundred rubles."

They drove up a long gravel road to a single-story building, not much more than a flat-roofed barn. A sign over the door said "White Dacha Collective Farm, Headquarters." Sergei used the key to open the door.

They were in a reception room. To Katherine's left was a desk with an old typewriter. Across from it, pinned to the wall, was a map of White Dacha and the surrounding villages. The room was empty. Katherine shivered; it felt colder inside the building than outside. The floor creaked beneath her feet, and in the air hung the vague smell of manure.

Sergei pointed to a phone on the desk, and sat down in the corner. Katherine went around the desk. She took a deep breath and picked up the phone. Sergei gave her the long distance code for Moscow. She dialed the code, then the seven digits she had memorized back in Ithaca. The phone began to ring.

"*The New York Times*," said a man on the other end in English. Katherine recognized the voice — it was Grayson Hines.

In Helsinki, Grayson had interviewed her for his story on Dr. Vladimir Ryzhkov's suicide. A few weeks later, Katherine called Grayson from Ithaca. She had done some research on Anton in Afghanistan and was trying to find out what organizations could supply her with specific information on troop positions. She didn't tell him why. She promised only to give him a story if anything came out of it. That was good enough for the reporter.

Hearing his voice now, she was overcome with the desire to cry: "Grayson! It's Katherine! Help me!"

But what could he do? He would only lead the KGB to her; foreign correspondents were themselves arrested from time to time. Whatever she had to do now, she would have to do it without Hines's help.

On the phone, Katherine deepened her voice. "Hello. I'm an American citizen and I need the phone number of the U.S. Embassy."

"We're not an information service."

"I realize that."

"One moment."

He gave her the number. Katherine said good-bye and put her finger on the cradle. She dialed the new number. Sergei studied her from his chair, a small smile on his lips.

The new voice said, "American Embassy Moscow."

"I'm trying to reach a man named Jack Sears, who is in Moscow," said Katherine. "I believe he is searching for his American daughter, who has disappeared."

"And who are you?"

"The daughter."

"I'll connect you with Consular."

The phone rang to an internal extension.

"Hello." A man's voice.

Katherine identified herself.

"Call back on this number," he said and gave her a new number.

She tried the new number.

A man, a different man, answered. "Is this Katherine Sears?"

"Yes."

"Well, young lady," he said jovially. "How nice of you to call. You have created quite a stir around here."

"I have?"

"Oh yes. But before we get into all that, I have someone here who would like to speak with you."

There was a pause. Then a new voice came over the line. "Kat, are you all right?"

The room got misty.

"Oh Dad! It's so good to . . ."

Her throat tightened. The events of the last few days crashed down around her like a collapsing building. Tears streamed down her cheeks. It was the first time she had cried since her abduction. Sergei started toward her, but she held up her hand to say she was okay. After a minute, that's what she told her father.

"Where are you?" he asked.

"I . . . I can't say. Somewhere safe."

"What is going on?"

"I don't know."

"I thought I saw you yesterday on the street."

"I saw you, too."

"And those men —"

"I'm safe now," said Katherine.

"Thank god. I came as soon as the State Department told me you were missing. We have to get you out of here."

Katherine grinned and sniffled. "I agree. How?"

"There may be a problem with that," he said. "I'll let the Embassy man explain."

The jovial voice that had answered the phone came back on. "Katherine? Yes. My name is Cameron Abbott. I'm a consular attaché. I'm very glad you called. Very glad. I've been to the Soviet Foreign Ministry three times already to speak directly with Deputy Foreign Minister Vsevolod Rulyov about your very case. I'm giving daily reports to the U.S. ambassador himself, by the way. The situation is very delicate, Miss Sears. Very delicate."

"Situation?"

"Hmm. Well. The Embassy can bring you in, of course. We have ways." He chuckled. "But, er, it may turn out that we would have to release you into Soviet custody. It seems you're wanted by the police in connection with a murder that took place at the Moscow port on the night you disappeared."

"Port? But I was never there."

"I'm very pleased to hear that. Very pleased."

Katherine suddenly remembered something: the cabin, the Tatar rushing out to intercept Sigmund.

"Is the port called *Rechnoy Vokzal* in Russian?"

"Yes."

"Who was killed?"

"His name was Pavel Danilov. Apparently, he was linked to an organization —"

"Soviet Psychiatry Watch."

"You *are* involved."

"Yes," Katherine sighed. "But not with the murder. The same people who killed this man tried to kill me. Twice."

"Who tried to kill you?" asked Cameron. "You can tell me. This is a safe line."

Katherine told him everything, leaving out only the details that could lead to Sergei and Soviet Psychiatry Watch. Her instinct now was to isolate herself. This was her folly, and she couldn't bear the thought of others suffering for it.

"How long can you stay where you are?"

"I don't know. I think my friend expects me to leave today."

"That's not a good idea," said Cameron. "This is not a normal diplomatic matter. No. No. I wouldn't want to risk your falling into Soviet hands right now. Not until we can straighten this thing out."

"How long will that take?"

"A few days. Maybe a week."

"A week! I don't think I can do that."

"I'm sorry. You're in a bit of a predicament. But the gears of justice grind slowly. Very slowly. You have to give the embassy time."

"I'll try."

"Maybe you should have stuck to astronomy, Dr. Sears."

"Put my father back on," Katherine snapped.

"Of course," he said unfazed. "If I may say so, you're very lucky to have your father here. I hope you'll listen to him. He's one of the best sovietologists in the world, you know."

Katherine was speechless. Was the diplomat really exploiting her predicament to suck up to her father? He obviously didn't know Jack Sears. There was nothing her father hated worse than an ass-kisser.

Cameron asked, "When will you call me back?"

Katherine put her hand over the receiver and asked Sergei when the phone was available.

"After nine o'clock every night," he said in Russian.

Katherine relayed that to Cameron and promised to call the following evening. Her father came back on the line.

"I don't like this guy," Katherine said. "Can we trust him?"

"Trust *me*," Jack said. "I know people — experts in Soviet law. We'll get them involved. You have to understand, justice has little meaning here. But where foreigners are concerned, the Sovs like to keep up appearances. They can usually be compelled to behave according to their own laws. These Soviet legal experts — they'll know what buttons to push. And if that doesn't work, I can get Washington involved. The secretary of state owes me a favor."

"Thank you, Dad," said Katherine. "I feel so much better just hearing your voice."

"We'll get you back, Kat. I don't know how this happened, but this isn't the time to get into all that. Just hang in there. Remember, you're Alice now, and you've gone down the rabbit hole to the Soviet wonderland. You remember my sermons?"

"Yes."

"Good. Trust no one. Not Victor Perov, and certainly not this man who is helping you now. It's easy to mistake Russians for human beings like us just because they have fair skin and seem to want the same things we want. Don't be fooled. These people have been dehumanized over generations. They are *homo sovieticus*. They would inform on their own mother for a few rubles."

Katherine had heard these speeches all her life, and she had no doubt her father believed every word of what he said. "I'm sorry to put you through all this, Dad."

"Forget it," he said. "It will all be over soon."

Katherine was beginning to have her doubts about that.

17

Victor was at his desk reading *Forensic Psychology* when Oleg came into his office that morning. Victor didn't see him at first; he was reading the same sentence for the sixth time.

The notion of insanity is negative in relation to sanity.

"There you are."

Victor looked up. Oleg stood in his doorway. He wore the expression of a father about to confront a son who has flunked out of school. It was the first time Victor had seen Oleg since last Friday, the day Victor shut the office door in his face. Victor had a pretty good idea what Oleg's long face was about.

The intervening days had passed in a torrent of activity and self-examination for Victor. Oksana and Grisha had moved back to their tiny flat in the southern Moscow suburb of Domodedovo. When Victor came home to his empty flat for the first time, he felt lost. He wandered the rooms sniffing the air for the smell of Oksana's perfume. As the long weekend wore on, he came to realize that as much as he cared for Oksana, there had been something self-destructive about taking her into his bed. He hadn't worked it all out yet, but he was certain he was better off in the role of Uncle Victor than as a lover and stepfather.

And then there was Katherine Sears. Strangely, Victor had fallen in love with Katherine twice. The first time was in their letters. It had been slow and idealized, the way a fan falls for a movie actress. Victor put her on a mountaintop where he could admire her but never touch her. She was safe. They were both safe. Even when he gave her Baba Raya's ring, it was the immature act of a distant admirer, not an adult declaration of love. He cringed to think of the shallowness of his emotion. But the bell tower in Zagorsk changed all that, for there he fell in love with Katherine Sears for the second time. This time was neither slow nor theoretical—it was sudden, real and overpowering, like nothing he had ever felt before. A connection to flesh and blood. She had come down from the mountaintop and stood before him. He could smell her sweat, feel her breath, sense her fear. Such courage she had shown in coming to Moscow! It shamed him—and invigorated him, for it was from the thought of Katherine's courage that he now drew the strength to begin his own quest to find Anton. He would finish the journey Katherine had begun.

"Good morning, Oleg," said Victor. "I'm rather busy. I'm expecting an important call."

Oleg ignored him. He dropped a newspaper clipping on Victor's desk. "You read English, I believe," he said.

Victor picked up the paper.

Rift over Science Award Widens
  By Grayson Hines
  Special to The New York Times
  MOSCOW — The son of a high-ranking Communist party official has broken ranks to say that a Soviet defector should posthumously receive a prestigious, international award for his work in astronomy.

  Victor Perov, son of Agricultural Minister Yevgenia Perova, presented a reporter Friday with eleven technical notebooks that appear to support his contention that Vladimir Ryzhkov contributed significantly to the work that led to the award.

  Haggling over the prize drove Ryzhkov to commit suicide last December in Helsinki, according to Finnish police.

  Ryzhkov, a former colleague of Perov's, embarrassed the Soviet scientific establishment last year when he defected while at a conference in Oslo. Since then, Soviet officials have played down Ryzhkov's significance, dismissing him as a "parasite."

  Perov's break with his country's scientific establishment is unusual in the Soviet Union where family members of high government officials are scrupulously uncritical of the government line.

  In December, Perov turned down the highest honor of the Hubble Foundation, saying he would not share the prize with Ryzhkov. In his speech, made in Helsinki with Ryzhkov present, Perov called his former colleague "a bureaucrat and a fraud."

  Perov gave no explanation for his change of heart.

  Perov's theories suggest that the universe may be repeatedly re-creating and then destroying itself in an endless series of Big Bangs and Big Crunches. Gunther Roder, president of the Hubble Foundation, has called Perov's theory "the most inspired example of original thinking I have seen in a decade."

  Perov is currently involved in a joint Soviet-American project with Cornell University to test his theories.

"So?" said Victor.

"You betrayed your comrades to the bourgeois West!" said Oleg.

The phone rang and Victor picked up. He put his hand over the receiver and said, "Excuse me, Oleg. I need to take this call."

Oleg's eyes bulged. "You need to . . ." He couldn't get the words out. "We . . . need to talk!"

"Yes. But not now."

"I could have you thrown out of here today, comrade."

"I don't think so," said Victor.

"Because of your mother, I suppose."

"What has my mother got to do with it?" asked Victor. "I am a full member of this institute. I am a member of the Communist party of the Soviet Union. I have a seat on the Academy of Sciences of the U.S.S.R. These are the reasons you can't throw me out. These are the reasons!"

Oleg glared at him. "We were friends once."

"We still can be," said Victor. "It's up to you. Now, if you will excuse me, I really must take this call."

Oleg started out of the room. Victor was about to put the receiver to his ear, when Oleg turned and said from the doorway, "Did you hear about Boris?"

"No."

"They found his body in the Moscow River last night."

"Jesus."

"He had a bullet in his head."

Oleg disappeared up the corridor. Victor went numb with shock. He stared at the spot where the director had stood.

A tinny voice called out through the phone. *"Allo? Is anyone there? Allo!"*

Victor was unable to move. He waited a few more seconds and then, at last, found the strength to lift the phone to his ear. It seemed to weigh a hundred pounds. "Dr. Bonderov? Yes, sorry about that. I . . ."

Victor's mind drifted again. A bullet in his head?

"Victor Borisovich?" the voice said.

Like Sigmund.

"I . . . Something . . ." Victor stammered.

Poor Boris.

"Are you there?"

We were friends once.

Victor composed himself and said, "Yes. Thank you for calling back."

Victor managed to suggest they meet for lunch at the Baku, a fashionable Central Asian restaurant on Gorky Street. Victor knew the head waiter there, and, by slipping him a few rubles, he could get a table anytime. Bonderov was interested. The meeting was set.

Victor arrived at the restaurant at one o'clock. Dr. Bonderov was already behind their table nibbling at fresh onion stalks. He rose to greet Victor, and a greasy wisp of hair fell into his face. He offered Victor a delicate hand. They shook.

"Shall we have a few drops?" Bonderov suggested.

He unscrewed the vodka bottle and filled two water glasses. They drank to their health.

Bonderov was about fifty years old with an average build, dark hair and a teenager's stringy mustache. He wore a wrinkled suit that was out of style by fifteen years. The tie was loose and pulled off center. None of this particularly bothered Victor, who was accustomed to working around the eccentrics of the scientific world, but somehow it was not what he had expected.

Oksana arrived, and both men got to their feet. Bonderov's eyes widened. She wore a dusty blue dress that showed her figure well and somehow made her skin appear even fairer than usual. Bonderov's chest swelled. Suddenly, he remembered his manners. He pushed his hair back up onto his head and apologized for having started without them. He suggested another drink in honor of "ladies present." He poured the vodka, holding the bottle over his glass a second longer than Victor's. Oksana smiled politely as the men drank to her.

They ordered their food and ate. The talk was idle. Bonderov told them about his work as a procurement officer at an institute Victor had never heard of. Bonderov was divorced. He had two kids whom he didn't get to see often enough. He described them as "the shining beacons in my perpetual night." The vodka had elevated his rhetoric.

Oksana mentioned Grisha, and Bonderov asked several questions about the boy's age, health and interests. He laughed. A nice laugh. It was the first curiosity Bonderov had shown in his hosts. Though an hour had passed, the subject of the meeting was still a mystery to him. Bonderov struck Victor as a man with nowhere to go.

The waiter cleared the table, took away the empty vodka bottle and brought coffee. Victor said, "Perhaps I should tell you why I invited you here."

Bonderov started, as though he had just remembered that they weren't all pals having lunch.

Victor said, "I need some information about special psychiatric hospitals."

Bonderov's expression did not change.

Oksana said, "I work at the *Izvestiya* archives. I found several articles about you in the late 1950s."

She put them on the table in front of him. One had a picture of a serious young man. Dark. Dashing. Same mustache. The caption read, "V. N. Bonderov."

He paged through the clips, his face blank, as though it were the first time he had ever seen them.

Victor said, "You were on a commission investigating Western claims that psychiatry was being misused in the Soviet Union."

Still no reaction.

"It *was* you, wasn't it?" Victor asked doubtfully.

Bonderov looked up. "Is it so hard to believe by looking at me?"

"Not at all," Oksana cooed.

Bonderov dropped the clips on the table. "If I had known what this was about, I would never have come."

"Why?"

"*Why?*" he mimicked as though he couldn't believe such a question. He lit a cheap cigarette and blew smoke out his nose.

"There was a lot written about the commission," said Oksana. "First Alexei Ulyanov, the dissident, convinced the Central Committee that psychiatry was being abused. That was 1955. The Central Committee assigned an investigative commission, and you were given a post. You had access to all hospitals, physicians, patients, records. The last article I found was one year later about how you had wrapped up your work and had submitted your recommendations. Then . . . nothing."

Victor leaned forward. "What happened?"

Bonderov shook his head. "What is your interest?"

"My husband has been committed," said Oksana.

"I'm sorry," said Bonderov. "Which asylum is he in?"

"That's what I'm trying to find out."

"You don't know?"

"Officially, he was killed in Afghanistan," said Victor. "We have received reliable information that he is alive, and in a psychiatric hospital."

Bonderov puffed furiously on his cigarette until he was visible only through a smoky haze. He shook his head. "I can't help you."

The restaurant was nearly empty now. Victor glanced toward the kitchen. Their waiter looked at them anxiously.

"At least tell us what happened with the commission," said Victor.

"The commission," Bonderov said dreamily. "All right. What could it hurt? The commission was theater. But no one bothered to tell us that." He shook his head. "We were so naive. Stalin was dead and Khrushchev was making reforms. We thought psychiatric hospitals would be part of it."

"What did you find out?"

"The charges of Ulyanov and the West were substantially correct. Poets, writers, intellectuals, musicians, all sorts of people were being systematically declared insane and put in psychiatric hospitals. They were being given dangerous doses of drugs without the slightest medical justification. Psychiatrists, installed by the

KGB, gave names to fictitious illnesses in order to make it all seem scientific. It was torture, really, but under the guise of psychiatry. For those of us in the profession, it was a terrible shock. These men had taken the Hippocratic Oath."

"What did the Central Committee say?" asked Victor.

"Nothing. We never heard another word. Days turned to weeks, then to months. After a while, my phone calls were not even returned. But I was young and eager. And stupid. I kept pushing. I tried to get another article published in *Izvestiya*, but the editors all refused. They had their orders. Eventually, because I was being so thick-headed, my bosses made it known to me that in the interest of my career I should let the matter drop."

"And you did, of course," said Victor. A note of recrimination crept into Victor's voice.

Bonderov's face flushed. "What have *you* done about it, comrade?"

"You're right," said Victor. "I'm sorry. It's not your fault."

"I'm not one of these goddamn dissidents. I'm a patriot. I tried to work within a system that I thought genuinely wanted reform. But the system didn't want it. Who am I to argue with that?"

"You did more than most," said Oksana.

Bonderov shrugged. "Anyway, I found out a couple of years later who killed the report."

"Who?" asked Victor.

"Khrushchev himself. He gave an interview, published in the newspapers in 1959."

Bonderov began to quote, as though from scripture:

" 'A crime is a deviation from the generally recognized standards of behavior, frequently caused by a mental disorder. To those who might start calling for opposition to communism, clearly the mental state of such people is not normal.' "

"*Khrushchev,*" Victor breathed. The former Soviet leader was like a god to him. In Victor's view of the Soviet Union — a view supported by his mother — all its present deficiencies began with the coup d'état that toppled Nikita Khrushchev and installed Leonid Brezhnev in 1964. Bonderov's picture of a repressive Khrushchev shocked Victor.

Bonderov said, "Khrushchev, our great reformer, gave us the foundation for punitive psychiatry. Its edict is: If you don't agree with us, you must be insane. And to think I bothered to go to medical school."

There was a pause and Oksana asked, "So what happened to you?"

Bonderov laughed bitterly. "I was the fall guy. The other members of the committee were astute enough to distance themselves from the report. They saved their careers. But I had gone too far with those interviews you dug up in *Izvestiya*. I got thrown out of the Party, then the institute."

"I'm sorry," said Oksana.

Bonderov shrugged. "So you see, I'm not the person to help you. If you're looking for a light bulb, I'm your man. I can't help you with this."

"Maybe I can help you," said Victor.

"How?"

"I could help you get a job. I know people."

"Who?"

"My college roommate was Dr. Igor Shamayev."

"Of the Nevsky Institute in Leningrad?" asked Bonderov. "That Shamayev?" He thought about that. "You would talk to him? You would do that for an old drunk like me?"

"Why not?"

Bonderov put out his cigarette and took a sip of his coffee. "What do you want?"

"I need to know everything about special psychiatric hospitals," said Victor. "Where are they located? How are people put into them? Who are the doctors? What are the drugs used? How are the patients treated? What is the security? What are the laws? Visitation rights? Mail privileges? I don't suppose there is a book —"

"A book?" Bonderov scoffed. "In the West, perhaps, but not in the Soviet Union. Maybe you would like to write one."

"Maybe I would."

Bonderov looked at Victor with astonishment. His gaze fell. "Would you really be willing to talk to Dr. Shamayev about me?"

"I said I would."

"I was a good psychiatrist, you know," said Bonderov. "Once. I got into the profession because I wanted to help people. And I did — while they let me. I've kept up with the technical journals. It would be nice to practice again."

Bonderov lit another cigarette. His eyes glowed, and he smiled slyly. "Maybe I could get you a copy of the commission's report."

"You saved a copy?"

Bonderov nodded. "But first, there are a few things you should know, just so you have a realistic view of your predicament. I'm afraid you really don't. You may have been feeling some relief that your brother is in a psychiatric hospital and not a prison camp. Most people do. Don't. A psychiatric hospital is far worse than prison. There is no term to your sentence, no realistic, legal recourse to indefinite incarceration. And while you are there, you are at the mercy of the whims of sadists — from the orderlies right up to the doctors. They are armed with powerful drugs and have free rein to use them. You know, I think the scariest single thing in our report was the existence of these monsters in white smocks. We found them at all the hospitals. They were drawn there like sharks to the smell of blood."

Bonderov looked at Oksana. She was looking at her hands in her lap.

"I'm sorry," he said. "I shouldn't—"

"No," said Oksana, raising her head. "Go on. Please."

"Okay. It all starts with the Serbsky Institute."

From the street, the Serbsky Institute could have been mistaken for a bakery.

It was nestled in a city block in a prestigious district of central Moscow, not far from one of the capital's most popular groceries, Smolensky Gastronom. Victor had been to the store many times for hard-to-find items, which lately had been almost everything. He had never suspected that extraordinary events were taking place next door.

The site was surrounded by a high cement wall with a guard at the gate, but what institute or factory in the Soviet Union wasn't? Even if a curious Muscovite bothered to read the metal plaque, "The Professor V. P. Serbsky Central Scientific Research Institute of Forensic Psychiatry of the Ministry of Public Health of the U.S.S.R.," how could he guess the truth—that the innocuous complex was the launching pad to the world of special psychiatric hospitals. The Serbsky was to psychiatric prisons what the KGB's Lefortova Prison was to the gulag.

The signs of the Serbsky's true purpose were obscure, but not invisible— especially for someone like Victor Perov, who had read the Ulyanov Commission's report. Valery Bonderov had come through on his word and given Victor a long-concealed copy of the secret report, so now, looking at the Serbsky from the street, the signs were unmistakable.

Standing across the street with his back to the Moscow River, Victor could just make out the roofs of the guard towers. Atop the wall, barbed wire was strung in five strands across posts that angled *inward*. Unlike the loose, rusty wire that might encircle a Moscow bakery, this wire was as taut as a guitar string. Its icy barbs seemed to scratch the sky. At the gate, the guard wore an Army uniform, not police. Bars covered the windows on the top floor of a long barracks.

Victor Perov shivered when he saw those bars. Not because bars don't belong in a mental hospital. The vast majority of people who passed through the Serbsky were genuinely ill. Some were dangerous to themselves and others. Some had committed crimes. Victor shivered because he had not wanted the Serbsky to exist at all. Having read the Ulyanov report, there was a part of Victor that held out hope it was a bizarre hoax. The bars brought the fiction to life.

It was four-thirty Thursday afternoon, the day after his lunch with Dr. Bonderov. That meeting had convinced him that time might be short for Anton. The drugs of punitive medicine produced a number of side effects, including memory loss, paralysis, alteration of personality, and psychoses such as schizophrenia, depression and paranoia. Anton's own independent spirit would be an enemy in the oppressive regime of a special psychiatric hospital. If they ever managed to break him, Victor doubted his brother could ever be brought back. A time bomb lay under his Anton, and Victor could almost hear it ticking. Already a week had passed since Victor's meeting with Katherine Sears in Zagorsk. Seven lost days. But Anton wasn't the only one living in the shadow of a ticking bomb. How much longer would the forces that held Anton — presumably the KGB — permit Victor to operate freely in his search. A month? Two months? It depended on so many factors. He and Yevgenia enjoyed tremendous standing within the Party, and people like Oleg would defend Victor — for a time. Then a lifetime of service would be discounted, and Victor would be no more immune to arrest than Anton had been. Yevgenia's power was far from unlimited, as the fate of Anton revealed. Victor would be counting the minutes now, for every one was precious until he located his brother.

That morning Victor had made an appointment with Dr. Petrus Bruk, the man Bonderov said was currently in charge of the Fourth Department, the KGB arm of the Serbsky responsible for "politicals." Bruk, a KGB colonel, dealt with the 10 to 15 percent of the inmates at the Serbsky who were not sick, not in need of treatment, but whose condition fit only Nikita Khrushchev's definition of mental illness. In the early 1970s, the U.S. government had labeled Bruk a "psychiatrist/murderer."

Oksana had paled when Victor told her about the appointment, but he had argued that it was the safest, indeed the only, way.

"Russians are suspicious when they don't know your motives," he said. "If I am going to do this, then I have to be up-front about it."

Victor circled the Serbsky complex until he reached the gate at the end of a quiet lane. An armed guard sat behind a Plexiglas booth. Beside him was a circular cage like the rotating door of an expensive hotel, only this one was made of cast iron and shaped into interlocking comb's teeth. In front of that stood a KGB guard holding an AK-47.

"I have a five o'clock meeting with Dr. Petrus Bruk."

"Papers."

Through a slot in the glass, Victor slid the guard his internal passport and Party card. The guard studied them and made a call. He hung up and slid the papers back.

"You can wait over there," he said, pointing to two chairs opposite the gate.

Victor sat down. People came and went. They flashed folding, cardboard identification cards at the guard. The check was not perfunctory as in most institutes — as in Victor's own institute. The guard examined each pass before pushing an invisible switch, which, with a click, allowed the rotating cage to turn.

After ten minutes, a husky nurse wearing a permanent frown appeared on the inside of the turnstile. The guard motioned for Victor to pass. Victor pushed his way through the cage and stepped onto the grounds of the Serbsky Institute.

The nurse clipped a white VISITOR badge on Victor's lapel and turned on her toes. She led Victor rapidly across a narrow outdoor walkway to the side entrance of a long building. The grounds were strangely silent. Wind whispered through the branches of a tree. But there was something else, too, a desolate cry like the howl of a faraway wolf.

"What *is* that?" he asked.

"What is what?"

"That crying sound."

The nurse stopped and listened a moment. "I don't hear anything."

They went on. Another armed guard was posted beside the entrance to the institute building. The nurse flashed her badge. The guard's eyes found the badge on Victor's lapel, and he nodded. They went inside and Victor was met by the unsettling, medicinal smell of a hospital. They climbed stairs to the third floor, a fact detailed in the Ulyanov report — the Fourth Department was located on the third floor of the Serbsky. It was a minor fact but it gave Victor the feeling he was entering a storm.

The nurse led Victor down a long hall to a reception room, past a secretary and directly into the office of the man who lived squarely in the eye of the storm: Dr. Petrus Bruk. He was not what Victor had expected.

Bruk rose from behind his desk. Not rose, really, because Victor had the impression that Bruk had simply slid off the chair like a child whose legs didn't reach the floor. Bruk had a round peasant face like an oversized beet root. He wore expensive gold-rimmed spectacles and, over his suit, a white hospital smock. In his early fifties, he was old enough to be seasoned, but not so old as to be obsolete. Despite his size — he couldn't have been over five feet two inches tall — he radiated respectability. If you were choosing sides for soccer, Dr. Bruk would be the last man picked. But if you were sick, Dr. Bruk was exactly the cut of man you wanted to step through the door, a stethoscope around his neck.

Bruk smiled the spare smile of a busy man who has made time for someone special. Victor shook Bruk's hand. It was the hand of a surgeon, delicate, recently manicured, perpetually scrubbed.

"It's not often we get astronomers with an interest in the psychiatric world," he said after he had climbed up onto his seat. "I'm afraid I know practically nothing about astronomy."

Behind Bruk was a wall of medical books. From where Victor sat, they seemed to prop him up.

"That's okay, I know very little about psychiatry. My interest is very recent."

"Really? Why is that?"

"My twin brother has been committed to a special psychiatric hospital."

Bruk frowned. "I'm very sorry. I hadn't heard that."

Victor believed him, and that presented a puzzle. Was there a back door to the psychiatric gulag?

"Nor had I until a week ago," said Victor.

"What was the diagnosis?"

"I have no idea," said Victor. "My brother is sane."

Behind the spectacles, the brown eyes narrowed slightly. "Are you saying there was a mistake in the diagnosis?"

"Yes."

"I see." Bruk scratched his chin thoughtfully. "Where is your brother now?"

"I don't know. Officially, Anton was killed in Afghanistan. And that's what I believed until I received information, reliable information, to the contrary."

"Which is?"

"That my brother is being held in a psychiatric hospital. Somewhere."

Bruk looked relieved. Whatever he had been expecting, this was not it.

"The information is wrong," said Bruk with conviction. "What you describe is quite impossible."

"This is Russia," said Victor. "The impossible happens every day."

Bruk snorted through his nose. "What makes you think he passed through here?"

"My brother was involved in some dissident activities in college."

Bruk nodded knowingly. "And based on that, you assumed the Fourth Department of the Serbsky had him committed. You seem to have a rather dim view of our work here, comrade Perov."

Victor's eye drifted to a portrait of V. I. Serbsky, the nineteenth-century psychiatrist who had sought ways of treating mental illness without confinement.

Victor looked back at Bruk. "My view of your work is irrelevant. I'm not a specialist."

"No, you're not."

"I have come here with one purpose: To inform you that Anton Perov is being held somewhere in your gulag, perhaps without your knowledge. As a matter of courtesy, I thought you should know that I will be looking for him."

Bruk sat back in his perch and tapped his fingertips together. "As I told you, we have nothing to hide. You will not find your brother among the sick. I do wonder, however, how you propose to conduct this little search."

Victor did not answer.

"You've been talking to the wrong people, comrade," said Bruk, as if he had guessed something about the source of Victor's information. "We have helped thousands of people here. But no one wants to talk about that. As for the nagging issue of the misuse of psychiatry, the West needed a human-rights propaganda tool, and they latched on to this."

"I suspect there is more to it than that."

"I'm surprised to hear you say that," said Bruk. He shook his head sadly and then leaned toward Victor as though he were confiding in him. "People want to believe the worst about our country. It's always that way. I was at an international conference in Costa Rica last year. While I was speaking, half the auditorium got up and walked out. And all because of this fucking human-rights bullshit."

Victor recoiled from the unexpected language.

Bruk went on calmly. "As I'm sure you can imagine, scientist to scientist, it was a humiliating experience."

"I doubt your feelings were their chief concern."

Bruk flinched, but his control was complete. He certainly knew who Victor's mother was, and he was not going to be provoked. He smiled.

"Comrade Perov. You seem like an intelligent man, but you're not thinking clearly. That's understandable. The bond between twins can be very strong, almost mystical. I'm sure you feel his loss very deeply. Perhaps, as a psychiatrist, I can help you."

"Is that a threat?"

Again, Bruk flinched. Victor wanted him to break into a rage. It would have made everything so much easier. But Bruk composed himself and went on. "Believe me when I tell you that you have been misled. Your brother is not in our 'gulag,' as you so provocatively put it. And even if he were, it would not be the result of a misdiagnosis here at the Serbsky Institute, as your new friends would have you think."

"How can you be so sure?"

"Because it doesn't happen," he said flatly. "I can tell you with all honesty that in my twenty-five years in psychiatry, I have never known a single case where a healthy person was diagnosed as insane."

And if Victor hadn't known better, he would have believed him.

A few minutes later, Victor was back outside the Serbsky. He knew little more about his brother than he had when he went in, but still he felt better. It was good to be doing something, and to know that the search for his brother was on.

18

It didn't take long for Yevgenia to hear about Victor's visit to the Serbsky. Belov called her that evening with the news. But by then they all had bigger problems.

Katherine Sears was alive.

Podolok played the tape in his office that afternoon. It was in English. Yevgenia read from a translation.

MAN'S VOICE: American Embassy Moscow.

WOMAN'S VOICE: I'm trying to reach a man named Jack Sears, who is in Moscow. I believe he is searching for his American daughter, who has disappeared.

MAN: And who are you?

WOMAN: The daughter.

"Is there any way Katherine could have known you were at the dacha that night?" Podolok asked.

Yevgenia shook her head. "She was wearing a hood. We used code words. I didn't even speak."

Podolok took a drag off his cigarette holder. "If she could link you to her abduction—"

"I just said it was impossible," Yevgenia snapped.

"So you said."

"How did she escape?" Yevgenia demanded.

"Nobody knows. Damn Belov. I should have left him in Leningrad. With the Americans involved, Director Shatalin will be looking for her too. He'd love to get his hands on this."

"I suppose Belov's hunting her down?"

"He's got some leads. Like a fool, she bolted for the American embassy, and his men grabbed her. But some taxi driver came along and rescued her."

Yevgenia snorted. "He lost her twice!"

"You think this is funny?"

"This whole business is funny. If you had left her alone, she'd be back in

America right now with her little secret. Now she's on the loose in Russia with a hell of a story to tell. And best of all, your only way of catching her is General Bumbler. It's a farce."

Podolok swept the tape recorder angrily from the table. It sailed through the air and crashed against the wall.

"Temper. Temper, comrade secretary," said Yevgenia. "I doubt you need to worry. Fate is on our side."

"How so?"

"She has no passport, no visa. She barely speaks Russian. And everyone — and I mean everyone — is looking for her. How far could she get? In our country, even the sky has eyes."

T h r e e days. Three phone calls.

"You said 'a few days,' " Katherine pleaded to Cameron Abbott from the empty headquarters of White Dacha. Katherine heard the edge of desperation in her voice. The American diplomat must have heard it too. It reminded her of Koos's prediction.

She'll wash up like driftwood on the steps of the American embassy begging for a Big Mac and fries.

"If you'll think back carefully you'll remember I also said it might take longer," Cameron said.

His joviality made Katherine want to reach through the phone and slap him. She pictured him in his office, his feet up on the desk, and she squeezed the phone so hard her knuckles turned white.

"I'm an American citizen," she said. "Doesn't that mean anything?"

More desperation. At least Sergei wasn't present to see this. Katherine was on her own tonight. Sergei had called a few hours earlier to say he wouldn't be up to Ivanovka. "My wife thinks I'm having an affair," he said.

Sergei had suggested Katherine go alone to White Dacha. At first, Katherine had declined. But a need to hear her father's voice — or any English-speaking voice, for that matter — had driven her from her self-imposed Ivanovka incarceration. Katherine walked alone along the narrow roads two miles to the house of Galina Tushchina in Bolshevichka. It was the same house Sergei had stopped at three days earlier to retrieve a key. Katherine put the key in her pocket and walked another fifteen minutes along the gravel road to White Dacha, rehearsing her lines for her daily phone call to Cameron Abbott.

"Of course it does," said Cameron. "It means a lot. But remember, as far as the Sovs are concerned, you are a fugitive."

"Thanks for reminding me."

"Yes. Well. I have something here that I thought might interest you. It's from Tuesday's *New York Times.*"

He read Grayson's article about Victor Perov and the notebooks. When Cameron finished, Katherine breathed, "Victor."

Victor. She and Sergei had discussed the possibility of contacting Victor again. But the more she thought about it, the more she was sure it was the wrong course. Just knowing that she was not safely back in Ithaca might compel him to come looking for her—and that would be disastrous. She was also determined to put no one else at risk on her behalf. The murder of Sigmund and the arrest of Lena Ryzhkova filled her with guilt. It was bad enough that her father had been dragged into this.

On the phone, Cameron was talking. "I had lunch with Grayson Hines about the article, and he had very little to add to what was written. But he did give me an advance copy of an article that appeared in today's edition."

Again, he read.

American Missing in Moscow
  By Grayson Hines
  Special to The New York Times
  MOSCOW—Soviet officials said Wednesday they have "mounted an all-out manhunt" to find an American scientist missing in Moscow for a fifth day.
  Katherine Sears, 32, an astronomer from Cornell University, disappeared from her tour group last Friday, the day she was scheduled to leave Moscow after completing a sightseeing tour. She was last seen Thursday evening getting into an elevator in her downtown Moscow hotel, according to a member of her tour group.
  Dr. Katherine Sears is the daughter of sovietologist Dr. Jack Sears, a conservative advisor to the Reagan administration. Dr. Jack Sears is recognized for his hardline stand against what he views as the Soviet threat. He is often credited as the behind-the-scenes force in President Reagan's "evil empire" speech.
  Dr. Sears is currently in Moscow to help with the search for his daughter.
  An official at the Soviet Foreign Ministry, who asked not to be identified, confirmed that Dr. Katherine Sears had violated the stay of her visa.
  A diplomat at the American embassy confirmed that Dr. Sears was missing, but refused to comment further.
  A Soviet official said the foreign ministry was giving "daily reports" to the American embassy.
  Both Soviet and American officials refused to speculate on whether or not Katherine Sears was the victim of foul play, or if her disappearance was in any way connected to her father's activities.

Vladimir Smith, a member of Dr. Sears's tour group, said by telephone from Utah that Katherine Sears had "sneaked away" from the group on one other occasion.

"When she didn't show up that last day we all just figured she had gone on walkabout again," he said.

"The American press corps is going nuts," said Cameron. "First Grayson scooped them on the Victor Perov story, and now this. They accused me of giving it to him, but I don't know how he got it."

"So what's next?" asked Katherine.

"I have to warn you: The Sovs know you're hiding somewhere outside Moscow."

Katherine's heart sank. "How?"

"I don't know. You called the embassy that first day on an unsecured line. It could have been that. They're asking some very peculiar questions. Very peculiar."

"Like what?"

"Like what you may know about Soviet psychiatric abuse, what was your real purpose in coming here, why you left your tour group on your first night, that sort of thing. You've told me everything, haven't you?"

"Yes! I have trusted you completely, for all the good it has done."

"I see. Tomorrow is the weekend. Nothing's going to happen till Monday. Call me back then. Here's your father."

Jack Sears came on the line. Katherine said, "Cameron thinks I'm involved with Sigmund's murder."

"I know."

"Do you think he's really doing everything possible?"

"Actually, yes. My legal experts are having no more success than Cameron. Someone is stonewalling, and it's impossible in this country to figure out who's behind it. But don't worry, I'll take your case all the way to the president if I have to."

"Thanks, Dad," Katherine said wearily.

They said good-bye and Katherine set the receiver in the cradle. She held the phone in her lap because the cord was so short that when she picked up the receiver, the whole phone came off the desk. Why would somebody build something with such an obvious defect? she wondered. And while she was on the subject, why color it such a putrid shade of orange? She put the phone back on the cigarette-scarred desk; it rocked on the uneven floor. Was no floor, no wall, no *thing* built properly in this country? Didn't Russians have pride? Or was that *defitsit* too? She looked around the dim, cold barn of White Dacha, and her gaze settled on the electrical cords that snaked over the floor. Why didn't someone

install some new electrical outlets — or at least tape down the cords before someone tripped on them? And why did the place have to smell like manure? Didn't
they have cleaning products in Russia? Mops?

Somewhere beyond the thin walls, out in the night, a cow bawled hauntingly.

Her father had given Katherine the words:

I hate this place.

I n the Moscow City Council Theater, KGB Director Shatalin finished briefing
Tarasov on Katherine Sears's status.

Tarasov listened thoughtfully. "She's savvier than anyone thought."

"How savvy do you have to be to outsmart Belov?" snorted Shatalin.

"Good point."

"So what are you going to do about it?" Shatalin demanded.

"Do?"

"She's alive!"

"So it seems."

"She's the key, you said so yourself. We have to find her before Belov does."

"Just like that," Tarasov laughed.

"How can you be so cavalier?" Shatalin asked.

"My attitude doesn't change the fact that foreign nationals on Soviet territory
are the jurisdiction of Counterintelligence, so Belov is within his rights to pursue
the investigation. There will be an all-out manhunt. He'll have every informer
within five hundred kilometers on the lookout. You're his superior officer, but his
power base is in the Kremlin, which means he can pretty much do as he pleases.
No, I believe I'll stick to my original strategy."

"And what has your strategy produced so far?"

"Give me one of those Winstons," said Tarasov.

Shatalin opened his cigarette case and tossed a cigarette into Tarasov's lap.
Tarasov lit it and drew a long breath.

"So? What have you got so far?" asked Shatalin.

Tarasov blew smoke out his nose. "Nothing."

Shatalin snorted and stood up. The guards posted at the two aisles spoke into
their walkie-talkies.

Shatalin inched to the end of the aisle. "One other thing," he said. "Victor
Perov went to the Serbsky yesterday raving that his twin brother was being held
in a psychiatric hospital."

"Why?"

"Jesus, Konstantin, who's working for whom here?" Shatalin exclaimed. "Try
giving *me* some answers for a change. You're the one who's supposed to be a
goddamn genius. Or did sitting in that *gaishnik* booth make you dumb?"

Tarasov didn't reply. Shatalin shook his head in disgust and went out without another word. The two guards turned after him.

Tarasov sat alone in the theater a long time, his Winston glowing in the dark like a red eye. Was it a coincidence Victor went to the Serbsky shortly after Katherine Sears disappeared?

Tarasov didn't believe in coincidences. He threw his butt on the floor and went out.

At 7:30 the next morning, Leo Yakunin came to Tarasov's flat.

"Sorry about the time," said Leo after Tarasov let him in. "I just got off the night train."

He grimaced at the tiny space. "Lord, what a shithole."

"Why are you back from Leningrad, Leo?"

"I got it. The link."

Tarasov smiled. "Like some coffee?"

"That would be great."

They went to the kitchen and sat down. Tarasov stood in his bathrobe over the coffeepot. It ticked as the water warmed.

"Go on," said Tarasov. "You were telling me about a link."

"Last year, on November 11 at 3:30 A.M., Yevgenia Perova was signed into the Leningrad KGB building by then-colonel Yuri Belov."

Tarasov thought. "The timing's about right. Good. How did you get this?"

"The log sheets. It stood to reason that if there was a connection between Yevgenia Perova and General Belov, then at some time she would have come to the building. And if she had, she would be required to sign in. Not even Belov could alter that."

"How did you get the log sheets?"

"They archive them, same as us. They're not even classified."

"So what brought the Iron Perova to Leningrad in the middle of the night?"

"I figured you were going to ask that, so I stuck around until I had the answer. I didn't want you to send me back up there."

Tarasov smiled. He poured the coffee into cups and set them on the table. He sat down opposite Leo.

Leo went on. "The time of the meeting suggested an emergency—I mean, 3:30 A.M.! Jesus. So I went through all the case files for two weeks on either side of that day. Nothing. It looked like a dead end. Then, by chance, I was having lunch in the KGB cafeteria and struck up a conversation with a border guard. All border guards for Finland and Norway are run out of Leningrad."

"Which was Belov's responsibility."

"Right. Anyway, this guard remembered a border shooting around that date."

"Border shooting?"

"Yes. So I went back to the archives for the case file on a border shooting on that date, but there was nothing."

"So there was no shooting?"

"Oh, there was a shooting all right. I phoned the head of the border guards up there, a fellow by the name of Captain Rodenko—one very bored, very unhappy Ukrainian. He said he had been assigned there about three months ago. He spent a half-hour talking to me about how I could help get him stationed in Kiev."

"You said he was new to the post?"

"That's right," said Leo. "The previous captain died in an auto accident on November 20."

Tarasov jumped to his feet. Ten days after Yevgenia Perova's visit to Leningrad."

"Right. So then I got real interested. Luckily, this Rodenko was anxious to help me, you know, so I could help him get out of Karelia. He put me on the phone with three of the border guards from the sector. One of them was the guy who actually pulled the trigger. He was real upset about it. Said the fellow ignored his warnings. All three of them remembered the incident, which surprised me—until I heard why."

"Why?"

"The man they shot had no nose."

"Excuse me?"

"He had no nose," said Leo. "Just a little stub where a nose should have been, presumably once was."

"A stub-nose man," said Tarasov. "Interesting."

"He was still alive when they got to him," said Leo. "Guess who did the interrogation."

"The captain who died in the accident."

Leo grinned.

"They remember anything else?"

"Siberia. He had escaped from exile in Oimyakon."

"And he made it all the way to the Norwegian border? A difficult journey."

Leo nodded. "He was quite resourceful, apparently. They said he had built himself two excellent little ladders. Remember the camp break in Yakutia in the 1970s?"

"Ladders."

"That must have been where he got the idea. Anyway, he made just one little mistake."

"What's that?"

"There are three fences on the border. He thought there were two."

"So he escaped into the forbidden zone."

"Right. Which is probably why he didn't surrender when the border guard called out for him to stop." Leo laughed. "Poor bugger thought he was in Norway."

Tarasov went back to his chair and sat down. He lit up a cigarette. It was Russian and tasted like rubber. "You got any foreign cigarettes?" Tarasov asked.

"I prefer *papirosy*."

"You kidding?"

"No. Really."

"Devil!" said Tarasov. He took a drag and said, "So let me get this right. A stub-nose man escapes from Oimyakon, flees to the border, gets shot—but not killed. He is interrogated. The captain informs Belov, who calls Yevgenia Perova in the middle of the night. She comes running up to Leningrad. They murder the stub-nose man and the captain, remove the file, and within months they both receive big promotions."

"That about sums it up."

"Why?"

"Without the file, I can't say."

"Oimyakon," said Tarasov. "That's in Yakutia, right?"

"The coldest place in the northern hemisphere. I suppose I get to go there next."

Tarasov grinned. "Don't forget your long underwear."

S h a t a l i n called Leo into his office the moment he arrived at Lubyanka. He told Leo about Katherine Sears.

"Tarasov refuses to look for her," said Shatalin.

"Figures," said Leo. "The guy's a loose cannon."

"I had forgotten what a fanatic he was. I never should have let him back in. Listen, Belov has formed a task force to find Katherine Sears, and I'm appointing you from my office."

"Yes, comrade director."

"I can't officially interfere with General Belov's investigation, but you can keep me informed. Perhaps an opportunity will present itself."

"What about Tarasov? He wants me to go to Yakutia."

"Yakutia! Jesus, what next?" Shatalin shook his head. "Let him go to Siberia himself. Tarasov's on his own from here on out. I promised him a month. He's got three weeks left. Then it's back to traffic tickets for him."

19

T h e idea came to Katherine on Friday night as she walked back to Galina Tushchina's house from White Dacha. She went straight back to the farm's headquarters and called Sergei. "I want you to get some things for me."

He took down the list and promised to bring the items the following evening. "We'll talk about this idea of yours then," he said.

It began to rain sometime during the night. When Katherine awoke Saturday morning and looked out the window, a new world greeted her.

Under the flat glow of the gray-black sky, a shadowless landscape had come to life. Everything was sharper, as though God had turned up the world's contrast knob. The last of the snow had been washed away. The brown dirt was stained muddy black. The weeds that grew in clumps in the fields had absorbed the night's moisture and now glowed phosphorescent. The bark of the birch trees shimmered white, as though someone had scrubbed them clean. And over everything lay the suggestion of fog. It was a morning from a fairy tale. It seemed to Katherine that mother nature herself was on alert, waiting for something to happen.

Katherine dressed quickly, washed and went out to help Baba Krista with breakfast. Katherine had a mission today, and as they sipped acid coffee at the kitchen table, she made her dramatic announcement.

"I go buying bread."

Baba Krista's wrinkled face curled into an expression of relief, as though she had been fretting over this strange young woman who lived like a prisoner in her home. Baba Krista found an umbrella, rubber boots only two sizes too big, and a clear plastic parka like those sold for a dollar at an American football game. Katherine looked like a genuine Russian peasant, circa mid-1980s, as she started off that morning for Bolshevichka.

The fragrance of this new, rain-washed world rose like menthol off the black earth. The air was so supersaturated with oxygen it made her dizzy to breathe.

The rain pattered gently on her umbrella as she made the half-hour march to Bolshevichka.

Bolshevichka, "Little She-Bolshevik," was not the Gomorrah that Sergei's sinister history of the fall of Ivanovka had suggested. It was a modest settlement of some two hundred wooden cottages and one five-story brick apartment block of the type Katherine had seen all over Moscow. A stream divided the town. There was a bridge for cars at one end; at the other, a high, swinging foot bridge. Beside the auto bridge stood a two-story stone building that looked out of place. Missing from the pastoral setting were golden onion domes. There was no church in Bolshevichka.

Katherine found the shopping district and began to browse. The shops—a produce store, a butcher, a dry foods store, a department store and a bakery—were clustered on the central "square," a spot where four cracked asphalt paths converged. The produce store sold two kinds of potatoes: dirty and clean. The butcher was closed, though the sign in the window read "open." The dry foods store offered three bins filled with unmarked cans reminding Katherine of donation barrels at a canned-goods drive. The department store sold a variety of things made of plastic: toilet bowl brushes, car fenders, plates and cups. The only things that weren't plastic were the washboards, about two hundred of them, all neatly faced so as to fill the shelves. An ordinary convenience store in the States would have offered Katherine a larger assortment than the entire "shopping district" of Bolshevichka.

Katherine went into the bakery. The sweet smell of the ovens hung in the air, but the room was empty—of people and bread. Crumbs in wooden racks on the wall attested to the presence of bread at some time in the not-too-distant past. She went outside and looked again at the sign. *Bulochnaya.* Yes, that was right. She went back inside.

"*Allo?*" she called out.

A middle-aged, bulbous woman in a white smock appeared behind the counter. She wiped her hands on her smock, blinked at Katherine and barked, "Who are you?"

"I want to buying bread."

"Foreigner. Humph."

"Can I buy bread?"

Katherine felt like a child who had been sent to the store for milk.

"Where are you from?"

"Latvia. I am from Latvia. Can I buy bread?"

The woman glared at her a moment. "No bread," she said and turned away.

"This is a bakery?" asked Katherine, but the woman was gone.

Katherine went outside and raised her umbrella. She stood miserably wondering what to do.

A middle-aged woman came toward her along the path. The first thing Katherine noticed was the woman's hair. It was precisely the shade of purple one finds in grape-flavored hard candy. She was built like a pear, big end down, and was supported by tree-trunk legs. Fat feet joined the tree trunks, but no ankle marked the juncture. The woman drew nearer. She had a young face, which made Katherine wonder if she were correct to assume the woman was middle-aged. She had a mole the size of a dime on the left side of her chin. Hair grew out of it. Her eyes were brown and shone hopefully.

"Yekatarina!" she said. "I thought that was you!"

It was Galina Tushchina, from whom Katherine got the key to White Dacha for her phone calls.

"Good day, Galina Alexandrovna," said Katherine, using the patronymic as a respectful form of address.

Galina frowned. "What's wrong?"

"No bread," said Katherine.

"Ach!" said Galina and spun Katherine around as though she were a child. She pushed her back into the bakery.

"Natasha!" Galina called out.

The plump woman came back from her ovens wiping her hands.

They began to argue. They spoke to each other at the same time in high falsetto voices, seemingly without pausing for air. Spit flew. It went on for a while.

At last, Natasha disappeared into the back room and returned with four loaves of black bread. She put them on the counter. She flipped the beads on her wood abacus and said, "Sixteen kopecks."

Katherine handed over the money and scooped up her loaves. She hugged them to her body. They were still warm. She dropped them carefully into her string bag.

Katherine felt as though she had won the lottery. Is this what she would have to go through every day to buy bread? She tried not to think about the effort required for something a little more luxurious, like a car, or tomatoes.

Natasha smiled and flashed two gold teeth. "Welcome to Bolshevichka. Bread is baked fresh every odd hour starting at seven."

She addressed Katherine as though she were talking to a dog. "You . . . un . . . der . . . stand . . . me?"

Katherine nodded and thanked her. Then Katherine and Galina went outside.

"What did you say to her?" asked Katherine.

Galina shrugged. "We were just chatting."

"I thought you were arguing," said Katherine.

Galina frowned. "What made you think that?"

"Never mind."

Then Galina seemed to remember something. "We have a Latvian in Bolshevichka. I was just telling her about you."

"Is that so?" Katherine replied sickly.

"I will have to invite you both over for tea and cookies and I'm sure it would be nice to speak a little Latvian though you really should work on your Russian and how is it possible that you went through our schools without learning better Russian it is the language of our country after all but I have heard that you Baltic people like to think of yourselves as independent and I hope you don't take offense to that because it's just something I read because I've never actually been to the Baltics and did you know that our institute has Russian courses and several foreign language courses as well which might be able to help you improve your Russian while you are here and perhaps I could help you to get enrolled and you're such a sweet dear of a girl a little helpless but with a face just like an angel and such a girlish figure . . ."

The words streamed out of Galina just like that, without punctuation. Their meaning took Katherine a while to work out. Understanding came later, after Katherine had said good-bye, after she crossed the swinging foot bridge and started across the big field toward Ivanovka, after she began to play back the words in the tape recorder of her photographic memory. And that's how it happened that, alone on a path in the middle of a field, Katherine Sears came to hear about the Institute for the Improvement of the Qualifications of Farmers.

T h e r e is an institute in Bolshevichka?" Katherine asked Baba Krista when she got back to the house. It sounded preposterous: a little village like Bolshevichka with an institute.

Baba Krista nodded. Now Katherine knew what that out-of-place stone building near the overpass was.

It rained the rest of the day, and was still raining that evening when Sergei's taxi pulled up in front of the house. Three days had passed since his last visit.

Katherine watched Sergei from the window. He tucked two bags under his arm, and then raced through the rain.

He bounded through the front door, and Katherine was there to greet him. It was great to see him, and she said so. He grinned and shook the water from his clothes. He gave her three kisses on the cheek. Next came Baba Krista, who shuffled up the hall exactly as she had that first day when Katherine arrived. He gave her three pecks as well.

They went into the kitchen, and Sergei unloaded a plastic bag. Sausage, a head of cabbage, bread and several potatoes spilled out onto the counter.

Baba Krista went to work immediately on a cabbage soup she called *shchi*.

Katherine and Sergei went into the living room.

"I have the books you asked for," he said. He spread them out on the table. There was a two-volume Russian-English/English-Russian dictionary, maps of the Soviet Union, Moscow and the Moscow region (which included a dot for Bolshevichka, but not Ivanovka). There was a textbook in English called *Russian in Exercises,* and another called *Russian As We Speak It.* Finally, there was a book on Latvia, in Russian, entitled *Soviet Latvia.*

Katherine examined each item. She ran her hands over the dictionary as though it were a gold-embossed, leather-bound special edition.

She thanked Sergei and said, "It occurred to me today, I don't know your last name."

Sergei smiled. "Gusin. My name is Sergei Sergeyevich Gusin."

Now he wanted to hear about Katherine's phone call the previous night. He listened with interest, and when she finished he said, "It looks as though you may be with us for a while."

"I'm afraid so," she said. "I have to learn to be more . . ." She stopped and reached for her dictionary. She found the word "independent." "*Samo-sto-ya-tel-na-ya,*" she read. Sergei corrected her pronunciation, and she put a check mark in red pen beside the word.

The dictionary was open the rest of the evening. Red marks began to scar the pages.

Katherine told him about her adventure in Bolshevichka. When she got to the part about the bakery, she said, "Galina Alexandrovna said that —"

Sergei winced. "Don't use the patronymic with her like she's an old woman," he said. "Galina, just Galina, is proper."

"I already called her Galina Alexandrovna."

"Then you offended her," he said, irritated. "She's only thirty-two years old."

Katherine gasped at that.

"If you want to live here," said Sergei, "you're going to have to learn some manners."

"I'm sorry."

"She's a friend of mine."

"I'm *sorry.*"

They were quiet a minute, then Katherine said, "There is an institute in Bolshevichka."

"Yes."

"Galina said she could get me enrolled for some Russian courses."

"Probably."

"Will you help me? I can't stay in my room forever. And I might learn some manners."

Sergei smiled. "I'm sorry. I didn't mean to be hard on you."

"No, you're right."

"You just don't know how insulting that sounds."

"You're right, I don't. So what about the institute?"

"I'll see what I can do."

Then Katherine told him about the Latvian in Bolshevichka.

Sergei groaned. "Of all the bad luck."

They modified Katherine's cover story so that she was from Latvia, yes, but the daughter of Polish immigrants. That would explain her bad Russian and nonexistent Latvian.

With that decided, Sergei said, "Now, let's discuss this idea of yours."

Katherine took a deep breath. "There is a ferry, the *Estonia*, that runs three days a week across the Baltic Sea from Tallinn to Helsinki—"

"How do you know that?"

"I was at the port in Helsinki. I checked the schedule."

Sergei nodded, and Katherine went on. She finished several minutes later, and Sergei said, "Nice idea, but I doubt it would work."

"But it might."

"It might not."

Katherine nudged him playfully. "Don't be such a pessimist. Besides, it's only a backup plan in case Cameron fails me. I hope I will never have to use it."

"Suppose for a minute that you actually did make it to Finland," said Sergei. "The Finns might just hand you back to the Soviets. They do it all the time."

"If I were a Soviet citizen, yes. But I'm American."

"You have no passport to prove that."

"I could arrange to have my father meet me at the port in Helsinki. He could have my papers already prepared. I don't think the Finns would dare turn me over then."

Sergei thought about it. "You will need Soviet documents," he said. "Two passports—internal and international—and an exit visa. Good counterfeits, not the usual stuff. These will have to fool a passport control officer."

Katherine recalled the thorough inspection her American passport had received at Sheremetyevo-2 Airport when she arrived two weeks earlier with her tour group. Sergei was right, the quality of the fake documents would have to be very high indeed.

Sergei said, "I may be able to get the passports, but the exit visa . . . that's practically impossible."

"Then we'll focus on the passports first."

Sergei bit his lower lip. "You realize, Katherine, this could take months."

"Then we had better get started."

20

I f one had to pinpoint the exact moment when Victor Perov's fall from grace began, it probably would have been that Monday morning when security guard Ivan Petrovich scowled at Victor and said, "Open your briefcase."

Victor stood at the security check to the SAPO Institute and gave Ivan a look of disbelief.

"Are you joking?"

In five years Ivan had never checked the contents of his, or as far as Victor knew, *anyone's* briefcase.

Ivan glared at him.

Victor shrugged and put his briefcase on the small inspection table.

"Open it, please," said Ivan.

Victor released the catches with a *snap* and stepped back.

Ivan approached the open briefcase as though it were a live bomb. He extracted a notebook and peered at it distastefully. He fanned the pages and set it gently on the table. He repeated this with the next notebook.

"What is this?" he asked.

Victor looked at the notebook. It was part of a calculation for X rays traveling in a gravity field. "Research."

"You often take such things home?"

"Every night."

"Hmm."

Two men came into the lobby. "Good morning," they said, and Ivan waved them through. Victor felt the back of his neck getting hot.

Then Ivan found something that seemed to really interest him. He held up a single sheet of paper. "What is this?"

Victor looked at it. "A list of items I need."

"No, *this*," Ivan said and pointed to a symbol at the bottom.

"That, my friend, is the letter 'X,' " said Victor. "It commonly signifies the end of a list."

"It looks like a swastika to me."

Victor lifted his head and laughed. Ivan's expression didn't change.

A group of three men came into the lobby. Ivan nodded at them, and they pushed open the swinging gate that led into the institute. As they passed, their heads turned toward Victor, his briefcase open on the table, its contents scattered about.

Victor blushed. "You think I'm a fascist?"

"I don't think anything," said Ivan. "I'm just the security guard."

"Come on, Ivan," said Victor. "Stop this. We're friends. At the summer picnic I looked after your daughter Katya while you played soccer."

"I am just doing my job, comrade," he said, still holding the list. "About this document, I will have to confiscate it and present it to the director for evaluation."

"Suit yourself," said Victor. He threw his papers into his briefcase, snapped it closed and then pushed his way through the gate. He slammed it behind him. The crash seemed to shake the whole building.

At ten-thirty a flyer went up on the bulletin board.

> *Respected Comrades!*
>
> *Our collective has been betrayed! Petty bourgeois interests have infiltrated our sacred workplace! Dear patriots! Make your feelings known at a special meeting of the worker's committee! Tonight at 19:30 hours in the Lenin Auditorium!*

Victor's heart sank when he spotted it. Five sentences, six exclamation points. Someone passed behind him in the hall, and he could feel his back being studied.

An hour later, Alexander Kaminsky stopped by to ask if Victor would be at the meeting. Kaminsky was the institute's director, and a longtime supporter of Victor's work. Three years earlier, he had stood up to Boris Orlov to push through Victor's Soviet-American project.

"I'm on the committee," said Victor. "Of course I'll be there."

The Worker's Committee had the power to expel any member of the collective. Victor's whole life had been devoted to getting into SAPO. To be thrown out meant never working as an astronomer again. He consoled himself with the knowledge that without a signal from the institute's Communist party cell, led by another loyal colleague, Pyotr Terolyov, it was unlikely the Worker's Committee would act. But he could have been wrong about that.

"People are likely to be a little hysterical," Alexander said. "Just try to stay calm. I'm sure we can work something out. You are a valued member of the collective. No one is going to forget that."

Victor came through the back door of Lenin Auditorium at seven-thirty. A woman shoved a piece of paper into his hand and then looked up at him. She gave a start to find herself face to face with the evening's guest of dishonor. Victor glanced at the paper; it was a Russian translation of Hines's article. He folded it and put it in his pocket.

The lecture hall buzzed with voices. At the front, four men and a woman sat at a long table. They looked out at the crowd blankly, their faces as dour as a government photograph. How many times had Victor entered this sacred auditorium with a tinge of excitement at a coming lecture, at the privilege of being in the presence of the greatest minds in the Soviet Union? He felt sick. He had thought he was ready for this moment. Now he feared he was not.

In the first five rows a tight cluster of about fifty people were huddled. Another hundred or so were scattered about the hall in small groups. Everyone held a copy of the paper. A few faces turned toward Victor when he came in, then looked away quickly. To Victor's left he spotted several members of the Helsinki delegation, including Dr. Mikhail Yakovlev, who had been with him in Stockmann's department store that day with Katherine Sears. Their eyes met and Mikhail dropped his gaze. Victor descended three steps, then inched along the narrow row until he found a seat alone near the edge of the auditorium.

Five minutes later, the chairman of the committee tapped his water glass with a pen, and the meeting was called to order.

"Respected comrades," he said. "We are here this evening to discuss an issue of great significance to our collective. All of you by now should have received a copy . . ."

The back door creaked, and Victor turned to look. A man stepped into the auditorium and stood a moment on the top step, surveying the room. He wore the uniform of a traffic policeman, a *gaishnik*. He was tall, with short blond hair and a powerful, bony face. He slipped into a seat in the back row.

Victor turned back to face the podium.

Someone was on his feet. It was a fifty-five-year-old technician from Victor's laboratory, a quarrelsome man whom Victor had recently helped earn a promotion.

"I am shocked by this article," he said. "It is nothing more than an exercise in anti-Soviet propaganda, imperialist lies and deceit. And they call it journalism!"

He sat down. The room murmured approval.

A thin man in spectacles rose. He was an astronomer who had been with Victor in Helsinki. He had spent most of the time drunk, watching porno movies in his room.

"I say Victor Perov has betrayed more than the institute, he has struck a blow to the future of world socialism!"

A few heads nodded, but Victor was relieved to see that quite a few of his colleagues looked uncomfortable. The evening, he decided, could still go either way.

"The chair recognizes comrade Dr. Oleg Ivanov."

Victor sat forward, as did the entire audience. Their heads moved like a wave. Ivanov was the elder statesman of SAPO. He had worked alongside some of the greatest astronomers of the twentieth century. Though two decades had passed since Ivanov had made a significant contribution to the progress of science, he was regarded as the spiritual guru of the institute.

The old man stood. He ran his fingers through his gray beard and then lifted his head.

"Esteemed comrades," he said, his voice rising to the pitch of an accomplished orator. "It is a sad day, and a sad, sad thing we now contemplate. But face it we must, or else bury our heads in the sand and dismiss the dreams of the founder of our great socialist state, our guiding light, Vladimir Ilyich Lenin. For the heinous act we consider today is nothing less than an attack at the very heart of our society: the collective. And for this savage, thoughtless and inexplicably petty betrayal, I am outraged."

He slapped his hand against the paper that carried Hines's article. "Not at this paltry, fleeting article, which is typical of the so-called free Western press, which as we all know is controlled by the military-industrial complex of our enemies. No, I am outraged that a trusted member of our collective, Victor Perov, a Party member, a man upon whom all the benefits and privileges of our Great Society have rained down, would place into the hands of the forces of imperialist repression the very instrument of slander against his own collective. For this crime, dear comrades, I can find no forgiveness in my heart."

The room erupted with cries of "hear! hear!"

The chairman raised his hands to quiet the room. He looked in Victor's direction. "Comrade Perov, your name has been invoked. This is a fair and impartial forum. Do you care to speak?"

Faces turned to Victor. Victor got slowly to his feet. The room fell silent.

"How can the truth slander?" Victor asked.

Victor stood facing Dr. Ivanov, but the old man avoided his gaze.

"Go on, comrade," said the chairman.

"What can I say to those who would call me a traitor?" said Victor. "I consider myself a patriot. I am truly sorry that some of you feel as you do, and especially my esteemed colleague Dr. Ivanov, whom I respect greatly. It was not my intention to slander this institute, but merely to rectify an injustice."

"An injustice in which you played a part!" This was Mikhail Yakovlev.

"All the more reason for me to be the one to set things right."

Mikhail was on his feet now. "Victor Perov has received every benefit this institute can offer. He has a private office, the demanding tools his work requires, an apartment, a good salary, and even foreign travel. He has repaid this generosity by betraying us to our enemies. This evening, the West laughs at the SAPO Institute, thanks to Victor Perov."

"Why are you so concerned with what the West thinks?" asked Victor. "Do they possess a moral authority our own people do not? Let our accomplishments speak for us. As long as the quality of the work here is excellent, no one will dare laugh at our great SAPO."

Several people nodded. *Why don't they speak up?*

The chairman said, "Are you willing now, before all of your comrades, to admit your mistake?"

"But comrade chairman, I do not consider my actions in helping to exonerate Dr. Vladimir Ryzhkov a 'mistake.'"

"But you went to our enemies," said the woman who sat beside the chairman. This was Dr. Raisa Mikhailova, one of Victor's closest friends. She had been to his dacha several times. He also knew her to be a dedicated scientist. "As far as I am concerned, *that* was your mistake. You should have come to us. You should have trusted your comrades."

"But I had no choice," said Victor. "Certain members of this institute perpetrated this injustice. I had no recourse but to find an outside channel."

Now Dr. Ivanov was on his feet. He looked at the chairman and stabbed a finger in Victor's direction. "How dare this . . . man . . . continue to slander our collective! Does he have no shame?"

A frail, middle-aged woman got timidly to her feet. She was vaguely familiar to Victor, but he couldn't place her.

"I have something to say," she said in a screechy falsetto voice, like a parody of a wicked witch.

"Yes, comrade," said the chairman. "All may speak here."

Dr. Ivanov sat down, and the faces of the auditorium turned to the old woman.

"Victor Perov is not one of us," she said. "I always said that. Very uppity, he is. I would come into his office sometimes, and he wouldn't even speak to me."

No one said a word.

"Would the speaker please identify herself," Victor called out.

She poked her chin in his direction and said, "Galinova, Lena Grigorevna."

That meant nothing to Victor. "What is your field?"

"I'm a janitor."

Victor nodded. So that was how he knew her. She emptied his trash can every day.

Dr. Igor Lunts, an astronomer, got to his feet. "I must agree with the esteemed Dr. Ivanov. Victor Perov has enjoyed every privilege of this institute and has repaid it with treachery. Recently, these privileges included research time on the most powerful radio telescope in the world. I motion now for a vote to withdraw his grant."

Victor shook his head at that. Lunts was bitter that his own proposals had been turned down.

Victor said, "Comrade chairman, that grant has already been approved by the advisory board of the Academy of Sciences."

"Not *approved*," said the chairman. "*Recommended* for approval. It is within our rights to consider a motion to refuse to follow that recommendation."

"I second the motion!" someone called out.

Victor was still on his feet. "Dear friends, don't do this. That experiment is not for me, or for the SAPO Institute or even for the Soviet Union. It is for *all* of mankind."

Victor looked around. "Doesn't anyone want to speak on my behalf?"

The auditorium was as quiet as a library.

The vote was taken. At the call of "For!" every hand in the audience was raised. At the call of "Against!" only Victor raised his hand.

"The motion is carried."

Tears filled Victor's eyes. "Look at what you have done! Look at *yourselves!* Are we scientists? Isn't our first duty to truth?"

Again, several of his colleagues looked uncomfortable. Just when it seemed some of them might rise to his defense a shrill voice rose self-righteously out of the silence.

"*My* first duty is to the motherland!"

It was Lena Galinova. The janitor.

Hear! Hear!

The denouncements came like machine-gun fire.

"He has a new car!"

"He has a four-room flat!"

"He takes confidential papers home."

"I saw him reading an English-language newspaper!"

"He sleeps with his brother's wife."

"He has a two-story dacha!"

Victor closed his eyes, and for some reason he thought about a Young Pioneers meeting when he and Anton were boys. Anton was about to be thrown out of the youth organization for absenteeism and insubordination. With Anton absent, Victor rose to his twin's defense. Victor denounced another boy, Dima, for having failed to read enough books during the previous month. For a Young Pioneer there was no more damning condemnation. Dima, a soft-spoken boy with thick glasses, lowered his head and said nothing — as Victor knew he would. When the minutes of the meeting were submitted the next day, Victor made sure Anton was credited with having denounced Dima. The record saved Anton from expulsion. Anton never knew about it. He would have been furious.

I deserve this, Victor thought.

At last, Dr. Ivanov rose. He cleared his throat, and the room quieted.

"Esteemed comrades," he said. "I have heard nothing tonight from comrade Perov that would alter my view of his reprehensible behavior. Frankly, I don't see how he can remain a member of this collective. I motion that we vote to expel him now."

"I second the motion," someone cried.

Hear! Hear! Hear!

Victor sank back in his chair. It was a lynch mob.

Alexander Kaminsky was on his feet in the third row. The room stilled.

"Comrades," he said. "Dear friends. I appreciate your feelings. But I would like to suggest that we postpone the question of expulsion. Perhaps our dear comrade Perov has indeed made a mistake—"

"Perhaps?" someone cried out.

"—but let us not rush to judgement. That, after all, is the mistake of the West."

There was a murmur of agreement.

In the end, the vote was postponed two weeks. No one needed to point out that by then the Communist Party Committee would have met and voted. That meeting was in one week. The worker's committee could then safely take its cue from the Party.

Two weeks. Time was running out for Victor Perov.

Konstantin Tarasov watched the chairman adjourn the meeting. People got to their feet reluctantly; some like angry spectators cheated by the referee who stops the boxing match; others like dazed witnesses of a public execution who have seen a thing that shouldn't have happened.

Victor Perov was the first to leave. He breezed by Tarasov without looking at him. Several minutes later, as the auditorium cleared, Tarasov got up and went out too.

He found Victor in his office, writing in a notebook. Tarasov leaned against the door frame and said, "You ever get the idea 'something is rotten in the state of Denmark'?"

Victor looked up. "Huh?"

"It's an English expression. *Hamlet,* if I'm not—"

"Who are you? How did you get in here?"

"My name is Konstantin Tarasov. Don't be fooled by the *gaishnik* disguise. I'm from the KGB."

"Victor snorted. Just what I need."

"As a matter of fact, I am." Tarasov pointed at the chair in front of Victor's desk. "May I?"

"I don't have time for games."

"I know that you think your brother is alive."

"And you've come to try to stop me from searching?" said Victor. "Well, you can't. Unless you're here to arrest me. Are you?" Victor held out his wrists. "Put on the cuffs. It would be the perfect end to a perfect day."

"I'm not here to arrest you," said Tarasov. "I'm here to help you."

"I doubt that," said Victor.

"I think you are right about Anton."

Victor's eyes narrowed.

"May I sit down now?"

Victor nodded. "What do you know about Anton?"

"I don't know where he is, if that's what you're asking. But I do know it's why Katherine Sears came to Moscow. I also know it's why Pavel Danilov was murdered on the wharf of Rechnoy Vokzal."

"Murdered?"

Tarasov nodded. "A terrible tragedy. He had a young wife and a four-year-old daughter."

"Bastards," Victor breathed. "Who did it?"

"You wouldn't believe me."

"Try me."

Tarasov lit a cigarette and looked hard at Victor. "Does a man with a stub nose mean anything to you?"

"Huh?"

"A man with a stub nose? It means nothing at all?"

"No."

Tarasov picked a flake of tobacco from his tongue. He flicked it on the floor and said, "Katherine Sears is still in Russia."

Victor paled.

"You didn't know that, did you? I wasn't sure until just now."

"I don't believe you."

Tarasov handed Victor a copy of Grayson Hines's article on Katherine's disappearance. "The people who killed Pavel Danilov have tried to kill her — twice. She's on the run."

Victor read it and collapsed in his chair. "Is she . . ."

"Dead? She wasn't four days ago. She may be now. The KGB is after her. Make no mistake, they *will* find her. She cannot hide for long."

"You said you could help?"

"Not with Katherine. I can help you find your brother."

"How?"

Tarasov pulled a scrap of paper from his pocket. He unfolded it and flattened it on the desk in front of Victor. It read:

Koos van der Laan. 332–4771

"What's this?" asked Victor.

"Call and find out," said Tarasov, nodding toward the phone. "When the man asks your name, say 'Fyodor Dostoyevsky.' "

Victor dialed the number. The line rang twice, and a voice answered in a foreign language.

Victor said in Russian, "May I speak to Koos van der Laan?"

"Who is this?" asked the voice in heavily accented Russian. The man's tone was guarded.

Victor looked at Tarasov and said, "Fyodor Dostoyevsky?"

The man's voice relaxed. "Koos is not in the embassy at the moment. He should be in tomorrow morning at nine o'clock. Is there a message?"

"No," said Victor. "I'll call back."

Victor hung up and looked at Tarasov. "That was the Dutch embassy, wasn't it?"

Tarasov nodded and smoked his cigarette thoughtfully. A cloud of smoke swirled around his head.

"Who is Koos van der Laan?" Victor asked.

"Pavel Danilov's contact," said Tarasov.

"The man who died on the wharf?"

Tarasov nodded. "The KGB has had him under surveillance for some time."

"I don't get it. Why are you telling me this?"

Tarasov needed time. Things were happening too fast for his liking. Belov was looking for the American. Victor was after his brother. Tarasov needed time to find the man with the stub nose, and he couldn't let others get to the answer before him. It was a long shot, but if Victor actually found his brother then Tarasov might get to speak to Anton before General Belov. And as for Katherine —she was a wild card. The only person in Russia she trusted was Victor Perov. There was always the chance Victor could lead him to her.

"I have my reasons."

"Why should I trust you?"

Tarasov snorted. "Don't trust me. Trust no one. It's a sorry day when you have to trust your fellow man. Believe me, I've been in this business long enough to know that—friends informing on friends for the sake of moving up the queue; colleagues denouncing colleagues in order to land a promotion. Trust is a luxury, and people like us can't afford it. But that day may yet come for you, comrade, when you will have to decide whom among the untrustworthy you trust more."

"And Koos van der Laan?"

"Go ahead and meet him," said Tarasov with a shrug. "I won't stop you. Others may, so watch your step. I will be away on business for several weeks. I will call you when I get back."

T h a t evening after Victor put Grisha to bed, after he told Oksana about Ivan Petrovich's fictitious swastika, after he told her about the committee meeting and about Alexander Kaminsky—after all that, Victor told Oksana about his talk with Konstantin Tarasov. Oksana's eyes flashed like knives in the dark.

"Stay away from that man," she said. "Promise me."

They sat beside each other on the sofa, and Victor turned to face her more squarely. There was an edge of fear in her voice.

"Why?" asked Victor.

"Just promise."

"It's possible he can help us find Anton."

"Anton wouldn't want that kind of help. Let him go to hell with the rest of them."

"Oksana!"

"Promise me!"

"My hands are not entirely clean," said Victor.

"Yours are not bloody," she said.

"What about Vladimir Ryzhkov?"

"That's not the same thing, and you know it," said Oksana angrily. "This man is from the KGB. The KGB! I lived under its shadow for my entire five years with Anton. We watched our friends sent to prison camps and psychiatric hospitals. We would listen to their stories after they got out and . . ." Her voice cracked. "They tried to lure us into informing on our friends. We refused, and so they turned our friends into informers against us. For five years, my stomach jumped every time there was a knock at the door. In the end, they got Anton. And how could they not? We had only our love for each other. What is that against the power of the KGB? So they put my sweet Anton in a psychiatric hospital and then told me he was dead. These men are not human. Now, I want you to swear to me that you will stay away from him."

"Even if he could help Anton?"

"I'm his wife!" she cried. Her face flushed, and her eyes were moist with rage. "He is the father of my son! No one wants him back more than me! But not if it means an alliance with this kind of man. Anton wouldn't want it. I *will not allow it!*"

She was panting with fury. Victor knew Oksana could be stubborn when she thought she was right. Victor called this side of her "the lioness," though he had seen it only twice before—once when Grisha had been sick and a pharmacist refused to sell her medicine, and once when Victor had suggested getting Yevgenia involved in the search for Anton. Now the lioness was on the hunt once again, claws exposed, fangs glistening. Victor knew he was no match for her.

"All right," he said. "I promise."

Her body relaxed, and she closed her eyes. She began to sob. Victor watched her. He longed to take her into his arms, but he did not. He feared where that touch might lead.

A few minutes later, they got up and went to their separate bedrooms. Victor opened the door to Grisha's room and stood a moment listening for the sound of his breathing. It came to him reassuringly. He backed out.

He went to his room, undressed, crawled into bed and turned out the light. He lay there a long time thinking about all that had happened to him that day — the argument with Ivan Petrovich, the committee meeting, Konstantin Tarasov, Oksana the Lioness. His mind went over it all for hours until he could think about it no more. He felt adrift. All his life he had things to hold on to — Anton, his work, Yevgenia, his comrades at SAPO, Oksana, Grisha, even his faith in the rightness of the Communist Way. Now, one by one, they were slipping away. The most frightening part was that they weren't just slipping away, he was pushing them away as he reached for someone who was probably forever out of his grasp — Katherine Sears.

Poor Katherine. Her predicament was all his fault. He had to help her. But how?

He fell asleep without having found an answer.

Once again, the nightmare came to him. This time it was clearer, more *detailed* than ever before. He was underwater, his lungs straining for air. He was climbing to the surface when he saw the shadow below him.

Should he rise or dive?

He went deeper. The shadow sharpened into an image. A boy. He was at the bottom of the river. He was clutching something.

A burlap sack.

Victor sat up in bed and screamed. He took a deep breath and then screamed again. Oksana came running from her room. She switched on the lights and sat down beside him.

"It's okay, Victor. It was just another dream."

Victor panted. "Oh god, Oksana. It's not a dream."

"Of course it is —"

"No, I remember now," Victor gasped. "It really happened, a long time ago."

21

It was the summer of 1960, the summer of the puppies.

Emma, the Perovs' collie, crawled under the gazebo floor minutes after the family arrived at their dacha for vacation. An hour later, out came four puppies — at least they were *assumed* to be puppies, those slimy, eyeless, oversized earthworms that wriggled atop the brown Russian clay. What else might Emma have squeezed into the world?

Emma's timing was a victory for the jinxed collie. She had disproved Mama's prediction that the puppies would be born ("hatched," as she put it) in the car on the way. Mama was not often wrong.

The puppies were mutts, the result of an unsanctioned union with a neighbor's boxer. The unfortunate beasts got the worst of each parent: The short hair of a boxer and a collie's long snout and tail.

"Good lord!" mama said when she saw them. "Emma had a litter of rats."

To Victor and Anton, the puppies were beautiful, a genuine miracle. They could scarcely believe their good fortune. One moment good old Emma, who couldn't even fetch a stick properly, disappeared under the gazebo floor, and the next, *presto!* she was surrounded by four newborn puppies. Emma lay beside them, her first litter, with the majesty of a queen who has produced an heir. To the boys, she was the Dog Goddess Emma, Bringer of the Puppies. The twins were eight.

Like most middle-class Muscovites, the Perovs went to their dacha every summer to escape the sticky heat of the Russian capital. The dacha, a two-story house with an outdoor toilet, was located about fifty miles from Moscow in the village of Petrovka. It was part of a community of dachas being built by the Communist party for middle-level officials in the Agricultural Ministry, located on land that was once part of the apple orchard of the boyar Ivan Kerensky. The rusty cable of Kerensky's raft ferry still looped across the river. The cables were embedded in the center of the poplars standing at either end. The previous summer, the boys had learned to go hand-over-hand out the cable and then, at the midway point, drop with a *plunk* into the swift Moscow River. They were looking forward to repeating the feat this year (and perhaps adding a flip?). Birch forests, rolling fields, clean air and the cool river made Petrovka an ideal spot for any family to spend its vacation, and especially for an upwardly mobile Communist party family like the Perovs.

What a glorious time to be a boy in the Soviet Union! The newspapers were filled with predictions of another record harvest. The war was nearly two decades in the past. Stalin was seven years in his grave. Sputnik had orbited the earth. Corn was growing in Siberia, thanks to the Komsomol, young communists not much older than the twins, who were helping to open up Siberia with hydroelectric dams and new railroad routes. Nuclear power plants were bringing safe, clean energy for the future. Communism was just around the bend. Soon, all the world would be communist. Just think, the West wouldn't have to suffer anymore from hunger and homelessness!

But for the Perov twins, the summer of 1960 was foremost the summer of the puppies, and they spent much of their time under that gazebo, covered with a layer of clay that soon became resistant to soap and water. They slept with dirt under their fingernails and the smell of the puppies in their noses. Though Victor loved the puppies, it was Anton who assumed the role of Puppy Master. He gave them their names: Yegor, Lena, Sergei and Dina, the runt of the litter. While Victor would come into the house at night to watch television, Anton would stay outside with the puppies, letting them crawl over him and lick his face. Emma must have thought she had a fifth pup.

If Mama was aware of any of this, she gave no sign. She was busy with her meetings, commuting nearly every day to Moscow on one of the suburban trains, the "Little Electrics." There were meetings of the Community Committee, the Dairy Products Committee, the Agricultural Worker's Union, the Communist party soviet, the Komsomol, the local soviet and even the neighborhood *zhek*. Everyone was in awe of mama's brilliance in these meetings. While most came merely to get their attendance book stamped, Yevgenia Perova took an interest in every detail. Inevitably, she was appointed chairman of any committee she joined. "If everyone worked like your mother, we would be living in communism already," Papa used to say when he wasn't too drunk to speak. Apartments had to be assigned, vacations awarded, dachas leased, quotas set, new policies defined. There was, as Mama always said, "much work to building the world's first socialist state." Sometimes the boys wished that being a mother was a greater part of that work.

Then one day near the end of the summer, the whole family — Mama, Papa, Baba Raya and the twins — sat around the picnic table on the dacha's front lawn. Mama used the moment to announce that the boys could keep only one of the puppies.

"Anton will choose the one," she said.

"Yevgenia!" said Papa.

"Let the boy learn how things are," said Mama. "There is no place for every living thing that wriggles into the world."

"He's eight!"

The sight of their father standing up to their mother left the boys wide-eyed.

Yevgenia said, "He's too sensitive."

"What will happen to the other three puppies, Mama?" Anton asked.

She didn't answer.

And then Victor knew. He didn't know how, but he knew. The idea grew in his head like a tumor.

He leaped to his feet. "She's going to drown them!"

"They're only mutts," said Yevgenia. "Nobody will want them. It's for the best."

Victor started to cry.

Anton just sat there. His eyes moved around the table—Mama, Papa, Victor, Baba . . . Victor knew the look. For Anton, the idea was so unbelievable that he might have heard that Mama wanted to kill *him*. His lower lip went out an inch.

"Anton will give us his decision on Sunday," said Mama. And then she got up and began to clear the table. Everyone else remained in their seats.

Anton never told me this story," said Oksana. She sat on the edge of Victor's bed as he paced the room.

"He probably didn't remember it," said Victor. "I had forgotten it completely, blocked it out, I think. The nightmares brought it back."

Victor was electrified by the resurrection of the long-repressed memory.

"Was it so terrible?"

"Listen."

Mama had made her announcement on Tuesday, which gave eight-year-old Anton four days to make his choice.

"I hate Mama," he said the next day when he and Victor were alone throwing stones into the river from the cable-raft dock.

"Don't say that!" said Victor.

"Well I do!"

Anton threw a stone, and they both watched it splash and sink below the surface. The current carried its wake downstream.

"What are you going to do?" asked Victor.

"If I pick one puppy, I sentence the other three to death," he said and began to cry.

Anton cried most of the rest of Wednesday and kept right on crying all day Thursday. On Friday, he refused to come into the house. He slept under the gazebo with the puppies. Mama decreed that no food be brought out to him. "We'll starve him out," she said. But Baba Raya snuck him some cheese and bread while Mama was working. On Saturday, they managed to get Anton into his bed, but then he wouldn't get up.

All Mama could do was cluck her tongue and say, "See what I mean? I'm worried about that one."

At three o'clock Saturday, Victor came to Anton's bedside and said, "Get up. I have a plan."

By the gazebo they met their neighbor Kostya, a pudgy, serious boy who had achieved the imposing age of nine and who would, one day, become Father Andrei. The plan was partly his.

"We're going to set them loose," said Victor.

"In the Silver Forest," added Kostya. "I know the place."

"What will the puppies eat in the Silver Forest, Victor?"

"Rabbits, I suppose," said Victor.

"And foxes and rats and mice, too," Kostya added.

Anton frowned. "They won't eat mice, will they, Victor?"

"They'll eat whatever they have to to stay alive," said Victor. "Now, Anton, you will have to choose. Three will go to the forest. One will stay with us."

"Then I choose Dina," said Anton. "He's the slowest. He would have the hardest time catching rabbits."

The boys put Lena, Sergei and Yegor into an old apple crate and strapped it to Victor's bicycle with the belt from Victor's pants. Emma watched dumbly from under the gazebo. Dina sniffed at the ground and took a bite of dirt. Kostya mounted his bicycle while Anton climbed onto Victor's handlebars. Victor swung his leg over the crate and put his weight down hard on the pedal. They were off.

They rode an hour and ten minutes along a packed dirt road until they reached a birch forest located along the railroad line. Sunlight shone down through the lime-green leaves, bathing the white bark in a shimmering light. It gave the place a magical atmosphere. The boys half-expected to see trolls and hairy-footed gnomes coming through the grass.

"The Silver Forest!" said Kostya.

The boys agreed it was a perfect spot.

They got the puppies out of the crate and played with them for about an hour. Then the boys got on their bicycles and left.

Anton rode behind his brother on the bicycle seat where the puppies had been, his arms around his brother's waist. Victor looked back over his shoulder as they rounded a corner. The puppies were chasing each other in the grass.

Anton hugged Victor from behind. "Thank you," he said.

When they got home, Anton told Mama that he had decided to keep Dina.

"The runt?" said Mama with disgust. "Lord! Why him?"

"*Because* he's the runt, Mama."

She shook her head at that. She went outside and came back a few minutes later. "Where are they?" she demanded.

"They ran away!" said Anton. "And I'm glad too!"

Mama bit her lip.

Two hours later, Kostya arrived at their dacha out of breath. "Come quick," he cried. "Your mama's down by the river. She has the puppies!"

The boys took off. They sprinted across the little community of dachas and plunged into the fields. They ran along the path past the boyar's old orchard, past the few bricks still standing from the mansion's foundation and then down the long hill to the river. There, where the raft ferry had once run, Mama was putting stones into a burlap sack. Victor halted a hundred feet away.

No!

Anton hit Yevgenia at a full run. The eight-year-old's body bounced off his mother like an underinflated ball thrown against a wall. He hit the ground and lay there stunned. Mama was knocked backward and lost her grip on the bag. One of the puppies' heads popped out of the bag. She pushed it back inside and then scooped up the bag. She tied a rope around the top and pulled it tight. She had just finished when Anton leaped onto her back.

The sack fell to the ground. The puppies squealed inside.

Victor charged to the point where his mother and twin brother were wrestling.

"Anton!" Victor cried. "Stop it! Get off Mama!"

Victor tried to pull Anton off his mother, but his brother was like a madman. He held tight with one arm and swung at his mother's chest with the other. Finally, Victor got hold of Anton's armpits and, with a mighty yank, dragged him free. They tumbled backward to the ground.

Yevgenia did not hesitate. She used the moment to pick up the sack and, *one-two-three!* she heaved it far out into the center of the stream. It splashed in the river, floated a moment downstream and then sank. Bubbles gurgled on the surface.

Victor stared in disbelief. He turned to his mother. She was panting from the struggle. She ran her hand through her disheveled hair and straightened her clothes.

From the river there came another splash. They both looked. Anton was swimming hard for the center.

"No!" cried Victor.

Anton reached the point where the sack had disappeared and then dove.

The water closed over him, and it was quiet again on the river. The water shooshed against brush that grew out from the banks. Far away, a crow cawed. Victor stared at the spot where his brother had gone down. He waited.

Anton did not come up.

"Mama!" cried Victor, but Yevgenia just stared at the river. She didn't move. She seemed to be thinking.

"MAMA!"

Victor sprinted to the dock and dove for the cable. He caught it in flight and swung a moment. He climbed hand-over-hand to the center of the river. It took another thirty seconds. Anton had been down a full minute.

Hanging high above the river, Victor could see to the river bottom. Anton was a brown shadow far down under the muddy water. He didn't drift with the current — that meant he was holding on to the bottom.

"I see him!" Victor cried out.

He let go of the cable, did a half-turn in midair and hit the water in a dive. He stayed underwater and swam to the point where he had seen his brother. Victor's eyes were open, but he couldn't find Anton in the murky water. The current dragged Victor downstream. He swam hard against it, but the current was strong. His lungs burned and cried out for air. And still there was no sign of Anton. The current carried him further downstream . . .

S o what happened?" asked Oksana.

Victor and Oksana were in the kitchen now. Oksana stood over the stove heating water for tea.

"I found him, of course," said Victor. "He had hold of the damn sack and was trying to untie Yevgenia's knot. He couldn't raise the heavy sack, so he was trying to free the puppies."

"My god."

"I pulled at his leg, but he would not let go. We fought. Then his whole body jerked, like a spasm, and I knew he had taken water into his lungs. He went limp, and I hauled him to the surface."

"Anton wasn't breathing when I got him to shore, about a quarter-mile downstream. All pioneers learn life-saving, and I was the troop leader, remember? I resuscitated him. Anton coughed and came back to life."

Oksana shook her head in wonder. "What about Yevgenia?"

"She arrived on the bank just as Anton started breathing again. Her face was blank. I've never understood her inability to act that day. I think she just panicked."

Oksana poured the tea and sat down.

Victor went on. "Until that day, Anton and I were more or less equals. Afterward, we assumed roles. It was understood that Anton would do any reckless thing that came into his head, and I would be there to look after him. And I was! Through all his pranks and radical politics I looked after him. Then came the day when I couldn't take it anymore, and I just stopped."

Oksana put her hand atop his. "Victor, you have to stop blaming yourself for that. I know all about your fight that day in the dormitory. Anton told me. After his arrest, he was tired of being your responsibility. He picked that fight with you. He was setting you free."

Victor jerked his hand back. "I know what he was doing!" he snapped. "But don't you see? I put him in this mess. The reason Anton could be so fanatical was that he knew he had his twin brother Victor the Survivor, to look out for him. What made me a survivor? Why was I able to carry on? Because I had Anton the Fearless, fighting my battles for me, that's why! We were like Siamese twins, still joined. And the terrible thing is, I knew it! I knew it, but I was such a coward I let it go on rather than take the kind of risks he was taking. It's so clear now: My whole life — my work, my privilege, my success — was built on Anton's sacrifice. Then Anton found you, and he was ready to have a normal life. So he broke the bond we had forged that day by the river. Only by then, it was too late."

Oksana sipped her tea. "So that's what the dreams have been telling you? That you have to rescue your brother because it's your fault? That doesn't make sense. You would have gone after him anyway."

Victor nodded thoughtfully. "You're right. That's not what the dreams are about."

"What then?"

Victor shrugged. "I wish I knew. There's something else . . . something I'm just not seeing."

22

Victor agreed to meet Koos van der Laan the next day at 4:30 P.M. in a North Moscow park, not far in fact from Rechnoy Vokzal. Victor knew the place. There was a natural spring there, which old Muscovites believed had healing powers. Baba Raya had often made the pilgrimage "to gather the waters of the spring of St. George," which made it sound like a noble mission. The reality was somewhat less exalted—a muddy pipe spewing water of questionable quality from the side of a hill.

Koos's instructions were succinct. If Victor believed he was free of surveillance, he was to fill a bottle from the spring and take it to a bench where the meeting would take place. If he was being followed, he would go directly to the bench and place the empty bottle beside him. Koos would be the bearded man carrying a green umbrella.

An empty Fanta bottle was already standing on Victor's desk at the SAPO Institute when Alexander Kaminsky phoned. It was two o'clock. Alexander asked Victor to come to his office immediately.

"I have an appointment in a half-hour," said Victor.

"This won't take long."

When Victor entered Alexander's office, Oleg Ivanov and Petr Terolyov were already seated. Victor was not surprised to see Petr—as head of SAPO's communists, Petr alone held the power to sway the decision for or against Victor. Petr was not a scientist, but he was a reasonable man as apparatchiks went. The institute was Petr's family, and he guarded it like a patriarch.

Alexander told Victor to sit "anywhere," but there was in fact only one seat, which was directly across the table from the three men. Victor sat down. He felt like an inmate at a parole board hearing.

"We have come up with a plan that should save you from expulsion," Petr said. "We have been working on it ever since the committee meeting last night."

Oleg said, "We've taken the liberty of writing a letter for you. It's just a rough idea. Feel free to change it around as you see fit."

Oleg spun a piece of paper on the table and pushed it toward Victor.

Victor read:

Dear editor of The New York Times,

A recent article in your newspaper misquoted me and, worse, drew wild conclusions from scant facts. I strongly disavow the opinion, given by Grayson Hines, that I had a "change of heart." To the contrary, I stand behind my consistent statements that Vladimir Ryzhkov improperly took credit for work done at the SAPO Institute. I repeat my position that I cannot accept the 1983 Hubble Prize until the name Vladimir Ryzhkov is expunged. It is true that I gave several technical notebooks to Mr. Hines, but these were for the Hubble Foundation to evaluate, a show of the SAPO Institute's commitment to fair and honest play in this matter, a matter into which politics should not be allowed to intrude. I regret that Mr. Hines chose to use these notebooks for precisely such ends.

Sincerely,
Victor Borisovich Perov
Research Fellow, SAPO Institute

"I won't sign this," said Victor.

Oleg said, "As I told you, feel free to change —"

"Burn it," said Victor. He crumpled the paper and tossed it at Oleg's chest. "This is beneath even you, Oleg."

Oleg's eyes opened wide. "How dare you —"

Alexander jumped in. "Victor, we're your friends. We're trying to help you."

"But this is laughable!" said Victor. "Everyone will see right through it."

"I have to chair a Party meeting on Monday," said Petr. "If I don't give them some show of remorse on your part I can't quiet the voices that would call for expulsion. I've been talking to them all day. They respect your work, and they want you to remain in the collective. But you're making that very, very difficult."

Victor sighed. Petr, like Yevgenia, was a believer. His genuine concern touched Victor, but it changed nothing.

"You want to help?" asked Victor. "Then let's be a scientific institute first, and a collective second."

Petr's eyes widened. "I don't believe you said that. The collective — it's everything."

Victor rose. "I have an appointment."

"You'll be voted out," said Oleg.

"I'll take that chance," said Victor. He crossed the room. The three men's eyes followed him as though he were an injured player being carried from the field.

"You'll lose everything," said Petr.

"I already have," Victor said. He left the room, closing the door gently behind him.

■

Stelskogo Park was a sprawling patch of green bordered on the north by the Moscow Canal, which, thanks to Stalin, connected the two main water arteries of the Soviet capital: the Moscow and Oka Rivers. The park itself was popular with Muscovites for its grass beaches, paddle boats and enterprising vendors who somehow were always well-supplied with Pepsi-Cola, shish kebabs, and a heavy beer called "Moskvich."

But in April, even the early bird sunbathers are still wrapped in winter coats, and the Moscow Canal carries only barges and ice water. So it was no surprise to Victor Perov that the beaches were deserted when he drove toward them shortly after four o'clock Tuesday. Victor parked beside a dirt path leading into a poplar forest. It was from here he would descend to the spring of St. George.

Koos van der Laan had chosen the meeting place well. Because of the back roads one navigated to reach the park, it would be impossible for a car to follow at a distance. And in the forest, the trees would make surveillance difficult.

As Victor walked, two women came toward him, bending under the weight of overflowing water bottles that sloshed and left a water trail back into the woods. He passed them. He followed the muddy trail for several minutes, until he reached a clearing where some steps descended a mud cliff. He went down. At the base of the hill, out of rock, water gushed from a pipe. A dozen people, containers in hand, stood waiting their turn at the pipe. Victor went to the end of the line.

Ten minutes later, he reached the spring. The cold water froze his hands as he held the narrow-necked bottle under the pipe. With the bottle filled he started back up the hill. He found the bench described by the Dutchman, and sat down to wait.

Koos van der Laan came up the trail, exactly on time, swinging a green umbrella. He was a short man with a full red-brown beard the color of copper ore. He strolled past Victor humming contentedly. A few minutes later, he returned from a different direction.

"Mind if I sit down?" he asked in Russian.

"Please do."

He smiled and flashed a set of perfect teeth. Foreigners always had such perfect teeth.

Koos offered his hand. "You must be Victor Perov."

They shook.

"Koos van der Laan," he said. "May we speak English?"

"Certainly," said Victor.

The Dutchman sat down and said, "Tell me about the wharf."

Victor told him everything.

"Shot through the head, you say? We suspected, of course. This business of his being drunk . . . well, we suspected it was a coverup. I'll pass the information

along to Amsterdam. Bloody awful business. Pavel knew the risks, but still . . .
Poor bugger. The KGB has already interrogated the wife, from what we've been
able to find out. She's free now. I hope Pavel didn't tell her too much."

"You'll pass my information along to her?"

"Absolutely not."

"Doesn't she have a right to know her husband wasn't drunk?" asked Victor.

"Of course. But it's not my place to tell her. You tell her."

"Maybe I will."

Koos shrugged. "What can I do for you?"

"I thought you knew," said Victor, surprised. "I need your help to find my
brother. He's being held in a psychiatric hospital somewhere —"

"Good heavens, I can't help you with that," said Koos, horrified. "I'm a com-
mercial attaché at the embassy of the Netherlands."

"But I thought you worked for Soviet Psychiatry Watch."

Koos winced. "My affiliation with that particular organization is something I
do because I feel it's important, and because I was inspired by Pavel Danilov's
bravery. Most of my fellow Dutch diplomats don't even know about it. Actually,
I'm just a courier. The ambassador admires the SPW's efforts, and we worked out
a kind of unofficial arrangement to use diplomatic pouches to smuggle communi-
qués. He allows me to make contacts such as this one today on an infrequent
basis. Other than that, we stay out of it."

"But you could get a message to Amsterdam for me."

"I could, but only if it related directly — and I repeat, directly — to the work of
Soviet Psychiatry Watch. We're not Western Union."

"Western *what?*"

Koos grimaced. "Never mind."

A chill wind blew, and both men tightened their jackets. "Let's walk a bit,"
said Koos. "Bloody cold, isn't it?"

They walked along a mud path that led away from the spring. The forest was
deserted.

Victor said, "Describe your system for communicating with Pavel."

Koos shrugged. "We had a monthly handoff. He gave me a report that I sent
by dip-pouch to the Dutch Foreign Ministry in The Hague. They checked it to
make sure it was SPW work and then passed it along to the SPW officer in
Amsterdam."

"Did you ever read the reports?"

"Always. I was instructed to withhold it if I deemed the material contrary to
the interests of the Netherlands."

"When did Sigmund, er, Pavel, first report he knew something about Anton
Perov?"

Koos thought. "February tenth. It was part of the regular handoff."

"So Amsterdam knows where Anton is," said Victor.

"No. Pavel gave almost no information about your brother—just what the American already told you. He was very nervous. Pavel was the only one who knew the truth. When he died, I'm afraid you lost your only source of that information."

"Besides Pavel's original source," said Victor.

Koos shrugged.

Victor thought a minute. "So the information about Anton—what little there was—was included in the February report."

"Not 'in,' " said Koos. " 'With.' The regular reports were databases. Rather dull, I'm afraid. The bit about your brother was part of what we call an SAR, 'Special Action Request.' In it, Pavel asked for someone to make contact with him under the code name 'Sigmund.' "

"Which would have signaled to him the matter was related to Anton Perov."

"Right."

"What is in a typical monthly report?"

"Information he had gathered that he wanted to get safely to the West," said Koos. "Names of new prisoners, new treatment techniques, evidence against various doctors and nurses."

"Were specific asylums mentioned?"

"It wouldn't be much good without them. Pavel was a fanatic about details."

They skirted a puddle and continued along the path.

"Where did he get his information?"

"Recently released inmates, mostly. He tracked them down and interviewed them, interrogated them was more like it." Koos chuckled. "He was as bad as the KGB."

"How many people did he interview in a month?"

"It varied. Sometimes none, other times more than a dozen."

Victor thought about that. "It stands to reason then that Pavel learned about Anton during one of the interviews he conducted during January and early February," said Victor.

Koos nodded. "Probably."

"And this same interview, presumably, would have produced other facts—other facts that would have been included in the notebooks he gave you on February tenth."

"Yes."

"So Anton is probably in one of the asylums mentioned in those notebooks."

"Unless the information about Anton was the only thing worth reporting from that interview."

"I will have to risk that," said Victor.

Koos thought a minute and then shook his head. "Nice try, but it won't work.

Even if you're right, I could never give you the notebooks. They contain the names of sources to whom Pavel promised confidentiality."

"I don't need the notebooks," said Victor. "I only need the list of asylums mentioned in them."

Koos nodded. "I'll pass the request to Amsterdam."

At that moment, two men came around a corner toward them. Victor's stomach sank. With a sick feeling, Victor realized that they had been talking too loudly —in English, no less. The two men came closer, seeming to pay no attention to Victor and Koos. They were dressed in muddy peasant coats. They looked like builders who had just left a construction site. The top of a vodka bottle poked out of one of their pockets. As they passed, Victor braced himself. He imagined their hands grabbing his arm and throwing him to the ground. Their knees would stab his spine as they slapped on the cuffs. Then the march off to Lubyanka, a show trial, then Siberia, or perhaps a psychiatric hospital . . .

The men passed. Their voices faded.

Victor thought of Oksana and Anton, who had lived with fear like that for three years. No wonder Oksana had been so upset the previous evening.

Koos went on, and for the first time his voice betrayed some impatience. "The next dip-pouch goes out on Thursday, so I can't get back to you sooner than one week from today."

"I understand. How shall I contact you?"

"You won't. We'll contact you. What's your home phone number?"

Victor gave it to him, adding, "It's probably bugged."

"We'll use the code name 'Yuri Nikolayevich.' Just pretend it's a wrong number. Then meet me here—with your Fanta bottle—the next day at this time."

Victor nodded.

Koos squinted at him. "You using a pay phone?"

"The first call was from my office, as I told you. This morning's call was from a pay phone."

"Near your flat?"

"Yes."

Koos shook his head. "Never use the nearest pay phone to your house."

Victor nodded. "There's one other favor, I'd like to ask," said Victor.

Koos looked at his watch. "What?"

"Katherine Sears, the American who carried Pavel's message to me, has disappeared in Moscow."

Koos's eyes narrowed. "Yes, I know. I told them she would get Pavel killed, damn her."

Victor stopped walking. "What did you say?"

"Before I gave her the codes, I warned—"

"*You* sent her to Moscow?" Victor said, astounded.

"Of course." Koos looked puzzled. "Wait a minute . . . you didn't know that?"

"No."

"But then, how did you get my name?"

"From a KGB agent."

Koos paled. "What!"

Victor told him about Tarasov.

"My god. Why didn't you tell me? I just assumed Katherine had given you my code name before her disappearance. Do you know what this means? This man Tarasov must be holding her somewhere. He got my name from her under interrogation, and then gave it to you."

A chill ran up Victor's spine. It made sense.

"I wonder what else she told them." Koos thought a moment. "This changes everything."

"What do you mean?"

"It means I'll be on the next plane to Amsterdam. My cover is blown."

"But what about the list? You promised to help."

"That's impossible now."

"But my brother! Katherine! You can't just abandon them!"

Koos peered into the forest anxiously. "The KGB could be watching us now. I can't understand how we can be together now if the KGB knows about me, unless . . ."

"Unless what?"

He glared at Victor. "Unless you're cooperating with them."

"That's ridiculous."

"This meeting is over."

"Please, you have to believe me . . ."

The Dutchman turned and walked away, stabbing his umbrella at the ground as he went. Victor watched him disappear around the bend, then found a bench a few steps away and sat down. He looked at the Fanta bottle in his hand and took a swig. The spring water was cool and tasted good.

The meeting had been a disaster. The Dutch now believed he was cooperating with the KGB. He couldn't count on their help. Victor was on his own without a plan.

Victor finished drinking and inspected the empty bottle. He shook his head. The old-timers were wrong about the healing powers of the spring of St. George.

He felt terrible.

23

Three days later, Konstantin Tarasov's plane set down at Yakutsk airport in Eastern Siberia. It was three-thirty in the afternoon, and the day was already moving toward dusk. Tarasov was irritable. Fifteen hours in overcrowded airplanes and filthy airport lounges had taken its toll on his nerves. Making matters worse, he had left his last pack of cigarettes on a table in a lounge in Novosibirsk—four long hours ago.

The plane taxied to a stop, and Tarasov jumped to his feet. He squeezed past slower-moving passengers and was the first to make it to the top of the ladder. The Arctic cold hit him like a splash of water. He blinked and his eyelashes clung together. His nose hairs froze, which caused him to sneeze. He pulled his coat around him and descended the stairs. A bus pulled up, its tires crunching the hard-packed snow like styrofoam. He scrambled aboard the bus.

A few minutes later, Tarasov was in the airport. A small man with brown skin, a flat face and Asian eyes came up to him.

"Comrade major Konstantin Tarasov?" the man asked.

"Give me a cigarette," said Tarasov.

"I don't smoke."

"Jesus Christ."

The man frowned. "You want to buy cigarettes? There's a kiosk here in the airport."

"Let's go."

He led Tarasov across the terminal, which had not a scrap of furniture, just a huge schedule board (broken) on one wall and a clock so high up he would have needed binoculars to read it. The place looked like an airplane hangar.

They reached a Plexiglas-enclosed kiosk. Tarasov knocked on the scratched glass and peered between the items against the window. Nobody was home.

"It seems to be closed," said the man.

"Lord, what a dump," Tarasov muttered.

"Excuse me?"

Tarasov pushed at the kiosk's window, and it slid open a few inches. Watching his hand through the glass, he navigated his fingers toward a pack of Astras—

cheap Moldavian tobacco, but if he didn't have a cigarette soon he would be smoking the feathers in his parka. He snared the Astras and tore open the pack.

"Uh, comrade," said his guide. "There's no smoking in the airport terminal."

Tarasov shook a cigarette from the pack, put it between his lips and lit it with a match. He inhaled deeply once, twice, three times.

"It's been four hours since my last cigarette," Tarasov said. "That's the longest I've gone without a smoke since I was seven."

"You started smoking when you were seven?"

Tarasov put the cigarette back in his mouth and studied the man for the first time. "What's your name?"

"Serafat Isyuking," he said. "Welcome to Yakutsk."

"Serafat, huh. That a Yakut name?"

"Well, yes," he replied. "I'm Yakut." He cleared his throat. "We have a car waiting. Shall we go?"

They made their way to a black Volga and were soon driving across a landscape of ice and snow. Wooden shacks appeared from time to time like alien spacecraft on an uninhabitable planet. The structures sank unevenly into the permafrost, giving everything a run-down appearance. Yakutia was the epitome of what people imagine Siberia to be — snow, Arctic cold, tundra, frozen rivers, Eskimos, reindeer and prison camps. Yakutsk was the capital of this sprawling swatch of tundra the size of Western Europe. Tarasov had never been to Siberia, and he took it in with the romantic fascination of a city boy in the frontier.

He thought about the stub-nose man. It was hard to believe anything that happened here could touch the nerve-center of the Kremlin. Who was the stub-nose man? What did he have to do with Secretary Podolok?

"You got a call from Moscow this morning," said Serafat. "Someone named Leo Yakunin. He wants you to call him."

Tarasov nodded and lit another cigarette. The car reached the city limits of Yakutsk, and romantic Siberia was transformed abruptly into a Soviet slum — concrete apartment blocks, empty shops and a large central square dominated by two government buildings, one for the legislature, the other for the security organs. It was to the second one Tarasov expected he would be going, but the car sped past.

"Where are we going?"

"The hotel."

"Why?"

"I thought you would want to check in, wash up, maybe have a rest —"

"Do I stink?"

"No. But after your long flight —"

"Who's the head of the center?"

"Colonel Novikov."

"Take me to him."

Serafat shrugged, and he and the driver spoke for a minute in a strange language. The driver did a U-turn headed back to the central square.

"Was that Yakut you were speaking just now?" asked Tarasov.

"Yes."

"Don't speak it around me again, okay?"

"Yes, comrade."

"And let's stop for cigarettes," said Tarasov. "These damn Astras are going to give me lung cancer."

Colonel Alexei Novikov was a big bear of a Yakut with a round, ruddy face and hair the color of coal dust.

"Welcome to Yakutsk," he growled and offered Tarasov a fat hand.

Tarasov sat in a chair in front of Novikov's desk. Portraits of Lenin and Konstantin Chernenko hung on the wall behind him. Tarasov spotted an ashtray and promptly produced a pack of cigarettes. He offered a smoke to Novikov. Tarasov lit both men's cigarettes.

Novikov inhaled and said, "Moscow warned us of your arrival, comrade. I trust you were received well at the airport."

"Yes, thank you."

"Your aide was mysterious about your purpose."

"A precaution," said Tarasov. "I'm here on an investigation."

"Is that so? What kind of an investigation?"

"Unofficial."

Novikov nodded. "I see."

"I was hoping I could count on your cooperation," said Tarasov. "I'm trying to find out about a man who escaped from exile last summer."

Novikov leaned back in his chair. "Stub-nose man, right? Killed trying to cross into Norway?"

Tarasov's mouth fell open. "How—"

"I went through all this last month with the other guys."

"What other guys?"

"Two boys from the Leningrad branch. Border troops. They were following up on the shooting. Perfectly routine."

"Do you recall their names?"

"Can't say that I do. I may have it written down somewhere. I can check it out for you."

"What did they look like?"

"One guy was huge—I'm talking polar-bear huge, if you know what I mean—

and you have to be pretty big to make that impression on me. The other one was more average. He had Mongol eyes. I'd say there was some Tatar blood in him."

"What can you tell me about the stub-nose man?" asked Tarasov.

Novikov shrugged. "His name was Stepan Bragin. He came out of the camps, Leslog-7, I believe. It burned to the ground in 1978 and they distributed the inmates between Leslog-9 and Leslog-11. But there still wasn't enough room, so they furloughed some of the inmates to exile in Oimyakon. It wasn't like they could shoot them: Those days are behind us, thank god. Anyway, Bragin was one of the lucky ones."

"Oimyakon?"

"It's a village in the region of the same name. It's about two hours' flight east of here. Only way in is by helicopter, or jeep from Ust-Nera, that's the regional capital for Oimyakon. It's all in the file, if you want to see it."

"I do."

Novikov pushed a button on his desk and asked a woman at the other end to bring the file. "It will take a few minutes," said Novikov.

They contemplated each other for a moment. Novikov said, "You have come a long way for a file, comrade."

"Perhaps I have," said Tarasov. "How did Stepan Bragin escape, anyway?"

"That's a big mystery," said Novikov. "There *is* no way out of Oimyakon, except by air. Jeep is theoretically possible, but only in the winter when the roads are frozen. Bragin disappeared in May, and besides, where would he have gotten a jeep? It's not like he could just walk out of there."

"Why not?"

Novikov laughed, a big, roaring, belly laugh.

"If you had ever been to Oimyakon, you wouldn't ask that," said Novikov.

They began to chat. Novikov said the KGB's main job in Yakutia was combating corruption. The gold and diamond mines were so rich, he said, "they would have made a thief out of Lenin." The remark gave Tarasov a start. In Stalin's time, it would have earned him a *tenner* — ten years in the camps — if not a bullet in the back of the head.

"You know what bothers us about you Lubyanka folks," said Novikov at one point. "You send people to our home as punishment."

Tarasov laughed. No one in Moscow dared talk so irreverently. Novikov had the relaxed speech of someone who lived very far from the yoke of Moscow. Tarasov liked the big Yakut.

There was a knock on the door, and a young Yakut girl came in. She looked distressed. "I can't find it."

"It's there," said Novikov. "Look again."

"I've already looked three times."

"Blast," said Novikov, shooting an embarrassed glance in Tarasov's direction. "You've misfiled it. Go back and find it."

"Don't waste her time," said Tarasov. "They took it."

"Who took it?"

"The border troops — only they weren't border troops. They pulled the same trick in Leningrad. That's why I had to come here."

"Bastards," said Novikov. "They have some nerve . . ."

"Is there a copy of that file anywhere else?"

"There might be something in Ust-Nera," said Novikov. "But the Leningrad agents went there too."

"Can you check it out?"

"I'll get right on it," he said snatching up the phone.

"Call me at my hotel."

Tarasov got back into the car with Serafat. They drove on, passing schools, a hospital, a gigantic statue of Lenin, a World War II monument and a large university. Everything was coated by a glimmering layer of ice like a fairy-tale village. On the streets, Tarasov saw some Russian nationals, but most of the people had the Eskimo faces of Yakuts. Despite the trappings of modern life, Yakutsk retained the spirit of a frontier town, though Tarasov was hard pressed to identify from where the impression sprung. Maybe it was the pipes that ran above ground, maybe it was the lack of signal lights, but most likely it was from the people themselves, who, like Novikov, radiated an openness, a *glasnost*. It suggested freedom.

Tarasov checked into the hotel and threw his bag onto the bed. He ordered a call to Moscow and was informed the call would be ready in an hour and a half. He lay down on the bed to think. The next thing he knew the phone was ringing. He answered, trying not to sound groggy. It was Novikov.

"The records are in Ust-Nera."

"I'm surprised."

"Oh, the Leningrad boys swiped the files there, too, all right. But they got unlucky. Part of the file was in Oimyakon at the time. It contains the material our agent there reconstructed after the 1978 fire at Leslog-7. A lot was lost in the blaze, apparently. Oh, and there's a tape."

"A tape?"

"An interview with Stepan Bragin in 1978. It was part of the effort to rebuild the files after the fire. Some of the inmates were real mystery people after the fire. Some had no records at all. It was a mess."

"And this tape is in Ust-Nera?"

"Yes," said Novikov. "There's a flight to Ust-Nera tomorrow. Shall I reserve a seat for you?"

"Thanks," said Tarasov and hung up.

Leo's call came through a few minutes later.

"His name is Stepan Bragin," Tarasov said over the crackle of the line. "He was exiled in Oimyakon. Before that, he was in the camps. There would have to be an arrest record in Lubyanka."

"I'm not working for you anymore," said Leo. "I told you. Shatalin said—"

"Just do this," said Tarasov. "It could be important."

Leo sighed. "All right."

"Call me in Ust-Nera tomorrow night, my time," said Tarasov. "Novikov will have the number. Remember, all communications should come over secure lines. Belov went to a lot of trouble to make sure the name Stepan Bragin never came to light. He wouldn't want me poking around."

S o now it was another plane, this time a twin-engine turboprop that whined and shook and seemed to fly slightly sideways, like a car whose chassis is mounted unsquarely on its frame. Tarasov was moving deeper into Siberia, and with every icy mile he could sense Stepan Bragin drawing nearer.

Tarasov used the time to perform what he called a "sanity check." The mind, Tarasov believed, was the body's laziest organ. Once it found a line of reasoning it liked, it was loath to go bounding off in a new direction, even if truth happened to lie that way. His goal now was to construct a theory that explained the events in Moscow, in Leningrad and on the Norwegian border that did *not* lead to Stepan Bragin. He could not. All roads converged on Stepan Bragin. His death was like a pebble dropped in a pool; everything else that followed was a result of that initial disturbance: Anton Perov's consignment to a psychiatric hospital, the changes to Anton Perov's file to make it look as if he was killed, Katherine Sears's trip to Russia and the subsequent attempts on her life, the murder of Pavel Danilov, the automobile "accident" of the captain of the border guards.

The plane rattled eastward impossibly, like a fat-bellied bumblebee. Tarasov looked out his window. A strange fog lay over the land.

"Ice fog," the man beside him shouted above the scream of the propellers.

"Ice fog?"

"Air freezes at fifty-five below. It makes fog."

Ice fog. The white earth was now even more desolate.

After two hours, the plane began to descend. White mountains rose in the east. The plane banked and a dirty settlement materialized out of the ice: Ust-Nera. It looked like a splotch of mud on a white carpet. The village was bounded on the east by the outline of a frozen river. From the air, Tarasov made out about fifty buildings, mostly huts, along two main streets. A half-dozen cross streets completed the black-and-white checkerboard. A tall smokestack towered over the western end of town belching tire-black smoke.

The plane landed, and this time it was not a black Volga but a jeep that was waiting for him.

The driver was a big Yakut with bad Russian. They bounced along the frozen roads in silence.

What passed by Tarasov's window was not a town, not a village, not even a settlement—it was a camp. While Yakutsk had the flavor of a frontier town, Ust-Nera *was* a frontier town. Tarasov didn't see a thing of substance that couldn't be hauled away on the inhabitants' backs. Just give them an hour's notice.

The jeep pulled up to a wood frame structure with a double placard that read: *Administrative Offices Oimyakon Region* and *Headquarters "Olyen" Collective Farm*. Tarasov followed the Yakut inside and was met by Fyodor Kagan, whom Novikov had described as a fine administrator and the only ethnic Russian for five hundred miles.

"Welcome to Ust-Nera," he said.

"You have a file for me?" said Tarasov.

Kagan led Tarasov to his office. Tarasov sat down at a small table beside a window while Kagan went to his desk. Kagan was about fifty years old, of average build. His face was pock-marked from acne, which gave him a rugged appearance. Thick blond hair was blown back permanently over his head, like a sailor facing a head wind. Kagan opened a drawer and withdrew a brown, accordion-style folder. He plunked it on the table in front of Tarasov.

"Dumb luck," said Kagan. "The case worker in Oimyakon had these sections, so the file wasn't here for the two Leningrad agents to remove."

Tarasov spun the file around to face him and flipped back the cover. A cassette tape lay atop a stack of papers.

"Would you like to hear the tape first?"

Tarasov nodded. Kagan got a tape recorder from his desk.

"The first voice you hear is mine," he said. "I did about forty of these interviews after the fire in 1978. I wouldn't have saved the tapes except that I never got around to making a transcript."

Kagan inserted the tape into the machine, slapped the lid closed and pushed PLAY.

From the little box rose the screech of a chair being pulled forward. And then a voice: Kagan's.

"What is your name?"

The second voice followed immediately, raspy but quite strong, like an old blues singer. It was a voice from the grave.

"My name is Stepan Bragin."

KAGAN: I will be asking you a series of questions. Some, I know the answers to. Others I don't. You won't know which. If I catch you in a lie, I will have to assume you are serving a twenty-fiver that began the day before the fire. Got it?

BRAGIN: Yes.

KAGAN: By the way, what happened to your nose?

BRAGIN: I lost it in the winter of '62. Frostbite.

KAGAN: You were here in '62? They say it was so cold ermine were dying.

BRAGIN: It's true.

KAGAN: I didn't realize Leslog-7 had been around that long.

BRAGIN: I was in Worker's Paradise Camp at that time.

KAGAN: I've never heard of that one.

BRAGIN: It was one of the first camps they built up here. It burned on January 4, 1962.

KAGAN: But you rebuilt it.

BRAGIN: Eventually. We lived in tents while we worked. One morning, I woke up and my nose was numb. The feeling never came back. It got red, then kind of gray, then white. Gents took it off.

KAGAN: Igor Gents? The prison doctor at Leslog-11?

BRAGIN: That's him. He used a kitchen knife. . . . Don't make that face. I never felt a thing. It was like snipping a fingernail, and I got seventy-two hours in the infirmary, which meant a wood stove and time off work, so it wasn't so bad.

KAGAN: Nineteen sixty-two? That was fifteen years ago. How long have you been in the zone?

BRAGIN: Since '56.

KAGAN: That's a lie. We all know the maximum sentence is a double tenner.

BRAGIN: I got life.

KAGAN: Nobody gets life.

BRAGIN: I did.

KAGAN: What was your crime?

BRAGIN: Subversion. I crossed myself on a square in Tallinn.

KAGAN: That's awfully stiff.

BRAGIN: You're telling me?

KAGAN: Well, Stepan. Because of overcrowding we are commuting some sentences to work furlough in the village of Oimyakon. You could work on the reindeer collective farm and even earn wages. Would you like that?

BRAGIN: Yes. Very much.

KAGAN: I'll see what I can do.

The sound went dead, and Kagan switched off the machine.

"I need a copy of that tape," said Tarasov.

"I'll have it made."

"I detected an accent."

"Estonian," said Kagan. "It's in the file."

"So he entered this work program?"

"Yes. I enrolled him. I felt sorry for the guy. He was the hardest of the hard-luck cases."

"How did he escape?"

Kagan blew a gust of air through his nose. "I've spent months thinking about that one. It's impossible."

"The impossible happened," said Tarasov.

"I know. Until those border guards showed up with pictures of Stepan—"

Tarasov started. "They had pictures?"

"Sure. I had to make the official identification."

"And it was him?"

"No mistaking that nose. It was Stepan. Quite dead, poor bastard. I wonder what the hell got into him. Anyway, if it hadn't been for those pictures, I would never have believed the old goat *did* escape. We all figured he just wandered off and died on the tundra—fell through some ice or got lost in a white-out, any number of possibilities."

"So how did he escape, then?"

Kagan shrugged. "Maybe, just maybe, he stowed away on a helicopter, which would have gotten him from Oimyakon to Ust-Nera. And then maybe, just maybe, he stowed away on an airplane that took him as far as Yakutsk. And from there, maybe, just maybe, he stowed away on another plane, avoiding police and airport security—"

"I see your point," said Tarasov.

"Like I said, it's impossible."

Tarasov lit a cigarette and turned his attention to the file. It consisted mainly of monthly interviews summarized by Stepan's case officer. The reports were terribly written, filled with spelling errors and bad grammar. A Yakut with bad Russian, Tarasov surmised. The reports were maddeningly sparse. Six years had been compressed into a few mundane summaries. There was a request for extra hours to earn more money, and a complaint about late wages. He was building a cabin, and he wanted to know how could he order materials. He wanted to know how to go about officially naming a river. *What the hell was that about?* There were several requests for a doctor to see his wife. Then he began to ask for medicine: His wife had ovarian cancer, and she needed morphine for the pain.

"Bragin had a wife?" Tarasov said.

He looked up, and that's when he noticed that Kagan was gone. Tarasov went out in search of him. He found him in the next room chatting in front of the desk of a fastidious-looking Yakut woman.

Kagan spotted Tarasov in the doorway and jumped to his feet. He introduced the woman. "Yermali is head of the collective that operates the Oimyakon farm where Stepan Bragin worked," he said. "She's also my wife."

The woman gave him a nod. Tarasov sensed a reserve in her. She didn't trust him.

Kagan said, "We were just recalling some of the stories about Stepan."

"He was a legend," said Yermali.

Something dawned on Tarasov. "*You* wrote the reports," he said.

"Yes," Yermali replied.

"The file said he had a wife," said Tarasov.

"Nadia Bragina," said Yermali. "It wasn't official, of course. Stepan was a bit old to be standing before a judge. He and Nadia just started living together, calling each other husband and wife. It's very common out here."

"They could have performed a traditional Yakut ceremony," Kagan added.

"She was Yakut?" asked Tarasov.

"Of course," said Kagan. "At least, I assumed so. Yermali?"

Yermali shrugged.

"What do you know about her?" asked Tarasov.

"She's another mystery," said Kagan. "We tried to find out about her after Stepan disappeared. But we came up empty. It's like she never existed. She died about the time Stepan escaped. I figure that's what triggered his decision to leave."

"Surely *someone* knows something about her."

Yermali flipped her dark hair over her shoulder. "Is this your first trip to a Siberian outpost, comrade?"

"Yes."

"I figured. You can't imagine how desolate it is. You can live an entire lifetime and never see another living soul."

"But you saw *him?*"

"Stepan's parole required him to work in our reindeer collective, so, yes, I saw him. The rest of the time he lived like a hermit. He built his house up on Suntar Ridge. Very difficult country. It takes eight hours by jeep over winter roads to get up there. In the summer, the roads are impassable."

"But I thought he worked in the village."

"Five months a year — September to February — when we do the slaughtering. The rest of the time he lived in his house. He loved that house. I imagine for someone who spent twenty-eight years in the camps to suddenly have his own house and a woman in it to make it a home must have been . . . well, it must have meant a lot."

Her tone suggested reproach. Tarasov let it pass.

Kagan said, "As long as Stepan kept turning up for work and his parole meetings, nobody cared to go out to his place. If Stepan hadn't mentioned Nadia in his parole meetings, we wouldn't have known she existed."

"Where did she come from?" asked Tarasov. "You must have a record of a Nadia Bragina somewhere."

Yermali smiled indulgently. "Nadia is a common Russian name among Yakuts. They take it because it means 'hope.' Stepan never mentioned her Yakut name."

"The file said she had ovarian cancer," said Tarasov.

"A doctor went up there just about a year ago," said Kagan. "The cancer was already pretty far advanced. She couldn't have lived much longer. He wanted her to go to the hospital, but she refused."

"I'll need to speak to the doctor," said Tarasov.

"I'll see to it," said Kagan.

Yermali said, "The two Leningrad agents said they found a fresh grave up by Stepan's place. They figure it was hers."

"They went to his cabin?" Tarasov asked, surprised.

"Oh, yes," said Yermali. "One of my assistants drove them up there. He said they tore the place upside-down searching for something. Then they found a fresh grave a few hundred feet from the house and that seemed to settle things for them. They must have thought Nadia would have it."

"Have what?"

Yermali shrugged. "Whatever they were looking for. They didn't say."

"So they didn't find it?"

"Not there."

T a r a s o v thanked Kagan and Yermali, and left. He took the file, cassette tape and tape recorder with him. His driver navigated the jeep through town and then came to a stop in front of a wooden barracks with a sagging roof.

"What's this?" asked Tarasov.

"O-tel," the driver grunted.

It was indeed the hotel, a dim barn with ten doors like horse stalls along a single corridor. Tarasov walked up to the reception desk and watched his breath congeal before him as he called out for the manager. A middle-aged Yakut woman with a deep scowl signed him in. She handed him an electric space heater and a key attached to six inches of reindeer horn. He walked down the unlit corridor to his room, unlocked the door and stepped inside. Six beds lined the cracked and peeling walls. The room reeked of garlic and cigarette smoke. There was no bathroom, just a rust-stained basin on one wall. A roach popped out of the drain hole, probed the surface a moment with its antennae and then disappeared back down the hole. Tarasov dropped his bag onto a bed and peeled off his parka and boots. He plugged in the space heater and placed it beside a bed. He lay down on his stomach and began to comb Stepan Bragin's file.

At eight o'clock, there was a knock at the door. "Telephone!"

Tarasov followed the Yakut woman up the hall. On the reception desk, a telephone receiver lay beside the phone. Tarasov picked it up.

"Lord!" said Leo. "You would be easier to find if you were on the moon."

Tarasov eyed the Yakut woman. She grunted and turned her broad back to him.

"What have you got for me?"

"Nil," said Leo. "There's no record of anyone named Stepan Bragin being sent to the camps."

"Why am I not surprised?" groaned Tarasov. "Could they have gotten to this file too?"

"No way," said Leo. "Not files in Moscow *and* Leningrad. Chernenko himself doesn't have that kind of access."

"Then they were lost."

"The KGB doesn't *lose* files," said Leo.

"So there never was a file," said Tarasov.

"Also impossible. Nobody goes to the gulag without an arrest order. There would be records of interrogations, confessions, sentencing. It's like he never existed."

"Then Stepan Bragin is lying," said Tarasov.

"Why would he do that?"

Tarasov grimaced and asked Leo about the Sears investigation.

"Belov's got us interviewing every taxi driver in Moscow. He's turning the whole city upside down. Apparently Katherine's father is giving up and going back to the States. Shatalin will be glad to see him go, I can tell you that. I don't think I've ever seen a foreigner bring so much pressure to bear on the KGB."

"But he gave up?"

"He wants to get Washington involved directly. So far, the Politburo has stayed out of it—not a peep from Chernenko. But if Jack Sears gets the American president involved, it could be another matter."

"So Belov knows his time is running out," said Tarasov. "He must be getting desperate."

"He's obsessed with finding her. He knows that if Chernenko turns the investigation over to someone else, then his involvement will come out."

"It'll never get that far," said Tarasov. "Belov will find her first. She can't hold out for much longer; I can't believe she's made it this long." Something occurred to Tarasov. "Shatalin must have you working on the investigation."

Leo ignored this. "I think we've covered everything. I really got to go."

Leo's haste gave Tarasov his answer. "There's one more thing I want you to do," said Tarasov. "Do you have a tape recorder on your phone?"

"Of course."

"Turn it on. I'm going to play a tape for you. I want you to get the accent analyzed."

When it finished playing, Tarasov put the receiver back to his ear. "Got it?"

"I'll get right on it," said Leo.

They agreed that Tarasov would call Leo the next day.

"Or maybe the day after," said Tarasov. "Don't try to call me. You won't be able to reach me."

"Why? Where you going *now?*"

"Just get that tape analyzed."

Tarasov hung up and went back to his room. He lay down again beside the heater. He stared at the cracks in the ceiling for a while and thought about the nonexistent arrest record.

Why would Stepan lie?

Tarasov went back to the reception desk and called Fyodor Kagan at home.

"I want to see the cabin," said Tarasov.

Kagan groaned. "I was afraid you would say that. I can get you to Oimyakon village by helicopter, three hours' flying time. I'll need Colonel Novikov's approval."

"You'll get it."

"Then the chopper will be ready tomorrow morning."

"That's not all. I want you to get on your radio set and call the commandant at Leslog-11. Tell him we're dropping by tomorrow."

"What?"

"It's possible, isn't it?"

"Sure," said Kagan doubtfully. "The camp is not that far out of the flight path."

"Tell him I want to talk to every prisoner there who knew Stepan Bragin while he was in the camps."

"The commandant won't like it," Kagan said. "He is God Almighty out there."

Tarasov ignored that. "Then I want to talk to this prison doctor, Igor Gents."

"What are you looking for, Major?"

"The Bragin identity."

It was 7:30 and still dark the next morning as Tarasov and Kagan walked across the snowy tarmac of Ust-Nera's airport. Snow crunched beneath Tarasov's boots. The helicopter was a C-9 cargo craft, "the truck of the north country," according to Kagan. Beside the helicopter, a young, rugged-looking Russian waited. He was only the second ethnic Russian Tarasov had seen in two days.

"Meet Vadim Klimov," said Kagan. "The best pilot in the north."

They shook hands and Kagan said, "Flying in the north requires the highest license a pilot can receive. The weather can change in seconds, and it's very easy to get lost, like flying over water. You need to know all about instruments and extreme weather." He hit Vadim on the back. "And that's why we northerners get pilots like Vadim."

The pilot grinned sheepishly. He bounded into the aircraft and climbed into the cockpit. He put on heavy headphones and was immediately absorbed in the preflight checklist. Tarasov and Kagan sat on facing benches in the cargo section.

And so, at 7:50 A.M. Sunday, by the purple twilight of predawn, the three men lifted off. They looped once over Ust-Nera, over the black-and-gray checkerboard, over the crumbling barracks that was the hotel, over the ten dozen shacks with their wood piled high against the walls, over the tangle of above-ground pipes and around the towering smokestack that spat soot into the air like black snow. They completed the loop, and the nose of the C-9 dipped and the engine roared a little louder and Ust-Nera fell away beneath them like a rodent dashing for its hole. They were heading east.

It grew warm inside the helicopter and Tarasov opened his jacket. He tapped his pistol anxiously in the holster beneath his arm.

"You called the warden at Leslog-11?" Tarasov asked.

Kagan nodded.

They flew for an hour over monolithic ice and snow. Gradually, the land began to rise. Scrubby trees appeared, clinging to the earth like grass to a sand dune. Then, with the suddenness of a plane passing from water to land, they were over forest.

"Taiga," said Kagan.

Tarasov looked down in awe at the landscape of ice and forest. It was breathtakingly beautiful but it gave him a lonely, homesick feeling.

"How do they get the prisoners up here?" Tarasov shouted over the roar of the rotors.

"Tunga River," said Kagan. "They come up in barges, like slave ships. That's in the summer, of course. In the winter, they walk."

On they flew. The land rushed away beneath him, land upon which no man had ever set foot. Tarasov had an urge to order Vadim to set down the chopper just so he could jump out into the snow and shout, "Here I am!" He tried to imagine how it must have been for the Cossack explorers who had opened Siberia centuries ago.

"When I was young," said Tarasov, "I used to dream about coming to Siberia to make my fortune."

"We get lots of those," said Kagan. He grinned. "How do you think I got here?"

"You?"

"I'm a Leningrader. I figured I'd work in the mines two years, earn enough money for a car and then go back. That was twenty years ago."

"What happened?"

"Yermali." He grinned. "A Yakut makes the perfect wife. They worship you like you're god on earth, work like horses, raise beautiful children and never boss you around the way our women do. You should try to find yourself one while you're up here."

"You have kids?"

"Two. One is in college in Novosibirsk. The other lives in Leningrad."

Vadim shouted from the cockpit. "There it is!"

Tarasov and Kagan rushed forward. Tarasov surveyed the sea of trees rushing at them. "Where?"

And then it came into view, first the guard tower peeking over the treetops. Then, five long barracks and a few other smaller buildings scattered about. Last of all, he saw two parallel rows of barbed-wire encircling everything. And that was it.

"You ever seen a camp before?" Kagan said.

Tarasov shook his head.

"Simplicity is its beauty," said Kagan. "If you will permit me to use such a word. The prisoners build the camp themselves. They cut the trees, lay the bricks, dig the latrines and stretch the barbed wire. They're not building too many new camps these days. But back in Stalin's time, during the great waves, they would march a group of a hundred or so prisoners, weak from months in the cattle cars, up to some spot more or less like all the others, and nail a sign to a tree. Presto! A new camp."

Tarasov frowned. He knew the stories. Who didn't?

"What types of prisoners are here?"

"All types, but common criminals, mostly," said Kagan. "Maybe a few politicals serving the tail end of their twenty-fivers. Don't worry, comrade. It's unlikely you'll have to face someone you sent away. These days, politicals go to the Urals for the most part. I guess we've grown more civilized."

"I didn't send anyone away," Tarasov said testily. "Judges do that."

"How many politicals do you know who were arrested and then later set free by the courts?" asked Kagan.

Tarasov didn't answer. They both knew. It never happened.

"I never dealt with politicals," said Tarasov. He was overexplaining himself now. He bit his lip and said nothing more.

The helicopter sat down, and Tarasov and Kagan scrambled out into the blizzard beneath the rotors. Tarasov's face froze instantly. Kagan's face was white as a snowman's. Tarasov would have laughed if he could have moved his mouth.

A man in a gray uniform came toward them along a trail. He carried a Kalashnikov machine gun.

"This way," he said and turned back toward the camp.

He led them along a path of trampled snow to an archway with a placard over it that read:

LESLOG-11 LOGGING CAMP
PRAISE TO LABOR

They passed into the empty camp. "Where is everybody?" Tarasov asked.

"Work detail."

Tarasov turned angrily to Kagan.

Kagan held up his hands. "I warned you."

The guard led them to the best building on the compound, a cement-brick structure with a wood-shingle roof. Smoke billowed from a chimney. They went inside and were led directly to the commandant's office. The guard stopped beside the door.

The commandant, a thin man about fifty years old with a grizzly beard and small eyes, rose slowly from behind his desk.

"Why aren't the prisoners in camp?" Tarasov demanded.

The commandant sat back down. His eye roamed his desktop a moment. Then he looked up at Tarasov as though he had just come into the room.

"I talked to OSO in Magadan," said the commandant. "They said to pass along a message. Here it is: 'Go to hell.' Got it?"

Tarasov glared at the warden. The OSO was the branch of the KGB that collected all the bad apples among the recruits, men too dim-witted to make it in the regular service, but still useful for their loyalty — and their ruthlessness. The OSO was notoriously autonomous within the KGB, an evil son everyone pretends doesn't exist until his services are required for a dirty job no one else wants. Tarasov knew they would not answer to reason.

"Take me to where the men are working," said Tarasov. "That's an order."

"Yegor," the warden said evenly to the guard at the door. "Throw these men out of here."

The guard took a step forward. Tarasov stepped to his right and spun around behind the commandant's chair. As he did, he pulled a pistol from beneath his parka. He placed it against the commandant's left ear.

"What the hell —" said the commandant.

"Major!" cried Kagan.

The guard froze, his machine gun pointed at Tarasov.

"I was thinking, maybe I should invite a geologist up here to go over your mining operation," said Tarasov. "I'm sure Colonel Novikov would be interested in the result of an audit."

"I've done nothing wrong."

"Yes, that's what they all say — just before the judge gives them a tenner."

"You're bluffing."

"You know what we say back at Lubyanka? Give me a man, I'll make a case." Tarasov cocked his pistol. "But maybe you'll save us all the trouble."

Tarasov used his free hand to take out a pack of cigarettes. He shook one free and lowered his head to take it between his lips. He lit it and took a long drag.

"So what will it be, commandant?"

The commandant's shoulders sagged. "What do I care? Yegor, refuel the snow-mobiles and take these men out to the work site. Tell Gents to cooperate. The prisoners can make up later for the work they missed."

Tarasov released the hammer and pulled back the pistol.

"Thank you for your cooperation," he said, and left the room.

Kagan followed him into the corridor. He opened his mouth to speak, but then he thought better of it.

They rode the snowmobiles out onto the taiga. The guard led the way, with Tarasov second and Kagan in the rear. Trees were spaced widely so the going was easy. At one point a rabbit crossed their path. The guard raised his machine gun and began to fire. *Rat-tat-tat*. The snow around the creature exploded. It stopped and darted off in one direction, then another. After twenty rounds, just when it seemed the rabbit would escape, the rabbit's body gave a jolt and it collapsed on the snow. The guard grinned and threw his gun over his shoulder. He drove his snowmobile to where the rabbit lay and scooped it up. He threw it into a leather bag and went on.

After what seemed like a very long time, Tarasov rounded a bend, and in front of him stood five men in uniform, machine guns raised.

Tarasov eased off the throttle. He had found the work detail.

24

What struck Tarasov hardest was the stupidity.

In a small clearing dotted with tree trunks, a hundred or so men in black-and-white striped hats cut trees with handsaws and axes. Another dozen men armed with machine guns stood guard.

The prisoners were too far away for Tarasov to see them well, but even from a distance it was obvious that they wore only patchwork quilts of tattered coats and bits of cloth and animal fur tied around necks and heads and faces and feet. Tarasov wondered how they managed; his own feet were already numb inside his Finnish boots.

Russians are such blockheads, Tarasov thought.

The guards gathered around him, and their guide, Yegor, relayed the commandant's orders.

"I thought this was a mining camp," said Tarasov.

"You can't mine gold in winter," said Yegor as though Tarasov were an idiot. "You need water for the sluices. So we come out here to cut timber."

The pace of the work was somnolent. Two men with chain saws could have done as much.

"It looks like a real efficient operation," said Tarasov. "Who is Igor Gents?"

A tall, muscular man with the heavily bearded face of a trapper stepped forward. His age was hard to guess, but he was certainly nearing sixty years old. He had large, weathered hands that curled around his machine gun as naturally as a baby held a teddy bear.

"You're a doctor?" Tarasov asked doubtfully.

"Does this look like a hospital to you?" asked Gents. "I'm a medic. Who the fuck are you?"

Yegor explained, and Gents looked at Tarasov doubtfully. He spoke to the guards a minute, and they headed out toward the prisoners. They began to shout.

"Zek 577!" one called. "Report!"

"Zek 339!"

"Zek 503!"

After fifteen minutes, a dozen shivering ghosts were lined up in front of Tarasov. They had hollowed-out faces and glassy eyes. Their gazes were fixed on Tarasov's feet. Tarasov wondered if they were so beaten by prison life they could not look a free man in the eye, or if perhaps they were merely interested in Tarasov's boots. Few of them had proper boots, just ordinary shoes wrapped in cloth. Their heads and faces were shaved. On their heads they wore only striped caps. Tarasov and the guards had fur hats with the flaps pulled down over the ears. The men stamped their feet as they waited to learn the reason for their summons.

Tarasov remembered the commandant's threat that the men would make up the lost time with overtime work. "Let's do this fast," he said.

He fired off a series of questions designed to find out who among them had known Stepan Bragin best at Leslog-7. Soon, he had narrowed the group to just four men. The others went back to work.

"Who can tell me about the day Stepan Bragin arrived at the camp?" Tarasov asked.

The men were silent.

"Speak up!" barked Gents.

"Let me handle this," Tarasov snapped.

"What happened to him?" stammered a man so thin he seemed lost in his clothes.

"He was killed," said Tarasov.

The prisoners were quiet a few seconds, then a small man with white whiskers and pale, colorless eyes spoke up. "I suppose I've been in the longest. I came to the zone in 1955, to Worker's Paradise Camp. But Stepan was already there. He was the cook's assistant. That's the most important job in camp."

"That's impossible," said Tarasov. "Bragin said he came in 1956."

A thin man, slightly hunched over, spoke up. "I doubt there is a man alive who can remember a time when Stepan was *not* in the camps. I heard he had been at Socialist Labor-66 Camp before Worker's Paradise. We all just assumed he was a fifty-eighter."

Tarasov frowned and looked at Kagan.

"*Article* fifty-eight," said Kagan. "A POW. After World War II, all Soviet soldiers who had been captured by the Germans were charged with treason under article fifty-eight and sent to the camps."

"But that would be 1945, at the latest," said Tarasov.

"Nearly forty years," said Kagan.

"No way was he in Socialist Labor-66 Camp," said Gents. "That was strictly for fifty-eighters. A tenner was a death sentence there. It burned in 1949. A lot of men died in the fire, including the commandant and a bunch of guards."

"Another fire," said Tarasov. "How long have you been out here?"

"I came in 1959 to Worker's Paradise Camp," Gents said. "By then, the Estonian knew his way around pretty good — all the scams. How to get an extra portion in the mess, how to get the special assignments. But I can't believe he was a fifty-eighter. That's just too much time."

"You just called him 'The Estonian.' Why?"

"That's where he was from."

"I know, but why not use his name?"

Gents thought about that. "That's what the old-timers called him."

"Not Stepan Bragin."

"No."

"Why not?"

"It was a nickname, I guess," said Gents.

Tarasov turned back to face the prisoners. "What else can you tell me?"

"Bragin was special," said a frail-looking man with a faint voice. He was the sickliest of them all. His cheeks caved in and his eyes were sunken so that when he spoke it was like watching a skull talk. It was impossible to guess an age. He might have been twenty-five; he might have been sixty-five. "Everyone understood Stepan was special. We didn't need to know why. You don't ask questions like that around here. But I remember one strange thing. We had an Estonian in the camp once, a general, a war hero. I forget his name."

"General Markus Tragertin," said the man with the pale eyes. "A big, arrogant son-of-a-bitch who tried to boss us around like we were just his grunts and he was still an officer. He bragged he was going to outlive us all."

The frail man went on. "That's him. I remember he was excited when he found out there was a fellow Estonian in camp. But after he met Stepan, he got disgusted and said Stepan was a fake. Everyone got angry at the general, and things went badly for him after that."

"How so?"

The frail man coughed. He broke into a fit of coughing, and the pale-eyed man picked up the narrative.

"He was always last in line for gruel, and the first chosen for general assignment work. Stuff like that. He worked hard, too, the stupid dolt. He kept burning up more calories than he took in. One day he just lay down in the snow and wouldn't get up. And that was the end of the big, arrogant son-of-a-bitch who was going to outlive us all. He didn't even make it through his first winter."

"But you believed him about Stepan?" asked Tarasov.

The frail man finished coughing. He nodded. "The thing is, the general bunked just over me, and he used to talk a lot, I mean, he did before he got so sick and we could all see he wasn't going to last. Then he kept to himself. But before that, he used to talk to me. And he talked a lot about the 'imposter.' That's what he called Stepan. He said the village Stepan claimed to be from didn't exist. Neither did his collective farm. And he swore Stepan didn't know a word of Estonian."

"What did Bragin say to that?"

"He didn't say nothing. What was there to say?"

Tarasov asked a few more questions, but there was nothing else the men could tell him.

"Let them go back to work," Tarasov said.

Gents dismissed them. As the frail man passed by, Tarasov slipped something into the prisoner's jacket. The man noticed it, and their eyes met. He walked on.

Gents said thoughtfully, "The only way a man could survive that long in the camps was if he got special assignment work. And Stepan *always* got special assignment work. Cook's assistant, bookkeeping, housekeeping. He was even medical assistant in the infirmary with me for a while."

"Why the special treatment?"

"Never could figure it out," said Gents. "It came down from the commandant. I always figured he was getting greased."

"Where's the commandant now?"

"Dead. Fifteen years."

"Seems everything to do with Stepan Bragin is either dead or burned."

Gents shrugged.

"We're finished," said Tarasov.

They started back to their snowmobiles. Tarasov was anxious to get out of the cold.

"Three fires," he said shaking his head.

"That's not surprising," said Yegor. "These camps are all firetraps."

Tarasov sighed. Three fires. Stepan had three chances to alter his identity. Stepan Bragin could be anyone.

Tarasov climbed aboard his snowmobile. His feet were numb and his fingers burned from the cold. He thought eagerly of Oimyakon village, an hour's flight away. He would have a hot meal and a bath and maybe take a nap before he called Leo.

Tarasov looked back toward the clearing. Gents had lined up the four inmates Tarasov had interviewed. The men were undressing.

"What's going on?" Tarasov asked Yegor.

Yegor shrugged. "Strip search."

"It's fifty below!"

"Regulations. They came in contact with you. They may have taken something."

Tarasov watched from the seat of his snowmobile as the four men stripped off layer upon layer of clothing. When at last they were naked, Gents circled them.

They held their hands over their genitals. Gents began to search the clothes. In the coat of the frail man Gents raised something up for inspection. It was the rabbit Yegor had shot.

Yegor whipped around to face Tarasov accusingly. "Son of a bitch." His snowmobile roared to life, and he sped off. Kagan followed.

Tarasov held back. He was stricken with a familiar sickness, a darkness that lay over his heart and paralyzed him. Beneath his clothes he began to sweat. He found it hard to breathe. He had nearly forgotten about these panic attacks, but now it all came flooding back . . .

Berlin, 1981. Tarasov was deputy intelligence chief for European operations and had been assigned to gather intelligence on the American Pershing missiles that President Ronald Reagan was deploying in Germany. The Kremlin was in a panic over the missiles, which represented a whole new kind of military threat. The American ICBMs were half a world away, while the MIRVs of the American submarine fleet were mostly invisible. But the Germany-based Pershings, so close, were like guns in their faces. KGB chief Yuri Andropov wanted intelligence on their deployment, and he wanted it fast. Tarasov arranged for the wife of an American officer to be caught in bed with one of his German agents, a former hockey star. After six brutal hours in a Berlin basement, Tarasov convinced the terrified woman that the only way to save her husband's career, and her marriage, was to cooperate with the Russians. Her recruitment was a real coup for Tarasov. It was unusual to turn a woman in this way — money was the usual inducement — and the CIA wouldn't suspect her. She had access to large areas of the base, attended many official receptions and made occasional visits to the embassy. Her husband's tour of duty was scheduled to last another three years, so she had great potential. Leo Yakunin was stationed in Berlin at the time, and he was assigned to run her.

Nearly six months passed before Tarasov saw the woman again. In that time, she had lived up to her promise, turning over hundreds of pieces of data from which the Soviet military had been able to build a picture of the Pershing's deployment. When Tarasov next saw the woman, he was horrified. She was a wreck — trembling, glassy-eyed and suicidal. After much questioning, Tarasov learned that Leo had unleashed a campaign of terror on the woman. He would call her at all hours of the day and night and insist that she meet him. Sometimes he would demand information she couldn't possibly get and then threaten to expose her infidelity; at other times he would force her to have sex with him. On one occasion, he forced her to have sex with three of his colleagues. Tarasov confronted Leo with her story, but he defended his actions as the best way to guarantee her continued cooperation. Tarasov went straight to Shatalin in Moscow, but the Foreign Intelligence chief refused to act. "The woman's delivering the goods. Andropov's happy. Why rock the boat?"

Tarasov had tried to forget about it, but he couldn't. As a KGB operative he had personally taken part in assassinations; he had ruined careers and destroyed lives. It was all part of the job. The Cold War was, after all, a war, even if there weren't men in uniform diving into bunkers. So why did he have scruples now? Perhaps he had been abroad too long and had begun to see his own country through more critical eyes. Or perhaps hearing his adolescent son recite idiotic communist propaganda as though it were fact had caused Tarasov to question his country's monopoly on truth. Whatever the reason, the image of the woman's frightened eyes haunted him. Suddenly, he felt like a man covered in blood. He had to get clean, to build a life for his wife and son on something solid. He decided to take a step that would be tantamount to professional suicide: He would go over Shatalin's head to KGB chief Yuri Andropov.

Andropov had raised his eyebrows at Tarasov's story of the American spy. "You're sure you want to go through with this?" Andropov had asked. "It would be a shame to ruin such a promising career over the fate of one American housewife, Major."

"I'm sure, comrade director."

Andropov acted swiftly. He recalled Leo from Berlin and gave Shatalin an official reprimand. Shatalin knew Tarasov was behind it.

Tarasov's career in the KGB was over.

Now he was back — and to his shame he was enjoying himself. When Shatalin had first insisted he work exclusively through Leo Yakunin, it had been a gut-wrenching turn of events. Tarasov was shackled to a monster, and no doubt this was part of Shatalin's revenge. But if one stares at the devil's face long enough, it starts to look like just another face. This was the genius of the KGB, and already, Tarasov was coming to respect Leo anew for his talents. Tarasov was reminded what a calm, calculating ruthlessness the KGB had devised. By involving tens of thousands in its reign of terror and then scrupulously documenting every torture, every forced confession, every summary execution, they made their unthinkable work seem as ordinary as accounting. Only, instead of ledgers, they used poison-tipped umbrellas, prison camps, psychiatric hospitals . . .

And rape.

Once again, black was becoming white. Evil was beginning to look *reasonable*.

His mind turned to Marina. He flushed when he thought of her marrying Titovo. Could he really blame her? The country had made whores of its people. As a Foreign Ministry attaché, Titovo had the pull to get Sasha a good military assignment when his draft came up next year. The son of a *gaishnik* got sent to Afghanistan: human fodder for desert snipers. Perhaps Marina was right — he had been selfish to leave the KGB. How could he allow his sweet bride to prostitute herself just because he awoke one day to find blood on his hands?

There on the Siberian tundra, Tarasov hardened his heart to the sickness he felt. He turned over the engine of his snowmobile and sped after Kagan and Yegor.

He's not Estonian," said Leo. "I can tell you that."

Tarasov was in Oimyakon village at the house of the local farm manager, where he, Kagan and Vadim would be spending the night. They had arrived at noon following an uneventful flight from Leslog-11. There had been no conversation. Each man was absorbed in his own thoughts. Within an hour of their arrival, they had eaten and bathed. Tarasov tried to put Leslog-11 out of his mind. He passed the afternoon going over what he had learned about Stepan Bragin, jotting notes and mulling over the theory that was taking shape in his mind. He waited impatiently for morning to arrive in Moscow, seven hours behind him.

At four o'clock, he was at last talking to Leo.

"Let me guess," said Tarasov. "He's a foreigner from a non-Soviet republic."

"How did you know?"

"Never mind how *I* knew. How did *you* know?"

"The tape. The analysis boys say the grammatical mistakes do not indicate a native Estonian speaker. Plus his 'Os' are all wrong."

"So where's he from?"

"They can't say," said Leo. "He's been in Russia too long."

"They must have a guess?"

"Those guys would rather chew glass than guess," said Leo. "You think he was a spy, don't you?"

"That's one possibility," said Tarasov.

"You have another?"

"I do. It's possible he has been in Yakutia since the 1940s."

Leo was quiet a moment. "A POW?"

"Yes."

"But why wouldn't he just tell the truth? He would have been amnestied."

"There is only one explanation: If it had come out who he really was, our mystery man would have killed him."

"Mystery man?"

"The man who's behind this whole thing. The one who put Stepan Bragin in the gulag in the first place nearly forty years ago. The man who gave him up for dead. The same man who, nine months ago, learned that this ghost from his past had risen from the dead only to be found trying to flee to Norway."

"You lost me."

"Okay," said Tarasov. "It's like this: A foreign POW in World War II gets thrown into a German POW camp along with our own boys. He knows something damaging about our mystery man. So the mystery man sends the foreigner to the

gulag along with the rest of our POWs, fifty-eighters, carrying his secret with him
—presumably to the grave, because he is supposed to die there. But he's tough,
and he stays alive. He lives every day fearing that he will be discovered, and the
executioner's axe will fall. Then the camp burns. The fire kills the warden and
many of the people who know about him. He helps build a new camp, and then
it burns too. Records are lost with each fire. Time passes and the guards who
knew the truth about Bragin's identity die or move on. Time is his ally. It is
erasing his past. Our man sees his chance. He assumes a new identity: The
Estonian, Stepan Bragin. But records still linger that could link him to the past.
And then a third camp burns. Now all trace of his past is gone, and new records
are constructed by men like Fyodor Kagan. He is furloughed to Oimyakon. He
builds a house. He gets married. He begins to live. Then his wife dies and some
madness overtakes him, and he decides to escape to the West, to go home. But
he is shot, gunned down in the forbidden zone, just a quarter-mile from freedom.
The border guards match his description with a fugitive reported missing from
Oimyakon, a man with no nose, Stepan Bragin. They investigate and suddenly,
after forty years, the truth comes to light."

"From the files that were removed from Leningrad," said Leo.

"The files Belov removed right after he realized what had fallen into his lap."

"I understand how Belov got involved," said Leo. "But what does this have to
do with the Iron Perova and her son?"

"I don't know. But let's leave that out for the moment. Now Belov and Perova
move quickly to rebury the past. They kill the captain who did the Bragin interrogation, remove the files, and put Anton Perov in a psychiatric hospital."

"It fits. But what did the man with the stub nose know?"

"I have no idea."

"If you're right about all this, then Bragin's secret died with him," said Leo.
"The coverup has worked."

"Not necessarily," said Tarasov. "The men from Leningrad were here last
month. They were looking for something."

Leo was quiet a moment. "You don't think he wrote it all down?"

"I do."

"Doesn't that strike you as terribly convenient," said Leo.

"No," said Tarasov. "Think about it. If you were Stepan Bragin and had been
sent to die in the gulag, wouldn't you want the world to know about it? Wouldn't
you write it down? You bet you would. Especially if you knew you were leaving
on a journey you probably would not survive."

"Maybe," said Leo. "So where are you going to find this last testament?"

"When I know how Stepan Bragin escaped from Oimyakon, I will have that
answer. And then we'll be ready—" Tarasov stopped.

"Ready for what?" asked Leo.

"I'll tell you tomorrow when I get back."

"Back! Where are you going now?"

"Bragin's cabin. Stay near the phone, Leo. I want to wrap this thing up quickly and get the hell out of here."

But Tarasov never got to make that call. In fact, months would pass before the two men spoke again, and by then the circumstances would be very different indeed.

M a j o r Konstantin Tarasov's C-9 helicopter crashed into a barren expanse of tundra called Upper Sharuleis Flat at 12:14 P.M. on Wednesday, May 2, 1984. Many things about the crash puzzled investigators from the start.

For one thing, only two bodies were found: Vadim Klimov, the pilot, and Fyodor Kagan, who was the Oimyakon regional Party boss. Tarasov's body was never recovered. It was possible an animal dragged it away. There were wolves on Upper Sharuleis Flat. And polar bears. In such a case, investigators noted, it would have been best for Major Tarasov if he had *not* survived the crash, as it had taken three days to locate the wreckage.

Another mystery was the cause of the crash. The engine failure was traced to a clogged fuel line, but how was that possible? Vadim Klimov was one of the best pilots in the north, and he had filed a checklist before takeoff. A fuel line as severely clogged as the C-9's should have been detected in the preflight check.

The craft had split into two pieces. The front section, which contained the bodies of Klimov and Kagan, had exploded on impact and incinerated the men. It was unlikely they felt a thing. The rear section was intact. If Konstantin Tarasov had been in the rear at the time of the crash he could have survived.

The final mystery was what they were doing up there. There was nothing on Upper Sharuleis Flat but ice and Eskimos. Klimov had filed a flight plan in Oimyakon village that would take them to a cabin on Suntar Ridge, near the Upper Tunga River — fifty miles *south* of where the C-9 went down. There was evidence that they had indeed visited the cabin, but then had traveled north from there instead of returning to Oimyakon village. Why? If the explanation was navigational error, then one of the Arctic's best pilots had confused north and south.

It took the investigators three months to complete their report. When at last it was ready, they presented it to the air safety commission review board in Yakutsk. The board was chaired by Colonel Alexei Novikov, MVD chief for all Yakutia.

Novikov listened for an hour. Then the big Yakut cleared his throat and said, "We may never know everything that happened that day, but clearly pilot error was involved to some degree. Regarding the matter of Konstantin Tarasov — we have witnesses to his boarding the aircraft that morning. I am satisfied that he was aboard the helicopter when it went down. As for his missing body, prints of wolves were found in abundance around the wreckage. It seems likely that his body was carried off. That is what the report will reflect, comrades.

"Any objections?"

The room was silent.

Novikov slapped his gavel on the pallet. "This case is closed."

That was August 2, 1984.

T h e morning of May 2 had begun well for Konstantin Tarasov. He awoke before dawn feeling rested.

It was quiet in the farm director's house. Tarasov hurriedly pulled on the same clothes he had worn the previous day and crept outside to have a smoke. The stars were fading in a violet sky. He stood for a half-hour enjoying the crisp air as the fragile dawn broke over Siberia.

An hour later, Konstantin Tarasov, Fyodor Kagan and Vadim Klimov lifted off from Oimyakon village's tiny airfield and started east toward the cabin of Stepan Bragin.

For thirty minutes they flew over monolithic tundra, like a frozen ocean, toward the white mountains of Suntar Ridge. The mountains seemed to stand still on the receding horizon. Then, quite suddenly, they were upon them. Vadim found a frozen river, the Upper Tunga, and followed it up into the folds of the ice-coated mountains.

The cabin of Stepan Bragin came into view a few minutes later. It rested in a tiny forest clearing where the falling land had leveled out to a narrow step. A frozen stream was etched in the ice beside the cabin. For miles in every direction, there was only rock and tree and ice. Tarasov shook his head in wonder to think that down there in that hovel, the most improbable place on earth, a foreigner had lived out the final years of his life. On lonely nights, with the Siberian winter beating at his window, did Stepan Bragin lament his brutal fate—the chain of events that had propelled him like a seed on strong winds to this bit of soil far, far from his homeland?

"Take us over it once," Tarasov told Vadim.

They looped around, and now they could see the cabin more clearly. It was strangely built, circular.

"A *yurt*," said Kagan.

"Yakut?"

Kagan shook his head, puzzled. "No. Mongolian."

A few hundred feet upstream from the cabin a mound rose out of the snow. Some rocks poked through.

"That must be the grave," said Kagan.

Tarasov nodded. "Okay, Vadim. Take her down."

The nearest place to land was a quarter-mile downstream. The helicopter set down and Kagan and Tarasov scrambled out onto the snow. They began to hike upstream.

The walk took fifteen minutes. Tarasov was just beginning to think they must have missed it when they stepped out into the clearing. They hurried to the cabin. Snow had piled roof-high on the uphill side. The door was broken and snow had drifted indoors. Tarasov went inside.

The *yurt* was hexagonal in shape. There was a single room with a wood-burning stove in the center. A metal flue disappeared through the roof.

"This is an Urguma house," said Kagan.

"Urguma?"

"Nomadic Eskimos. There are fewer than two hundred of them left in all the world. They drive their reindeer herds into the mountains in summer, and then west to the taiga in winter. They build houses like these at each end of their migration."

"Why would Bragin build an Urguma house?"

Kagan shrugged. "Maybe it's something he picked up in the camps. It's very practical, as you can see. A single stove heats everything. No dividing walls. Very simple."

The room had been ransacked, exactly as Yermali's assistant had said. Pots and dishes lay on the floor. Tarasov took a step forward, and a bit of plate crunched beneath his boot. A new-looking pine bed was turned on its side against the far wall. Its mattress lay beside it, slit open. Pine needles oozed out like blood from a wound.

Kagan looked at the mattress and said, "A pine-straw mattress — just like the *zeks* make in the camps."

Tarasov circled the room. When he reached the upended bed he spied something on the floor and bent to pick it up. It was a candlestick holder made of barbed wire.

"A strange souvenir for a victim of the gulag," said Kagan.

Tarasov pinched his lips grimly. "Not a victim, a *survivor*. This would have reminded him of that."

"Not much left of the place," said Kagan. He shook his head. "How did he live up here? It must have been a nightmare."

"It was a dream come true," said Tarasov. He pointed to a flower box over the kitchen table.

"He loved this place enough to bring in flowers," said Tarasov. "He was very happy here."

"Perhaps."

"Let's take a look at that grave," said Tarasov.

They went outside and started uphill. The grave site was pretty much what they had seen from the air: a pile of rocks partially buried by snow.

They stood over it a minute. Suddenly Tarasov clapped his mittens together and let out a laugh. "That's it!"

"What?"

"What a fool I've been! It's not the man who makes the home. It's the woman."

"What does that—"

"I know how Bragin escaped."

T h e y lifted off and turned north along the western edge of the mountains until they were once again over tundra.

Tarasov cursed himself for not having figured it out sooner. The answer was there all along. The timing! It was the only clue he should have required. Stepan Bragin had disappeared in May, but he hadn't turned up on the Norwegian border until November. Six months! Where had he been all that time?

The helicopter raced north. They had six hours of daylight left, and Kagan assured him it would be plenty of time to test Tarasov's theory.

Tarasov went over it in his mind. Stepan Bragin had, after all, *walked* out of Oimyakon. He had traveled with the Urguma Eskimos, his wife's tribe, taking part in their annual migration from the eastern highlands to the western taiga grasslands. And if Tarasov's theory turned out to be right, then it was also possible that Stepan had given some member of the Urguma tribe the very item sought by the Leningrad agents—the item Tarasov felt certain was a document, a testament that would clear up the mystery of the stub-nose man.

In the helicopter, Kagan explained that, ordinarily, it might take weeks to locate a single Urguma tribe on the tundra. Their migration varied each year and followed no timetable. But by chance, Kagan had sent a helicopter to the Urguma camp just three days earlier on a medical emergency, the very medical emergency that had prevented Tarasov from interviewing the doctor who had examined Nadia Bragina. The camp, Kagan informed them, was in a place called Upper Sharuleis Flat.

"It's not far," said Vadim. "We'll be there in a half-hour."

Tarasov felt the need for another sanity check. He left Kagan and Vadim in the cockpit and went to the rear of the helicopter. He sat down and went over it all one more time, attacking his theory from every angle. It held up.

If all goes well, thought Tarasov, by evening I will know the great secret Bragin knew about Podolok—*and* the link to the Perovs.

He was about to rejoin the others in the cockpit when the first jolt came. It felt like a car hitting a pothole. Then, almost immediately, there was a second jolt, bigger, and the floor of the helicopter fell away. Everything in the compartment rose off the floor as though weightless.

Kagan was shouting, "Get her up! Get her up!"

"She won't respond!" said Vadim.

Tarasov grabbed hold of a bar on the wall and tried to climb forward through the body of the craft. But the helicopter was shaking so badly he was swept off his feet. He flew backward and crashed against a wooden crate. He struggled to his feet. It was strangely quiet in the craft, and with a chill Tarasov realized why: The engine had died. The rotors were freewheeling.

"We're going down!" Kagan cried.

The tundra filled the front windshield, and Tarasov threw himself behind the crate. In the last instant before impact, Tarasov was thinking about Sasha. He was suddenly glad Marina was marrying Titovo. His wife and son would be taken care of.

The craft exploded. A sharp pain bit his left arm. There was a curious *snap* from his rib cage as it was crushed like kindling.

Then . . . blackness.

Tarasov awoke on his back. Bits of twisted metal and debris lay all around him. Part of the rotor lay a few feet away. A brown vinyl seat stood ludicrously beside him. He didn't know how long he had been unconscious, but the aircraft was still burning somewhere nearby. He couldn't see it, but the black smoke swirled over his head. The smell stung his nose. His left arm ached, and he suddenly remembered the sharp pain he had felt on impact. He turned to examine it. There was nothing there. The arm was gone. It had been ripped away along with the sleeve of his parka . . .

He opened his eyes and looked around. The smoke was gone now, so he must have been unconscious for a while. He decided not to look at his missing arm. It was difficult to breathe. He felt as though someone were sitting on his chest. He wondered about Vadim and Kagan. They must be hurt badly, too; perhaps they were even dead. Why else wouldn't they have come? He looked up into the clear sky for sign of a rescue plane. He lay like that for a long time, watching the sky, listening to the wind, shivering. He was still watching as the sky changed from blue to black.

The wolves came sometime in the night. Tarasov held them off with his pistol. He fired his last bullet at dawn.

By then he no longer felt the cold, and his body had stopped shivering. Death was near. It wasn't so bad. He closed his eyes and waited.

Death came to Konstantin Tarasov in the form of a reindeer goddess, a strange angel of the north with the head of a woman and the body of a reindeer. He had been dozing when he sensed her presence. He opened his eyes. It was daytime — he couldn't say if it was the same day. The angel hovered over him, a shimmering silhouette in the blinding brightness of the sun. He squinted, and her face came into view, a gentle Eskimo face. He smiled. She laid her hands upon him, and he began to rise. Together, they floated up into the light.

part iii

Inmate 222

25

V i c t o r Perov sat alone in the last row of Lenin Auditorium as the vote was taken. He made no speech. He had done all his speech-making a week earlier, during the Communist party meeting, when it might have mattered. The outcome of that meeting had sealed the outcome of this one. Victor came this evening only in order to see the final vote for himself, and to force his comrades to look at him as they voted to cast him out.

"All in favor?" the chairman called out.

"All against?"

Victor went back to his office and opened the door. He recalled the last time he had returned to his office after a committee meeting. That was two weeks ago, when he had met Konstantin Tarasov. Victor half-expected to see the magnetic KGB agent leaning on his office door frame, that cocky smirk on his face. But he didn't come. Tarasov had vanished, and that surprised Victor. He had not expected to get rid of the KGB man so easily. Tarasov didn't strike Victor as the type to give up without a fight.

Victor fell into his chair. He was exhausted. In the ten days since he met Koos van der Laan in Stelskogo Park, he had barely slept. Along with Oksana Filipova and Valery Bonderov, he had been working day and night to try to crack the shell of secrecy that surrounded the gulag of Soviet psychiatric hospitals. But Bonderov had been right that day at the Baku restaurant: It was a desperate task. Not only was he unable to find solid information about the ayslums' number and whereabouts, he couldn't even confirm their *existence*. Victor began to appreciate what a valuable man Pavel Danilov had been, and what a loss to the cause of justice his murder was that night on the docks of Rechnoy Vokzal. That realization was part of a disturbing shift in Victor's thinking. He had embarked on a quest that began as a search for his brother, but already it was becoming much more. It was a journey into the dark recesses of a system he had spent his life helping to build, but that now he realized he had never truly known. Anton had fallen into a pit, and before Victor could rescue him, he had to admit that such a pit could exist, and that he himself had helped dig it.

Meanwhile, Victor was running out of time. In a matter of weeks, the net that encircled him would finally close, and not even Yevgenia would be able to free him. Next to be lost would be his membership in the Academy of Sciences. Then his membership in the Communist party itself. His life was a tower of bricks he had once thought to be as solid as the Great Pyramid. Now it was collapsing beneath his feet at a pace that left him dizzy.

In the race to find his brother, Victor was losing. Something drastic had to be done, and there was only one option left: He had to convince Yevgenia to help. But before he could do that, he had to get permission from Oksana, and that wouldn't be easy. Victor winced when he contemplated the showdown, but he couldn't shirk it anymore. Yevgenia was their last hope. He had asked Oksana and Valery to meet him that evening at his flat in order to make his case.

Victor glanced down at his feet. Two empty cardboard boxes sat on the floor beside him. He looked around his office at his awards, his equipment and his books. The time had come to pack it all up neatly into those two boxes and walk out of his office for the last time.

Victor lifted the photograph from his desk. It was his most prized possession, a picture of his father, Yevgenia, Anton and himself at Lake Sini on vacation in 1979, the year before his father died.

He took a last look around his office and went out. He pulled the door closed and stabbed the key into the lock like a dagger in someone's chest. He went down the long corridor, past the telescope his friend Vladimir Ryzhkov had loved so dearly, down the stairs toward the security check. He said good-bye to it all as he went, for he knew he would never see any of it again. But it wasn't to a building or to an institute or even to astronomy that he said good-bye. It was to a dream he had held since Anton gave him that telescope on his twelfth birthday, a dream he had worked for, realized and flourished within. That dream had given Victor's life its structure and direction. Once so potent, it had become as thin as broth. What unnerved Victor as he strode down that corridor for the last time was not that he was turning the final page on this chapter of his life, but that the next chapter had not been written. Before him lay a blank page.

Victor descended the stairs to the security check, and Ivan came out of his booth, his eyes eager. These twice-daily searches of Victor's papers had given new meaning to Ivan's dull existence.

Victor came toward Ivan and held out his hands, "Sorry to disappoint you, dear friend," said Victor. "But I have nothing for you to search today."

Ivan's eyes fell. He spotted the picture frame in Victor's hand. "What's that?"

"A family photo." Victor held it up for inspection.

"I will have to confiscate it."

"Don't be ridiculous."

"You are not permitted to take anything from the building. Those are my orders."

"Get out of my way," said Victor, and he pushed through the gate.

As Victor passed, Ivan grabbed his arm. Victor jerked free. Ivan lunged for the photo. He nearly got it, but Victor slapped away his hand at the last moment.

Now on the other side of the security check, Victor turned to face the security guard.

"Are you out of your mind?" Victor asked.

The two men looked at each other. Ivan had a strange, confused look on his face. Then his hand went slowly to his holster, and he drew out his gun.

"Jesus," breathed Victor. "You *are* out of your mind."

Ivan pointed his pistol at Victor. His hand shook. "Give me the photograph."

Victor turned his back to Ivan and walked toward the outer doors.

"Stop!" shouted Ivan.

Without looking back, Victor asked, "Or you'll shoot?"

He threw open the glass doors and stepped out into a snowy, mid-April night.

And that was how Victor Perov bade farewell to the SAPO Institute.

A n hour later, Victor stepped into the foyer of his Moscow apartment and shook the snow from his coat.

"We're in here," Oksana called out from the living room.

Victor hung his coat on a peg and went to the living room. Oksana and Valery were seated side by side on the floor behind a coffee table covered with maps, transportation schedules, telephone city codes and bits of paper with the names and addresses of physicians, nurses, hospitals, prisons — anything possibly connected to special psychiatric hospitals.

Victor looked at them and said, "Planning a trip?"

Oksana's eyes searched Victor's face. "How did it go at SAPO?"

Victor shrugged. "Like we expected."

"I'm sorry, Victor."

Valery looked up, realizing suddenly that Victor had entered the room. "What?"

Victor smiled. Valery was like a new man. Victor's old roommate had offered him a clinical job in Leningrad starting in the fall. Valery was barely recognizable as the tragic drunk Victor and Oksana had met two weeks earlier in the Baku restaurant. On this evening, he wore a loosely woven sweater with the words "1980 Olympics" on it. It was tacky but new. A clean collar poked over the top. His hair had been cut recently, though the locks on his hairline still fell onto his brow whenever he dipped his head. He was forever pushing them up. A teacup was beside him.

"Nothing," said Victor.

Oksana put a newspaper in Victor's hand. It was the evening edition of *Izvestiya*.

"What's this?"

Oksana grimaced and said, "Page three."

Victor opened the paper and stared in disbelief. There, under a story about the murder of an ambulance driver at Rechnoy Vokzal, was a picture of Katherine Sears. The article went on to describe how the American tourist was wanted in connection with the murder. She was believed to be hiding somewhere outside Moscow. All Soviet citizens were urged to report anything connected to her whereabouts. A telephone number was given.

"Jesus," said Victor when he finished reading. "They're trying to use the public to find her."

"The KGB must really be desperate," said Oksana.

Victor nodded. A crime report in the Soviet press was almost unheard of. According to communist propaganda, crime did not exist in the U.S.S.R.

Valery said, "A foreigner doesn't just 'hide out' in the U.S.S.R. How is she doing it?"

"She must have help," said Oksana.

Victor paced, shaking his head. "At least we know she's still alive," he said.

"Why doesn't she try to contact you?" asked Valery.

Victor looked at the picture in the newspaper and sighed. "She's protecting me."

"Poor Katherine," said Oksana.

They were all quiet a moment, and then Valery cleared his throat. "You said you had something you wanted to discuss?"

Victor nodded solemnly. It was time to convince Valery and Oksana that the Iron Perova was their only hope.

The telephone rang. Victor hesitated: He was reluctant to be distracted now that he had resolved to act.

"It could be my mother," said Oksana. "She's with Grisha."

Victor nodded and picked up. *"Allo?"*

A man's voice spoke in heavily accented Russian. "May I speak to Yuri Nikolayevich?"

Victor started. "Who?"

"Yuri Nikolayevich." The accent was ridiculous.

"There's no one here by that name," said Victor. "You have the wrong number."

"Sorry." The person hung up.

Victor put the receiver in the cradle and stared ahead. His heart was pounding. Oksana and Bonderov watched him.

"What's the matter?" asked Oksana.

Victor looked into Valery's eyes, then Oksana's. "That was the Dutch Embassy. They want to meet me at Stelskogo Park tomorrow afternoon."

Oksana said, "I thought the Dutch thought you were a KGB spy."

Victor shrugged. "So did I."

He gave his name as Titus Waal. He was a spidery man with a bony face and deep-set, serious eyes. He sat down on the park bench beside Victor and his Fanta bottle — exactly as Koos van der Laan had done at the previous meeting.

"I was surprised to receive your call," said Victor.

"I need your help," Titus said.

"*My* help?" Victor exclaimed.

"It's about Katherine Sears."

"What about her?" Victor asked anxiously.

"She's in trouble."

"I know. I read *Izvestiya*."

"You don't know how *much* trouble. Someone has tried to kill her — twice — and she only narrowly escaped. She can't hold out for long."

"How do you know this?"

"She's in regular telephone contact with an American diplomat. Her father has been working to get the Soviets to waive her arrest warrant, but he has hit a stone wall. Katherine can't be helped from the outside. She needs someone *inside*."

Victor frowned. "How do I know this isn't a trap? The Dutch Embassy thinks I'm cooperating with the KGB."

"I'm not with the Dutch Embassy."

"What!"

Titus gazed anxiously into the forest. "Listen carefully, because we don't have a lot of time. Last year, after you contacted Katherine in Helsinki, she came to me for help in finding out what happened to your brother. I told her you would never have wanted her to get personally involved. Your message that day in Stockmann's department store, the plea for help you embedded in friendly chatter, was intended for your old colleague Vladimir Ryzhkov."

"That's right!"

"But you know Katherine — she insisted. I told her it was a long shot, but I put her in touch with all the usual human-rights groups — Helsinki Watch, Amnesty International, the Red Cross and others — including Soviet Psychiatry Watch. When Pavel Danilov sent a special action request to Amsterdam saying he had located your brother, no one was more surprised than me. But Pavel was terrified because of your family name, and Koos van der Laan considered it too dangerous to try to make contact. I convinced him that Katherine could be trusted, and he agreed to reveal Pavel's contact code name, "Sigmund," only if Katherine herself went in. I became her coach for the mission, and a pretty poor coach I turned out to be. This is all my fault."

Titus looked miserable.

"You mean you're here as a private citizen?" Victor asked, astounded. "You don't have diplomatic immunity?"

Titus nodded.

Victor grimaced. "But if you're not a diplomat, then how did you get the code word, 'Yuri Nikolayevich'?"

"From Koos."

"Why would he give it to you? He thinks I'm a spy."

"I convinced him you are not."

"How did you do that?"

Titus looked hard at Victor. "Katherine showed me the ring, Victor."

Victor stiffened. Katherine wouldn't have told anyone but a true confidant about that. "Give me the name of the American diplomat. I'll call him."

"His name is Cameron Abbott. He has a secure telephone line, just make sure you call from someplace safe."

"Understood."

Titus gave Victor the number.

"Katherine's an amazing woman," said Titus.

Victor nodded slowly.

Titus took a piece of paper out of his pocket and handed it to Victor.

Victor unfolded it and read. On the paper were the names of six special psychiatric hospitals scattered throughout the U.S.S.R.

"What's this?" Victor asked.

"It's the list you asked Koos for."

Victor gaped at it. This was the list of asylums mentioned in Pavel Danilov's final report to Soviet Psychiatry Watch! If Victor's theory was right, Anton was in one of these six asylums.

Victor looked up. "How . . ."

Titus smiled grimly. "If Koos seems like a bastard, it's because he's a soldier in a war. In truth, he cares deeply about the victims of punitive medicine. Why do you think he has devoted so much of his life to it? Did you know Koos is a communist?"

"What!"

Titus chuckled. "He hates the Soviets almost as much as he hates the Americans. He's a troubled man, but I will say this about him: He cares deeply about justice. And that's all Pavel Danilov was looking for when he submitted his special action request about your brother. He knew the risks yet he took them because he was moved by your brother's plight. Koos doesn't want Pavel's death to be in vain. This list is a gift from both of them. The rest is up to you."

"What about you?"

"Me? I'm just a simple academic. I'm doing this for Katherine."

Victor shook his head in awe. "Katherine Sears has some amazing friends."

Titus smiled thinly. "That's what I'm counting on. At this moment, friends are all she's got."

26

Katherine Sears was in the stairwell that morning, a textbook under her arm, when the director of the Bolshevichka Institute for the Improvement of the Qualifications of Farmers came through the fire door.

"*There* you are," she said as though Katherine had been hiding.

Maya Timofeyeva was an officious, self-important woman of fifty. Sergei had warned Katherine to avoid contact with her. "She's dangerous," he had said. "She's the sort of woman who makes everyone's business her own. Unfortunately, our country is filled with such people."

Katherine tried to sound busy. "I was just on my way to class."

"I know. I need you to stop by my office after class, Yekatarina. There's something I really must talk to you about."

Katherine's heart sank. "What is it?"

"After class." Maya tapped her watch. "You don't want to be late."

Katherine sighed. As if she didn't have enough to worry about.

She went upstairs and found the classroom. The class was a continuing education school for farmers who sought management positions within their collectives. The program was funded by the Agricultural Ministry, and was free to students who received recommendations from their collective. When Katherine arrived, most of the other sixteen adult students were already in the room. She sat in her usual chair, beside the window, second from the front.

Katherine took off her *platok*, babushka scarf, and shook her hair. She kept on her coat; it was cold in the room. In fact, it was cold everywhere, all the time. Since coming to Ivanovka three weeks earlier, Katherine had been in a near-perpetual state of coldness. "Near," because there had been that time, about a week earlier, when Katherine had been caught outdoors in *slyakot*, Russian for "slush falling from the sky." There was no English word for it. Drenched and cold to the marrow, Katherine had come into the drafty house and set to work immediately on her bath. She astounded Baba Krista by spending an hour heating kettles of water on the stove and then dumping them into the bathtub. When the tub was full, she slipped neck-deep into the water and stayed that way for two hours, steam rising around her, a grin of utter contentment on her face. She had been warm then. That was the only time.

Katherine watched from her desk as her energetic, twenty-six-year-old Russian-language teacher bounded into the classroom and went straight to work on the blackboard. Katherine opened her textbook to the chapter on verbs of motion and prepared for her usual battle, hoping only that she wouldn't embarrass herself too badly. She was by far the worst student in class. The other students were fluent Russian speakers, peasants who had trouble with grammar. Katherine had never before been in a class where *she* was the one holding up progress. She was determined to acquit herself well despite her slow start. She spent her evenings behind her textbooks, peppering Baba Krista with questions. Learning Russian, even with the benefit of her photographic memory and her childhood tutorials, was turning out to be more daunting than Katherine had imagined. The Russian language was not a scientific question that could be submitted to the rigors of mathematics and then explained. It was a monstrous universe where laws were made and then broken without apology. It was like trying to master the violin in a few lessons, when all she could do was scratch out scales.

Katherine sat in the classroom that morning and tried to focus on what Irina Mikhailova was saying, but her mind drifted to the matter of the director's summons. What could it mean? Katherine began to imagine the worst.

What if the KGB had found her?

Hadn't Sergei warned her about informers?

"Knockers, secret helpers, little patriots, informers," Sergei had said before her first day of class. "Our country is crawling with them."

"I can't stay home all the time," Katherine had protested. "I'll go crazy. I'll just have to be careful."

"How?" he exclaimed. "The only way to be careful is to associate with as few people as possible. You can't know if someone is an informer. I could be one, for all you know. And you'll never know until it's too late and maybe not even then, so don't even try to guess."

Sergei paced the living room at Baba Krista's. Katherine watched him from her chair beside the stove. His face was all tangled up and tense like a towel being wrung of water.

"What's the matter with you tonight?" Katherine asked.

Sergei collapsed into a chair. "Men were at the taxi park asking questions today. I think they were KGB."

"What kind of questions?"

"They wanted to know who was working three weeks ago on Tuesday."

Katherine thought about that. "That's the day . . ."

Sergei nodded.

"I want you to make me a promise, Sergei. If men ever come for me, you must pretend that you didn't know who I was. Tell them I was your mistress, I don't care. Turn me in if you have to."

"I can't do that."

"Then I'll turn myself over to the KGB today," Katherine said fiercely. "I will not have another person's life at risk for me. Now give me your word. Or do I go to Lubyanka now?"

Katherine's voice trembled with emotion. This was not a bluff, and she was determined that Sergei know that.

He shrugged. "You win. I promise."

Katherine relaxed. They were both quiet a moment, and then Katherine asked, "How are the documents coming?"

"Will you forget about the documents!" he exclaimed. "That will take months, Yekatarina. You don't have months."

Katherine glared at him. He was right, of course, but she needed to do *something* besides wait for her father to save her. She had an urge to throw herself into the arms of the Russian police and take her chances. But too many people — Victor, Titus, Koos, Maxim, Lena and Sergei — could get hurt.

She resolved to treat her predicament as though it were an astronomical endeavor — define the problem, construct a theory, test the theory and so on, until the original problem was no longer a problem. She had used this methodology all her life, and it had served her well. But then, she was a scientist, not a spy. Could she really expect to impose a structure on such a violent and irrational world?

Sergei's shoulders sagged under Katherine's stare, and he said, "It's going about like I'd expect. In sixty days I should have everything — except the exit visa, of course. What do you plan to do about that?"

"I'll think of something."

"Naturally." Sergei's voice showed his exhaustion and worry.

"I'm sorry," said Katherine, "for all the trouble —"

"No. No. It's okay. I'm . . . it's just this terrible business at the taxi park . . ."

"I promise to be careful, Sergei."

"But you insist on going to these Russian classes?"

"I have to, Sergei. If my escape is to succeed at all, I will need much better Russian than I have now."

Sergei did not argue that point.

In the classroom, the voice called out her name, and she had a feeling it was not for the first time. "Yekatarina?"

Katherine looked around. The eyes of the class were on her. She had been daydreaming.

"*Izvinite,*" she excused herself. "I, uh, was not hearing."

"Was not *listening*," the teacher corrected.

"Right."

"Now, repeat after me . . ."

Class broke up at eleven o'clock, and Katherine went directly to Maya Timofeyeva's office. She knocked on the door.

"Sit down," Maya said, and sat down beside her. She looked troubled.

"I know I'm holding the class back," said Katherine. "If you want me to drop out, I will understand."

"Drop out?" Maya said surprised. "Good heavens, no. You must stay with it. You must double your efforts. Russian is the official language of our nation. If you are to be a good citizen you must improve your Russian. Do you want to be a good citizen?"

"Of course. I just hate holding up the class."

Maya shook her head. "You have a very competitive, very *capitalist* view of education, Yekatarina. Is that Latvian?"

Katherine gulped.

"Now," said Maya, slapping her hands on her thighs. "I understand you know some English."

Katherine felt the blood drain from her face. "Why do you think that?"

"Yulya Sergeyevna saw you listening to the English-language broadcast of Radio Moscow. She said you were speaking along with it."

Katherine's heart sank. Yulya Sergeyevna! Who needs informers when you have gossips?

With her father out of the country, and her calls to Cameron Abbott down to one per week, Katherine had been desperate for her native tongue — hence the Radio Moscow broadcast. Sometimes it seemed that if she heard one more word of Russian her head would explode.

"I speak a little bit, I guess," Katherine said.

"Oh, don't be modest. Yulya Sergeyevna said you spoke beautifully."

Katherine ground her teeth. "She's too kind."

"How would you feel about teaching English here?"

"Excuse me?"

"As you no doubt know, Katya Grigorevna has left to be with her son in Leningrad, and we have no one to teach our summer semester."

"But I'll only be in Ivanovka a few more months," said Katherine. "Then I have to go back to Latvia."

"That's perfect. I only need someone to fill in until I can get a proper replacement. I have twenty students registered for our summer semester, and I can't just turn them away."

"I wouldn't know how to teach English."

"We have a syllabus. Just follow it."

"I don't know . . ."

Maya shrugged. "I can't force you, of course. At least promise me you'll think about it."

"I'll think about it."

N o. No. No. Absolutely not," said Sergei that evening.

"I'm so bored most of the time," said Katherine. "It would be nice to feel useful."

"Out of the question."

Katherine saw the fear in Sergei's face and relented. "Okay. I won't do it unless you agree. I don't want to put you or Baba Krista in any more danger than I already have."

Sergei relaxed.

"Shall we go?" asked Katherine.

It was Monday night, time for her weekly phone call to Cameron. She and Sergei got into his taxi, and he drove her to the collective farm. He sat in his usual chair in the corner. Katherine went around behind the secretary's desk and dialed the number.

A moment later, she was talking to Cameron.

"Your father got out okay," Cameron said cheerfully.

"Good," breathed Katherine.

"He's already raising hell in Washington. I heard he has a meeting next week with the secretary of state. He certainly has access. You know, I doubt I'll be surprised when I see him standing beside the president whispering in his ear, 'What about Katherine Sears, Mr. President? What about Katherine Sears?' "

Katherine didn't laugh. "Me either."

"Now, have you thought about what you want me to say to Victor Perov? He'll be calling me this evening."

"Tell him 'thanks, but no thanks,' " said Katherine. "He can't help me, and it would be risky for us to try to meet. Tell him I'm glad he's making headway with his search. Thank him for helping Lena Ryzhkova and Maxim Izmailov. It means a lot to me to know that they're both okay."

"Is that all?"

"Tell him I suggest we work out a way to meet in case it should become necessary in the future. I'll leave the details to him."

A w e e k later, Katherine spoke to Cameron again, and this time he had a new message from Victor.

"He says, and I repeat exactly, 'If Anna Akhmatova ever wishes to discuss poetry with Victor Perov, she may do so on the ascension of the Large Magellanic Cloud. Anna will know the place.' "

Katherine smiled. Victor had just thrown a life preserver into the alien sea of Russia. She didn't intend to use it, but just knowing it was there, that she could reach out to Victor Perov if the need arose, made her feel less alone.

"Understood," she said.

"Not to me!" said Cameron. "What does it mean?"

"Good night, Cameron."

"Wait a minute! Just tell me one thing: Who the hell is Anna Akhmatova?"

On the way back to Ivanovka, Katherine fell into reverie. Sergei must have sensed her mood because he was quiet also. As they drove through Bolshevichka, Katherine stared at the rickety houses with their roof-high wood piles. She had been inside a few of those houses. It seemed to her that a long time had passed since she had come to Ivanovka. A month.

Snow fell on the windshield and melted as soon as it touched the warm glass. The crumbling wipers streaked the dirty glass, and Sergei had to stop once to throw snowballs at the windshield. He smeared it with an oily rag and went on. She watched him and thought: It's already summer in Ithaca. On the Cornell campus, students would be studying outdoors in the grass and playing Frisbee barefoot. She was overwhelmed by an odd melancholy. In the absence of news of the outside world, Katherine could easily have imagined that time was suspended. What a strange isolation a Russian peasant endured. And what a blessing! That isolation was all she had to protect her.

Sergei pulled the car up to Baba Krista's house and turned off the engine. They both sat quietly for a minute listening to the ticking of the engine as it cooled. Finally, Sergei spoke.

"Do you even know *how* to teach English?"

27

Yevgenia's phone call to Victor came as no surprise. A month had passed since their last conversation, which had ended in his refusal to sign Oleg's letter to *The New York Times*.

Now Yevgenia wanted him to come to her apartment that evening. It was his first invitation to her home, but the timing was not good. Valery Bonderov had just returned from the Urals, where he had interviewed an orderly at the Orel asylum. Plus, Oksana had set up an interview with a former inmate of Little Rock Special Psychiatric Hospital, one of the six asylums. Two weeks had passed since Victor got the list from Titus Waal, and the search was progressing. The KGB-run asylums were fortresses, but their security was intended to keep inmates in. They were quite unprepared for the trio's brazen assault. Soviet citizens knew so little about what went on behind the walls of the asylums that there was little need to guard against a curious public. So far, the size of the country and the very secrecy surrounding the asylums had worked in Victor's favor.

Already, the three had logged one thousand combined miles of travel around the U.S.S.R., using an array of pretenses from simple surveillance, to interviews of workers, to bogus visits to patients. But for all the effort, only one asylum had been eliminated: Smolensk. Victor had gone there himself and found a sympathetic nurse. She had checked the admissions records and found no record of an Anton Perov.

Victor felt himself getting impatient with their plan. Under most circumstances he was a patient man. Compared to the time spans demanded by a single astronomical survey, this task was proceeding with the ease of taking out the garbage. What had changed was Victor's own understanding of Anton's predicament—the drug overdoses with the risk of permanent brain damage, nerve damage, loss of memory, kidney shutdown, death. At first, the nightly stories of sadistic orderlies, nurses, doctors and fellow inmates had merely horrified him. But with each new interview, a rage grew within Victor. Sometimes he wondered how he would ever quell it.

Despite the busy evening, Victor accepted Yevgenia's invitation. There was something he, too, wanted to talk to her about.

The apartment was located near Patriarch's Pond, one of Moscow's most prestigious districts. The building was a twelve-story, red-brick monolith surrounded by
a wrought-iron fence. Victor turned his car into the gate and was stopped by a
uniformed guard. Victor gave his name, and the man checked a clipboard. He
nodded. "Go ahead."

In the lobby, he was met by another guard in uniform. Again, Victor's name
was checked off a list.

"Tenth floor, comrade," said the guard. "Straight ahead to the elevator."

The elevator was German-made and glided silently as it rose. Soviet-made lifts
banged and clanked as if to remind you of their labor.

He got off on the tenth floor and stepped into a spacious lobby of red and
green Dagestani carpets. A tsarist chair sat against a wall beneath a mirror and a
chandelier. A door swung open, and Yevgenia stood before him. She moved aside,
and he went into the apartment.

Victor kissed her cheek.

"You look good, Yevgenia," he said. And he meant it. She wore an Italian-made
gray suit with a high collar and a big bow at the neck: a bit dowdy, but classy in a
way Victor usually associated with capitalist women. She wore her makeup less
heavily than in the past, with softer colors more suited to her fair skin. Had
someone taught Yevgenia Perova, at age fifty-five, how to properly apply makeup?
Victor tried to imagine it, and the thought made him smile.

They went to the living room and sat down in facing armchairs.

"So you really did it," she said.

"Did what?"

"Got yourself thrown out of the institute, out of the *Party!*"

"You have it backward. They threw me out."

"You gave them plenty of provocation."

"I can't agree with that."

"The Party doesn't make mistakes, Victor."

Victor raised his head and laughed. "A Central Committee member, yes, but
still the little peasant girl."

Yevgenia bit her lip. "Don't call me that."

"That's what Papa always called you."

"I didn't like it then."

"Liar," Victor said with a smile.

Yevgenia contemplated him a moment. "You've changed."

"*I've* changed," said Victor. "Look at this place! Even the sofa's imported! Is
Soviet furniture not good enough for you anymore?"

"Don't be petty, Victor," she said. "It doesn't suit you."

Victor sighed and sank back into the chair. "Why have you called me here?"

"You have made things very difficult for me."

"I'm sorry about that," said Victor. "I had hoped it could be avoided. It's why I have kept you informed all along."

"Am I supposed to be grateful? It would have been better if you had done what you were told."

"I was told to lie, Yevgenia. And to hurt people I care about."

"Don't be insolent. My god! The son of a candidate-member to the Politburo cast out of the Party, the guiding light of our society . . . it's a scandal. I am fighting for my political survival."

"Your *political survival?*" Victor repeated incredulously. "We should be talking about Anton's *physical* survival."

Yevgenia rolled her eyes.

"Why can't you believe that my career, the institute, the Party — it all means nothing without Anton?" asked Victor.

"Anton is gone."

"We'll see."

She got to her feet and walked to the window. "I can't help you, you know."

"I don't need your help."

She turned to face him. "This is difficult for me to say, Victor. I've dedicated my life to the building of communism. And at the same time I have tried to be a good mother."

"I know you have."

"As a woman I have had to shoulder extra responsibilities that a man doesn't have: the raising of our next generation, our shining future."

"You're quoting Lenin."

She ignored that. "But I've always been a communist first. I put my country before everything else."

Victor nodded. "I learned to accept that a long time ago. We all did. Me, Papa, Anton."

"Not Anton."

"No, I suppose not Anton," Victor said. "He wanted a mother who was a mother first."

"But you didn't?"

"You are what you are, Yevgenia," shrugged Victor. "I sometimes wished it were different, sure. But I was always proud of you."

Yevgenia dropped her eyes. "I hope you can understand what I have to say now. My whole life has come down to a simple choice: You or the State."

Victor frowned. "How so?"

"My comrades in the Central Committee tell me that the only way I can possibly stay on in my present post is to sever all ties with you. To disown you, if you will."

"Disown me?"

"Just officially, of course."

"You really wrestled with this one, didn't you, Yevgenia?"

"Don't be sarcastic," she said. "It has been a very difficult decision." She was quiet a moment, and Victor considered the possibility that her anxiety was genuine.

"From now on, Victor, you are completely on your own. You will be treated no differently than any other citizen."

"I'm not afraid of that."

"You should be," she sighed. "You've grown up privileged."

"Yevgenia, I don't know what to say to you. I never meant to hurt you, and I'm sorry if I have. I know what the socialist cause means to you. All I can say is: Do what you have to do, just as I'm doing what I have to do." He paused. "But I want you to promise me one thing."

"Yes?"

"When I find Anton, you will help me get him free."

"You will not find Anton!"

"I'm saying if I do—"

"Goddamn it, Victor! I forbid you to carry on with this."

"Forbid?" asked Victor with exaggerated incredulity. "But Yevgenia, you disowned me, remember? You can't forbid anything."

"Don't be cruel."

"Promise."

"It's a stupid promise, and I will not dignify it."

Victor felt the blood rise to his face. "Do you know what goes on in these asylums? Torture, beatings, isolation. And the drugs, my god—"

"I won't listen to this."

"I do, almost every night. It makes me sick. I want to put my hands over my ears and say, 'No, it's a lie. It's all a lie.' And not just because of Anton. But because of how it has cheapened everything the Soviet Union has accomplished. We're supposed to be the shining beacon of socialism in the world, the next step in human evolution, and here we are, the great Soviet state, behaving like some paranoid Latin American dictator with his midnight death squads."

"It's a lie."

Victor sighed and went to Yevgenia. He kissed her on the cheek.

"Believe what you want," he said. "I used to. I just can't do it anymore."

He started for the door. Yevgenia called after him. "Son?"

Victor whirled around. He could not remember the last time she had called him "son."

"Yes, Mother?"

Her eyes danced over his face.

"What is it?" Victor asked.

"Do you miss it?"

"Miss what?"

Deep wrinkles criss-crossed her forehead, and suddenly she looked much older. "The institute. The Party."

"I feel as though someone cut off my right arm," he said.

She sighed. The reply seemed to settle some doubt. "So why did you do it?"

"To save the rest of me," Victor said and went out.

V i c t o r was late, so the interview was already underway when he stepped into Oksana's living room.

The decision to use the tiny flat as the command center for the search was one of the trio's first decisions. From the start, their campaign was designed for speed, not secrecy. It was the reason Victor had gone to the Serbsky to announce his intention to find his brother; and now it was the reason they conducted their campaign so openly in Oksana's apartment. The KGB would know what they were up to, but it would move cautiously as its agents strained to balance the competing threats of Victor's search and the power of the Perov family name.

For once, the cowardice of the Soviet bureaucracy was working in their favor.

An old man sat on the sofa talking softly to Oksana and Valery. They all looked up when Victor came in. The man's left eye found Victor's face, but the other one wandered off. The man had a stubbly beard, gray streaked. His hair was still short from when it was shaved in the asylum.

Victor already knew the man's name, Gennady Obolensky, a Jew repeatedly denied permission to emigrate to Israel on the grounds that he had once worked as a machinist in an aerospace factory. Gennady had retaliated with a campaign of letters to foreign embassies, news organizations and a succession of Soviet leaders: Brezhnev, Andropov and Chernenko. He had been incarcerated in a number of different prisons and psychiatric hospitals over his seven-year-long campaign for freedom. His last arrest was six months earlier, as he tried to break into the American embassy. This time he had been sent to Little Rock asylum, which Pavel's list told them was located in the Urals. Already, they had learned that Little Rock was the most secretive of all the asylums, and was reserved for the hardest cases.

Valery had a pen in his hand and a notebook on his lap. Oksana was seated beside him. Victor remained on his feet in the doorway. He was too wound up to sit.

"Go on," said Valery, checking his notebook. "You were describing a 'wet wrap.'"

"They wrap you in a wet bedsheet and then lay you on your bunk," the man said, his errant right eye wandering around the room. It bobbed like the eye of a ventriloquist's puppet. "After a little while, the sheet begins to dry and shrink. You can't imagine the pain. It crushes you from all directions all at once. Some people pass out. I've heard of people suffocating. You scream and scream and the orderlies and the nurses just stand there laughing . . ."

"Enough!" said Victor.

The three of them looked up. Valery shot Victor a hard look.

Oksana mouthed, "What's the matter?"

Victor frowned and went sullenly to the corner. He threw himself into a chair.

"And they did this how often?" Valery continued.

"To me, three times. But there are people who get wet wraps almost every week. They're the ones the nurses don't like. They let the orderlies do whatever they want."

"And the orderlies are picked from the prison population?"

The man nodded. Victor got up and began to pace.

"What about the doctors?" asked Valery.

"We almost never saw the doctors. Once a month, at most."

"Okay," said Valery, turning a page in his notebook. "Now let's talk about the drugs . . ."

Victor took a step forward and shoved a picture of Anton before the old man's eyes. "Have you ever seen this man?"

"N-No," the man said reflexively.

"Look at it carefully," said Victor. "You've never seen this man?"

The old man studied it and shook his head. His eye, his one good eye, went to Valery like a plea for help.

But Victor pressed on. "Have you ever heard of a patient named Anton Perov?"

"No."

"Never?"

"No."

Victor grunted and pulled back the picture. Valery glared at Victor, who took a step backward and then went back to the corner. He sat down again.

In his best clinical voice, Valery said, "Now, about the drugs . . ."

The interview went on for another half-hour. Victor watched from the corner. The old man's voice cracked and trembled—not from emotion, for he had a strange detachment from his words, as though he were describing things that had happened to someone else, but as an aftereffect of drug-induced Parkinson's disease, his antitherapy for the past six months.

When it was over, Valery thanked the old man and closed his notebook.

Victor blurted out, "How old are you?"

The old face with the roving eye turned toward him. "Thirty-two."

The room went silent.

"I'm tired," said Gennady.

"You can sleep here, tonight," said Oksana.

Gennady lay down and Oksana pulled an afghan over him. Then she and the two men went into the kitchen and sat down on stools.

Oksana faced Victor and asked sharply, "What was that all about in there?"

"Thirty-two!" said Victor. "My god, the man looks sixty—"

"Shh," said Oksana. "He'll hear you."

"There's a rhythm to an interview," Valery explained patiently. "You disrupted it, Victor. It nearly cost us the information we need."

"Sorry," said Victor. "Tell me about Orel. You talked to the orderly?"

"Yes, but I don't think we can rule out Orel. Not yet."

"Why not?"

"The orderly never saw the actual patient records. All he can say is, based on his own work routes, there is no Anton Perov in Orel Special Psychiatric Hospital."

"Oh, I don't believe this!" said Victor. "You went all the way to Orel and *that's* what you came back with?"

"Victor!" Oksana scolded.

"Why *didn't* he get into the records?" asked Victor.

"They're in a locked room," said Valery.

"So tell him to pick the lock. Steal a key. Break it down and make it look like a theft. But don't come back with this! Now I have to go back and start over from—"

"That's enough, Victor!" said Oksana.

Valery looked at Victor, hurt. "The man did what he could."

Victor jumped to his feet so suddenly that his stool fell backward with a crash. Without picking it up, Victor stormed out of the kitchen. He crossed the living room, past Gennady, who was already snoring, and onto the balcony because there was nowhere else to go. The balcony was so packed with boxes and toys and tricycles and bicycles that there was barely room to stand. It was cold and Victor wished he had put on his coat. He looked out at the back of another building, exactly like the one he was in. Frozen clothing hung stiffly on a dozen balconies. Some balconies had been enclosed, a common upgrade, but the workmanship was poor and the effect was to make everything even more dreary. It was urban poverty. His Moscow.

Oksana came beside him and put her arm around him. She laid her head on his shoulder. It was the first time they had touched in over a month.

"I'm sorry," said Victor.

"It's not me you owe an apology to."

He hung his head. "I know. It's just that . . . I can't listen to any more of these interviews."

"It's getting to all of us," said Oksana. After a moment, she asked, "How was your talk with Yevgenia?"

Victor shrugged. He shivered.

"You're cold," she said. "Let's go inside."

She moved for the door, but he stayed in his place.

"How's Grisha?" he asked.

"Good. He's still with my mother."

"When we find Anton, are you going to tell him about us, or do you want me to do it?" asked Victor.

"We didn't do anything wrong, Victor. We thought he was dead." She sighed. "Soon this will all be over."

"Will it?" Victor asked.

"What do you mean?"

"I've been thinking," said Victor. "What kind of a man goes into a burning nursery and only rescues his own child from the flames?"

Oksana took a step back from Victor. "What are you saying?"

"I don't see how this can end with Anton."

"Where *will* it end?"

Victor squeezed the cold railing with his bare hands and looked out into the night. "Maybe it never ends."

Oksana got quiet. When Victor turned to her a moment later, she was gone. He stood alone several more minutes and then went inside. He found Oksana in the kitchen with Valery.

"So," Victor said. "What do we do about Little Rock?"

Oksana and Valery exchanged glances. Valery said, "Gennady swears Anton is not there. It's pretty solid information."

"But Gennady was only in the 'A' and 'V' wards," said Victor. "Anton could be in one of the other three — 'B,' 'G' and 'D.'"

"Perhaps. But on cold days, the wards were often mingled during exercise time — so that the guards could quickly get back indoors. There's a chance they just never crossed paths, of course. But still . . ."

"You're saying we should eliminate it."

"I wish we had something more solid, but the place is a real fortress," said Valery. "This may be the best information we ever get out of Little Rock."

Victor stood a long time thinking. What should he do?

If it were a cosmological survey, what would you do?

The answer came clearly: When time is limited and the problem is large, identify the likeliest candidate and eliminate the rest.

"I agree," said Victor. "Little Rock is out. We'll concentrate on the others."

28

"In-mates! At-ten-tion!"

The cry ricocheted through B ward of Little Rock Special Psychiatric Hospital like a trapped bullet. The voice belonged to the Uzbek, chief orderly for the asylum. He had earned the nickname not because he was from Uzbekistan, but because of his enthusiasm for the old khanates of Central Asia, and, in particular, their embrace of slavery, torture, public executions, stoning, public humiliation, rape and the cutting-off of hands and feet. He would often glare at a prisoner and say, "You know how they would have handled this in Bukhara, don't you?"

The Uzbek stood in the precise mathematical center of B ward, a point marked with a red dot. The ward itself was an open two-story structure, like a brick airplane hangar. On all sides, metal doors with peep slots, locked by sliding bolts, faced him. From where the Uzbek stood, he could see the outside of fifty-seven doors. Behind them were fifty-seven eighteen-foot-by-twenty-one-and-a-quarter-foot cells, home to two hundred and thirty-two inmates.

Following the Uzbek's command, the ward grew still. The Uzbek had a baton in his hand and he swung it against his palm. *Smack.* He took a breath and raised his head.

"Pre-pare your-selves!"

His cry was followed by shuffling, like the flapping of a hundred birds' wings, which was the sound of prisoners moving behind the doors of their cells, getting out of beds, pulling on clothes, whispering to each other if they dared. Then came the *jingle* of keys in orderlies' hands followed by the *clank-clank* of stubborn locks and the *creak* of reluctant doors. There were fifty-seven doors to be opened in B ward so the jingling and the clanking and the creaking and the smacking went on for some time.

Then out they came, upright-walking, jittery beasts, blinking as though coming into a bright light. The smell came with them, damp tobacco, urine, sweat and the spoiled-beef smell of rotting teeth. They wore dusty-blue pajamas and round caps atop their shaved heads. Some had the dancing eyes of frightened horses. Others stared blankly ahead, as though the nerves connecting the eyes to the brain had been severed. Those on the second floor stepped out of their cells onto a catwalk and put their backs against the wall. On the first floor, they found a yellow line the color of goldenrod and placed their toes on it. Their slippers covered the line completely, but did not cross over. Never before in the history of mankind had a straighter row of upright-walking, jittery, blinking, foul-smelling, rotten-toothed beasts been assembled than the one that toed that goldenrod-yellow line.

"Right face!"

The prisoners turned.

"Move!"

The prisoners moved, shuffling toward the little passageway at the end of the building.

It was exercise time at Little Rock.

E v e r y o n e was already in the muddy yard when Inmate 222 came outside, led by a square-faced female nurse. He looked unsteady on his feet, and the nurse supported him by the arm. They took a few more steps together and stopped. He nodded at her, and she turned and left.

The sky was gray, and it was cold, but the air had already lost its winter chill. Inmates stood in groups in the small yard, not much larger than a basketball court. It was pie-shaped and bounded by the wall of B ward on one side, A ward on another and a brick wall on the third. A guard tower rose over the fat end of the wedge, and they could all plainly see the barrel of a machine gun aimed unspecifically in their direction. Beyond the walls, the gentle Urals rose in all directions.

Not far from Inmate 222, a group of six prisoners stood together awkwardly, like shy kids at recess not quite sure what to do.

"Look!" said a man with a tumor in his neck the size of a plum. "There he is!"

They all looked at Inmate 222.

"The unluckiest bastard in Little Rock," said a man with eyes that darted over the ground as though he were looking for something.

The prisoners only saw Inmate 222 once a week, as often as he was allowed in the yard. Most inmates had daily exercise rights.

"Je-Jesus," said a dwarf. "H-He looks t-t-terrib-b-b . . ."

"Shut up!" said a man with a dark, angry face.

Like the others, Inmate 222 wore pajamas. The right side of his face hung limply on his skull. Sagging skin partially covered his right eye. He looked like a boxer who had lost a fight.

"The anti-Christ," said a fourth man, fairly young, with strange, dark eyes that were almost black. "He is. For in my dreams I have seen . . ."

"Shut up!" said the man with the angry face.

". . . his eyes being pecked out by ravens . . ."

"Shut up!"

"P-P-Poor ba-ba-ba . . ."

". . . his skin crawling with the maggots of . . ."

"Shut up!"

". . . stard."

". . . his own decay . . ."

"Shut up!"

Inmate 222 stood strangely twisted, favoring his right side. His right hand was turned into a hook. He began to look around.

"What's he looking for?" asked the man with the tumor.

"Shut up!"

"His fr-fr-fr . . ."

"Shut up!"

". . . friend."

"The anti-Christ! He is. For in my dreams I have seen . . ."

A short distance away, two orderlies also noticed the appearance of Inmate 222. The first was a large man with long dark hair. His name was Felix Tulikh, and he was supposed to have beaten his wife to death for having flirted with a neighbor. He had been serving his sentence at the regular part of the prison when he was recruited as an orderly in the asylum. The second orderly's name was Stanislav Surikov. He had an average build, an oval face, and hair the color of beach sand. He was not a convict but a professional guard, which was unusual. It was rumored that he had been transferred to the asylum as punishment. No one knew for what. So now Stanislav worked side by side with some of the same men he had once guarded.

"Jesus, look at him," said Felix.

Stanislav shook his head. "Nerve damage. All down his right side."

"He's on your rounds, isn't he?"

Stanislav nodded solemnly. "Lazda really has his hooks in him."

"What do they have him on?"

"Insulin shock. Sodium Amytal."

Felix whistled. "I wonder what he did."

Little was known about Inmate 222. His identity was a secret, guarded by the inmate himself, who seemed to do so against some kind of threat. But Little Rock was a place of a thousand secrets, and the two orderlies gave no more than a passing thought to the matter of Inmate 222's identity. It was enough to know that he was a prisoner in Little Rock. After that, what else mattered?

"What's he looking for?" asked Felix.

Stanislav pursed his lips grimly. "He *hasn't* heard."

"You're right! He *hasn't* heard."

"Poor bastard."

"Come on," said Felix, and he started toward Inmate 222. Stanislav followed.

When they reached him, Felix asked, "Looking for someone?"

Inmate 222 stared at them. He didn't recoil from Felix's voice the way most inmates did. This seemed to irritate Felix, who barked, "Speak up, scum! Are you looking for someone?"

"Niko-wai Do-gan," Inmate 222 said. He had begun to lisp in the last several weeks.

"Nikolai *Yuseyevich* Dolgan?" grinned Felix, emphasizing the Jewish part of the name. "The history professor?"

The prisoner didn't respond, and Felix slapped his baton into his palm. "Speak up or you go to the infirmary!"

"Yes."

"You two were friends, weren't you?"

"W-were?"

"Your friend is dead."

Inmate 222 looked at Felix in disbelief.

Felix held up his right hand, fingers together, palm out. "Swear to god."

"It was suicide," said Stanislav. "I'm sorry."

"Crazy son-of-a-bitch sucked the ends off of 365 match heads," said Felix. "The Uzbek made me count them. Tough way to go. Hell of a bellyache."

"Shut up, Felix!" said Stanislav.

"But h-how—"

". . . did he get the matches?" said Felix. "He was issued one match a day to light the oven. He worked in the kitchen, as you know. He used a flint and pocketed the match."

"You're saying he planned this . . ."

"For exactly one year," said Felix.

"How long have you known him?" asked Stanislav.

"Three mo-months."

"And he never said a thing?" asked Stanislav.

Inmate 222 didn't answer. His masklike face was twisted into an expression that might have been grief. He turned and limped away.

"Hey!" barked Felix, disappointed. "Where the fuck do you think you're going?"

"You're a bastard, Felix," said Stanislav.

Felix grinned.

Stanislav watched Inmate 222 walk away. After a few steps, Stanislav called out, "Two-twenty-two?"

He turned.

"You okay?"

He lowered his head and went on.

A week later, Stanislav Surikov went onto night duty. On his first night, as he made his rounds in B ward, a voice called out to him from Cell 37.

"They say you have debts," it whispered.

"Quiet in there!" he hissed.

"I can help you."

"I said, quiet!" He tapped his club against the door.

"Let me help you with your debts."

"Don't make me open this door," Stanislav warned.

"You won't be sorry."

"That's it!" said Stanislav. He fumbled with his keys and pulled open the door. He raised his club, and was about to strike the man before him. He froze.

"You?"

It was Inmate 222.

"I hear you have debts."

The orderly shook his head incredulously. "I ought to crack your skull."

There were five other prisoners in Cell 37, all lying on their bunks under a red light. Some were snoring. One had his eyes open, but that's how he always slept.

"You have to help me," Inmate 222 whispered.

"I don't *have* to do anything."

"I have money."

"You don't have piss."

"I have nine uncut diamonds. Big ones."

Stanislav grabbed the prisoner by the arm and dragged him out onto the catwalk. He threw him against the wall and put the club to his chin.

"Move and you die," he said.

He got out his keys and locked the door. He grabbed the prisoner and pushed him to the end of the catwalk. Stanislav pulled open a door and threw the prisoner inside. He followed him into the dark room and closed the door. He flipped a switch and a dim light illuminated a small, brick-walled room with a single chair and a table. It was an interrogation chamber.

"Bullshit," said Stanislav.

"They were given to me, right before I was arrested," said the prisoner. "I hid them. They're yours if you help me."

"Where are they hidden?"

"Karelia."

"What the hell good are they to me up there?"

Inmate 222 took a step toward Stanislav, and the orderly raised his club in defense.

"They're worth over a million rubles," said Inmate 222. "That's worth the trip north, wouldn't you say? You're not a convict, like the others. You could get out of this place."

"Maybe I like it here."

The prisoner stroked the dead side of his face. "They say you have debts to black marketeers."

"Do they?"

"They say you got caught stealing from the prison, and that's why you were assigned here. But your debts remain."

"I can take care of myself," said Stanislav. "I don't need help from some political."

"Okay," shrugged the prisoner. "Maybe you'll get lucky and they'll only break your legs."

Stanislav's eyes narrowed. He seemed to be thinking. After a minute, he shook his head. "I can't help you."

"L-Look at me," said Inmate 222, his stutter suddenly getting worse. "Look at what they're doing to me! Half my f-face is dead. My kidneys ache all the time. I'm beginning to f-forget things. Three more months of their th-therapy and I'll be dead. Or w-worse."

Stanislav looked at the prisoner a long time. "What do you want?"

"There's a man in Moscow. Nikolai told me about him. I have a letter for him."

"Mail it yourself."

"Lazda would never let it get through the post. It must be delivered from the city post office."

"You have this man's address?"

"It's about a year old."

"Why send it to him? Why not to your family?"

"I have a three-year-old son, who my wife is raising alone. I can't take a chance of him losing both his parents."

"Don't you have any other family?"

The prisoner was quiet a moment. "A brother," he said finally. "I have a twin brother."

"Why not send the letter to him?"

Inmate 222 shook his head. "My brother is a great man. He would sacrifice his life for me, or his work, which is the same thing. I can't let him do that."

"I think you should worry about yourself."

The prisoner didn't respond.

"What's the name of this man you want to get the message to?"

"Pavel Danilov."

"I should report you — and him — to the Uzbek."

"Then you'll never get the diamonds."

"Sure I would. I can get the information from you under interrogation."

"You would have to bring in the Uzbek or Dr. Lazda. They would get the diamonds."

Stanislav was quiet a moment, calculating. "And what if they're not where you say they are?"

"Then you will kill me."

"You got that right," said Stanislav, and he swung his baton into his hand. In Inmate 222's weakened condition, two blows from that baton would end his misery. "How can this Danilov help you?"

"He can get word to the West."

"That might make things worse for you," said Stanislav.

Inmate 222 stared at him. "How could things get any worse?"

29

Katherine followed her father's misadventures in Washington through her weekly phone calls to Cameron Abbott.

Jack Sears's meeting with the secretary of state did not take place as scheduled, or even the week after that, as rescheduled. Following the second cancellation, an aide refused to set a new date. The secretary had a long-scheduled tour of Central America, and Jack should try to schedule something after he got back. No promises.

"Dad must be going crazy," said Katherine.

"No," said Cameron. "He's going to Costa Rica."

"An ambush?"

"That seems to be the general idea."

In spite of herself, Katherine laughed.

That conversation with Cameron took place the day her father was supposed to have returned.

"I'm sorry things are going so badly," said Sergei when he heard about it.

"Not badly," said Katherine. "Just slowly. At least the KGB hasn't returned to the taxi park."

Sergei nodded. "They were just fishing. They've been to every train station in Moscow."

"How do you know that?"

Sergei just smiled.

That night, after Sergei left for Moscow, Katherine went out onto the grassy street of Ivanovka. The night was still, with only the faint howl of a dog to break the silence. The air was brisk, and Katherine jammed her hands into her coat pockets and pulled her arms against her sides. Katherine knew she should be in her room preparing for her first English lecture the next day, but there was something else she had to do. She stood a moment, scanning the heavens. In remote Ivanovka, far from lights and pollution, the night sky was a display of unbelievable richness. For an astronomer like Dr. Katherine Sears, such a sky was like a favorite book she could open up at random and read for hours.

But Katherine had come out into the cold this night with a purpose, and it didn't take her long to find what she was looking for. In the east, suspended on the border between Capricorn and Aquarius, hung a faint star that, in fact, wasn't a star — the Large Magellanic Cloud. Katherine shivered to think that in a strange way, this subgalactic clump of stars located outside the Milky Way was the impetus for all that had happened to her. After all, it had brought her to Victor Perov.

Katherine smiled. Leave it to Victor to use the ascension of the Large Magellanic Cloud as the timetable for their meetings. It was their personal, secret language. Approximately once a month, the Large Magellanic Cloud would move from one sign of the zodiac to the next, a process known as ascension.

On this night, the Large Magellanic Cloud was making its ascension.

The next day at precisely noon, Victor would climb the bell tower in Zagorsk and wait for her. She wouldn't come, but it made her feel less alone to know that he would be there, and that each month for as long as she was in the U.S.S.R., he would make the climb up the spiral staircase.

Katherine stood a while longer looking up at the formation, imagining that Victor, too, was looking up from wherever he was. Their love of astronomy had brought them together, and now it was the only way they could be together. There was something fitting in that.

Katherine felt her finger for the place where her amber ring had once rested. Sergei had long since sold the ring to pay for Katherine's counterfeit documents. She missed the ring, but she was sure Victor would have understood her decision.

She took a last look at the sky and then, almost reluctantly, she went back inside.

Katherine had butterflies in her stomach that morning as she stepped into room 203. Twenty Russian faces looked up at her — farmers' faces, young and old, skin coarsened by outdoor work. Clumsy, callused hands clutched pencils. The men wore suits and the women wore dresses, but still, they looked like farmers going to church on Sunday, the mud of the potato field still beneath their fingernails.

Their eyes, however, were eager; they wanted to speak English. Well, Katherine would see what she could do about that.

She put her books on the desk, turned to face the class and said, in English, "Good morning."

The room was quiet a moment. Then one voice said, "Goot mornink."

Katherine turned toward the source of the voice, a man of about thirty-five with rather thick glasses. "You speak English?"

"A leettle."

"No one else?" she asked in English.

She surveyed the blank faces. She smiled grimly and took a breath.

"Good morning *znachit 'dobroye utro.' Povtorite, pozhaluista*," Katherine said. "Good mor-ning."

The class repeated. "Goot mornink."

"Very good," said Katherine Sears. *"Ochen khorosho."*

And so it went. After class, Katherine went to Maya Timofeyeva's office.

"How was the first day?" Maya asked.

Katherine shrugged. "I got through it. There are a few things that would help. First, a dictionary of agricultural terms. These students not only want to learn English, they want to be able to talk about fertilizer and wheat combine mechanics."

"I'll see what I can do," said Maya.

"Also, one of the students said the foreign-language library in Moscow subscribes to farming trade journals in English."

"That's possible."

"I would like to borrow them."

Maya sighed. "Let's not go overboard, Yekatarina."

"A lot of these students want nothing more than to be able to read about Western farming techniques."

"Our books are just fine for that. I appreciate your enthusiasm, but, please, just stick to the syllabus."

The next evening, Sergei came to Baba Krista's. It was Friday, so they made their weekly drive to the collective farm office. Along the way, Katherine asked if he could help her get a library card to the foreign-language library in Moscow.

"Absolutely not," he said.

"I would need documents?"

"Yes," he said tiredly.

"Then, perhaps you could check out some materials."

Sergei groaned and rolled his eyes.

Katherine didn't respond. By now she had learned that Sergei, no matter how much he complained, loved intrigue. It was why he drove a taxi, it was why he dabbled in the black market, and it was at least partly why he was helping her. A fanciful part of Sergei saw himself as a Russian romantic in the eighteenth-century tradition, seated on a horse, arguing about the Enlightenment, poetry and the injustice of monogamy for males. Given his way, Sergei would die in a duel. But there was more to Sergei's desire to help Katherine than whimsy. Something boiled within Sergei, something as hot and furious as lava. It compelled him to take these risks. She was Sergei's weapon, and he was using her to get even.

For what?

Someday, Katherine hoped to ask precisely that.

A few minutes later, they arrived at White Dacha. Katherine dialed Cameron Abbott, and a moment later she was speaking English to the American diplomat.

"Your father missed the deputy secretary in Costa Rica," Cameron said. "Now he can't get an appointment with him for three weeks."

While Katherine was digesting this information Cameron said, "There is some good news. A hard-line senator from your state gave a speech on the floor of the Senate about you."

"Really?"

"Not about you, *per se*. But he cited your case as an example of Soviet treachery and diplomatic incompetence. I guess that got some journalists wondering, because after that your story appeared in several newspapers. Grayson Hines interviewed me today for a feature he's writing for the Sunday magazine."

"You didn't—"

"No, I didn't say anything about our talks. But he does want to know if he can interview your father."

"That's up to my father," said Katherine. "Will all this publicity help?"

"That's the good news—it already has. The ambassador has an appointment with the Soviet foreign minister in three weeks. Your case has been put on the agenda. With a little luck, Katherine, the Soviets will drop their charges and issue you an exit visa. You could be home for the Fourth of July."

In the office, Katherine gave Sergei the thumbs-up sign.

"Thank god," she said.

T he following week, Maya Timofeyeva came to Katherine's English I class and took a seat in the back.

She began with the homework: verb conjugations. On the blackboard, Katherine wrote:

I sit. You sit. He sits. We sit. They sit.

After going through four more verbs, they moved to pronunciation.

Irena Kilitova, a collective farm director from Stavropol, raised her hand. "Are we learning the English variant or the American variant?"

"I guess you could say I'm more familiar with the American variant."

"What's the difference?" asked Yegor, a quiet young man whose interest in English was closely linked to an interest in the Beatles.

"The accent," said Katherine.

"The English spell differently," said Igor, who was always eager to show his knowledge of the West. In fact, all the class, even the dour, communist types like Irena Kilitova, showed a barely contained fascination for anything Western.

"That's true," said Katherine.

"I wonder if there are different dialects even within the United States," said Yegor.

"Of course there are," said Katherine.

Something about the way Katherine said that made everyone inch forward in their seats. The room got quiet.

"How so?" asked Katya, a pretty local girl, who was working toward a degree in accounting.

Katherine said, "In the New England states, for example, they have a—"

"New England? Where's that?"

"You don't know . . ." Katherine began, looking at the curious faces. She smiled thinly. "Of course you don't."

Before she knew what she was doing, Katherine had stepped over to a map of the world and was pointing to the United States of America.

In the back of the room, Maya Timofeyeva scowled.

"In the northern states," said Katherine, "they speak a harder dialect. Harder vowel sounds. Sharper consonants. In the south," she went on, "they use softer vowel sounds. Longer. It's very pretty."

Forty eyes were glued to her. She had the class's complete attention.

"Can someone from the North understand someone from the South?" asked Katya.

Katherine smiled. This was as close to travel as Katya would ever get.

"Sometimes it's difficult," she said.

Maya came up to Katherine after class.

"Your knowledge of American dialects is quite impressive."

"Yes?" asked Katherine gathering up her books and papers. "It's kind of a hobby, I guess."

"You've departed from the syllabus, Yekatarina."

"The syllabus is terrible."

"Be that as it may, these students have to take standardized tests."

"They do?" Katherine asked surprised.

"Of course! How is it that you don't know these things?"

"Tell me about the tests," said Katherine.

"They take them in August. If they don't pass, they have to wait another year, maybe two, for a place in this class—and that's assuming their collective would vote to send them here again, which is doubtful."

Katherine thought about that. "Do you have copies of these tests?"

"Old ones."

"May I have them?"

T h a t Friday, when Katherine called Cameron Abbott, a familiar voice answered the phone.

"Oh, Dad!" said Katherine. Tears clouded her eyes, and her throat tightened. "It's so good to hear your voice."

A month had passed since they had last spoken.

"Yours sounds good too, Kat-Kat."

For once, the endearment didn't strike her as condescending.

"I heard about your trip to Costa Rica. I'm sorry about all that."

"No trouble at all," he said. "When this is over, maybe we'll write a book."

Katherine laughed. "Who would buy it?"

"Are you kidding? You're famous."

"I am?"

He told her about the senator's speech. "I had just seen him two days earlier. I told him about the problems we were having with the Embassy and it seemed to strike a chord. He called the foreign service 'a breeding ground for ticks on the butt of the taxpayer.' "

"That sounds like him," said Katherine. "And to think I never liked him."

"After his speech, reporters started calling."

"What did you tell them?"

"I thought the senator said it well, so I stuck pretty close to his view of things. All I said about you was that we had reason to believe you were still alive. Grayson Hines wrote the best article. His story is the only reason the sons-of-bitches around here are doing anything, pardon my French."

Katherine smiled.

Jack said, "The ambassador's meeting is in two weeks. It's almost over, Katherine."

"I sure hope you're right."

"Of course I'm right! I told you I'd get you out of here. You just hold on and do like I said. Keep your head low and trust no one, you hear?"

Katherine didn't reply.

A **q u a r t e r - m i l e** from the American embassy, inside a KGB apartment on the Moscow Ring Road, two large spools of tape turned slowly on an upright recording machine. A man wearing headphones sat before the machine. He listened to the words "wait and see," and then parting expressions of love followed by a promise to "touch bases" at the same time the following week. Two clicks signaled the end of the conversation.

The man pushed STOP and picked up the telephone. A voice answered, and the man said, "Leo Yakunin, please."

The line began to ring again. An irritated voice answered.

"It's Eduard," said the man at the recording machine. "We got another one."

"Good," said Leo. "What about a trace?"

"It was a secure line."

"Naturally. Anything significant in the transcript?"

"Perhaps. She told him they would 'touch bases' next week."

"What the hell does that mean?"

"I have no idea."

"I thought you knew English."

"I do. It's not English. A code, perhaps?"

"Get the cipher boys working on it. It may be important. And send the tape and transcript to me as soon as it's ready."

30

T w o psychiatric hospitals down, four to go. That's how May began for Victor Perov.

On the May Day holiday, Victor, Oksana and Valery settled on their assignments. Valery would take Moldavia; Oksana, Kazan; Victor, Leningrad.

"With any luck," said Victor, "by the end of the month, we'll know where Anton is."

On May 10, Victor left on the night train for Leningrad. In one hand he carried a suitcase for clothes and papers; in the other was a six-foot-long, hundred-pound wooden case.

By ten o'clock the next morning he had checked into a hotel and was standing on Arsenal Street outside the Leningrad Special Psychiatric Hospital. He looked up at the guard tower and the walls topped by barbed wire. He recalled his visit to the Serbsky Institute in Moscow and how he had been chilled by the sight of the barbed wire. It no longer had that effect on him. Not after Smolensk. Not after all the late-night interviews.

Victor went into the guard booth and presented himself as a visitor. Each patient was permitted two visits per month.

"Patient's name?"

"Anton Perov."

The guard checked his clipboard. "We have no patient by that name."

Victor hadn't really expected it to be that easy. But by identifying himself at the outset, he was guaranteeing that a record of his visit would make its way back to the KGB. It was as he told Oksana the day he went to the Serbsky to confront Petrus Bruk: "Russians are suspicious when they don't know your motives."

The KGB was a paranoid organization. Its agents would always imagine the worst, and then act as though the worst were true. For Victor, the safest course was to defuse that paranoia by announcing his intentions openly. The KGB wouldn't arrest a Perov so long as his only motive was to find a brother everyone knew had been killed in Afghanistan. As far as the KGB was concerned, Victor was a harmless nuisance.

"You must be mistaken," Victor said to the guard with mock incredulity. "I've been here before."

The guard checked the list again. "No."

"Show me the list."

"Get lost, buddy."

"Then just show me the part of the list where 'Perov' should be."

The guard flipped some pages and pushed the clipboard in Victor's eyes. "See?"

The list went from V. Petrovich to S. Pozniak.

"You're right," said Victor. "Sorry to have troubled you."

He left. The next day, he came back and presented himself to a different guard.

"Patient's name?"

"Vladimir Petrovich."

The guard checked the list and frowned. "We have a Valery Petrovich."

"That's what I said: Valery Petrovich."

"And who are you?"

Victor handed over his internal passport. The guard opened it up. Inside lay ten rubles. The guard closed the passport and said, "I'll have to hold on to this while you're inside."

From his research, Victor knew that Leningrad Special Psychiatric Hospital had been an ordinary prison before its conversion in the 1960s. The asylum was still operated by the Ministry of Internal Affairs. The ministry, called the MVD by its Russian initials, was the U.S.S.R.'s security organ. It encompassed everything from the KGB, which was technically just a committee within the ministry, to the traffic cop who stood on the asphalt ruining his arches.

Inside the asylum, the ceiling rose five stories like the atrium of a ritzy Western hotel. Along the edges were cages filled with people, who looked like wounded animals. Some just sat with their backs to their cell walls, curled up and rocking themselves. Others moaned, and their dissonant pitches clashed in the open cave. One man had his penis out and was masturbating. One lunged at Victor as he and his escort passed.

Victor winced. He wanted to find Anton, but not here, not in this snake pit.

Victor lagged behind the orderly systematically scanning the cages. His eyes could cover only a fraction of the men in that five-story atrium, perhaps 5 percent. Anton was not among that fraction. Victor was led to a room and left alone. A short time later a nurse came in with a tall man with a neck like a garden hose and a huge, pyramidal head.

"Who is this?" Victor asked.

"Valery Petrovich," said the nurse.

Valery Petrovich's head jerked in a spasm at the sound of his name, and he gazed blankly at Victor. One glance told Victor that the man was seriously disturbed.

"No it's not," said Victor.

"It most certainly is," said the nurse.

"Well, it's not *my* Valery Petrovich," said Victor haughtily. The nurse huffed and took her patient out of the room. A few minutes later, the orderly led Victor back through the exercise yard to the guard booth. While in the yard, Victor surveyed the rooftops of buildings outside the compound. About a quarter-mile away, he spotted a yellow-and-white apartment building that would serve his purpose.

The guard gave Victor his passport, minus the ten rubles. Victor stepped through the prison gate and was back on Arsenal Street, where he had begun less than fifteen minutes earlier. He took a deep breath and felt what every visitor to a prison feels once he has left the compound. *Thank god it's not me.*

It made him ashamed.

The brief tour of the prison told him one important thing: There was only one prison yard for the entire ward. That simplified things considerably. It was time to get to work.

The next morning Victor stood at the base of the sixteen-story yellow-and-white apartment building he had spotted from the prison yard. Over his shoulder was a backpack, and in his right hand was his heavy wooden case. He went into the building—there was no security—and rode the elevator to the top floor. From there, he ascended the staircase another half-floor to a dead end at a chain-link door. For once, Victor was grateful for Soviet prefabricated construction. All these buildings were the same, which had guaranteed that Victor's assumption about the layout of this particular building would be correct. The door was locked with a puny padlock that Victor snapped easily with a metal rod from his backpack. Victor stepped through the door and wound his way through the maze of boxes and tools. He reached a steel ladder that rose a half-story to a metal grate in the ceiling. He set down his wooden case and climbed to the grate, pushed it aside and, a moment later, stood on the roof. He looked around. It took him several seconds to get his bearings and locate the psychiatric hospital. It was a distant speck between the smokestacks of a factory. He went back down the ladder and hauled the heavy wooden case to the roof. He found a place near the edge of the roof and snapped open the catches and lifted the lid. Inside lay the body tube of the telescope Anton had built for him twenty years earlier, along with all the lenses, counterweights, stand, locking mechanisms and other hardware. It took Victor ten minutes to set it up. Using the finder scope, he located the asylum and then moved his eye to the powerful main viewer. He used the positioning screws to zero in on the exercise yard. The scene came in clearly. He smiled. He could make out puddles, even a discarded soda bottle. Fanta. He locked the telescope in position. He got a thermos from the backpack and poured some coffee. He sat back to wait.

An hour later, the first group of prisoners filed into the yard. Victor moved the viewer slowly over the faces, back and forth, sweeping and identifying, sweeping and eliminating.

Victor spent the next seven days on the roof, peering through the eyepiece of the telescope. The inmates were brought out in shifts, so Victor's days were long. A couple of times he thought he saw Anton, but with later inspection he was proven wrong. By the last day, he knew the exercise schedule of the Leningrad Special Psychiatric Hospital better than the prison personnel themselves.

Victor was now sure. Anton was not in Leningrad.

V i c t o r returned to Moscow pleased that he had succeeded in eliminating one of the Soviet Union's largest special psychiatric hospitals from his list, but depressed that he had not located Anton. Three hospitals had now been eliminated, but Victor had heard nothing from the others, and he wondered how their assignments were going.

He got off the train in Moscow at nine o'clock in the morning and went straight to the long-term parking lot to get his car. He was driving west along Kalininsky Prospekt when an on-foot traffic policeman waved his black-and-white baton at him. Victor pulled over.

"Documents," the *gaishnik* demanded.

Victor handed over his registration, proof of insurance, proof of inspection and internal passport. He no longer had the red Party card.

The policeman took the documents and went behind the car. He spoke into the radio attached to his shoulder. He came back and asked Victor to open the hood.

"What's the matter, Inspector?"

"Just open the hood, comrade."

Together they found the identification number on the engine block. The policeman radioed it to the dispatcher.

"Where did you get this car?" the policeman asked.

"I bought it about six months ago."

"How?"

"Through the SAPO Institute."

"SAPO?" said the policeman impressed. "You work there?"

"Not anymore. Why?"

"This serial number is on a list of stolen vehicles."

Damn Oleg.

"It's a mistake."

"No doubt," said the officer sympathetically. "But I will have to impound the vehicle until it is sorted out."

Victor handed over the keys knowing he would never see his car again.

Victor retrieved his telescope and bags from the trunk and hailed a taxi. He got back to his apartment an hour later and threw open the door.

"I'm home!"

No one replied. He had hoped to find Oksana and Grisha there. Their absence probably meant that Oksana was still in Kazan. Victor went directly to the phone to call Oksana's mother. Grisha would be with her, and Victor hoped to bring him back to the flat that evening. He missed the little guy. Victor picked up the telephone.

The line was dead.

On June 24, the same day that Katherine Sears began teaching English in Bolshevichka, the day the Large Magellanic Cloud ascended into Aquarius, Victor ascended the steps of the bell tower in Zagorsk. When Katherine Sears didn't come, he passed the rest of the afternoon visiting with Father Andrei. Victor told him about his dreams.

"You remember that day at the river?"

"Certainly. I got there just as you were reviving Anton."

"Can you add anything at all to what I've told you?"

Father Andrei frowned. "Like what?"

"I don't know," Victor said miserably. He must have sounded like a fool.

Two days later, Victor took Grisha to Kazansky Station to meet Oksana. Her mother had told him that Oksana would be arriving on the 3:12 P.M. express. That's all he knew.

Victor spotted Oksana in the crowd on the platform. She wore a red beret on her blond hair and was impossible to miss. Their eyes met. They searched each other's faces for a moment, then their eyes fell in the knowledge that Anton was still missing.

Grisha spotted his mother and dashed toward her. She scooped him into her arms. The three-year-old began a lengthy report on the many shortcomings of his new day-care center. He had been forced to leave the posh one near *Izvestiya* a week earlier. Victor picked up Oksana's bag, and they headed for the subway entrance.

"You didn't bring the car?" Oksana asked.

"I'll tell you later."

That evening after they had put Grisha to bed, Oksana related the story of her two-week-long ordeal at Kazan Special Psychiatric Hospital.

The first two days had gone disastrously. She was turned away at the gate and later threatened by a local police detective.

"He said I would be arrested if I was caught within a hundred yards of the hospital," she said.

Next, she stalked nurses at the nearest bus stop, trying to find someone sympathetic to her problem. Not only was she turned down but someone reported her. This earned Oksana another visit from the detective, who by now had a copy of a KGB report that identified her as the wife of a dissident. Now, she was banned from talking to anyone from the hospital.

Ten days had already passed and Oksana was desperate. She charged into the guard station and threw herself on the mercy of the men. She began to weep. "My husband is in here! Please help me! Are you not men?"

"I was hysterical, and the two guards rushed to console me," Oksana recalled. "They kept telling me to calm down. Calm down."

They checked their records and assured me that they had no Anton Perov in Kazan Special Psychiatric Hospital. Then I just broke down totally. This time it was not an act."

The two guards, at a loss about what to do with this inconsolable female, called for help. It arrived in the form of the asylum's chief of staff.

"I guess they thought I needed a doctor," said Oksana.

The psychiatrist led her through the compound to his office. He made several calls, which verified the guards' contention that they had no Anton Perov. When that still didn't satisfy Oksana, the psychiatrist, at his wits' end, agreed to take her on a tour of the compound.

The guards joined them so the four went about the hospital like an inspection team, peeping into every cell.

"God, Victor, it was horrible," said Oksana. "A dumping ground for human beings. I don't care how sick they are, they . . ." She didn't finish the sentence.

She recovered and went on with her story. She had finished the tour of the asylum and turned to the men, saying, "You know, maybe I *am* mistaken."

"As I left the asylum grounds I turned to say good-bye to the guards," recalled Oksana. "You've never seen such relief on men's faces."

Victor and Oksana laughed, but the laughter was grim. For unspoken between them was the knowledge that only two hospitals now remained — Moldavia and Orel.

And already, six weeks had passed.

31

I t was called a chat. Two diplomats would meet for a few hours away from the usual diplomatic regalia and just talk man to man. The theory was that as men they could sweep away the political dust and see their way clearly past the problems of the day. It didn't always work that way. The trouble with men is that men get hung up on ideas. In the diplomatic world, ideas are about as welcome as a cockroach on a dinner plate.

But the myth of the diplomatic chat endured, and so it was that U.S. Ambassador Raymond Stevens and Soviet Foreign Minister Oleg Bitovich were scheduled to have a diplomatic chat on July 26, 1984, in the ambassador's private residence, Spaso House. Among the issues they would discuss — eighth on a list of nine — was the fate of an American fugitive by the name of Katherine Sears.

"It's a mansion on a quiet downtown street," Cameron told Katherine by telephone the day before the meeting. "They'll have dinner. Some California wine. New England pot roast. The point is, it will be a relaxed atmosphere."

Katherine was alone at the White Dacha headquarters. It was Wednesday, not the usual day for her call, and Sergei was in Moscow. She had walked thirty minutes from Ivanovka just so she could hear these excruciating details of the next day's meeting. Katherine wouldn't normally have been interested in a diplomatic dinner menu, but, this evening, no detail was too small. For his part, Cameron seemed pleased to have such an interested listener. He relished his role as diplomatic insider tossing off tantalizing glimpses of the glittery world of international diplomacy.

"We've absolutely forbidden the ambassador to bring up human rights," Cameron laughed. "It infuriates the Russians, just infuriates them. Anyway, the affair should be a great opportunity to talk about unusual things such as —"

"Such as me."

"I didn't mean it like that."

Katherine smiled. "You're all right, Cameron."

He was an annoying little fellow, but Katherine couldn't help it — he was growing on her.

Cameron went on to say that the meeting would touch on a wide range of issues. The specters of Afghanistan and Iran loomed large, of course. But there would be ample time to give her case its due attention.

"And what if the foreign minister agrees to issue me an exit visa?" asked Katherine.

"Then you'll be in the embassy tomorrow night. You could be back in Ithaca the day after tomorrow."

Katherine took a deep breath. It was impossible not to get her hopes up.

"The meeting should break up at about ten o'clock, and I'll be briefed immediately," said Cameron.

"I'll call you at eleven," Katherine said.

It was settled.

The next day in class, Katherine faced her students feeling like a traitor. She pictured Igor, Yegor, pretty Katya and all the others coming to class on Friday, their homework completed, and waiting with growing concern for a teacher who would not come.

"It's not like her to miss a class," they would say. "Is she sick? Has some tragedy befallen her?"

As far as they would know, their teacher, Yekatarina Yurgina of Riga, would have simply vanished. For their own safety, and hers, Katherine could tell them nothing.

After class, Katherine took a stroll through Bolshevichka. She walked along the river to the swinging bridge and then crossed to the center. She leaned on the wire railing. The muddy water ran swiftly below. The river was smooth and silent, but she could judge its speed by the sticks and bits of grass that rushed by.

She recalled that first day, back in April, when she had crossed the bridge. Patches of snow had clung to the banks. The day had been faintly magical. But today was summer ingenuous. Katherine had never really considered that Russia might have a summer. Such a summer! Clouds drifted in a blue sky the color of an Italian fresco. Sparrows, warblers and a dozen other birds unknown to her sang from branches hidden by the lush greenery. White seed-pods from poplars drifted in the air like summer snow. The Russians called it *pukh*, fluff.

Upstream a group of children plunged into the river. They screamed and splashed each other. She heard a curse below and noticed an old man fishing on the bank. Katherine went on across the bridge and followed the river to the clump of cottages where Galina Tushchina lived. Katherine needed the office key so she could make her late-night phone call.

Galina's hair, which had been grape purple when they first met, was now luminescent copper, roughly the color of a shiny American penny. Galina invited Katherine to stay for tea, and the two women had a pleasant conversation about nothing that Katherine could recall later. Katherine left, checked her watch, and went directly to the bakery. It was three o'clock — an odd hour — and the fresh bread loaves would be coming out of the ovens. She recalled with a smile her first attempt to buy bread from the Bolshevichka bakery three months earlier.

After Katherine bought her loaves, she went outside and stood on the square, saying a silent farewell to Bolshevichka. It really was a fine little village, she decided, even if the hardware store had never been open (you could always borrow a tool from the collective farm); even if queues for sausage stretched an hour and a half (at least you saw your neighbors); even if bread was only available every other hour (it gave you someplace to be, and it was fresh).

Katherine walked toward the river. She crossed the swinging bridge, cut across the beet field stepping carefully from rut to rut so as not to harm the young stalks, and turned north along the single-lane road to Ivanovka where Baba Krista would be waiting.

Baba Krista, of course, knew nothing about Katherine's reasons for being there, or her impending departure. The old woman had merely accepted her new roommate as a grandmother accepted a troubled grandchild.

As Katherine's Russian had improved, she had enjoyed many talks with Baba Krista. The talks were leisurely, peppered with long pauses and unexpected resumption. They were the sort of conversations Katherine could not recall having had in her native language. They talked about the cat, children, what was on sale that week in the shops, why men never help with the house chores, why men shouldn't be allowed to help with the house chores, the perils of vodka, Sergei. They never talked about careers or money. And only once about politics.

On that occasion, Baba Krista had, in passing, referred to the communists as *revolutioniks*, as though they might fade from the scene at any moment. It had struck Katherine as uncharacteristically irreverent, and she had asked Baba Krista about it one afternoon while they were drinking coffee.

"Oh my, dear," said Baba Krista as though she were addressing someone who had just said the world was flat. "The Bolsheviks were newcomers themselves not that long ago. I remember it well. All puffed up and self-important they were, building monuments to themselves." Baba Krista sighed, and her ancient eyes glistened.

"Back then, everyone was calling them the New Russians. Never forget, Yekatarina, someday, they, too, will pass. Then it will be on to the next new thing, and as sure as snow falls in Siberia people will begin all over again talking about the 'New Russians.' Ha!"

Baba Krista took a sip of her coffee, and her eyes grew thoughtful. This was one of those pauses when it seemed that the conversation had ended. Katherine knew better and waited. The old woman went on.

"There is no such thing as New Russia or Old Russia. There's just Russia timeless. Everything else is just a flea on an elephant. He hitches a ride, and then, when the elephant decides to turn, he cries, 'Look at me! I'm controlling the beast!' "

Baba Krista was napping in her armchair when Katherine arrived that afternoon with her loaves of warm bread. Katherine smiled at the sleeping woman and went to her room. She got out *Soviet Latvia* and began to read. The propaganda-laced Russian-language book was the primary source of Katherine's growing vocabulary. She forced herself to read five pages a day, looking up every word. The book, now half-finished, was filled with underlined words and definitions scratched in the margins. Today, however, Katherine had trouble concentrating and put the book down. She lay back on the bed and, as she had done that first night in Ivanovka, fell asleep staring into the Red Corner, at the icon of St. George and the Dragon.

Sergei arrived at nine o'clock. They ate fried potatoes, sausage and black bread and then went outside. Darkness didn't fall until eleven o'clock, so the sky was still light. They took a walk up the grassy street, as they had that first day when Sergei told her the story of Ivanovka's decline and fall.

Sergei said, "I'll think of something to tell Baba Krista and the rest of the town after you've gone."

"Thanks," she said. They were quiet a moment, and then Katherine said, "Maybe you were right. I shouldn't have started teaching."

"No," said Sergei. "They're really going to miss you over there. Maya Timofe-yeva is bragging to anyone who will listen that she has the best English teacher in Russia."

"Really?" said Katherine. "I thought she didn't like me."

Sergei smiled. "She does complain about your unorthodox methods." He shot her a sideways glance. "She is also boasting about how much your Russian has improved."

Katherine laughed. "Now I know you're joking."

Sergei remained serious. "Have you forgotten how it was?"

Katherine realized abruptly that she had. Three months ago, she certainly couldn't have dreamed of teaching a course in English. Nor could she have conversed with him as effortlessly as she was that evening. All along, her impatience with the pace of her progress in Russian had been an impediment to learning. In the last weeks, almost without realizing it, she had slipped into fluency.

"I guess you're right," she marveled.

"You have a real gift for language," he said. "I can't believe you're an astronomer. That trick you do of replaying conversations in your head is spooky."

Katherine smiled and took Sergei's arm. "It's time," she said.

He nodded, and they walked back to the house. They rode in silence to White

Dacha's headquarters, arriving at a few minutes to eleven. Sergei went to the corner, and Katherine sat down behind the desk. She took a deep breath. She was nervous.

"Good luck," said Sergei.

She dialed and Cameron answered.

"Yes, Katherine. I thought that would be you. Well. I'm afraid I have some bad news. The ambassador raised the subject of the Nicaraguan freedom fighters. It was not on the agenda, a kind of sneak attack ordered by the president himself. They spent more than half the evening on that alone. That put them behind schedule. Then the ambassador brought up the refuseniks, which sounded like human rights to the Russians, and well, all hell broke loose. I'm afraid the ambassador never got around to discussing your case."

Katherine couldn't speak. She was numb.

Cameron said, "There is another chat scheduled in six weeks. We'll get you on the agenda, then. I promise."

Katherine's ears had begun to ring, and she could barely hear him. Had he just said, six weeks?

"Six weeks?"

"I'm very sorry," said Cameron.

How could I have let my hopes get so high?

She would have expected to fall apart, but strangely she accepted the news calmly. Her eyes fell on Sergei, and she smiled thinly at him.

"Katherine?" said Cameron. "Are you there?"

"Is there any guarantee this won't happen the next time?" asked Katherine.

"I assure you, I will do everything I can —"

"But there's no guarantee."

"No," said Cameron. "No guarantees."

"Thank you," said Katherine. "At least, now I know what I have to do."

32

O n a hot day in July, Victor Perov stood in a dark corridor before the door of Pavel Danilov, the man he knew as Sigmund. He knocked and when his widow failed to answer his knock, he knocked again. *A second time.* And but for that minuscule act, he would not have found his twin brother. It was enough to drive a person mad! How very differently things would have turned out! Life was revealed to be infinitely interwoven — Katherine Sears, Konstantin Tarasov, Pavel Danilov, the man with the stub nose, Yevgenia, Oksana, Valery, Anton, himself. They were like cables in a suspension bridge, each bearing its share of a great burden. Cut any single cable and the forces in the remaining cables adjusted instantaneously to keep the bridge standing. The bridge stood, yes, but its mathematics were altered all across its span. An engineer with a calculator and several weeks' time could have estimated the changes. But the bridge performed the calculation immediately and precisely, like a gigantic, mechanical computer. And so it was when Victor Perov knocked a second time — the great bridge trembled, and the forces changed. Fate was altered.

Or was it? Could Victor have walked away from the door without having met Pavel Danilov's widow? Perhaps, after all, this was how God manipulated the universe, with levers as small as the least decision of an inconsequential man. In a single moment, Victor's old certainties vanished into a fog of doubt.

Valery Bonderov had another theory — they were "due for a little luck."

Victor Perov had begun that fateful July day in Oksana's cramped south Moscow flat. Victor and Oksana were in the kitchen, sitting on stools, drinking tea from cracked cups and talking about everything but what was on their minds, which was:

It's all up to Valery.

Valery was due any minute from Orel, and he had promised to come directly from the train station. When the door buzzed, they both jumped as though it were a fire alarm. Oksana got up to answer it. Victor followed her up the narrow hall into the foyer. He was filled with dread.

Valery came through the door carrying a sports bag with a broken zipper. His clothes were wrinkled and his hair was uncombed. He looked like someone who had slept in his clothes, which was probably the case.

Valery threw his bag on the floor and shook his head with disgust. "He's not in Orel. I'm . . . I'm sorry. Goddamnit."

Nobody spoke. At last Victor said, "Tell us about it."

Victor only half-listened to Valery's story. Valery had done his job, no better and no worse than he and Oksana had done theirs. What consumed Victor's thoughts was that Orel, the final asylum, had been stricken from the list. At the moment, there *was* no list.

"I was thinking," said Valery. "Danilov might have waited a month before informing Amsterdam about Anton. That means the asylum would be, not on our list, but on the previous month's list."

Victor nodded perfunctorily. That had occurred to him too.

"But how would you get it?" asked Oksana. "Didn't the man at the Dutch embassy say you should never call him?"

"The problem," said Victor, "is not getting a new list. I'm prepared to go to every asylum in the Soviet Union if necessary. The problem is time. Time is the enemy."

For the moment, there was nothing else to say. Oksana announced she was leaving to pick up Grisha from her mother's apartment. For now there was no asylum to rush off to.

"That's Vykhino, right?" Victor asked. Vykhino was a suburb east of Moscow. It reminded Victor of something.

Oksana nodded.

"I'll go with you," he said.

They walked to the subway line and rode the train north for thirty minutes. It was Saturday so it was not crowded, and they sat side by side staring straight ahead. The train rocked them gently. When they reached the city center, they transferred to an eastbound train.

Victor thought about the search. Where had they gone wrong?

The answer was: It could have been anywhere. Anton's asylum might not have been in Danilov's February report. Perhaps, as Valery suggested, it was in the January report. Or the December report. Or perhaps it was in no report at all, as Koos van der Laan had warned that day in the park. Or perhaps it was in the February report after all, and they had simply not been thorough enough in their search. Anton could have died in the asylum. He could be in solitary confinement. He could be imprisoned under an alias.

Or perhaps Anton Perov had died in Afghanistan, after all, just as Yevgenia had said. Perhaps she was right, too, about Victor's motives—he was so desperate to have his brother back that he was prepared to believe anything.

Perhaps. Perhaps. Perhaps.

After another twenty minutes, they neared Elektrozavodsky Station.

"This is my stop," said Victor.

Oksana looked at him curiously. "What's here?"

"Something I've been meaning to do for a long time," said Victor. "I'll tell you tonight."

He got off and watched the subway train speed away into the tunnel. It grew quiet on the platform, and he got out his wallet. He found a scrap of paper. It said:

> *Maria Danilova*
> *15/3 Little Decembrist Street*
> *Apt. 77*

Pavel's widow. This was the vow he had made to Koos van der Laan that day in the park.

> *"You'll pass my information along to her?" Victor had asked.*
> *"Absolutely not," said Koos.*
> *"Doesn't she have a right to know her husband wasn't drunk?" asked Victor.*
> *"Of course. But it's not my place to tell her. You tell her."*
> *"Maybe I will."*

F o r weeks, Victor had intended to visit Maria and her young daughter. But he had procrastinated. He had lots of excuses. It was far from the center. It was a bad neighborhood. He was busy with his search. But the truth was, he hadn't known what to say to her. Now, he thought perhaps he did.

The Elektrozavodsky region was one of the Russian capital's worst districts. Muscovites called it "proletarian," which had once meant righteous but was now a disparagement. Muscovites had become snobs, and Victor supposed he, too, was a snob. But what human being would choose freely to live in such an antiparadise? Factories and people existed side by side in a way that appraised human beings only as components of factories. A scientist by nature, Victor easily imagined the mathematics of the Kremlin's Great Planner:

Car Factory + Food + Water + People → Cars + More Food + More Water + More People

The machine was regenerative. Hail the socialist miracle!

For the living components of the socialist miracle, Elektrozavodsk was an urban ghetto of a peculiarly Soviet sort. There was no starvation, no homelessness, no drugs, no gangs, no prostitution, little random crime. Children went to school and learned to read. It would indeed have been paradise on earth but for the squalor. And the desperation.

The region was a veritable jungle of unsound buildings, aboveground pipes, rusty playground equipment, old cars and exhaust-spewing trucks. The people Victor passed on the street were all dressed poorly. They appeared to be less healthy than the average Muscovite but still more healthy than the average Russian. Though it was early afternoon, Victor saw at least a dozen people staggering under the effects of alcohol. Poplar *pukh* lay over everything.

Victor asked directions three times, trying to locate Danilova's building. At last, he found it and went inside. It reeked of decaying garbage. He climbed the chipped, concrete stairs three flights and crossed a dim corridor until he stood before a wooden door marked "77."

Victor knocked and waited. His mind wandered to that night on the wharf — the ambulance racing toward him, the vehicle sailing silently off the side of the wharf, the splash, the icy cold of the water when he jumped in, and Pavel Danilov, husband and father, sinking down into the cold, black Moscow River, a bullet in his head . . .

No one answered the door. He raised his fist and knocked again.

A petite woman with bleached hair and a round, attractive face pulled open the door. She wore a threadbare robe and fuzzy pink slippers. She contemplated Victor Perov with wary brown eyes.

"Maria Danilova?" Victor asked.

"Yes?" she asked, slightly out of breath. She arranged her robe and fastened it with a sash.

"My name is Victor Perov."

Her eyes narrowed.

"I spoke with your husband —"

"I know who you are," she said coldly. "What do you want?"

"To talk."

"I don't want to talk to you."

"I will only be a minute."

"This apartment is being watched by the KGB," she said.

"So am I."

She glared at him. "My daughter is in the bath. I'm surprised I heard you knock at all."

"I can wait."

"No." She started to close the door.

Victor whispered through the gap, "Your husband was murdered."

The door stopped. Her one eye peered at him.

"What did you say?" she asked.

"Don't make me talk about this in the corridor," Victor said. "May I come in?"

She looked over his shoulder, her face stolid, then opened the door just wide enough for Victor to turn his body and slip through.

It was a small apartment, nearly identical to the one Oksana had in south Moscow. Every inch of wall space had been converted to shelving, which was crammed with books. The effect was of a cozy reading room in a library.

"Thank you very—"

"You're in," she snapped. "Now, tell me what you just said."

"Pavel was murdered."

"How do you know this?" she demanded.

"I was there."

"No one was there."

"I was. We were supposed to meet that night at Rechnoy Vokzal. I tried to pull him out of the ambulance before it sank. But he was already dead. He had been shot."

She looked at him with a blank expression he could not read.

A child's cry rose from the bathroom.

"Excuse me," she said. "Have a seat. I'll be right with you."

She hurried out. Victor went into the living room. Hundreds of books rose from floor to ceiling. Half were medical books, most related to psychology. Victor spotted *Forensic Psychology*, the same text he had read before he began his search for Anton. The rest of the library was a hodgepodge of literature, science, the complete works of Marx and Engels, and a dozen novels in English. Victor was still browsing when Maria came into the room.

Maria said, "She'll play alone in the bath a while. I don't want to talk about this in front of her."

"Of course."

Maria sat down on the sofa. She lit a cigarette and turned her head to exhale. "They told me he was drunk. Pavel didn't drink."

Victor nodded. "How did you know about me?"

"The KGB," she said. "One of the fuckers told me that the son of a 'higher-up' —you—was involved, so if I didn't want my daughter to grow up in an orphanage I had better stop asking questions and start answering a few. So I told the son-of-a-bitch everything. What do I care?"

So, after all, it had been Maria who had given the KGB Koos van der Laan's phone number and code name. Koos had been wrong in the park when he speculated that Konstantin Tarasov had gotten the information from Katherine Sears under interrogation. That meant Tarasov had been exactly what he said he was that day in Victor's office: a KGB detective looking for an ally in Victor Perov.

Victor told Maria Danilova everything he knew about the death of her husband. When he finished, Maria said, "So you're saying Pavel was murdered to prevent him from telling you where your brother is?"

"Yes."

She glanced anxiously toward the cupboard. She seemed to be thinking about something when a large splash came from the direction of the bathroom. Her daughter laughed.

Victor nodded toward the bathroom door. "What's her name?"

"Julia," Maria said. "She still asks for him. 'Where's Daddy? When's Daddy coming home?'"

She shook her head and smoked her cigarette. "Bastards."

"Is there anything I can do for you?"

"Can you bring Pavel back?"

"No."

"Then what can you do?"

"I don't know."

"Soviet Psychiatry Watch gave me some money," she said. "Some Dutchman met me in a park and gave me a little envelope with some money. I lost my husband so I guess that means I have some money coming to me. I took it for my daughter's sake. I don't need money. I need my husband."

Victor watched her for a while and then said, "I'm going to carry on his work."

"You?" she scoffed.

"Somebody has to."

"Why you?"

"That's the trap, isn't it?" asked Victor.

She shrugged. "Suit yourself. Throw away your life. You won't change a thing."

"Pavel did," said Victor. "Thanks to him, I know my brother is alive."

"You found him yet?"

"No."

"So what's changed?" Her eyes darted toward the cupboard again. She seemed troubled.

Victor asked, "Why did Pavel work with the SPW?"

Maria snorted and sat back in the sofa. "I don't think Pavel knew. At first, I think it was only because he could, or because he was a Jew and couldn't get into medical school. It might even have been because his father was a Stalinist, and he wanted to hurt him."

"I wish I could have met him. He sounds a little like my brother. Anton is a father, too, you know. He has a three-year-old boy, Grisha. He doesn't remember Anton. Sometimes he gets confused, and he thinks I'm his father."

"Why is that?"

Suddenly, Victor needed Maria to understand. Her predicament was so similar to Oksana's that he found himself explaining more than he had intended. "His mother and I had an affair."

Maria blew smoke out her nose and stared at him.

Victor went on. "It was after they told us Anton was killed in Afghanistan. The grief was unbearable. I didn't know anything could hurt so much. We shared our pain, and then one day our grief turned to love. Or at least I thought it was love. Now I see it was just more grief, but in a new form."

"What about the woman?"

"Oksana? I'm not sure," Victor said. "She must have known what we had wasn't really love. But she's very practical. It's difficult to raise a child alone."

Maria nodded.

"It may have been nothing more than gratitude and a certain fondness. I think women are just naturally more practical than men."

"Not women," said Maria. "Mothers."

Maria snubbed out her cigarette and got to her feet. She went to the cupboard behind Victor and found a shoe box. She sorted through some papers until she found an envelope. She dropped it in Victor's lap.

"I got it about a month ago," she said.

Victor looked at it. It was addressed to Pavel Danilov. The postmark was Perm, in the Urals. It was already open.

"What is it?" Victor asked.

"It's about your brother," she said.

A half-hour later, Victor Perov stood at a taksifon not far from Maria's apartment. He spoke to Oksana, who was still at her mother's in Vykhino. Something in Victor's voice must have alarmed Oksana. "Victor, what's wrong?" she asked.

"I have a letter from Anton!" he cried into the cracked mouthpiece.

"What are you talking about?"

"We didn't find him," Victor said. "But he found us! Oh, Oksana! God knows how he did it, but he found us! Anton's alive, and I know where he is!"

33

B u t their elation was extinguished as quickly as a match struck in a strong wind. The contents of the letter pretty much guaranteed that.

Dear Pavel Danilov,

I am writing to ask for your help.

My name is Anton Borisovich Perov. I am at present Inmate 222 at Little Rock Special Psychiatric Hospital. I have been here since November 12, 1983, when I was arrested for attempting an illegal border crossing into Norway. At the time, I was a deserter fleeing my regiment in Afghanistan. I was being falsely accused of killing a fellow soldier, and when I realized they intended to have me executed I fled.

The circumstances of my arrest may have some bearing on my case, and, therefore, I will relate them to you.

On November 9, 1983, I was on the Kolsky Peninsula near Norway. I was making a survey of the border fortifications in advance of my escape attempt the next day. By chance I saw a man gunned down as he fled across the forbidden zone. I escaped back into the forest on the Soviet side, but somehow the KGB found me, and I was arrested the next day. Two days after that, I was sent to Little Rock and put under the care of Dr. Lazda. I never had a trial or a commitment hearing.

My life here is a daily nightmare. My first month, I was interrogated every day under the influence of sodium Amytal. That was only the beginning. After that, the treatments began in earnest. For three months, I was given large doses of insulin that gave me seizures and left me in shock. I awoke from these seizures with severe memory loss. I would recover my memory as time passed, but never completely. Parts of my body fall numb from time to time and remain that way for weeks.

After three months, I don't know why, they changed my treatment and started me on aminophenomyl three times a day. It makes me so lethargic. I find it hard to concentrate. It is so painful to the muscles where they give the injection that I can't sit or lie down for hours afterward. Though I am tired all the time, I stay awake at night because, in my drug regimen, that is the only time when I have full use of my faculties. It is at such an hour, with the asylum asleep, that I write this letter begging your aid.

I do not believe that I can live much longer under these conditions. The only thing that keeps me from taking my own life is the hope of seeing my wife and son again. I ask you to get word to Western agencies, to ask them to publish the details of my plight. Perhaps Western pressure can protect me in ways our own laws have failed to.

Do not inform my family about my conditions. I have my reasons for this, and I ask you to respect them. If I die in here, then let them think I died in Afghanistan, as Dr. Lazda assures me they have been told.

I am sorry to lay this burden on you. But I do not know where else to turn.
Sincerely,
Anton Borisovich Perov

The letter was dated April 10, 1984.

Almost three months ago.

"Do we go to Yevgenia, now?" asked Oksana that evening at Victor's apartment.

"No," said Victor. "I have to see him first. It's the only way. I'm going to Perm tonight."

"I'm going with you."

T h e r e were no seats on the eastbound night train from Moscow's Kazan Station, so Victor bribed a conductor. Oksana slept in the conductor's cabin, while Victor was put in a compartment with three steelworkers who drank vodka and ate smoked fish all night.

They arrived in Perm at noon, carrying two large backpacks and Victor's telescope. They hailed a taxi and paid the driver handsomely to take them to the asylum. Victor's money had run out weeks ago, and he was now living off money from the sale of household goods to black market vendors Valery knew. So far, Victor had sold a full set of Czechoslovakian china, a Polish crystal bowl, and two oil paintings by the celebrated impressionist Sergei Fuzin. The items were all Yevgenia's, and there would be hell to pay when she discovered them missing.

The taxi driver took them east out of Perm into the countryside. After a half-hour, the land began to rise, and the road narrowed. They were moving into the Urals. The air grew cooler as their altitude rose. At last, the car came over a rise, and the driver pointed into a valley.

"There it is," he said.

Little Rock.

"Stop the car," said Victor.

They got out and Victor surveyed the scene. Little Rock Special Psychiatric Hospital was nestled in a shallow depression in the hills. A cement-and-barbed-wire wall enclosed five barracks, a guard tower and several other smaller buildings. It was just as Gennady Obolensky had described that night in Oksana's apartment.

"Where do the workers live?" Victor asked the driver.

"There's a village about a mile east of here."

"What's it called?"

The driver shrugged. "I don't think it has a name. We call it the 'village near Little Rock.' "

The road ahead wound another mile to the asylum's front gate and then around the compound. It disappeared over a hill in the distance. To the east, along the road to the asylum, a lonely hill rose to a rocky outcrop.

"Take us there," Victor said pointing.

"Bald Top," said the driver, and they got back in the car.

They reached the base of Bald Top, and the driver pulled onto the grassy shoulder. Victor paid the fare plus a generous tip. They stood on the roadside with their backpacks and telescope as the taxi did a U-turn, spun its wheels in the gravel and sped away. It got very quiet. Wind howled through the valley like air blown into a soda bottle.

Victor and Oksana hiked for an hour to the summit of Bald Top. Then Victor crawled to the edge of the cliff and peered down. About a quarter-mile away stood Little Rock.

After they put up the tent, Victor assembled the telescope. He positioned it behind a boulder, which provided natural cover. The tent was far enough back on the summit that it would be invisible from the asylum. They had chosen a perfect observation point.

An hour later, and just twenty-four hours after Maria Danilova had pulled Anton's letter from a shoe box, Victor was peering through his telescope at the exercise yard of Little Rock Special Psychiatric Hospital.

The days passed like a long, miserable road trip. The first night, the temperature dropped to forty-six degrees. It was even colder the second night. On the third day it began to rain. It continued to rain, day after day, without pause. After a while, everything was so soaked it seemed that the rain was rising out of the ground. They could get neither warm nor dry. When they weren't taking their turn behind the telescope they were huddled in their sleeping bags. Oksana shivered so badly sometimes that she had trouble keeping her eye over the eyepiece. She never complained, and Victor was too fearful of the lioness to suggest he relieve her before her shift was over.

They used heat tablets to boil water for coffee, since they didn't dare build a fire. They ate like mice, nibbling on a slab of cheese roughly the size of a cement block. They also had a dozen sausages that Victor sliced with a pocket knife. On the back slope of Bald Top, Oksana had found mushrooms and dewberries, which, along with six loaves of bread and the water Victor brought from a stream two miles away, completed their diet.

The asylum's regimen revealed itself early along. Prisoners were brought out in shifts to one of two yards bounded by the wards themselves. First came A ward, then B ward, V ward, G ward, D ward, and so on, according to the Russian alphabet.

The first day, the inmates were outside for half-hour shifts. Anton was not among them. After that, the shifts were cut to fifteen minutes because of the rain. Again, Anton was not to be found. The rain kept up, and soon it was their new enemy.

On the last night of the first week, Victor lay in the dark tent in his damp clothes in a damp sleeping bag listening to the hiss of rain on the canvas. He was just wondering if Oksana was awake when she blurted out, "Perhaps he was moved."

They both understood what she was really saying: Anton was dead.

"How the hell would we know?" Victor snapped. "This goddamn rain —"

"Victor!"

And so began the second week.

On the tenth day, the rain stopped. Victor awoke with excitement and threw open the flap of the tent. He peered out, groaned and fell back inside. Thick fog lay over everything. Victor didn't even bother to set up the telescope that day, or the next day when the fog persisted. They stayed in the tent most of those two days, finishing up the sausage and bread.

The twelfth day broke sunny. Victor and Oksana scrambled out of the tent and went to work. Victor went to fetch water while Oksana prepared a breakfast of cheese, mushrooms and coffee.

She handed Victor a metal cup. "That's the last of the coffee."

"If he's here, they'll bring him out today," said Victor. "This is the first decent weather in ten days."

B ward came into the yard through the east door at exactly 11:25 A.M. Bent over and looking through his eyepiece, Victor could make out puddles in the yard, footprints of the inmates, and even the muzzle of the gun in the guard tower. Visibility was excellent. The inmates filed out in a line and then scattered. They reassembled in small groups. There were several men in wheelchairs. They were a motley bunch, full of twitches, tumors, disturbed expressions, pocked complexions and bad teeth — at least as bad as Victor had seen in Leningrad.

With Oksana beside him, Victor scanned the faces in group after group in the yard. It took fifteen minutes. Nothing. But since the day was sunny, the men remained in the yard. Victor used the extra time to go back over all the faces. He was moving from one group to another in the yard when his tunnel vision fell briefly on a middle-aged man in a wheelchair. Something about the man made Victor pause. The man's hair had been shaved off like all the prisoners'. He had a dull stare, and his head was tipped strangely to one side as though its weight was too great a burden for his feeble neck. Victor frowned and looked at the face. For nearly a minute, he squinted into the eyepiece. Then a cold chill crawled up his spine. He gasped and lifted his eye from the viewer.

"What's wrong?" Oksana asked.

He didn't speak. He just stood there. She pushed him aside and peered into the viewer.

"It's just a . . ." she began, and then grew quiet.

Victor stood numbly beside her for two minutes while she looked. Then she stepped back from the eyepiece and turned her face toward Victor. Tears streamed down her cheeks.

"No!" she cried, and threw herself at him. He put his arms around her. She struggled like an animal in his grasp.

"Who did this?" she cried and beat her fists on his chest. "Who did this? Who? Who?"

At last, exhausted, she collapsed. He held her close while she sobbed. Victor looked over Oksana's shoulder, down at the distant asylum. He made himself a promise.

I will find out who did this. And when I do, I will make him pay. By god, he will pay.

part iv

The Little
Peasant Girl

34

I t took Katherine Sears four months and six days to confront her memories of that night at the KGB safe house.

That was still a lot sooner than she would have liked.

All during those slow summer months in Ivanovka, Katherine was haunted by half-images and scraps of dialogue from that night. They flashed before her eyes like a strobe light, and left her trembling and disoriented. Almost anything could trigger an episode — a word from a student, the sight of a distant forest line at night, even the smell of a Soviet space heater. She felt like one of those Army veterans who dove for cover whenever a car backfired. A particularly bad flashback had come during a lecture, and she was forced to sit down while Igor rushed to get a glass of water. Instead of fading with time, the flashbacks were becoming clearer and more frequent. The reason was obvious — and terrifyingly unavoidable: As her knowledge of Russian grew, she was capable of understanding more and more of what had transpired that night. The memory was like a cut weed that kept coming back stronger because the root was intact and growing far underground. Her photographic memory, which she had always claimed as a gift, had become a curse.

Still, until that afternoon in late July when Sergei uttered the word that broke down her defenses, Katherine had managed to keep buried the memories of her ordeal — and with them the terrible truth about who was behind Anton Perov's imprisonment. But with that single word from Sergei, she could resist no longer. It was as though a door opened, a magic door that could only be unlocked with the magic word.

The word was *zhelezo*.

It meant "iron."

I t was August 29, a month after the diplomatic fiasco between the American ambassador and the Soviet foreign minister. For Katherine, the month had passed in a lazy succession of sunny days and peaceful, cricket-chirping nights. Katherine lived by the natural rhythm of Bolshevichka: never hurried, never idle. During her days, Katherine taught English and attended her Russian classes. In the evenings, she prepared her lectures, did her homework and read *Soviet Latvia*, which she was using to build her vocabulary as well as to learn enough to maintain her cover as a Polish Latvian. Occasionally, she visited with friends, spending long evenings around a table of tea, cookies and sliced cucumber. Bit by bit, Bolshevichka came to life for Katherine, filling up with brave struggles and petty intrigues, courageous hopes and drunken desperation. At times, it seemed to Katherine that Bolshevichka life was more rural than Russian. At other times, as when someone would talk offhandedly about losing a family member to famine or Stalinist repressions, she was reminded of just what a stranger she was. She couldn't figure out if Russians valued life less than Americans, or if they simply accepted suffering in a way Katherine never could.

So came the day at the end of August when Sergei and Katherine made a special trip to White Dacha. It was Wednesday, and Katherine was expecting news from her father about his last-ditch effort to force action from the State Department. She had expected to be connected immediately with her father, but Cameron Abbott had some surprising news.

"Victor called," he announced. "He found Anton."

Katherine closed her eyes and whispered, "Thank god."

Cameron went on for several minutes. Anton was in a place called Little Rock Special Psychiatric Hospital. Victor had bribed an orderly to stop the treatments and then gone to his mother, Yevgenia, who was using her considerable influence to get Anton transferred. From the orderly, Victor was already getting rave reports on Anton's improving condition. Deadened nerves were healing, memory was returning. Anton no longer needed the wheelchair. Victor hadn't seen Anton yet, but he hoped it would only be a few more weeks until Yevgenia could work that out.

"He said to say 'thank you,' " Cameron said.

Katherine recalled all that she had read in Ithaca about special psychiatric hospitals. She shuddered.

"So it has not been for nothing," she said.

"Victor also said to remind you he's always ready to discuss poetry with Anna Akhmatova on the ascension of Magellan," said Cameron, adding, "whatever that means."

Katherine smiled. "Let me speak to Dad."

Her father came on the phone. "Katherine?"

"Hi, Dad."

"How are you, Kat-Kat?"

"I'm fine. So, what did they say in Washington?"

Jack groaned. "Washington — the place is a nest of rattlesnakes."

"It's all right, Dad. It's not your fault."

"You've been put on the agenda for the ambassador's chat in two weeks."

"I understand. Listen, Dad, I have a favor to ask."

"Yes?"

"It's a big favor, and I want you to promise me you'll do it."

"What is it?" he asked suspiciously.

"Promise."

"Okay. Okay. I promise."

"Go home."

"Home?" he exclaimed. "No!"

"Please, Dad."

Time was running out. Katherine could feel her enemies closing in. As time passed, she came to truly appreciate just how many different ways she could be tripped up. Someone could recognize her face from the newspaper, the phone line could be bugged, her repeated calls from White Dacha could arouse suspicion, her link to Sergei's taxi park — anything could spell the end.

"I can't leave you alone."

"I'm not alone."

"You're not trusting these people?" he exclaimed. "I told you —"

"*Ya znayu to, chto ty skazal*," Katherine snapped. *I know what you told me.*

"Katherine?" Jack said, confused. "What the hell . . ."

She went on in Russian. "I've learned a few things since I've been here, Dad. I haven't forgotten your sermons, but they can't save me now."

Jack Sears was quiet a moment. "You speak Russian like a peasant," he said in scholarly Russian.

"Promise me you'll go home."

"All right," he said resignedly.

Katherine returned to English. "Thank you."

"For what?" he asked miserably.

"I love you, Dad."

"I love you, Kat."

I n the car on the way back to Ivanovka, Sergei bubbled with nervous excitement. "So, it's set. There's no turning back."

Katherine shook her head, unable to share his enthusiasm. She was worried about her father; she had never heard Jack Sears sound so beaten as he had on the telephone.

"Don't go soft on me now, Yekatarina," Sergei teased. "This was your idea, after all. Where's my *zheleznaya amerikanka?*"

Katherine froze. Sergei had just called her his "Iron American." Iron. *Zhelezo*. The word ricocheted in her head.

Zhelezo. Zhelezo. Zhelezo.

A door burst open and memories poured through. Katherine felt sick.

Sergei looked at her and said, "Yekatarina. Are you all right? Yekatarina . . ."

Z h e l e z o can go to my prick!" said the big guard. "The *amerikanka* doesn't speak Russian. What difference does it make?"

"We must stick to the prescribed precautions," said the doctor. "No slipups."

They were in the cabin. Katherine was in a chair with a hood over her head. Her hands were tied behind her back. The Tatar had left ten minutes earlier to intercept Sigmund. Katherine had the impression, even without knowing the language, that he had left on the orders of a fourth person: The leader, the one who whispered, the one they called Zhelezo. Katherine had heard him come into the cabin an hour before, and she had felt the tension in the room rise. Zhelezo was particularly interested in what Katherine had told Victor. Then Zhelezo was gone, leaving Katherine alone with the doctor and the big guard.

"This is Zhelezo's operation," said the doctor.

Zhelezo, again.

No, Katherine's memory was tricking her. The doctor hadn't said *zhelezo*. He had said *zhelezy*. The last letter had changed to "y." Why?

The flashback went on.

"Whore," cursed the guard.

Now they were outside, walking along the path, dodging slushy puddles. Katherine was in the lead . . .

Marching to my grave.

She looked up at the stars. Her eye searched instinctively for the Large Magellanic Cloud. But it was invisible below the horizon.

In a few minutes, I'll be dead.

The big guard poked his shotgun into her back, and she almost fell.

"I wonder if she-foreigners are any different," he said ponderously.

The doctor was quiet a few seconds and said, "Forget it."

"She's built nice."

"Yes," agreed the doctor. "But what if Zhelezo finds out?"

"How would we get caught?" asked the guard.

"I don't know . . ."

"Listen. It's simple. We have some fun, and then we do the job. Who's the wiser? Who's going to tell Zhelezye?"

Here was a *third* pronunciation of *zhelezo*. This time, the guard added a "ye" to the end. Why? It didn't make sense.

And then Katherine knew. In the Russian language, word endings mutate depending upon the position of a noun in the sentence, the way, in English, an

"M" is added to the word "who" in the interrogatory form "to whom." In Russian, the grammar is far more complicated, with six possible singular endings for each noun. The endings depend not only on the position of the word in the sentence, *but also on its gender*. *Zhelezo* was a genderless word, yet the endings the two men had been using were feminine. That's when Katherine understood. The doctor and the guard had unwittingly, with the instinct of native speakers, assigned a gender to *zhelezo*. The endings they had used — "y" in one case, "ye" in another — were feminine. Only now, after three months of Russian grammar at the Bolshevichka institute, did Katherine know enough to explain the mutating word, *zhelezo*: Zhelezo was a woman.

"Yekatarina?" Sergei was saying in the car. "Yekatarina?"

But Katherine did not answer. She was back in Ithaca, two years earlier, reading Victor's letter advising her to go home for Christmas.

"I know about exacting parents," he wrote, "my own mother is known as the Iron Perova."

Iron.

Zhelezo.

Katherine gasped. "My god. I know who was in the cabin that night."

"What are you talking—"

"I've got to warn Victor," she said. "Turn the car around!"

"I don't understand."

"Please. Now!"

Sergei shrugged and hit the brakes.

They sped back to the collective, and a few minutes later, Katherine was back on the phone with Cameron.

"I've got to speak to Victor," Katherine said.

Cameron was groggy. "What? What's happened?"

"It's urgent."

"I don't know how to contact him," Cameron said irritated. "He calls *me*, remember?"

"He never left a phone number?"

"What am I, the Yellow Pages? I thought you said it was too dangerous for you two to meet. What's going on?"

"I . . . I don't think I should say. It's . . ." She was having trouble organizing her thoughts. Her mind leaped from memory to memory like a barefoot man on hot pavement — the sound of Zhelezo whispering, the feel of the shotgun in her back as the men calmly discussed raping her, the big guard lying on the floor with his chest blown open . . .

"What?" Cameron asked impatiently.

"I have to speak with him in person."

"Tell him at your next meeting, *Anna Akhmatova*."

Katherine thought a moment. "But the next ascension is over three weeks away!"

"Is it so urgent?"

"I'm not sure," she said, and she wasn't. After all, Victor had told Cameron that everything was all right. But what if Yevgenia had gotten to the orderly? What if the reports Victor was receiving from him were bogus? What if Anton's treatments were continuing? They could even be accelerated . . .

Katherine said, "If Victor calls, tell him . . ."

Tell him what? To meet was a risk. To not meet might be a bigger risk. To wait three weeks might make the decision irrelevant.

She made up her mind. She would have to trust that her news could wait three weeks. After all, it had waited this long.

"Tell him Anna Akhmatova is anxiously looking forward to discussing poetry next month."

35

Tell him Anna Akhmatova is anxiously looking forward to discussing poetry next month.

General Yuri Belov hit STOP on the recorder and looked up at Anatoly Podolok. "That's it, comrade secretary."

"And the Americans don't know we've tapped this line?"

Belov shook his head. "They think it's still secure. We had agents examine over twenty thousand phone lines before we found this one. It was an unprecedented search."

"Did you get a trace?"

"Partial. The call originated in the Yaroslavl Oblast."

"A pretty wide area. It would take weeks to find her."

"Four, I figure. Of course, we might get lucky."

"Only if our luck changes," Podolok said morosely. He took a drag off his cigarillo and leaned back in his desk chair. "Double the agents on the case. Cut the search time to two weeks."

Belov nodded. "What are we going to do with her when we find her, comrade secretary? The Americans will know we have her."

Podolok blew smoke up into the room. "She will resist arrest. When she does, an unfortunate accident will befall her."

On the third floor of Lubyanka, Leo Yakunin made his report to KGB Director Oleg Shatalin.

"Yaroslavl Oblast, huh?" said Shatalin. "The second Belov gets his hands on her I want to know about it. With Konstantin Tarasov dead, Katherine Sears is the only person who can tie together General Yuri Belov, Anatoly Podolok and the Iron Perova. I have to talk to that woman before Belov does something to shut her mouth — permanently."

36

Katherine knew something was wrong the moment the stranger came into the classroom. By then it was too late to run.

It was a week after Katherine's last talk with her father. In that time, the last pieces of her escape plan had begun fitting into place. She had already received her counterfeit internal passport and international passport. Two items remained to be gathered—the exit visa from the U.S.S.R., and the entry visa to Finland. Sergei had learned that the entry visa was a simple matter of applying to the Finnish Embassy. But first, she would need an exit visa, and Sergei had spent the last week combing the darkest recesses of the black market looking for a source. He was not optimistic.

"For a Soviet citizen like Yekatarina Yurgina to leave the U.S.S.R. you must possess a chain of paperwork a kilometer long," said Sergei, who had spent weeks investigating the procedure. "I never knew what prisoners we all were until now. You can't get an entry visa to a foreign country without an exit visa from the U.S.S.R. You can't get an exit visa without an international passport. You can't get an international passport without an internal passport. You can't get an internal passport without a letter from your employer. And you can't get a ticket on a ship without all of that. And every step of the way, there are queues leading to locked offices, corrupt bureaucrats, contradicting rules . . . ach!"

The morning the stranger came to class had begun as usual. She arrived at the institute at eleven o'clock for her Russian class. Her own English I class was at one o'clock, so she had passed the free hour rehearsing her meeting with Victor in two weeks' time in the bell tower in Zagorsk. How would he react to her news that Yevgenia Perova, his own mother, was the voice in the cabin that night, that she had ordered the execution of Pavel Danilov, the incarceration of Anton and, presumably, Katherine's own death?

Katherine was at the front of her class when the door opened and Maya Timofeyeva and the stranger came through. The stranger was about forty years old, bald, wearing a gray polyester suit like all middle-level Moscow bureaucrats. He looked exceedingly serious. Her heart sank.

"Excuse me for invading your class," said Maya. "But someone has come all the way from Moscow to make an important announcement."

Katherine stepped aside to make room for the stranger. She rolled a piece of chalk nervously between her fingers.

The man cleared his throat. "Comrades. I have indeed come all the way from Moscow." He turned to Katherine. "I have come to meet *you*, Yekatarina Yurgina."

The chalk broke in Katherine's hand.

"I am the All-U.S.S.R. director for adult continuing-education schools. I have just seen the scores for the proficiency exams in English I. This class got the highest average score of any class in the entire Soviet Union. Three of the top ten scores came out of this class. For such an extraordinary achievement I felt I should come up and give the news in person. Congratulations."

The class was applauding. Maya was applauding. Katherine saw that the man had put out his hand. She raised her hand numbly toward him. He gripped it and shook enthusiastically.

She was only half-listening as he went on to describe the honor she had won — the chance to represent Soviet teachers of English at an international teaching conference.

Later that evening, when she told Sergei the news, he let out a whoop that surprised her.

"What?" she asked.

He was grinning. "Don't you see?"

She shook her head.

"The conference is in East Berlin!"

"Yes . . ."

"Germany!"

Then it hit her. "My god."

He laughed. "That's right. You've got your exit visa."

T h a t night Katherine and Sergei sat at the kitchen table drinking coffee and going over the details of her departure.

It was perfect. She would hunker down four more months and then leave the country as an honored Soviet teacher. Once in Berlin, she would simply go to the American consulate and declare her true citizenship. The next day, Katherine would tell Maya Timofeyeva she needed the exit visa early; Sergei insisted she get the paperwork in hand as early as possible.

Katherine sipped her coffee. The coffee's bitterness heightened her senses, and she found herself thinking about Sergei. The last weeks had taken a toll on her friend and savior. Gone was the sparkle in Sergei's eyes that had made her trust him that first day at the train station. The man was exhausted.

And no wonder! His wife was staying at his dacha south of Moscow, so he was traveling hundreds of miles each day from his apartment in Moscow, to Ivanovka, to his dacha, to various ministries and embassies in Moscow, and then back to Ivanovka. Somewhere in this schedule, he managed to work a few hours at the taxi park at Paveletsky Station.

"Thank you," she said.

"For what?"

"For everything."

"Oh." He smiled thinly. "My pleasure."

"Someday, I'll pay you back," said Katherine, but the words sounded hollow.

There was a knock on the cabin's front door.

Katherine and Sergei exchanged anxious glances.

"Who would be calling at this time of night?" Katherine asked. It was nearly midnight.

"You stay here," said Sergei and got up. She heard him open the door and then speak a moment with someone. He came back into the room looking shaken.

"What's wrong?" she asked anxiously. "Who's there?"

"I think you had better go to the door," he said.

Her heart pounding, she got out of her chair and went up the narrow hall. On the stoop was Maya Timofeyeva and four other teachers from the institute.

"Maya Grigorevna?" Katherine said.

"May we talk to you, Yekatarina?"

"Of course. Please, come in."

"No," said Maya, waving her hand. "It's late and we can talk more on Monday. We're just so excited we wanted to come over immediately."

Katherine held on to the door for support. "What is it?"

"We've talked it over among ourselves, and I talked to the directors in Moscow, and I know we're just a small institute for farmers, and Bolshevichka is not much of a village compared to a big city like Riga, but, well, we would be honored if you would consider joining our collective as a permanent member."

For the citizens of Bolshevichka, there was no greater honor. Katherine gaped at them as her eyes filled up with tears of gratitude.

She couldn't think of a thing to say.

T h e following week passed in a blur of paperwork. A bottle of Georgian cognac convinced a man at the Foreign Ministry to put his stamp on the visa despite Katherine's absence. A carton of American cigarettes convinced a man at the Education Ministry that Yekatarina Yurgina, though not a certified teacher, was entitled to represent the U.S.S.R. at the conference. No bribe could expedite the

KGB, which had to certify that Yekatarina Yurgina's departure from the Soviet Union posed no threat to national security. That line went for three days.

At last, Wednesday arrived — the day before Katherine was to see Victor in the bell tower. She awoke refreshed and went to the kitchen for her usual large breakfast of potatoes, sausage and coffee with Sergei and Baba Krista.

When they finished, Sergei offered Katherine a ride to Bolshevichka. He was on his way to Moscow that morning to see a diplomat in the Finnish embassy.

"No thanks," she said. "I feel like walking."

She left a few minutes later, stepping out onto the creaky floorboards of Baba Krista's front porch. The door slammed shut behind her, and she looked into the sky for clues about the weather. Cotton ball clouds dotted a pale sky. A breeze played with her hair and carried a smell that said "summer" but whispered "autumn." There wouldn't be too many more days like this one. Not this year.

She decided to walk along the river bank to the institute. It would take a little longer, but it was a beautiful day. She crossed the beet field to the line of trees that marked the river and then disappeared into the narrow band of foliage that hugged the river on either side. A dirt trail maintained only by the passing feet of fishermen and swimmers wove through the poplars, birches and scrubby pines, up and down the bank, two miles to Bolshevichka.

She felt good as she started along the trail. Her departure was all but certain. Four months of easy living in Ivanovka was all that stood between her and freedom.

She made her way along the bank, past the swinging bridge, toward the institute. The poplars closed in around her as the trail climbed up to the road. She had just stepped out of the trees when she froze. Two police cars idled in the parking lot. She took a step back into the cover of the trees and peered up through the branches. A black Volga was parked beside the police cars. Her heart raced.

It couldn't be! Not now! Not when she was so close!

A strange man came through the front door. He glanced at his watch and looked up and down the road. He looked straight ahead, and his gaze fell on the foliage around her. She stopped breathing. He looked at his watch again and went back inside. She exhaled.

She took a few more steps backward, keeping the trees between her and the institute. A twig snapped under her foot, and she almost screamed. The institute disappeared into the foliage. She stood there a second, the river gurgling beside her. A crow cawed in the distance.

Her documents. She had to have her documents. They were in her room, stuffed between the pages of *Soviet Latvia*. She turned and walked swiftly along the bank. She began to jog, and then to run. How did they find her? Her phone calls to Cameron — they must have traced the line. Sergei had warned her about that.

How much time did she have? She calculated. The men would wait a while at the institute, maybe a half-hour, then they would realize their ambush had failed, and they would go in search of her.

She stayed on the river bank, using the trees for cover. When she reached the clearing where the swinging bridge crossed over, she stopped and peered up the arc of the bridge. No one. She sprinted for the trees on the other side and kept on going, running as fast as she could, over the rocks, up the steep bank, then down to the flats. Her bare ankle brushed some nettles, and she was only vaguely aware of the sting. After twenty minutes, she reached the White Dacha beet field that stretched to Ivanovka. She came out of the protective trees and started across the field. She was in the open now so she walked, trying not to attract attention. The road was on her right, and Ivanovka was visible about a quarter-mile straight ahead. She drew closer, and Baba Krista's house came into view along the grass street.

She was about a hundred yards away when she saw the man on Baba Krista's side porch. He was smoking a cigarette and gazing at the horizon.

Katherine dropped down into the dirt. Just as she did, his eyes went to where she had been standing. He stood still a minute, looking, and then he paced around the corner to the front of the house. He was out of view.

Now Katherine guessed what must have happened. They had come for her right after she had left for the institute. Because she had taken the long way along the river, they hadn't been able to find her. So they sent men to the institute to wait for her. Sergei's taxi was gone, which meant that Sergei, too, had left before they came. They now had men positioned at both ends of her route. She was trapped.

But she had seen them first, and that was something. It might still be possible to go back to the river, follow it another half-mile to the road and hitch a ride to Moscow. And then what? She could go to Zagorsk the next day and ask for Victor's help. But even if he could hide her, what would she do next? Assume a new alias and start all over again to get new passports, a new exit visa — this time without Sergei? No. If she acted fast, perhaps she could make it to Tallinn before the KGB realized that Katherine Sears, alias Yekatarina Yurgina, had an exit visa and might be trying to flee the country. Once they knew that, her documents would be of no use. Every passport control officer in the Soviet Union would be on the lookout for Yekatarina Yurgina. She had to move fast. And she had to have her documents.

A picket fence ringed Baba Krista's yard. In the back, it opened up into a vegetable garden. There was an old shed that had once been the outhouse.

Katherine got slowly to her feet and, hunched over, sprinted toward the house. She crept up to the foot of the fence, using the shed for cover. She squatted and peeked around to the front side of the house. The man was still on the porch smoking. He was an enormous man with a face that seemed to be slipping off his skull. A holstered gun was strapped to his side.

"Comrade general Belov!" someone called from inside the house.

He flicked his cigarette to the ground and disappeared into the house.

So there were at least two of them.

She circled the fence to the back yard and found the gate, gingerly lifting the latch and pushing it open. She checked the three windows on the back side of the house. Baba Krista passed in front of the middle window. She was at the kitchen sink (filling the tea kettle for her guests, perhaps?). Katherine waited until Baba Krista turned away, and then, keeping low, she sprinted through the garden toward her bedroom window. When she reached the house, she put her back against the shingles directly below the window and forced herself to slow her breathing. After a long minute, she peeked up through the glass. There was her bed, the icon of St. George on the wall and, through the door, the hallway and the bathroom. A man came through the bathroom door, still zipping up his fly. She ducked down. She waited a minute and then peered over the sill again. On the small table beside the bed lay *Soviet Latvia*. She stood up and gently pressed up on the window. It didn't move. She tried again, a little harder. Nothing. She looked up through the glass at the latch and saw why. She had locked it the previous evening.

She slid back down to the ground. There was only one thing to do. She inched along the house to the kitchen window. She could hear someone moving around inside. Baba Krista? She raised herself up and looked in. Baba Krista was at the stove, leaning over a kettle of tea. Katherine stood so that her head and shoulders were visible. Baba Krista's eyes caught the movement, and her head turned. Their eyes met, and the old woman froze. Then she raised three fingers and pointed behind her.

Three men. In the living room.

Katherine nodded and then mouthed the word "passport." Baba looked at her quizzically. Katherine repeated it, but Baba shook her head. She didn't understand. With her finger Katherine wrote "PASPORT" in Cyrillic letters on the window. Baba Krista read it and nodded. Katherine was about to wipe it away when a man came into the kitchen behind Baba Krista. Katherine ducked down as Baba Krista turned. PASPORT was still written on the glass.

On the ground, her body trembled as she waited for the sound of voices raised in excitement at the discovery of what was written on the glass. A moment later she heard a tapping at the window and looked up. "Where?" was written on the glass.

Katherine erased what she had written and so did Baba. Katherine held out her palms side by side, then closed and opened them like a book. Baba Krista nodded. There was no question about *which* book Katherine was indicating. There was only one book in Katherine's life, *Soviet Latvia*.

Katherine slid down and waited. Minutes passed.

Then, over her head, she heard the window open.

A hand appeared over the sill. It was the bony, clawlike hand Katherine had watched so many nights knitting in the living room. It clutched two passports. Peeking out from the cover of the international passport was Katherine's exit visa.

Katherine reached up and gave the old hand a light squeeze before it disappeared through the crack in the window.

There was no time to lose now. Katherine backed out of the yard through the gate. She heard the familiar squeak of the front door being opened. Someone was coming! She darted for the shed. The porch floorboards groaned, and she dove into the dirt. She lay there a minute panting, bracing herself for the shouting that would indicate she had been spotted. Nothing. She listened hard, and she could hear men chatting. She didn't dare peek around the corner of the shed; the men were just fifteen feet from her. She just lay there, waiting. They stayed on the porch for what seemed a very long time, and then a cigarette butt landed six inches from Katherine's hand. She heard the men moving again on the creaky porch. The door opened and then slammed shut. She waited. It was quiet.

Katherine got to her feet and inched back along the fence to the beet field. She reached it and, with a last glance toward the house, began to run toward the line of trees at the river. A minute later, she reached the trees and fell panting onto the river bank. She lay like that for a while. Then she got to her feet.

Now what?

She looked across the beet field toward the road, and her heart leaped. About two hundred yards away, moving very slowly toward Ivanovka, was a yellow taxi.

Sergei.

He was looking for her.

She realized in an instant that if she hesitated, he would pass by. She had two choices. She could hurry along the path to a point where the river passed close to the road. This option had the advantage of keeping her hidden, but she was also likely to arrive too late to intercept Sergei. A straight-line course through the open field was her only chance. She leaped out of the trees at a full run. The ground was soft, and her pace was slower than she had anticipated. She came nearer, but the car didn't slow. She could see the back of Sergei's head now; he was looking the wrong way. He was already past the point where she had calculated they would cross paths. Desperation overtook her, and she tried to force her legs to move faster, but they only sank deeper in the loose soil. She waved her arms and screamed.

"Sergei!"

His head whipped around, and the car screeched to a stop. The passenger door flew open. She reached the pavement, went around the back of the car and leaped in. Before she could even get the door closed he hit the gas.

"They found me!" she cried over the roaring engine.

His jaw was set, and his hands clutched the steering wheel.

He shook his head. "They found *us.*"

37

Sergei drove a quarter-mile past Ivanovka and then turned onto a tractor path.

"Where are we going?" Katherine asked.

Sergei kept his eyes straight ahead. "We have to get around the roadblocks."

"Roadblocks?"

Sergei nodded. "That's how I realized what must have happened. I saw the roadblock and looped back to the institute. I saw the police cars there and hoped you were somewhere en route."

He took the taxi along the path. Weeds scratched at the side of the car. A wood building, crumbling and half-burned, loomed ahead.

"What is this place?" Katherine asked.

"The old Ivanovka railway station."

They circled the station house. A sign lay tilted in the dirt. It said "IVANO." The rest had decayed. Sergei took the car up a slight embankment to the railroad tracks. To Katherine's amazement, Sergei turned right and started through the weeds along the old railroad corridor. She braced herself for the rattle of the railroad ties. It didn't come.

"It's smooth," said Katherine in wonder.

Sergei nodded. His eyes were fierce with concentration.

"They pulled up the ties a few years back," he said. "They needed them somewhere else."

They went slowly along the old track. Trees lined both sides of the corridor. Neither of them spoke. After twenty minutes, they reached a crossing on the main road to Moscow. Sergei stopped, put the car in neutral and lifted the emergency brake. He shifted in his seat and, for the first time since she jumped into the car a half-hour earlier, he faced her.

"That should put us clear of the roadblocks," he said. "Now, what I recommend —"

"Take me to Tallinn," Katherine said.

"Tallinn?" Sergei exclaimed. "You don't have your . . ."

His voice trailed off, and his eyes widened with astonishment. Katherine was waving her passports at him.

"You went back," he said with amazement.

She nodded.

His eyes narrowed thoughtfully. "Your entry visa for Finland won't be ready until next week."

"By then my papers will be invalid," said Katherine.

"They found you! Your papers are invalid *now!*"

"Maybe not in Tallinn," said Katherine. "It's another republic, far from Moscow."

"Not *that* far."

"Just listen a minute, comrade pessimist. It stands to reason that they can't get word everywhere immediately. Even if they know I'm fleeing—"

"They know."

"—they won't know how or where. I could be planning to swim to Turkey for all they know."

Sergei said nothing.

"There is a ferry out of Tallinn tomorrow at two o'clock," said Katherine. "If I can just get on the ship before they receive word from Moscow about me, then I can have someone from the embassy waiting for me at the port in Helsinki when I arrive."

"I don't know," he said doubtfully.

"What choice do I have?"

Sergei didn't answer.

Katherine said, "Now, if you could just drop me at a train station, I could—"

"Train station!" Sergei exclaimed. "That's the first place they'll look for you. You wouldn't get through the front door."

"I'll take my chances."

"No you won't," he said. "I'll drive you."

She shook her head. "No, Sergei, you've done enough."

"How will you get a ticket for the ship? You don't even have a Finnish entry visa."

Katherine winced. This was the weak link.

"I don't know," she said.

"Listen, I'm not going to just abandon you like this. These bastards can't get away with this. I won't let them. You know you need me. For god's sake, let me help you."

Katherine closed her eyes. Sergei was right. She'd never get through without his help.

She opened her eyes and looked at him gratefully.

"Good!" he said and then gazed thoughtfully up the road. "Two o'clock tomorrow you say?" He looked at his watch.

"Can we make it?" she asked.

He released the emergency brake and put the car in gear. "We'll see, won't we?"

He took the car off the railroad corridor and turned north on the single-lane road.

They made their way northwest, snaking through rural, European Russia. Through the dirty windshield, Katherine watched it roll past. Some of the villages still had their musical, old-Russian names like Dolgorukovo (Long-Armed) and Sosnovka (Little Pine); others, like Bolshevichka, had clunky, Soviet names such as Elektrozavodsk (Power Station Town). But apart from the names, the villages were pretty much the same. Along the road stood heavily latticed wooden cottages in need of paint. They had roof-high wood piles with rickety picket fences and busted gates in front. Old women in babushka scarves and house slippers bent under burdens worthy of mules, while young men with dirty fingers and eager eyes squatted around bottles of vodka and plates of pickled garlic. And everywhere people worked in the dirt — not in the barren, rolling fields that stretched in every direction, but in the tiny, bountiful plots within the picket fences. This was the Russia Katherine had come to know in Ivanovka and Bolshevichka. To her, this *was* Russia. Moscow was an aberration.

On they flew. Katherine felt as though a stone had been thrown into a pond and now she was the fish trying to swim ahead of the expanding ripples. She had a head start, but would the ripples overtake her before she got to Tallinn? How long would it take the search for Katherine Sears, alias Yekatarina Yurgina, to engulf the Tallinn port?

They drove a long time, stopping only to fill the gas tank from two aluminum canisters that Sergei, like all Russian drivers, kept in the trunk. After three hours, Sergei pulled up to a gasoline pump at a collective farm. The pump was closed, so Sergei wandered off into the village to look for the station operator.

Katherine found a market and bought bread and a can of tuna. Sergei returned a half-hour later, grumbling. He had failed to get gas.

From a taksifon, Sergei phoned his neighbor at the dacha. He left a message that he was away on business and would be back in three days.

"Will the KGB question her?" Katherine asked.

He shrugged. "She'll tell them I have a mistress."

Katherine frowned. "Is that what she thinks has been going on?"

"That's what I let her think."

"But why?"

"Because she would believe it," he said.

Katherine didn't ask if that meant Sergei had taken mistresses in the past. At her evening tea parties in Bolshevichka, Katherine had heard enough stories about Russian men's infidelity, of young girls' complicity, and of Russian wives' tolerance of it. The whole thing confused Katherine. She knew Sergei adored his wife. Why would he cheat on her? Was it all part of his romantic view of himself? He had certainly never tried to take advantage of Katherine in that way. In her vulnerable position it would have been easy enough. There had been times when she had caught him leering at her in a way that made her wonder. She had worried at those times that there would be a confrontation, but Sergei had always behaved like a gentleman.

So Katherine didn't ask Sergei to explain. She accepted now that there were things about the Soviet Union she would never understand.

They drove on. She used Sergei's pocket knife to cut the bread and spread the tuna for sandwiches. They ate as they drove. Sergei kept glancing toward the gas gauge and muttering. Just as the gauge slipped into red, a tractor came around a bend toward them. Sergei flashed his lights and held out three fingers. The farmer flashed back.

"Ha!" Sergei cried victoriously.

He did a U-turn and headed back up the road. They found the tractor pulled onto the shoulder a few hundred feet beyond the spot where Sergei had flashed. Sergei came beside it, and the farmer siphoned gas into Sergei's tank and the two canisters. Sergei paid him triple the official rate, and the man put the money in his wallet. They were off again.

"That should get us to Tallinn," he said.

She began to fret about the Estonian border. Would there be a document inspection?

At 2:00 A.M. they rounded a corner, and a wood hut came into view beside a red-and-white-striped crossing gate.

The border.

She saw at once that the hut was dark, and the gate was raised. Sergei rammed on the accelerator, and they blew past the gate at eighty miles per hour.

"Welcome to Estonia," grinned Sergei.

Sergei urged Katherine to sleep, but she declined — as she had done repeatedly since they set out. She was determined to stay awake to keep him company, not that he was very receptive to conversation. Sergei had been tired when they started the journey, and he had been driving hard now for twelve hours. Still, sometime after they passed the border to Estonia, Katherine gave over to exhaustion. She fell asleep, half-dreaming, half-thinking about Victor in the bell tower.

Somewhere overhead, the Large Magellanic Cloud was in ascension.

This was to have been the day.

S h e awoke to daylight.

"Good morning," said Sergei.

She looked at her watch — 5:30 A.M.

"Where are we?" she asked, stretching.

He pointed ahead. On the horizon, an enormous crane rose.

"Tallinn," he said.

It was the loading crane for the shipyard.

Signs directed them to the port, and they came to a stop in an empty parking lot. They walked to the port authority building, and Sergei rattled the doors. "Locked," he said.

Katherine didn't hear him. Her eyes were on the ship that towered over the two-story building, a ship she had seen once before — in Helsinki.

The *Estonia*.

Katherine gaped at it. She felt a rush of butterflies.

Her freedom ship!

The port opened at eight o'clock, two hours away. They decided to have breakfast, and got back into the car and headed toward the city.

Tallinn sat atop a hill surrounded by medieval walls. Sergei parked outside the stone wall, and they walked through an ancient gate into the city. The sensation was of entering a castle. It had everything but a moat.

Inside, Katherine found a fairy-tale setting of narrow cobblestone streets that wound as leisurely as footpaths through a maze of stone buildings. The skyline was like a bed of nails — dozens of near-vertical steeples stabbing the sky. After the self-effacing charm of Russia, outspoken Tallinn was something alien. It was hard to believe it was part of the Soviet Union — with one exception: the dilapidation. Ancient buildings on major streets stood empty. Bits of glass lay on the ground beside shattered windows. It was as though forty years ago, when the republic was absorbed into the U.S.S.R., Tallinn's residents ceased to care, and became squatters in their own homes.

Sergei found a basement café, and they sat down in a dark booth.

Katherine studied Sergei across the table and said, "You look dreadful. You have to get some sleep."

"I'm fine," he said. "I just need coffee."

The waiter brought brewed coffee, American-style, and Sergei grimaced when he tasted it. "This isn't coffee."

To Katherine also, now accustomed to Russian coffee, it tasted as weak as tea.

Sergei drank three cups, and they both devoured eggs, ham and toast. The food revived them. Katherine hadn't had such a satisfying breakfast since Ithaca. No kasha. No fatty sausage. No fried potatoes. Even the service was good.

They sat quietly for a while, enjoying the afterglow of a good meal, their minds occupied with thoughts of the ordeal that lay ahead. Strangely, it was not the risk of being caught that absorbed Katherine, but the realization that if everything did work out for the best, then she would never see Sergei again. There was so much she didn't know about her benefactor, her savior, her friend.

There was one thing she *had* to know. She had waited through all their months together, hoping for the right moment, and now she realized if she didn't ask the question right then, she would never get another chance.

"Why did you help me?" she said suddenly.

Sergei frowned. "I told you. I can't let these bastards get away—"

"No," Katherine said firmly. "I mean from the very beginning. That day in the alley, and every day since. Why?"

His face hardened. "I have my reasons."

"What reasons?"

"It's not important. Forget it."

"It's not about me, is it? Or, at least, I'm only part of it."

"Katherine, we have so much to worry about, why start—"

"Please."

Sergei dropped his eyes. She saw his chest rise and fall through two deep breaths. "Everyone's got a story," he said quietly.

"What's yours?"

Sergei lifted his gaze, and what Katherine saw made her heart skip. His face was twisted with pain. His lip twitched as he struggled to contain his emotion.

"I'm a Russian," he said. "The great-great-grandson of a Cossack ataman—did you know that? Pure Russian. Every drop in my blood; every cell in my body—Russian. They . . ." he said, invoking the Russian *Oni* to signify the communists, "they have made me ashamed of what I am."

His voice trembled as he spoke. Katherine listened frozen, afraid any movement would break the spell.

"This country—we call it the motherland, and that's how I feel about it, like a son toward his mother. It gave me life. It protects me, comforts me, gives me a sense that I belong to something important, something beautiful. And how I love her! Her wide-open spaces, her rugged winters, her more-rugged people. I would give my life to protect her; it wouldn't even be a question. Any Russian would."

He sneered and pretended to spit. *"Phoo* on these communists. Look what they've done to Russia. We're a basket case. Corruption everywhere, the bureaucracy, the special privileges for Party members, the drunkenness, nothing works, nobody wanting to work. . . . You think we don't know this? You think I haven't seen the way you turn up your nose at our empty shops, at our tiny flats, at our bad teeth, at the way our people smell of cheap soap—"

"Sergei, I didn't mean—"

"No, you're right! It's shit! Russia is shit!"

"It is not."

"Oh no? I've picked up Helsinki television broadcasts in Estonia, so I've seen how it is in the West, maybe not everything, but enough. We've all heard foreign records at one time or another—the Beatles, Elvis Presley, jazz—and we can hear the freedom in the music. We know."

He shook his head ruefully. "You want to know how stupid they are? Whenever one of your newspapers prints an article critical of U.S. policy, *Pravda* reprints it *word for word*. The idiots! They don't think we'll marvel that an American paper has the freedom to print such things. Such is their contempt for us, the People, the proletariat. God, how I hate them."

Sergei looked exhausted now, and he put his head in his hands. He rubbed his eyes.

He said, "You think we don't know these things? We know. I wish with all my heart we didn't."

Katherine remained still, waiting for Sergei to go on. But he was finished. He had no energy left.

"What does this have to do with me?" Katherine asked.

"You're their enemy."

"And any enemy of theirs is a friend of yours."

"Something like that," he said.

"So, in a way, you've been using me."

"Does that bother you?"

She thought a moment. "No. It makes it easier. I'm sick of playing the damsel in distress." She looked down at her hands and said, "I was worried that . . . well, not worried really, but I thought, maybe . . ."

"What?"

She flushed and looked straight into his eyes. "You know."

He smiled, his blue eyes glowing with a light of their own in the dim room. He nodded slowly. "That might have been part of it."

T h e doors to the port building were standing open when they returned at eight o'clock. They went straight to the ticket counter. Behind a Plexiglas booth, a young woman blinked at them with heavy lids.

"Sold out," she said and looked down at the table in front of her as though the matter were settled.

Katherine's shoulders sagged. Sergei was undaunted.

"Who's in charge of tickets?"

The woman rolled her eyes. "Ferry line captain."

"Where is he?"

"He's not here."

"Why not?"

"Too early."

"When does he arrive?"

"It varies."

"Usually?"

"Eleven."

"So late?"

"Maybe twelve." Shrug.

Katherine wanted to scream. The horrid woman rolled her eyes after every question. After every answer she looked back down at her desktop. Katherine had an impulse to reach across the desk, take her head between her palms and force the woman to meet her eye. Perhaps it was no extravagance that the woman's booth was encased in Plexiglas. She would need the protection.

In any event, her behavior didn't seem to bother Sergei. Katherine wondered what gave Sergei the strength to calmly face the daily ignominies of Soviet life. Was it acceptance, or merely ignorance of the alternatives? It didn't really matter. In the Soviet Union, endurance of the unendurable was currency.

"Where's his office?" asked Sergei.

She rolled her eyes and pointed over their heads to the open-air second level.

They started toward the stairs.

"Sergei, if there are no tickets—"

Sergei waved his hand with irritation. "Getting a ticket is not your problem."

They found the director's office and sat down to wait. Those three hours passed like torture. In fact, physical torture might have been preferable to the mental parade of scenarios her mind forced her to abide, all against a backdrop of those ripples, those dogged ripples moving outward on the Soviet pond toward Tallinn, toward the port, toward the *Estonia*, while she sat like a fool on that oil-stained vinyl chair staring up at a door with a rectangular sign that said, "Captain Markus Yolonsky, Director, Estonia Line." Steadily, a queue of about twenty people formed behind them.

Three hours later, at precisely eleven o'clock, a strikingly handsome man of about forty breezed up the hall toward the office. His powerful frame was encased in a neatly pressed navy uniform. Several insignia pins were attached to the uniform on the shoulderboard, the lapel and the chest.

The crowd bunched up behind Katherine and Sergei, forcing them against the office door. The smell of body odor and bad breath was stifling. Without a word, the captain pushed through the bodies to his office door. He unlocked it, went inside and then closed the door behind him. After another ten minutes the door swung open again, and the captain ushered in Katherine and Sergei with the air of a boyar consenting to entertain the grievance of one of his serfs.

The captain listened quietly as Sergei explained their problem. When he had finished, the captain looked at them with his blue eyes and said in a way that seemed to leave no doubt:

"We're sold out."

"My friend really has to get to Helsinki," Sergei said.

The captain looked at Katherine and shrugged. "What is to be done?" The captain rose. "Perhaps tomorrow—"

"What about seats for VIPs?" asked Sergei.

The captain sat down again. "Those are for VIPs."

"Sell us one of those tickets," said Sergei.

The captain sighed dramatically (ah, the burden of command!) and reached for one of the three phones on his desk. He began to speak in Estonian. Katherine's heart was pounding. She knew that this was all part of a game, but the knowledge didn't help.

After a minute, the captain hung up and said, "It will cost you triple fare."

"Done," said Sergei.

The captain opened his desk drawer and pulled out a pad of empty tickets. As Katherine watched, he began to write. He was selling her a ticket!

But it was too early for celebration, and Katherine knew it. This man worked for the ferry company. Of course he was happy to sell another ticket and put the money in his own pocket. Sergei was right, getting the ticket was not the problem. Passport control was the problem. Katherine recalled the cold gaze of the passport officer in Moscow's Sheremetyevo-2 Airport when she had arrived more than four months earlier. She shivered.

Without looking up, the captain put out his palm. "Documents."

Katherine handed him her papers. He studied the international passport, then the exit visa.

"Finnish entry visa?" He said.

"I don't have one," said Katherine.

The captain put down his pen and looked up. "What?"

"She doesn't have one," said Sergei.

"Then she can't get on the ship."

"All we're asking you to do is to sell us the ticket. Let us worry about the Finnish authorities."

"What's the point? The Finns won't even let her disembark."

"You mean they won't let me through Finnish passport control," Katherine corrected.

"No," said the captain, irritated at Katherine's presumption. "They won't let you off the ship. The Finnish immigration officers motor out to the *Estonia* in the harbor, board her, and then check everyone's documents before she puts in. We're not cleared to dock until everyone has been cleared. We've had a lot of problems with defectors. You understand."

"I thought I would at least be able to get off the ship," Katherine said miserably.

Her plan had been to have American Embassy officials meet her in the Helsinki port. But if she couldn't even get down the gangplank . . .

"The ferry is Soviet territory," the captain explained. "The Finns aren't going to let you leave Soviet territory until they know you have a visa to enter Finnish territory."

Sergei and Katherine exchanged glances. Katherine imagined herself on the ferry, looking out over Helsinki, but unable to leave the ship, trapped within Soviet territory for the lack of a single document. It was infuriating. The Finnish entry visa, of all things — it was the one document that was supposed to have been a formality.

"Sell me the ticket, anyway," said Katherine.

"What's the point?"

"Let me worry about that," said Katherine.

"No," said the captain. "I will worry about that. It looks bad when our people don't have the right paperwork."

Our people.

Katherine pushed the money across the desk to him. "Really," she said. "I know what I'm doing. Please. Just sell me the ticket."

"Sell the girl the ticket," said Sergei.

The captain glared at them both a moment. His eyes fell to the money, and he pulled it to him. He slipped it into his pocket.

"I have a feeling I'm going to regret this," he said and picked up his pen.

He finished writing the ticket and then tore it from the pad. It was blue and yellow, about the size of a dollar bill. The paper was thin and soft, almost like newsprint. Across the top, it said in Russian, "Welcome Aboard the *Estonia.*" She slipped it inside her passport with her exit visa.

"Bon voyage," said the captain without any enthusiasm.

They got up and left.

In the corridor, Katherine looked at her watch. It was 11:45 A.M.

An announcement signal, three descending tones, echoed through the hall. Then a voice on a loudspeaker said, in Russian:

"The *Estonia* is now boarding for Helsinki. All ticketed passengers are requested to proceed at this time to customs inspection."

"That's you," said Sergei.

Katherine nodded numbly. They went downstairs into an open hall like a small airport terminal. They stopped beside a metal barricade. Ahead, a man in a bright-blue uniform stood behind a high table. He was searching a man's suitcase. Customs inspection.

"This is where we say good-bye," said Sergei.

Katherine nodded. "You know what to tell Cameron Abbott?"

"Yes."

Katherine smiled. "Sergei, I don't know how—"

Sergei raised his hands. "Before we get into all that, I have a kind of going-away present for you."

Katherine almost laughed. "What!" They had fled Ivanovka as though it were under bombardment. A present?

Sergei held out his hand and opened it up. In his palm lay Katherine's amber ring.

She began to cry; she couldn't even say why. Maybe it was because the escape was nearly over, and she was relieved. Maybe it was because passport control was in front of her, and she was frightened. Or maybe it was because, from this point on, she would be on her own, without Sergei. Whatever the reason, she wept. She fell into his arms, and they held each other for a long time. They must have looked like lovers about to be separated.

They released and stepped back from each other. Sergei slipped the ring onto her finger.

She looked at it through blurry eyes.

"You didn't sell it," she said.

He smiled. "How could I do that?"

A rage at her own impotence rose up inside her. Maxim Izmailov, Lena Ryzhkova, Grayson Hines, Sergei, the blond in the Novodevichy convent, Cameron Abbott, her father—a chain of people to whom she owed a debt she could never repay. Where would it end?

She started to pull the ring off her finger. "I can't let you—"

Sergei placed his hand over hers. "You'll pay me back someday."

How? she wanted to cry out.

The one way she could repay him and everyone else who had helped her was to make it safely out of the U.S.S.R. The thought gave her strength. They embraced one last time. Then she turned and walked past a metal barricade toward the customs official.

Behind the tall tabletop, the agent watched her approach. Sergei stood a few feet away as the man inspected Katherine's counterfeit Soviet passport. He flipped through the empty, crisp pages and asked, "First time abroad?"

Katherine nodded.

"Open your bag," he said.

"I have no bag."

"Money?"

She took out her wallet and opened it. He counted out exactly fifty U.S. dollars, the maximum a Soviet citizen was allowed to carry abroad.

He stamped her declaration, and then turned his attention to a woman who had come in behind her.

So far so good. She walked to the end of the customs area. To her left was a long corridor that went down to passport control. She could see the dreaded booths at the far end. That part of her journey would be invisible to Sergei, so she paused at the corridor entrance and waved. Sergei smiled and waved back. He pointed above his head telling her that he would be up on the observation deck. From there, he would be able to see her board the ship. Assuming she made it that far.

She started down the corridor. It went along for a hundred feet and then narrowed at the end to a swinging metal gate. Katherine stopped a few feet from the gate, behind a red line on the floor. Two people were ahead of her.

The passport control officer sat in a Plexiglas booth to the left of the gate, high up on an unseen stool. Katherine could see his profile through the glass. He was young, about twenty-five, with traces of acne on his jaw. He wore an olive-green uniform and a cap with a shiny black bill. On the front of the cap a gold military medallion glistened.

The boy had the heartless look of the officers in Moscow, all right. He spoke only to demand documents. He only looked up from his paperwork in order to squint at the face in front of him as he compared it to the passport photos.

Katherine's heart raced as she fretted about all the things that could go wrong. The passports could be detected as fraudulent. The officer could notice that the date on the exit visa had been altered. Or, as Sergei had warned, Yekatarina Yurgina's name could already be on the "black list" of people sought by the KGB. Every passport control officer in the U.S.S.R. had a black list. How often was it updated? Sergei didn't know. If her name was on the list, she would be arrested immediately. That much was certain. For a passport control officer to approve a black-listed person's exit visa was unthinkable; it would probably mean his own arrest.

At last, the little gate swung open and the man in front of Katherine passed through. It was Katherine's turn.

She stepped up to the gate and put her documents onto the shoulder-high counter.

"Hello," she said in Russian.

The boy did not look up.

He slid the internal passport back to her and took the international passport, the ticket and the exit visa.

He worked at his desk a minute and then looked up to study her face.

It's normal. Stay calm.

He looked down again and went on writing. Then, quite suddenly, his expression changed from bored to interested. He raised his head. Her heart sank.

He said something to her. The language was strange.

Had she just forgotten Russian? No, it wasn't Russian. Why would he be speaking to her in a foreign language?

He repeated himself, and his face grew suspicious.

Katherine felt her palms go clammy. Then it occurred to her. Of course! He was speaking Latvian! She was Yekatarina Yurgina of *Latvia.*

In Latvian, exactly as she had memorized from *Soviet Latvia,* Katherine said, "I do not Latvian so well speak."

"No," he said switching to Russian. "You sure don't. *I'm* Latvian."

"Oh," she said. She felt sick. During her long months in Ivanovka, she had pored over the pages of *Soviet Latvia* for details to round out her background cover story, but she had never really expected to need it. She had never tested it on any of the citizens of Ivanovka; she had not even checked it out with Sergei, who was a native of the Baltics. She had no idea now whether it would hold up, especially to a Latvian — an immigration officer, no less! Of all the lousy luck . . .

"You must be Russian," he said.

"Polish," she said.

"From Riga, I suppose."

Katherine nodded.

"Me, too. Whereabouts?"

Katherine pictured the map in the back of the book. She saw the main street.

"Rainis Boulevard," she said.

"The historic district?" He frowned. "How is that possible?"

She pointed at the glass. "It's hard to hear you through this. Rainis Boulevard is where I work."

"Really? Where?"

"Café Luna."

According to *Soviet Latvia,* Café Luna was a "must stop" for the Riga tourist.

"Marvelous! How did you get that job?"

"It wasn't hard," she shrugged and hoped he didn't notice the sweat forming on her brow.

"Oh, come on," he said. "You must have some great connections."

She took a breath. This was agony. Any minute she would get tripped up on one of her lies. The line was backing up behind her, and she could feel people's impatience. She had already been at the booth twice as long as either of the other two people before her. The officer was oblivious to it.

"My father is a manager at the television factory," she said, remembering what she had read.

"The Ruben factory?"

She nodded.

"Why are you going to Helsinki?"

"Shopping. Stockmann Department Store."

"Naturally." He seemed satisfied and went back to his desk work. Katherine watched him, her pulse pounding in her ears. She waited for the thunder clap of stamps that signaled approval. But it didn't come.

He looked up at her, and his face was troubled. "Come with me, please," he said.

"Is something wrong?" she asked.

He got off his invisible stool, and came around the back side of his booth. He took her arm.

"Just come with me," he said.

Katherine allowed herself to be led away. Her feet glided over the floor without touching.

He took her into a small room with cushioned walls. Two rows of fluorescent lights buzzed like flies. He closed the door and turned to her.

"Excuse me for asking," he said. "But if I gave you some money, do you think you could pick up a pair of blue jeans for my girlfriend?"

Katherine's throat constricted, and she almost choked. "Why, yes," she stammered. "I could do that."

The deal was done, and Katherine left the room a minute later with fifty dollars of the boy's money and a scrap of paper with the words: *Levi's — Size "S."*

They went back to the gate. He stamped her visa and passport. He gave back her documents and nodded to her. The gate gave off a little *click*, and she pushed it open. She was through. She walked outside onto the wharf, and towering six stories above her was the *Estonia*. She spotted the gangplank and started up toward the ship. At the top, she stepped through a port door onto the carpeted deck of the *Estonia*.

A steward smiled broadly and said, "Welcome aboard the *Estonia*."

At exactly two o'clock, the ship's mighty horn blew, and the deck began to vibrate beneath her feet as the giant engines stirred. The water around the ship began to boil. From the railing, Katherine waved at Sergei, who stood behind a railing on the observation deck. She kept waving as the *Estonia* backed out of Tallinn harbor, and she was still waving as it turned north toward Helsinki.

The other passengers went inside, but Katherine stayed on the deck, her arms folded on the railing. She breathed the cool, salt air and watched the foam move south past the steel hull.

An hour later, she was still on the deck when the coast of the Soviet Union sank like a wounded ship into the slate sea.

38

I n a small apartment near the American embassy in Moscow, a buzzer erupted.

A man leaped to his feet from the sofa and sprinted to a recording machine. He hit RECORD and two large spools began to turn. He pressed one side of a headset to his ear.

A voice in English said, "Hello?"

The man knew this voice. It was the diplomat, Cameron Abbott.

"Are you Cameron Abbott?" the second voice asked in Russian. This new voice was unknown to the surveillance man. He slipped the headset over both ears and sat down.

"Who is this?" asked Cameron, switching to Russian.

"I'm calling for Katherine Sears."

"Is she okay?"

"She's fine. Listen carefully. She is at present on a ferry out of Tallinn. It's called the *Estonia*. She will arrive—"

"Is this some kind of a joke?"

"No joke. Listen. She is arriving in Helsinki at 18:15 hours today. She has counterfeit Soviet documents under the name Yekatarina Yurgina. She has no Finnish entry visa."

"My god," Cameron breathed.

"She asks that you have someone from the American consulate meet her at the port before the Finns can—"

"I understand," said Cameron. "Consider it done. We'll be there. Absolutely." He chuckled. "How did she manage it?"

"That is all."

The line went dead.

In the KGB apartment, the man pushed REWIND and stripped off his headset. He dialed the telephone beside the machine as the big reels wound backward. The line began to ring.

"General Belov. What is it?"

"Eduard here. Katherine Sears is on a ferry out of Tallinn."

"Tallinn!" Belov exclaimed. "She couldn't have made it that far!"

Eduard played back the tape of the phone call.

Belov listened and then snapped his finger on the phone cradle. He released the button and spoke to his secretary. "Get me our station director in Tallinn. It's an emergency."

He consulted the Aeroflot flight schedule. A few seconds later, Belov was speaking to the head of the Tallinn branch of the KGB.

"You have a ferry currently on its way to Helsinki?" said Belov.

"Yes," the man said. "The *Estonia*."

"I want you to turn that ship around."

"Excuse me?"

"Turn it around. There's a fugitive on board. Under no circumstances is she to leave the Soviet Union."

"The ship *is* Soviet territory. She hasn't gone anywhere."

"I intend to keep it that way."

The man thought a moment. "Let me radio the captain. We'll put your fugitive under arrest. He'll be back in Tallinn with the ship the day after tomorrow."

Belov paused. He looked at the Aeroflot schedule again and nodded. "That's acceptable. Listen carefully. No one is to talk to her, not one word. This is critical."

"Understood. I'll need a description of the fugitive."

Belov gave it to him from memory, and added, "Under no circumstances is she to be allowed off that ship until I arrive to take her off."

"You're coming to Tallinn?"

"No. Helsinki. There's a flight leaving in ninety minutes."

"I see. If that's the case, you should arrive ahead of the *Estonia* by at least an hour. I just want to add that—"

Belov hung up and dialed his secretary. "Call the flight schedule director at Vnukovo-1 Airport. There's a plane to Helsinki in . . ." he looked at his watch ". . . eighty-seven minutes. Make sure I get a VIP seat. Then call the embassy in Helsinki. Tell them to have a man at the airport with an entry visa for me and a car to take me directly to the port. And then tell my driver to be ready to go in five minutes. Tell him he had better have fuel in the car this time or I'll have him assigned to driving dog sleds in Siberia."

"Right."

"And get comrade secretary Podolok on the line."

The line rang twice, and then a voice barked, "*Da*, General."

"Thought you'd want to know. We got her."

■

At that very moment, a white Chevrolet Blazer leaped through the front gate of the American embassy and turned south on the Garden Ring Road. Inside the vehicle, Cameron Abbott was shouting instructions to the driver.

"I've got to make that flight."

"Vnukovo-1 is forty minutes even without all the stoplights."

"Stoplight?" Cameron cried. "No stoplights. No speed limits. We've got diplomatic immunity, now's the time to use it." He looked at his watch. "Damn, it's going to be close. Go!"

39

Finland rose in the north, a delicate bluish band barely distinguishable from the sea. As the ship drew nearer, the band grew and hardened into a coastline of white granite cliffs that held off the angry water like the walls of a cell.

Katherine watched from the deck. After the Soviet coast had faded from sight, she switched to the port side of the ship, climbing to a small deck, six stories above the sea. As the cliffs of the Finnish coast took shape, so, too, did her thoughts. They turned to the coming ordeal over her missing entry visa. It hung over her head like a lie about to be exposed. By now, Sergei would have talked to Cameron. The KGB might or might not have recorded the conversation. It was out of her hands now. It was up to the Americans to convince the Finns that Yekatarina Yurgina should be allowed off the ship.

She looked at the cliffs and wondered—was she really any closer to freedom? If she was not allowed off the ship then she was still technically in the U.S.S.R. The Finns wouldn't be involved at all. That made her status a U.S.-Soviet affair, as it had always been. In a way, though she had come far, Katherine was no closer to freedom than she had been in Ivanovka.

A small fishing trawler, its nets rolled onto gigantic spools after a day of fishing, motored off the port bow about a hundred yards from Katherine. An old man and a young boy busied themselves on the deck. She watched them for a long time. Seagulls hovered over the trawler's stern, cawing and diving. After about ten minutes, the boy noticed Katherine alone on the deck and waved. She waved back.

The voice came from behind her.

"Yekatarina Yurgina?"

She turned. Two men in the blue uniforms of the crew looked at her.

"Yes?"

"We've been looking all over the ship for you."

"Is something wrong?"

"Come with us, please."

They each took an arm and started to lead her away. She resisted, but their grip only tightened. "Ow! You're hurting me."

"Then don't give us any trouble."

"What's going on?"

"You are under arrest."

They yanked her from the railing and part-led, part-carried her across the deck toward a small door. The door, a portal, was closed and marked "Staff Only" in Russian. Katherine had reached the deck by metal stairs at the opposite end. For passengers, it was the only way onto the deck. No wonder the men had trouble locating her.

They reached the portal and pulled open the door. The man on her right started through.

In that moment, an overpowering fury rose within Katherine. It boiled with the desperation of her long months in hiding; the Embassy's inability to help her; her own failure to contact Victor about Yevgenia; the horror of the rape attempt.

Was this how it ended? With freedom in sight?

She thought of Sergei, of the risks he had taken for her. She pictured Victor, going from asylum to asylum, giving up his beloved science in his courageous quest to save his brother.

It was so unfair! To be so close, and now have it all slip away — it was more than she could bear.

Katherine's breathing grew shallow, and she began to hyperventilate, her upper lip being drawn in and out with every breath. The man in front of her turned to see what was wrong, but he was too late.

"NO!" she screamed and threw her weight onto his back.

He fell forward. His foot caught the bottom lip of the portal door, and he went down. His grip on her arm did not relax, however, and he pulled her down with him.

Katherine got to her feet and darted for an inner door. The first officer swung his hand at her ankle and grabbed hold. She kicked backward and brought her heel down on his fingers. He cried out and let go. She sprinted for the door and jumped through.

"Get her!" cried the man on the floor. She slammed shut the heavy steel door and fumbled with the latch. But the men were too fast; they reached the door, throwing their bodies against it. She was propelled backward.

She screamed and sprinted across some kind of navigation room. A map lay on a long table, and a man was studying it. He looked up in amazement.

"Stop her!" they cried, but Katherine had already found a staircase and was heading down. She reached the bottom, just as the men appeared at the top. The first man put his feet on the edges of the ladder and slid down. She turned and ran on.

She was in the staff part of the ship, and nothing was marked. She fled wildly in a direction she believed to be toward the bow. She had an idea, but if it was to work, she would have to put some distance between herself and the men.

She reached a long corridor and ran on, squeezing past a wide-eyed sailor in his boxer shorts. She scampered down another ladder. At the bottom, she spied a swinging door with a small, head-high window. She pushed through.

She came into the ship's main dining hall. About fifty passengers sat at tables covered with glasses of beer and plates of sausage. Happy chatter filled the room.

She wove through the tables toward the far door. The men burst through the swinging door. "There she is!"

Katherine glanced back, colliding with a table occupied by four diners. The table was bolted to the floor, and she doubled over the top, sending drinks and plates crashing. She rolled off the side of the table and fell at the feet of a wide-eyed woman whose blouse was now covered with mustard, beer and sauerkraut.

Katherine looked back. The men were nearly upon her. As she watched, a woman with a tray of food stepped into the men's path. They collided, and the woman shot off the floor as though fired from a cannon. Beer and food filled the air. Both of the men went down.

"Devil!" one of them cried.

"Someone stop her!"

Katherine was back on her feet running for the door. She passed through the doorway and sprinted along another corridor, this one carpeted and heading back toward the stern. She passed a duty-free shop and then entered the casino. She kept on going past a short row of slot machines. A few gamblers looked strangely at her, but the rest didn't seem to notice.

She spotted a door leading onto the deck. She pulled it open and dove outside.

The sun was still high, but the air had taken on a late-afternoon chill as she came onto the deck. The sound of the ship's mighty engines was different now, less muffled, as the propellers churned up the water and sent the bow crashing through the waves. Seagulls screeched overhead, and the smell of the ocean filled Katherine's nose.

She looked left and right to get her bearings. She was on the starboard side. Damn! She needed port.

She ran along the deck toward the bow. People sat in lounge chairs drinking beer and watching the Finnish coastline grow. As she passed a door on her left, one of the men lunged through. His hand raked down the back of her shirt. She screamed and ran on, his feet pounding in pursuit. She looped around the bow of the ship and started down the port side along the shoulder-high railing. The man was only a few steps behind her now. She could hear him panting.

A few feet ahead, a door opened and the other man jumped out in front of her, his arms open as he prepared to tackle her.

Trapped!

She slowed her pace and put one foot on the lowest rung of the railing at the edge of the deck. She swung herself over the side and threw her body out into nothingness.

She fell.

She hit the water feet-first, wind roaring in her ears. The sea felt like concrete and her feet and ankles exploded with pain. The sea closed over her.

She might have passed out but for the cold, which drove her to dig upward, lungs burning. It seemed to take forever, but at last her head broke the surface, and she sucked the salt air into her starved lungs. Her feet and ankles throbbed. Her ribs ached. She trod water and looked up. The giant stern of the *Estonia* was moving away. On deck, three stories up, her two pursuers hung over the railing shouting and pointing. She could tell by the wild gestures of their arms that they were giving directions to someone. A life preserver sailed over the side of the ship. It splashed a few yards away. She looked at it and then turned the other way.

From six stories up on the observation deck, the sea had looked peaceful. On the surface, it was menacing. Land had vanished. The horizon was a jagged waterscape of whitecaps. The sea, which had been blue, was now black. For a full minute, she trod water and squinted over the waves that lifted her and then dropped her, and still she couldn't find what she sought.

Panic rose. The water was as cold as slush, and she recalled something she had once read about hypothermia — it could kill in seconds if the water was cold enough. She was injured; every breath brought new pain to her chest. She feared she had broken some ribs. How long could she last?

A wave lifted her and at last she saw it: the Finnish fishing trawler with the old man and the boy. Then it disappeared again below the jagged horizon.

She kicked off her shoes and began to swim in the direction of the trawler. It was hard going. The pain in her chest was excruciating. After several minutes, a wave lifted her, and she saw the boat again. It was moving away from her. Desperation seized her. She wouldn't make it. She gave up swimming and trod water.

Just then, the great horn of the *Estonia* sounded, and a speaker cried out in Russian, "All hands! Man overboard! Port side! All hands!"

She turned back to the fishing trawler. The boy had climbed up on the gunnel of his trawler and was now scanning the surface of the water.

"Help!" she cried and waved her arm.

It took a moment, but the boy finally saw her and pointed. The trawler churned a slow arc in her direction, its bow crashing against the waves, the staccato *putt-putt* of its engine growing steadily louder in Katherine's ears. Katherine was weakening now, and it was all she could do to keep her head above water. At last, the boy threw a life preserver into the water. It bobbed with the waves, impossibly small, impossibly far away in the cold confusion of the sea. With the last of her strength, she swam toward it and slipped her arms through. The boy reeled her in like a fish.

The boy pulled her over the side of the trawler, and she collapsed onto the deck like a mackerel. She lay on her stomach, spitting sea water onto the deck. She gasped desperately for air. She had never been so tired in all her life.

She lay like that a long time, until her breathing grew steady and her strength returned. Then she rolled over and looked up into the astounded faces of the two Finns.

The old man looked to be about sixty, while the boy was no more than twelve.

"You almost drowned," said the boy in English.

English!

Katherine didn't answer. She rested another minute and then lifted herself up enough to peer over the bow. The *Estonia* was about a quarter-mile away and fading. She fell back onto the deck.

"My name is Katherine Sears," she said in English. "I am an American citizen."

The boy and the old man stared at her, their mouths agape.

"Take me to shore," she said.

"That's where we are going," said the boy.

40

The Aeroflot jet reached the gate at Helsinki's airport, and the pitch of the engines' whine began to fall.

Cameron Abbott unfastened his seat belt and jumped to his feet. An Embassy limousine was waiting on the "Arrivals" curb, and if he hurried, he could still beat the *Estonia* to the port. He had just bent over to retrieve his briefcase from the floor when someone plowed into him so hard that he was thrown forward into the narrow space between the seats.

A stewardess appeared over him. "Are you all right?" she asked anxiously. "That pig—he just bowled you over!"

Cameron struggled back to his feet and looked up the aisle in time to see an enormous Russian turn out the cabin door.

"Who was that?" he asked.

The stewardess looked both ways conspiratorily and then raised her index finger to her lips.

Cameron understood.

KGB.

Outside the airport, General Yuri Belov jumped into the passenger seat of a Russian Zhiguli sedan with diplomatic plates. His enormous stomach pressed against the front of the dashboard, and he shifted a moment trying vainly to get comfortable. Two other men were in the car—both KGB agents employed as diplomats at the Embassy.

"To the port. Fast!" Belov barked.

"There's been a change, comrade general," said the man behind the wheel. "The American is no longer aboard the *Estonia*."

Belov's face flushed red. He tried to speak, but his throat had tightened into a knot. All that came out was a hiss like air leaking out of a tire.

41

Katherine was on the deck of the trawler shivering beneath three blankets when the speedboat appeared. She clutched a thermos cup of tea and watched fatalistically as the boat closed with the speed of a bloodhound pursuing an escaped convict. As it neared, a loudspeaker called out in Finnish.

"What's he saying?" Katherine asked the boy, her voice trembling from the cold.

"They want to board us."

Katherine knew that by coming aboard the trawler, she had legally passed into Finnish territory. All that remained was to convince Finnish authorities of her true citizenship.

"Tell your grandfather to do exactly what they say."

The trawler slowed. The police boat, with two men in uniform aboard, came alongside. A tall Finnish policeman leaped into the trawler and went directly to Katherine.

"You are under arrest by the authority of the republic of Finland," he said in Russian. He spun her around and cuffed her hands behind her back.

"My name is Katherine Sears. I'm an American citizen."

He didn't reply. He led her to the side of the boat and the second policeman steadied her as she climbed out of the trawler. She sat down on a cushioned bench in the bow of the speedboat. Katherine looked up at the boy and the old man.

"Thank you," she mouthed, and then she was off again, racing toward shore.

After ten minutes, they drew up to the end of a long pier. A half-dozen Finnish policemen and three men in poorly fitting suits were waiting for them. One of the policemen tied the boat's bow line to a cleat. The other helped Katherine out of the boat onto the wooden pier.

She was in Finland.

A husky man in a police uniform stepped forward. He had a blond beard and the air of command.

"I am Lieutenant Pose of the Finnish police," he said in passable Russian. "Yekatarina Yurgina, you are under arrest."

"My name is Katherine Sears. I am an Amer—"

"You are charged with attempting an illegal entry into Finland."

To her left, Katherine heard someone speaking Russian. She turned to face the men in suits. The man in front looked familiar. He was the man she had seen smoking on Baba Krista's porch, the day before.

Katherine addressed him in Russian, "Good evening, General Belov. Have a nice flight?"

"How did you know my name?" he demanded in Russian.

Lieutenant Pose observed the exchange and turned to Belov. "What's going on? What are you saying to her?"

"I'm an American citizen," said Katherine in English.

"She's lying," said one of the Russian diplomats in English. "She's Latvian. Check her papers."

"If you don't mind, I'll handle this matter without Soviet interference."

"This woman is wanted by the Union of Soviet Socialist Republics in connection with a murder," said the diplomat. "I will not leave her side until she is turned over to Soviet authorities."

"The passport is counterfeit," said Katherine. "I'm not Soviet. I'm American."

"Don't listen to her," said the Russian diplomat.

"Call the consulate. Check it out. My name is Katherine—"

"Shut up!" hissed Belov in Russian.

Lieutenant Pose said something in Finnish to his men. A policeman took her shoulder, and they all started up the pier.

"You're making a big mistake," Katherine protested, but they weren't listening.

Belov came in behind her and whispered, "You came a long way for nothing."

His sour breath warmed her neck, but it inspired no action. Wounded and exhausted, Katherine was beaten. If the Finns were determined to hand her over to the Russians, then there was nothing she could do to stop it.

At that moment, a black limousine screeched to a stop at the end of the pier. A man in a blue suit leaped out and ran toward them. He was short with wire-framed glasses.

"Hold it!" he cried in English, his tie flying. "Stop right there!"

Katherine's heart leaped. She knew that voice. "Cameron!"

He held a diplomatic passport in front of him and said, "I am from the American Embassy! This woman is an American citizen!"

"She's Soviet. I have her passport."

"It's a fake."

"She is under arrest!" said Belov. "She is going back to Moscow."

"Shut up!" barked Lieutenant Pose.

"I was just saying that—"

"I know what you were 'just saying.' This is a Finnish matter. This woman is in Finnish custody." He turned to Cameron. "What were you saying?"

"She's American. I insist that you release her into my custody."

"He's lying!" cried Belov.

Lieutenant Pose's eyes bulged. "I told you to shut your mouth!" He shook his head, exasperated, and took a deep breath. "As far as the lady's nationality is concerned, she could be bloody Martian for all I care. She attempted an illegal entry into Finland. It's really not at issue."

"But it is!" said Cameron. "If she's American then no crime has been committed."

"What are you talking about?"

Belov was yelling at the diplomat in Russian. All the diplomat could get out was a feeble, "Don't listen to him."

Lieutenant Pose glared at the three Russians. "One more word out of you and I'll take the cuffs off of her right now." He turned back to Cameron. "You were saying?"

"American citizens have the right to apply for an entry visa upon arrival in Finland. Is that not correct?"

"It is."

"I would like to apply for a visa now," said Katherine.

Lieutenant Pose nodded slowly. "He's right. Her nationality is an issue. But first, we must establish—"

"This is insane," said the diplomat, throwing his hands in the air. "We have international treaties that require you to hand her over to the Soviet Union! This woman is an American spy and I am not leaving Finland without her!"

Lieutenant Pose gaped at the diplomat. "You *acknowledge* that she is American?"

The diplomat seemed to realize his mistake. "I acknowledge nothing. As I said, I have orders to bring her—"

Lieutenant Pose turned to Belov and said in English, "Finland is a nation of laws, comrade. I am releasing this woman into the custody of the Americans until her identity has been sorted out."

"You can't just let her go!" the diplomat cried.

"I'm not letting her go," said Lieutenant Pose, irritated. "She will be free under a restraining order that forbids her—"

"Restraining order!" the diplomat groaned.

Lieutenant Pose went on. "—from leaving Finland until it has been determined whether or not she is guilty of a crime. If she is, she will be taken back into custody."

"This is nonsense!" the diplomat shouted. "I order you to arrest her."

Lieutenant Pose ignored him and motioned to one of his men to remove the cuffs. The man pulled a small key out of his pocket. He went around behind Katherine.

Belov cried out in Russian, "Get her!"

The two Russians leaped at Katherine. Before anyone could react, one man had hold of Katherine's legs while the other had her shoulders. They started to drag her away.

"Are you crazy!" cried Lieutenant Pose. "Put her down!"

But the men were already moving away with Katherine in their arms. She was still handcuffed, so she could only wriggle her body in her own defense. The pain in her ribs was like a knife. If the Russians could get her to their car. . . . God, it was the courtyard in Moscow all over again.

"Stop them!" Cameron cried. "They're kidnapping her!"

Lieutenant Pose gave a signal and the policemen charged at the Russians. Pose raised his baton and brought it down with a crack on the head of the man who held Katherine's feet. He collapsed to the ground. Belov rushed at Pose. The big Finn raised his baton again. Belov froze.

"Soviet arrogance!" Lieutenant Pose spat.

The Russians were outnumbered three to six, and in seconds the Finns had them pinned to the ground. Cameron stood off to the side, watching with wide eyes. Katherine got back to her feet and went around behind Pose, hiding like a child behind her mother.

"*Oy!*" cried the Russian diplomat. His back was being stabbed by the knees of the Finnish policeman atop him. "That hurts! Let me go, you idiot! I have diplomatic immunity."

Lieutenant Pose nodded, and the policemen got off the men. The Russians scrambled to their feet and faced the six Finnish policemen, who now formed a line between the Russians and Katherine. The Russian who had been struck by Pose's baton massaged his head behind the ear.

Belov glared at Lieutenant Pose. The general's hair was tousled, and his face was as red as a ripe tomato. "You're making a big mistake," he said in Russian. The diplomat translated and together they all stormed away. They piled into a Zhiguli sedan and sped off.

A policeman uncuffed Katherine. She massaged her wrists.

"Are you all right?" asked Lieutenant Pose.

"I think I may have broken some ribs," she said.

"We'll get that checked out," said Cameron.

"You may go with him," said Pose, motioning to Cameron. "I won't hold you. But you are forbidden to leave Finland until this is sorted out. Understand?"

Katherine nodded.

"Come on," said Cameron. "Let's get out of here."

He led her to the black limousine parked at the end of the pier. She got in first and slid over. He sat down beside her.

He closed the door, and the chauffeur pulled away.

"Well, that was exciting," said Cameron.

"You got my message," said Katherine.

"Yes," he said. "Apparently, your Russian friends did, too." He chuckled. "I sat beside that man you called General Belov all the way from Moscow."

"They almost got me," said Katherine.

Cameron nodded gravely. "I was at the port when we heard you had jumped ship. I came here as fast as I could."

Katherine couldn't think of what to say.

Cameron said, "By the way, it may interest you to know that this car is considered American soil."

"Really?"

He put out his hand. "So permit me to be the first one to say, 'Welcome to the U.S.A., Katherine Sears.' "

42

It was midnight in Moscow, and the mighty bells of the Kremlin tower clanked out their signature melody. Then, solemnly, the clock counted the hour.

In her office, Yevgenia Perova listened as the twelfth gong tolled and fell silent. She sighed. At any minute, General Belov and Anatoly Podolok would step through her door to discuss the execution of her son Anton.

The unthinkable had happened—the American had escaped. It didn't matter that Belov's incompetence was at fault. Katherine's secret was now in the West, and sooner or later, it would make its way back east to KGB Director Oleg Shatalin. Then he would find Anton in Little Rock, and the truth about the man with the stub nose would come to light. They would all be ruined.

Yevgenia was beyond caring about her own career, but Podolok and Belov would never allow Anton to jeopardize their secret. Katherine's escape was the signature on Anton's death warrant.

How had it come to this?

She found herself thinking about her husband. Boris would have known. He had been a flawed man, a drunk, but he had a gentle common sense she missed. And needed. She remembered something Victor had said a few months back—he had called her *krestyanochka*, "the little peasant girl." Boris had coined the secret endearment back when they were still teenagers. Later, she thought he did it to get under her skin, something he could do better than anyone. Now Yevgenia saw that there was more to it than that—he was reminding her of her roots: her parents who fled the famines of the 1930s to settle in Leningrad; the squalor of their proletarian ghetto; the wretched life of a Soviet textile worker.

Then came the war . . . and the siege. Something happened to Yevgenia as she watched her neighbors, her friends, her teachers starve, while she secretly collected rats in the sewers. She supposed it was there, down in the sewers, that she invented the Iron Perova.

Where had the *krestyanochka* gone? Yevgenia looked into herself, and she could find nothing of the little peasant girl. All that was left was the Iron Perova.

When had fiction become fact?

All these years she had told herself she needed no one, just the Communist party, the socialist cause, but now she feared she was wrong. She longed to talk to Victor about it. Only a year ago, they had lived together under the same roof. Now, she could never talk to him again. He would find out what she had done, and he would never forgive her.

It was time to face the truth — she had made a mistake that night when General Belov called from Leningrad about Anton. And now she was doomed to pay for it with the loss of both of her sons.

She reached into her desk and pulled out a framed picture of her family standing beside a canoe on Lake Sini, the same picture Victor had kept on his desk at SAPO. She rubbed her thumb over the faces — Boris . . . Victor . . . Anton. How happy they all looked. She had always secretly sympathized with Anton's campaign to rescue that lake, a passion almost certainly connected to his romantic memories of that summer. Of course, even then, there had been problems: fights with headstrong Anton and arguments with Boris about his drunkenness. But somehow the summer in that picture had been different. For a few weeks they had been a family like other families — no demanding ideologies, no meddling Marxist theory — just blood ties binding together four very different people. The writings of Lenin were Yevgenia's bible, yet it occurred to her with a start that, in all forty-four volumes, not a single word celebrated the simple wonder of the family.

Her hands began to tremble, and she felt as though she were about to cry. It had been ages since she wept, and she was terrified. She stared at the picture waiting for the tears. She waited, but they didn't come.

After a while, her hand grew steady again, and she put down the picture. Her thoughts went to that evening ten months ago when she first encountered the man with the stub nose.

It had begun with a phone call.

I'll get it," said Yevgenia, and she put down her book. Victor was at his desk writing a note to Katherine Sears about his survey.

Yevgenia put the phone to her ear. "*Allo?*"

"Comrade Perova. Sorry to bother you at home. My name is General Belov."

"Who?"

"Belov. I'm calling from Leningrad. I'm with the security organs, you understand?"

He was KGB. "Go on."

"We have a bit of a problem up here. It involves your son."

"Which one?"

"Anton. Naturally, I called you the second I realized who he was. I'm afraid the situation is rather . . . delicate."

"Delicate."

"Yes. He was picked up in a restricted area near the border with Norway. It looks as though he was trying to flee the country."

Yevgenia was on the next flight to Leningrad. She had no need to explain herself to Victor: He was used to her sudden, mysterious departures on matters of state. By 3:30 A.M. she was in the KGB center on Arsenal Street shaking the hand of General Dogface, Yuri Belov. He was polite and eager to please. She knew the type too well: The bureaucracy was packed full of ass-kissers like Belov.

He took her to an observation room where she could see Anton through a two-way mirror. He lay on a cot staring at the ceiling. His beard was grizzly and his clothes were soiled with red clay. He looked like hell.

"Let me talk to him," she demanded.

"Of course," said Belov hesitantly. He didn't move to open the door.

"What's the matter with you?"

"The situation has gotten a little more complicated than it was a few hours ago," he said.

"How so?"

"Come with me. I want to show you something."

He took her through a maze of corridors to a small infirmary. The beds were all empty, except for one.

Yevgenia walked to the bedside and looked down at the unconscious patient, an old man. She grimaced in revulsion. The man had no nose.

"What happened to his nose?"

"We don't know," said Belov. "We assume frostbite: He was in the camps for years. He's in a coma now. Last night, one of our border guards shot him trying to escape into Norway, not far from where your son was found. We believe they may have spoken."

"So?"

Belov looked down at the man with the stub nose. "One of our officers, a captain, interrogated him before I brought him here. Before you see your son, I think you should take a look at the transcript of the interrogation."

They went back to Belov's office, and she sat down behind a long table. She began to read. The story was compelling and a little hard to believe — a foreigner surviving all those years in the camps, burying his identity. Then, on the last page, she came upon a name that made her stop reading and gasp.

"Andrei Vlasov?"

Belov snorted through his nose. "It kind of jumps out at you, doesn't it?"

Yevgenia shook her head in amazement.

General Vlasov was the Soviet Union's Benedict Arnold, a Soviet officer who had changed sides during World War II and fought alongside the Nazis. He recruited heavily from German prison camps, creating a rag-tag regiment that ultimately saw little combat. After the war, Vlasov and his men were turned over to Stalin.

Yevgenia stood and began to pace. "But Stalin executed all the vlasovites in 1945."

"That's what we thought. I've been looking through some of the files, just the ones we have up here in Leningrad, and I came across this."

He handed her a document, yellowed with age. Yevgenia read. It was a transcript from a KGB interrogation of a Soviet POW just before his execution. In a desperate attempt to offer information to save his life, he told of how a vlasovite officer had come to the German POW camp where he was being held, Stalag 33. "The Red Army was only a day away, and everything was in chaos," said the man. "I was working in the records office, and this vlasovite comes in and takes my German superior aside. Next thing I know, they come out, and they want my register book. I could see what was going on: The vlasovite rat bribed the Germans to substitute records. The numbers add up, but we got the wrong guy. There was a swap. Man, I feel sorry for that poor bastard!"

"The mythical missing vlasovite," Yevgenia snorted. "It's folklore, Stalinist propaganda. The old man loved anything that made us all suspect each other."

"Maybe not. The stub-nose man couldn't have known about this file, yet his story matches perfectly. He says he was in a German POW camp. He says that on the day before it was liberated by the Red Army, a vlasovite officer came and substituted records, and he was shipped out with the other traitors."

"Which camp?"

Belov smiled. "Stalag 33."

"The same one," Yevgenia breathed.

"Think about it. This vlasovite, sensing the war was going against Russian traitors, went to the camp and substituted the stub-nose man's records for his own. How hard could it have been with the chaos of the retreating German Army? Then the stub-nose man disappeared into the gulag, and the vlasovite faded back into the Soviet army."

Yevgenia shrugged. "And the vlasovite might have survived the war and lived happily ever after—he might even have become a member of the Party for all we know!"

"Right."

"Did the stub-nose man happen to mention who this vlasovite mystery man was? You blacked out the name on the copy you showed me."

Belov smiled faintly. "He did."

"Well?"

Belov spoke the name. Yevgenia's jaw dropped.

"So you see," said Belov, "the opportunities here are infinite for someone who plays his cards right."

Yevgenia nodded thoughtfully.

"There's just one little problem."

"What's that?" she asked.

"Your son, Anton. He knows too much."

Yevgenia put away the picture and folded her hands across the desk. She sat facing the door, waiting.

Belov and Podolok arrived a few minutes later. They looked resolute, and Yevgenia knew she had to take the upper hand, or all would be lost. This was not a time for pondering the mistakes of her life. It was a time for action. It was time for the Iron Perova.

"I'm glad you've come," she said. "Something has to be done."

Podolok and Belov remained standing not far from the door. "I'm glad you see it that way," said Podolok.

"I had hoped it wouldn't come to this," said Yevgenia.

"I think we both felt that way, comrade," said Podolok. "But now there is no other—"

"I've been talking to Dr. Lazda quite a lot lately," Yevgenia went on. "Anton's long history of trouble stems from a condition called 'compulsive truth-seeking disorder.' It's an actual disease. It's related to creeping schizophrenia—I looked it up." She shook her head. "It describes Anton perfectly."

She began to quote what she had read so many times in the textbook Dr. Lazda had loaned her.

"The compulsive truth-seeker views his struggle as quite justified, and the road he chose as the only true road. If a doctor attempts to dissuade him, he becomes irate, angry, and tells the doctor that the meaning of his life is in the struggle, that he foresaw the possibility of arrest, but it never stopped him because he cannot renounce his ideas. Yet he still considers himself mentally healthy."

Podolok sat down heavily on a chair and pulled out a cigarillo. Belov lit it.

Podolok spoke across the room. "Anton is schizophrenic?"

Yevgenia nodded solemnly. "Lazda warned me that his condition could resist ordinary drug therapy. It has. I had hoped I could avoid this. It's desperate, but Dr. Lazda assures me—assures me—that it is totally justified."

"What are you talking about?" asked Podolok.

"There is just no other way," she said.

"What?"

"A frontal lobotomy."

"Jesus."

Yevgenia turned to face Podolok. Belov sat down beside him.

"It's not like it sounds," she said. "We all think of it as a kind of personality removal, making people into human vegetables, and all that. But Soviet medicine has come a long way from those voodoo days. You know, Dr. Lazda says they may even use a laser! So you can see how far we have come. Dr. Lazda says our specialists can now surgically remove near-term memory with only a minimum of collateral damage. It should also cure Anton of his compulsive disorders."

Podolok smoked his cigarillo and looked at Yevgenia a long time. She wondered what he was thinking. A small smile came to his lips.

"How will it be done?"

"Normally, he would be transferred to the public hospital in Perm, but in this case, I thought that would be — "

"Not a good idea. What's the other option?"

"We fly in a surgeon, the best, and he does the operation there at Little Rock."

"You have someone in mind?"

Yevgenia nodded.

Podolok got to his feet. Belov rose beside him.

"Do it," said Podolok and left the room.

Yevgenia called Dr. Svyatoslav Schmidt the next morning. He was less than enthusiastic.

"This is outrageous!" he exclaimed. "You can't just order me around like a secretary. We have procedures. I have patients."

"Consider it a house call."

"Find someone else. I don't do this sort of thing."

"You do now."

Dr. Schmidt paused, as if calculating how he would fare in a showdown with a junior Central Committee member. "What you're asking me to do isn't medicine," he said. "It's butchery."

"In the hands of an ordinary surgeon, perhaps."

"In any hands."

"Listen to me. This is a special patient. He must have the best our country has to offer. Like it or not, that is you."

Dr. Schmidt sighed and said, "I'm extremely busy right now."

"Naturally. When are you free?"

Yevgenia heard him flipping through the pages of an appointment book.

"I can be at Little Rock in four weeks," he said with disgust. "I'll do the surgery then."

"Very good," Yevgenia said. "I'll fly in myself to observe."

43

T h e American embassy in Helsinki was housed in a historic building on a quiet street on the city's north side. Its fenced-in grounds had become Katherine Sears's new home while the lawyers and diplomats sorted out the legal mess of her status in Finland.

"Do not leave the embassy grounds," Cameron Abbott told her shortly after their arrival. "The Sovs may try a kidnapping. General Belov's gone back to Moscow, but the others are still skulking about. I know you're anxious to go home, but this is going to take a while."

"How long, Cameron?" she asked.

"Two weeks. Maybe three."

Katherine nodded. "Can I use the telephone?"

Cameron smiled. "The code for the States is 071."

A minute later, Katherine was on the phone with her father.

"Dad?"

"Kat?" he said groggily. It was 3:30 A.M. in Princeton. "Is that you?"

"I made it, Dad. I wanted you to know, I'm safe."

"Where are you?"

"Helsinki."

"Helsinki? My god. I'll be on the next flight there."

"No, Dad. Stay put. I'm okay. Really. I'll be home in a few weeks, I promise."

Katherine hung up, a bit pleased, a bit troubled.

She slept that night on a firm mattress in a guest suite in a small wing of the embassy. She awoke early, showered, dressed and went to the cafeteria, where she dined alone. Afterward, she wandered the perimeter of the embassy and tried to reflect on her experience in Russia. Already it felt disconnected from her, like a dream that fades the more you think about it.

Cameron found her wandering and led her indoors, past the Marine guard post, to the ambassador's grand office. Flanked by a photograph of President Ronald Reagan and the American flag, a middle-aged man in a double-breasted suit and horn-rimmed glasses rose wearily and came toward her.

"So you're the one," he said distastefully. "You've had half the Embassy up all night, little lady."

Katherine glanced at Cameron and then back at the ambassador.

The ambassador pulled at his lapel. "This is one helluva diplomatic mess, I'll tell you that. The Sovs are raising a huge ruckus, and the Finns — well, they can't hold out forever. They just want you out of the country, fast, and they don't particularly care which direction you go — east or west."

"How are the arrangements coming?" Katherine asked.

"There's a hearing three weeks from tomorrow."

"Then what?"

"There's a flight out the next day. You'll be on it."

Katherine passed the intervening weeks nursing her bruised ribs and meeting a lot of people whose names she didn't even bother to learn — CIA agents, Finnish police, physicians, psychologists and a slew of lawyers and embassy officials. She told them just enough to make them go away. She wasn't sure if they believed her story, but she didn't care. The time would come when she would want to say more, but for now she wanted only to get home.

Grayson Hines called one afternoon. Katherine didn't ask how he had heard about her escape. He got right to the point. "If you ever feel like talking to the press —"

"The story is yours, Grayson," she said. "I promise."

Later that day, Katherine was in a small conference room talking to some men who had flown up from Moscow, when Cameron came in.

"There's someone here to see you," he said.

Titus Waal stepped through the door.

"Titus!" Katherine exclaimed.

Titus was beaming. "Katherine Sears, as I live and breathe."

They rushed toward each other and embraced.

"I was so worried," said Titus. "I thought . . ."

"I know."

The men from Moscow left, and then Titus, Cameron and Katherine began to exchange stories. For the first time, Katherine told everything. At one point, without thinking about it, she lapsed into Russian. There were parts of the story in Ivanovka that Katherine could only express in Russian. The men listened in astonishment.

"Your Russian," Titus exclaimed. "It's fluent."

"I finally found a way to learn Russian. Of course, it's not for everyone . . ."

They all laughed.

Katherine was fascinated to hear about Titus's meeting with Victor in Stelskogo Park.

"Koos really came through with that list," Katherine said, astonished. "You know, he's the hero in this — him and Pavel Danilov."

"Don't underestimate your part, Katherine," said Titus. "Victor never would have met me in the park if you hadn't gone to Russia. Only you could have made him doubt his country." Titus shook his head. "In a way, I feel sorriest for him. Imagine learning that everything you believed was a lie. He's going to have to be awfully strong to follow this to the end."

Katherine nodded. In some ways, Victor's journey was more profound than her own.

Katherine decided it was time to tell the two men what she had deduced about Yevgenia Perova.

"So you think Anton may actually still be in danger?" asked Titus, after she had finished.

"Maybe. I can't know for sure."

"I'll pass it along to Victor — if he calls."

If he calls.

Katherine was about to protest, but she stopped herself. What else could Cameron do? What else could *anyone* do? Her duty was done. It was time to get on with her life.

A hearing the following day would resolve the cloud over her status, and then she would be free to go. Back in her room lay her new American passport and, tucked in the pages, a plane ticket.

She went out that night and sat against a tree, gazing up a long time at the stars. In the east, the Large Magellanic Cloud hung on the edge of Virgo. In two days, it would make its ascension to Pisces. But that no longer mattered. She was going home.

A n hour later, Titus found her beneath the tree. Katherine looked at his face in the dim light and knew something was wrong.

"Cameron said you'd be here."

"What's the matter?" she asked. "What are you doing here?"

Titus was supposed to be in a hotel in town.

"Koos just called me from Amsterdam." He paused. "He got a new dispatch from our orderly at Little Rock. It's about Anton."

Katherine jumped to her feet.

Titus grimaced. "I wonder if I should be telling you this."

"What? Tell me what?"

Titus sighed. "Anton's treatments have *not* stopped, just as you feared."

Katherine went numb.

"I'm afraid that's not all. He's been scheduled for surgery."

"Surgery?"

"A frontal lobotomy, Katherine," Titus said apologetically. "A neurosurgeon is flying in from Moscow—"

Katherine shook her head. "My god, she's a monster."

"You were right. I'm so sorry."

"Does Cameron know?"

"Yes. I told him before I came out here."

"What did he say?"

"What could he say? If Victor calls—"

But Katherine was already gone, sprinting over the manicured grass and past a Marine guard to the back door of the embassy.

Cameron was waiting for her in his temporary office. He was seated behind a large mahogany desk with nothing on it but an American flag paperweight.

"Katherine, I know you're upset, and I'm sorry, but—"

"Sorry?" Katherine exclaimed. "Don't you see what's happening? Yevgenia is controlling the information Victor is getting. He doesn't realize it. And now, because I escaped and blabbed to everyone about Anton being alive, she's scheduled this lobotomy. It's all because of me!"

"You don't know that."

"We've got to do something."

"*We?*"

"Okay, *you*. You've got to get a message to Victor."

"How?" Cameron said, annoyed. "You know what that place is like. It's not as if I can pick up the phone and call him. I'm an attaché of the American Embassy, and he's the son of a Central Committee member. Come on, Katherine. Be reasonable!"

Katherine paused. "Maybe he'll still call you," she said doubtfully.

"Actually, Katherine, that's not possible." His tone became apologetic. "We disconnected the phone line you were using."

"What! How could you—"

"We figure it was bugged," he said defensively. "That's how the Russians traced you to Ivanovka. It's how they knew you were on the *Estonia*."

"Jesus, Cameron! When were you going to tell me about this?"

"Frankly," he said coldly, "I didn't realize it was my responsibility to keep you informed of the workings of the Embassy."

Katherine ignored that. Something occurred to her. "Does Victor know I'm out of the U.S.S.R.?"

"I don't see how he could."

"Cameron, remember what I told you about our rendezvous in the bell tower in Zagorsk on the ascension of the Large Magellanic Cloud?" she asked excitedly.

"Yes."

"Well, there's a meeting there in two days. That's still three days before the lobotomy is scheduled, time enough to stop it. As long as Victor thinks I'm still in the Soviet Union, he will go there. Someone from the embassy could go to the bell tower and warn him!"

Cameron thought about that. "I'll talk to the ambassador."

It was late afternoon the following day when Cameron came to Katherine. She had spent the day pacing the compound like a caged lion, deep in thought, mumbling to herself. By the time Cameron appeared, the shadows from the trees had already plunged the embassy into twilight and the temperature was dropping fast toward the cold Finnish night.

"You're wearing a path in the grass," he said.

Katherine ignored the attempt at levity.

"What did he say?" she asked.

"The Finns have dismissed the charges."

Katherine frowned, confused. Then she remembered — the hearing.

"Oh, that's great news," she said unenthusiastically.

Cameron threw up his arms. "That's all the excitement I get? Katherine, you're going home! There's a flight out tomorrow morning at nine o'clock. You'll be dining in New York tomorrow night!"

Katherine nodded. "Thanks, Cameron," she said with all the graciousness she could muster. "Thank the ambassador . . . everyone."

"I will."

"Now, please, tell me what the Moscow ambassador said about Anton?"

Cameron grimaced. "He said 'No.' "

Katherine gaped. "No?"

"He feels that meeting Victor is beyond the scope of our mission. Sorry."

"My god, Cameron! He has to change his mind!"

"He won't. In the first place, he says your theory about Yevgenia Perova is just — "

"It's not a *theory!* She was in the cabin that night! I know it!"

"Even if you're right, no one really knows quite what to make of it. The ambassador feels the U.S. government would be reckless to get involved without knowing all the facts."

"What facts does he need? Doesn't he know what's going to happen to Anton if Victor doesn't get that message?"

"You have to understand, our mission has a very narrow scope—to further the interests of the citizens of the United States."

"Won't *you* do it for me, Cameron? As a personal favor? Just go to the tower—"

"Katherine, I *can't*. In fact, the situation is even worse than I have told you. If Victor Perov were to call me, say through the central switchboard, I'm forbidden to say anything about this to him. I can only say that you are no longer in the country. I'm sorry, but those are my orders."

Katherine turned on her heels and left the room.

My god. It WAS all for nothing.

That night, Katherine lay in bed for hours, staring at the ceiling and listening to the tick of the clock beside her bed.

A terrifying idea was taking shape in her mind. She was almost afraid to think about it; sometimes thinking led to doing. She got up and went to her dresser, where she found her counterfeit documents in the name Yekatarina Yurgina—the Soviet internal passport and the Soviet international passport stamped with a departure from Tallinn. She turned the documents over in her hand and went over the idea again, looking—almost hoping—for a flaw.

Yekatarina Yurgina was a Soviet citizen, and a Soviet citizen didn't need an entry visa for her own country. She would simply flash the passport and be waved through passport control. Of course, there was the issue of the "black list," but surely that was only for people *leaving* the country. Who would expect Yekatarina Yurgina to *return?*

The *Estonia* ran from Helsinki to Tallinn every Wednesday at 7:00 A.M. She would kill a day in Tallinn and take the sleeper train to Moscow. She would lose an hour when she entered the Moscow time zone. That would put her in Leningrad Station in Moscow about nine o'clock in the morning. Then two hours by taxi from the station to Zagorsk. Eleven o'clock. She would arrive at the bell tower of St. Sergei one hour before noon on the day of the ascension of the Large Magellanic Cloud.

It was possible to warn Victor. Theoretically. But only if she could really get a ticket and . . .

And what the hell was she thinking about?

T h e sun rose promisingly on a clear morning in Helsinki. In his suite on the embassy compound, Cameron Abbott whistled happily as he dressed for his trip to the airport. Along with an escort of four Marine guards and four Finnish policemen, he would be putting Katherine Sears on a morning flight to New York City. After seven months of supervising one of the most trying cases of his career, he was hours from victory over the Soviets.

He was just knotting his tie when the Marine guard knocked at his door.

"Come in."

"Sir, we have a problem," said the Marine.

Cameron straightened his tie, checked his image in the mirror and turned to face the visitor.

"She's gone," said the Marine.

"Who's gone?"

"The woman — Dr. Sears. We can't find her anywhere."

"Don't be ridiculous," Cameron scoffed. "Did you check outdoors? She likes to walk —"

"We looked everywhere. Her room is empty. She took her Russian clothes, and all her things, including her Russian documents. All we found was this."

He put something in Cameron's hand. Cameron looked down at it — Katherine Sears's new American passport. Tucked inside the passport was her plane ticket.

Cameron closed his eyes in defeat.

Katherine had gone back to the U.S.S.R.

44

V i c t o r Perov woke that Thursday morning feeling like an athlete the day after he scored the winning goal.

He jumped out of bed and went to the bathroom to shave. As he did, he had an idea.

He found Oksana in the kitchen in her bathrobe. She had the coffee on the table and was frying potatoes for breakfast.

She must have read something in his face because she said, "You talked to Yevgenia last night, didn't you?"

Victor grinned. "Next week. She said Anton will be transferred out of Little Rock to Perm Hospital on September 26."

"We can see him?"

Victor nodded.

"And the charges . . ."

"Dropped. He'll spend a few days at the hospital under observation, and then we can bring him home."

"Oh, Victor!" said Oksana. "He's really coming home."

Victor went around the table and took his place behind the cup of coffee.

"I was thinking," he said. "We should all go together to Perm to see him."

"Grisha too?"

"Of course. Anton will want to see him. It could be the best medicine."

Her face was radiant. *She* was radiant. A lump swelled in Victor's throat. Anton had a lot to come home to.

Victor took a sip of his coffee. "I have my rendezvous today."

Oksana nodded. "Any word from Yekatarina?"

He shook his head. "I called the embassy, but the line was disconnected."

"Maybe that means she got out."

"Maybe."

"We owe her a lot," said Oksana.

"More than I can ever repay," said Victor. "The least I can do is keep my promise until she gets word to me, somehow, that she's safe. Anyway, Father Andrei is expecting me."

Oksana smiled mischievously and stirred the potatoes in the oil. "Are you becoming religious, Victor?"

He shrugged. "Maybe I am."

They were both quiet a moment, then Oksana said, "I still can't believe it's really over—"

At that moment, the hot oil in the pan exploded. Drops sailed into the air and landed on Oksana's arm. She jerked her hand reflexively, and the pan crashed to the floor. Potatoes and oil spilled onto the linoleum.

In the other room, Grisha began to cry.

Father Andrei and Victor Perov had found the kind of friendship that perhaps only boyhood friends share. They could talk on any subject with complete honesty. They disagreed, sometimes bitterly, but it was inconceivable that the friendship could suffer. Father Andrei had a strength that expressed itself as steadfastness, not to be confused with calm, for the priest could be fiery when roused. He was like a ship onto which you could pile a great load and yet the water line would barely sink. Waves could swell around him, but the mighty bow of his character just cut right through. In this respect, Father Andrei reminded Victor of Anton. But Anton had been troubled and often angry. Father Andrei could be troubled, yes, but even then he was buoyed by a reserve of strength that Victor assumed came from his faith. It mesmerized Victor like a painting he didn't understand, but somehow fathomed.

On this day, they talked mostly about Anton. As noon neared, Victor spoke briefly of his plan to continue Pavel Danilov's work for Soviet Psychiatry Watch.

"That's fine, Victor, but remember: Bars do not imprison men," said Father Andrei. "Our minds do. There are men in prison camps more free than you and me."

Victor nodded. "I think I know what you mean."

At that moment, the bells of St. Sergei rang to life. The sound startled Victor; he had lost track of time.

"You had better go," said the priest. "We can talk more when you come back."

Victor got up and went out through the rectory doors. As he crossed the courtyard alongside the cemetery, something up in the bell tower flashed in the corner of his eye—movement, a bit of color. He stopped and looked up. The platform was still.

He shrugged and walked on. He reached the tower's door and went inside. It was cool and musty-smelling, like a basement. He climbed the stone steps to the second-floor chapel, found the spiral staircase and began to climb, round and round. He reached the first overlook and went immediately to the next level of the staircase. He climbed on. He reached the second overlook and stepped out onto the tiny platform.

Her voice came from behind him, in Russian.

"Nice of you to make it, Victor."

45

V i c t o r Perov is eight years old. He stands on a river bank in the hot sun on a perfect August afternoon. He squints at a spot on the swift-moving surface of the Moscow River. It is the spot where his twin brother has dived down after a burlap sack of puppies. Time has passed. Too much time. The boy-Victor takes his eyes from the spot and turns to his mother. She is beside him. She, too, stares at the spot.

Why doesn't she do something?

He looks at her the way any eight-year-old boy looks at his mother. She is beautiful in a way that defines beauty. She is his universe. Her arms are the arms that hold him when he is hurting. Her face is the face in the dark room after a nightmare. Her lips are the lips that kiss him and tell him everything is all right. Her body is the body that gave him life.

Why doesn't she do something?

The boy-Victor sees in her face an expression he knows—a set jaw, a shimmer in the eye. It is the look of hard decision. The Iron Perova.

There by the river, he sees that look on his mother's face, and he recognizes it. But he does not acknowledge it. For he is a boy and this woman is his mother, and what kind of mother would wish her own son to die?

V i c t o r now knew the answer. For until Katherine Sears had finished telling him what had happened in the cabin that April night in Lubertsi—that Yevgenia had been there supervising the interrogation—Victor had never rid himself of that eight-year-old boy's vision of his mother.

Now, with the eyes of a man, Victor looked back on that scene by the river and understood it perfectly.

And he knew what he had to do.

But first he needed permission from Oksana. He would have to break a promise.

46

KGB Major Konstantin Tarasov had turned up on Victor's doorstep nearly five weeks earlier, shortly after Victor and Oksana returned from their two-week camping odyssey on Bald Top. Victor was coming home late one night after a meeting with Yevgenia. He turned the corner to his apartment, and there was Tarasov, the mysterious, vanishing KGB man, sitting on the stairs. It gave Victor a start.

It was Tarasov, but it wasn't. He was like a different man, and not just because of the lost arm. He looked beaten, desperate, no longer the cocky detective who had stood in Victor's office doorway the night after the meeting of the SAPO collective. He was in hiding, he said, and could not even go to his wife, who had, in any event, married another man. He had been betrayed by someone in the KGB. Someone had sabotaged his helicopter. He thought he knew who.

Tarasov's words tumbled out fitfully, between furtive gazes up the corridor when he would listen warily for the sound of pursuit. Then he would relax and go on.

Victor agreed to listen to Tarasov's story only because he knew the KGB man had not been involved in Katherine's abduction. Maria Danilova had "blown" Koos van der Laan to the KGB — not Katherine, as Koos had assumed that day in the park. Tarasov had been telling Victor the truth that day outside his SAPO office.

Victor was puzzled that Tarasov should come to him. Why? What did Victor have to do with KGB internal intrigue?

Then Tarasov sprang his surprise: He had information relating to Anton. It involved a foreigner who had been killed near Norway last November while trying to cross the border.

At once, Victor made the connection to Anton's letter:

> *On November 9, 1983, I was on the Kolsky Peninsula near Norway. I was making a survey of the border fortifications in advance of my escape attempt the next day. By chance I saw a man gunned down as he fled across the forbidden zone . . .*

A coincidence?

Tarasov went on to say he had evidence of a scandal that went all the way to the Politburo. He didn't know the connection to Anton, except that there certainly was one. He said he hoped they could help each other.

Victor had sent him away: There was the matter of his promise to Oksana that he would never ask for help from anyone in the KGB.

But before he left, Tarasov had given Victor a way to contact him. Now, with Katherine Sears in Moscow and Yevgenia days from supervising a frontal lobotomy on Anton, Victor was ready to do just that.

That afternoon, Victor took Katherine, Oksana and Grisha on a suburban train to his old family dacha in Petrovka, two hours from Moscow. He left them at eleven o'clock that night, saying only that he had to meet someone. Oksana and Katherine were on the sofa, deep in conversation. Initially, there was some suspicion between them, but it quickly disappeared. They seemed to have hit it off.

Victor found Tarasov in a cabin south of Moscow, right where he had said he would be. Tarasov ushered him inside enthusiastically. The cabin was small, with a tidy garden out front and two small rooms upstairs and down. In the corner of the living room, stacked six feet high, were hundreds of books—thrillers, one after another. Victor tried to picture the KGB agent passing his days reading spy stories, cooking and working in his garden. Victor gave up: It didn't fit. Could Tarasov have changed so much?

Tarasov offered him tea from a samovar, and they sat at the kitchen table talking far into the night, swapping information. Tarasov leaped from his seat when Victor told of Anton's letter. This was the link Tarasov had been looking for: Anton had witnessed the shooting of Stepan Bragin.

They began to construct a plan. Victor admired Tarasov's ruthless mind, but he found it a bit unnerving too. Tarasov's eyes glowed fiercely as he plotted his revenge, and Victor could believe that he had once been a very good KGB agent. Perhaps Tarasov had not changed so much after all.

Victor returned to Petrovka at dawn and slipped into bed for a few hours' sleep. At 9:00 A.M., he gathered Katherine and Oksana in the living room. Grisha played out back in the very gazebo where the collie Emma had once given birth to a litter of puppies. The two women sat together on the sofa facing Victor.

Victor began to talk. He told them about Tarasov and what the KGB man had found out. He told them what he thought it meant. Finally, he told them his plan.

Victor watched the women carefully. Katherine was captivated: He could see her mind calculating, weighing risks, looking for holes—ever the scientist. Oksana's face was impenetrable. It was like a Greek bust of Aphrodite, beautiful, but cold. For the plan to succeed, Konstantin Tarasov would have to tame the lioness. Victor did not envy him.

Victor said his piece. It took an hour.

"So you have already contacted this KGB man?" asked Oksana.

Victor nodded. "Last night. We talked for five hours."

"I see," said Oksana.

"I won't do anything without the consent of both of you," he said. "All I ask is that you hear the man out."

Katherine and Oksana exchanged glances. Katherine shrugged.

"You know how I feel," Oksana said to Victor. "But if Katherine agrees, then I'll listen."

"Let's hear what he has to say," said Katherine.

Victor went to the window of the dacha and raised the shade.

A minute later, there was a knock at the door. Victor pulled open the door, and into the dacha stepped Konstantin Tarasov.

Katherine took her cue from Oksana and did not get up. She watched the KGB man from the sofa. Tarasov wore peasant clothes: a loosely woven sweater, gray polyester slacks and cheap black shoes. He looked like a poor collective farmer come to the big city. His cheeks and forehead were raked with pink scars from his helicopter crash. His left sleeve was sewn closed at the bicep. Katherine's eyes were drawn to his stub the way a person's gaze is drawn irresistibly to human deformity. The little stub moved as though it still believed it slung a heavy arm.

Victor nodded to Tarasov and motioned him into the living room.

"Good morning, ladies," Tarasov said with a smile. It was an engaging smile, and Katherine realized suddenly that though Tarasov bore the scars of a terrible ordeal, he was still a handsome man.

"Good morning," said Katherine.

Oksana said nothing. Her arms were folded across her chest.

Tarasov came toward them. He put out his hand to Katherine. "So you're Katherine Sears. It's a pleasure to meet you at last."

Katherine shook his hand. Women in Russia are expected to offer limp handshakes, but Katherine defied convention and gave him a good old American handshake—three pumps, one-two-three.

Next, Tarasov offered his hand to Oksana. "And you must be Oksana Filipova."

She stared at his hand as though it were a rotten fish under her nose. He withdrew it and looked around awkwardly for a place to sit. No one spoke, so he sat in the armchair at the end of the coffee table. Victor sat down in a chair across from the women. So now the four of them—Victor, Katherine, Oksana and Konstantin Tarasov—formed a square around the small coffee table.

The room was quiet.

Tarasov looked at Victor. "You're on," said Victor.

Tarasov cleared his throat. At that moment, in spite of herself, Katherine felt a little sorry for the KGB man. What could he possibly say to convince them that he deserved a place in their square?

Then Tarasov began to tell the most remarkable story.

47

T h e reindeer goddess's name was Kamala Tuchana. It was an Urguma name.

She found Konstantin Tarasov, near death, in the wreckage of the C-9 helicopter on Upper Sharuleis Flats. She had been traveling on foot with her husband, three children and a small herd of reindeer when she spotted the black smoke. The weather was good, so the family decided to detour across the flats. It took them two days to reach the crash site.

Kamala's husband lifted Tarasov from the wreckage. The other men were dead, so he left them. He carried Tarasov to their *chum*, a tiny wooden hut on a reindeer-drawn sled. In the old days, *chums* were tepees made of reindeer hide. Nowadays, Urguma preferred something more solid. They kept the traditional name, though.

They traveled for two weeks across barren tundra. The weather was good, and their pace, six miles a day, was about maximum for an Urguma family with a *chum*, an injured Russian and twenty-seven reindeer.

Tarasov remembered little from the journey. He was delirious most of the time, with a few snapshotlike moments of clarity. He would awake in the *chum*, which was not much larger than a large outhouse, and listen to the jingle of the bells on the reindeer and the *shhh* of the snow gliding under the sleds. The Tuchanas talked among themselves—and to the reindeer—but their language was strange. It would blend with his dreams, and then he would fall back into his delirium.

They joined the tribe on the fifteenth day. By then, Tarasov's fever had broken, but he was still too weak to get out of bed. He felt sick every time he looked at his empty sleeve.

Already, Tarasov was a child of the reindeer. The herd sustained him, as it sustained all the Urguma. At first, Kamala had given Tarasov reindeer milk to keep up his strength. Later, she added reindeer meat to his diet. Kamala rubbed a salve made of ground reindeer horn into his wound. He lay beneath a blanket of reindeer hide. Kamala's coat, hood, pants, boots and mittens were all made of reindeer hide. It was why, when Tarasov had lain delirious and near death in the wreckage of the helicopter, he had mistaken Kamala for a reindeer goddess.

Chief Yulan came to his bedside that first night in camp, the Tuchanas clearing out of their *chum* in anticipation of the meeting.

The sight of the chief was a disappointment to Tarasov. He wore the same reindeer-hide clothing as the other Urguma. There were no extra beads, no necklaces, no hats, nothing at all to distinguish him from everyone else in the tribe—except for his age, that is, which was certainly greater than those of the others. But how much so? Tarasov, who prided himself on his detective's eye, could not guess. What were the dynamics of aging out on the tundra, where a warm day was zero degrees and the nearest tomato was five hundred miles away? The chief might have been a hundred; he might have been forty. He had a round, weathered face that was as tight as an aging movie actress's. He had eyes as black as onyx, frozen into a perpetual squint.

"You are able to talk?" he asked Tarasov, and his breath was visible in the dim *chum*. His Russian wasn't good, but it was understandable.

"Yes."

"Then you must tell us who you are."

"I'm a KGB agent."

The chief nodded grimly. "That accounts for the gun." The chief rose. "We have a radio. I'll call Ust-Nera and—"

"No," said Tarasov.

The chief sat back down and waited.

"Don't call anyone. Please. Not yet."

"Your arm needs professional attention."

"My helicopter crash was not an accident."

The old chief contemplated him. Something in his gaze told Tarasov that one didn't lie to the chief. "Why do you think this?" the chief asked.

"Because of what my death would erase," said Tarasov.

The chief looked at Tarasov a long time, and Tarasov had the distinct feeling he was looking deep inside him. It was unsettling. After several minutes, the chief stood up and went to the door. "I will think on your request," he said and left.

The chief was a slow thinker, and the weeks passed. Meanwhile, Tarasov grew stronger. Kamala moved him to his own *chum*, where he remained in bed. From Kamala, Tarasov learned that the tribe was made up of fifty people, ten families so interrelated that they were really like one family.

"In all the world, there are only sixteen hundred of us," Kamala told him one day as he lay in bed eating. At least he was feeding himself now. "Half our people don't even know our language. Only about two hundred of us still live by the old way, and as you see—" she smiled. "—it's not quite the old way."

The children, she said, went to Russian schools in Ust-Nera. Helicopters came to collect them.

"Few want to return to the old life once they've lived in the outside world," she said. "They're glad that some of us still keep the old ways alive. But they think we're crazy."

"What do you think?" Tarasov asked.

She thought a minute. "It's a hard life on the tundra, that's true. But I have noticed that few of our people find happiness in the outside world. They're not part of that world. I don't think you can just say, 'Up until now I've been one person, now I'll be another.'"

"Do they ever come back?" Tarasov asked.

"Some. But by then, they're not part of our world anymore, either. A lot of them are alcoholics. It's like they're stuck in a place that is neither here nor there."

"A forbidden zone," Tarasov said to himself.

Kamala looked at him strangely. "You talk in riddles, Konstantin Tarasov. Perhaps we will make an Urguma of you yet."

The logic of Urguma life was the logic of animal husbandry. Reindeer grazed on frozen grass beneath the snow. That grass was so sparse that each reindeer needed many acres of land just to survive. As a result, the reindeer herders moved constantly over enormous distances.

A week passed, and they moved. Three days passed, and they moved again.

"Why doesn't the chief answer?" Tarasov asked Kamala one day.

"He is greatly troubled by you," she replied. "He looks into your soul, and he sees blackness."

So they moved again. Tarasov learned that they were moving west, toward Olengorodok, where part of the herd would be given over to the collective for slaughter. Technically, the Urguma were members of a very large collective farm. They tended the collective's herd, for which they received wages. They migrated between slaughterhouses at the two endpoints of their migration — Olengorodok in the west and Oimyakon in the east.

In the fifth week, Tarasov got out of bed. Kamala gave him a reindeer-hide coat, boots and a single mitten for his right hand. She had sewn closed the left sleeve just over his stub. He fumbled with the clothing for a half-hour, but at last he was dressed. He went outside. Kamala saw him and giggled. He looked at himself miserably.

"I look ridiculous," he said.

"Like a white Urguma." She laughed.

So he began to train himself for his new life with one arm. He learned to button a button and to lace his boots. It was maddening. Tarasov tried to help with the herd, but there was little he could have done even if he had both arms. The animals shied from him. He did help with chores by cutting reindeer meat with a bone-handled knife. That proved to be a source of amusement for the tribe, since it was considered women's work.

"At least I'm good for a laugh," he said morosely to Kamala.

In that time, Tarasov thought a lot about his predicament. The world believed he was dead, and for the time being it would have to stay that way. Marina would marry Vladic Titovo, and there was nothing he could do about it. Tarasov felt keenly the pain of the ruin of his family: It was as if he had lost his other arm. But he consoled himself that at least young Sasha would be provided for. Marina was doing her duty as a mother in the only way left to her. Now he would do *his* duty. He turned his mind to the helicopter crash. The conclusion was inescapable: The helicopter had been sabotaged in Oimyakon, or perhaps the previous day at Leslog-11. And that meant he had been betrayed by someone in the KGB. But who? Leo was the only person who had known he was in Siberia. What did Leo have to gain by his death?

One day, as he walked among the herd with Kamala, he asked about Stepan Bragin's wife, Nadia.

"Never speak this name to the chief," she said sharply.

"Why?"

But she would say no more. And that was the end of the matter until one day in August, just a week from Olengorodok, when the chief called Tarasov to his *chum*. Tarasov went, and they sat on opposite sides of a tiny picnic table.

"I have watched you," the chief said. "And I have looked every day into your soul. Now I see that your arm was the source of your darkness. This is why it was taken from you: In order to save the rest of you."

Tarasov didn't know what to say to that.

"There are things you have not yet told me, yes?" asked the chief.

Tarasov nodded. "When the helicopter crashed, I was coming to see you."

The chief nodded as though this didn't surprise him. "Why?"

"I have been warned not to speak this name to you."

"Speak it."

"Nadia Bragina."

The chief gave no reaction. "What do you know of her?" he asked.

"I know she died of cancer. I know she was married to a foreigner who spent many years in the camps."

"How do you know this?"

"I was at their *yurt*. I saw her grave."

Again, the chief looked at Tarasov a long time.

"You are a puzzle to me," said the chief. "I cannot help feeling that an evil has been delivered to us, yet that this evil is also part of a purpose that is good."

"Look, Chief," said Tarasov, shifting in his seat. "I am grateful to you for saving

me and hiding me here. I think I have been very patient. But I can't wait forever.
I need to know things. And I need straight answers. No more riddles."

"What do you wish to know?"

"You helped Stepan Bragin escape from Oimyakon, didn't you?"

The chief stared at him.

"The man with the stub nose?"

He said nothing.

"Answer me!"

The chief just stared.

"I know you did," said Tarasov. "Do you realize you could be arrested for giving
aid to a fugitive? Now that he is dead, shot while trying to escape —"

"Enough!" said the chief, and for the first time Tarasov saw the old man angry.
"I see now I have acted foolishly with you. When we reach Olengorodok, I will
inform the police of you."

"You would sign my death warrant," Tarasov said fiercely. "And your own."

The chief glared at Tarasov, absorbing the veracity of the threat. Then, without
a word, he turned and went out.

That night, after the camp went to sleep, Tarasov slipped out of bed. He
dressed quietly and got his bone-handled knife from the table. He went out the
door of his *chum*. It was summer so the sun shone low on the horizon. The only
sound was the jingle of the bells of the reindeer and the crunch of the snow
beneath his deerskin boots. He crept to the chief's *chum* and pulled open the
door. The old man was asleep with his head beside the entrance. One of his
daughters slept with her young son on the opposite wall.

Tarasov knelt beside the chief and put the knife to his old throat. The onyx
eyes snapped open and looked at Tarasov with alarm, and then sadness.

"You cannot kill me," he whispered.

"I have killed before."

"So you believe."

Tarasov paused. "What are you talking about?"

The chief sighed. "Put away your weapon, Konstantin Tarasov. I have already
decided to give you what you seek."

The chief slid out of bed and got dressed. His daughter awoke and looked at
him with concern. He said something to her in Urguma, and she rolled over and
went back to sleep. The chief retrieved something from the cupboard and slipped
it into his pocket. They went outside and started to walk toward the herd.

"Yes," said the chief. "I helped Stepan escape Yakutia. He traveled with us
exactly as you are traveling with us now. We took him to Olengorodok. From
there, he traveled with the Yevenki Eskimos, who passed him to the Dolgani
Eskimos, who took him all the way to the Urals. From there, he made his own

way to Norway. At least, that was the plan. I never worried about Stepan. He was the only white man I ever met who knew more about life in the Arctic than an Urguma."

"Why did you do it?"

"For my daughter."

"Nadia."

The chief nodded. "She left the tribe to marry the foreigner. I was against it. Not because I oppose the outside world. Our life is not for everyone. But Nadia was special. She had a deep connection to the spirit world, like a shaman. But shamans are men. It was very puzzling."

They reached the herd and began to move among the animals. From time to time, the chief would brush a reindeer's nose or pull at an antler the way a mother fusses with her child's hair even when it's fine. The chief was leading him somewhere, and Tarasov wondered where.

"Nadia believed that Stepan was kept alive all those years in order to fulfill a purpose. You have told me he is dead. This saddens me, but I believe you speak the truth. So, I wondered, was my dear Nadia wrong? For a while, I doubted her. But then I realized I was making the same mistake as you white men, who see death as an ending. That is why I was so angry when you told me Stepan was killed."

"I'm not following you."

"Stepan's death is part of his purpose."

"How?"

"I don't know." The chief sighed and looked hard at Tarasov. "But I am forced to accept that you are part of it, too, Konstantin Tarasov. And that is why I have decided to give you what you want — not because of your knife."

The chief stopped beside a large pine tree. It had a low branch that bent almost to the snow. A boulder lay just beyond the tip of the branch. It looked as though the tree were straining to touch the boulder.

"Before she died, Nadia asked me to help Stepan with his journey. It's an Urguma belief. You can't ascend to heaven unless your body is buried in the ground of your birth. Stepan was worried that he would fail to complete the journey, so he gave me something, which he said I should keep safe."

The chief reached into his pocket and pulled out two leather-bound books. He held them in his mittens and waved them.

"This is what you're looking for," he said.

"What is it?"

"Stepan's memoirs. He worked on them all summer as we traveled to Olengorodok: He was as useless with the reindeer as you are. He gave them to me exactly one year ago on this very spot." He slapped the boulder. "He said if I ever learned that his quest had failed, then perhaps these could help him see it through."

"How?"

"I don't know."

"You haven't read them?"

"I can't. They are in English."

Tarasov's eyes widened. "English!"

The chief nodded.

"I read English," said Tarasov.

The chief handed the books to Tarasov. "So let us begin. Read."

With his one hand, Tarasov fumbled to open the first book. On the inside page, in carefully printed letters, was written:

The diary of Stepan Bragin. Volume 1

The two men sat down side by side on the boulder. Tarasov flipped the page and began to read aloud, translating simultaneously into Russian for the chief:

> *My name is Stepan Bragin, but it was not always so.*
>
> *I consider myself a lucky man. For how many men can claim to have lived three lives?*
>
> *My first life began with my birth on February 12, 1923, in Rochester, New York, in the United States of America.*

Tarasov stopped reading. "My god! Bragin was American!"

"Yes," said the chief. "Read on."

> *My parents were John and Sarah. They gave me the name I used throughout my first life: Donald Mortimer Turnhill. As I recall, Mortimer was my great-grandfather's name. Growing up, I showed no special talents, but I could fix a car pretty well. When I was old enough to work, I got a job at the biggest auto garage in Rochester. I was saving money to open my own garage. Such were my dreams. At nineteen I married Martha. A year later, we had a son, David. My son was not yet one year old when I left for Europe to be a navigator in the war. I flew reconnaissance missions for three months. On September 19, 1944, my plane was shot down near Prague. And that was my first life.*
>
> *My second life began in a German prison camp and went on for a long time as I was moved from one camp to the next. By then, I was in Siberia. I lived under many identities. The last one was Stepan Bragin. This was my second life, and the longest one. It lasted for thirty-two years.*
>
> *My third life began on May 1, 1979, the day I married Yelichuri Yulan, the daughter of an Urguma tribal chief, my Nadia. I had been released from the camps six months earlier and was living out an epilogue to my second life. But*

we fell in love and, as I said, we got married. So I found myself, at age fifty-six,
beginning a third life. It was my best life. It was also the shortest. It ended the
day she died—April 4, 1983.

So those were my three lives. I have no wish for a fourth. I have no bitterness
about my fate. Four years of happiness is more than most people can claim. And
I have learned that a minute of happiness, true happiness, wipes away a year of
pain. So, to my amazement, as my time with Nadia passed, the bitterness that
had accumulated over my long, second life melted away like an ice cube left out
in the sun.

So, you ask, why write these memoirs? It is not vanity, and it is not out of a
desire that my story be told. In fact, it is my wish that the contents of these diaries
be kept secret, and that when my promise to Nadia is fulfilled, the person in
possession of these recollections burn them and then cast the ashes over my grave.
Let the relatives of the man who was called Donald Turnhill believe he died in a
plane crash all those years ago. In a way, he did.

I am putting my story to words now because I carry a terrible secret. This secret
is the crux of my life—indeed, it is the whole logic of my life. I leave behind this
journal in order that this secret not perish with my death. What I desire from this
journal is only that it help fulfill the final wish of my beloved Nadia, whose name
in Russian means "hope," and who was my hope. It is this: that my bodily remains
be buried in the place of my birth, the United States of America, so that we may
be joined in eternity. This is her belief, and my sacred vow to her before her death.
If I fail in my quest then it is my hope that this journal can be used to fulfill the
vow that, in life, I left undone.

What follows are my recollections from the three lives of Stepan Bragin.

In the dacha in Petrovka, Tarasov stopped and looked at the faces of Victor,
Oksana and Katherine. They stared at him as though under a spell.

Tarasov pursed his lips. "So, for the next week, sitting on the very boulder
where Bragin had given his memoirs to Chief Yulan, I read aloud the story of the
three lives of Stepan Bragin."

The room was quiet.

"What did it say?" asked Oksana. It was the first she had spoken since Tarasov
had come into the house. With her question, Katherine felt the icy mood in the
room thaw.

Tarasov must have felt it too, because he smiled appreciatively. He reached
into his pocket and pulled out two leather-bound books. He dropped them on
the coffee table.

"See for yourself."

48

T h e Borovitsky Gate was a thirty-foot-high archway hollowed into one of the Kremlin's twenty red-star-topped towers. It served as the staff-only entrance to the seventeenth-century fortress turned twentieth-century office complex that was the seat of power for the Soviet Union.

Victor Perov stood at the gate while the guard checked his pass. It was 3:00 P.M., a few hours after Konstantin Tarasov finished his story of his six months with the Urguma Eskimos. Victor waited, going over in his mind once again what he was going to say. At last, the guard waved him through, and Victor started along the driveway to the grounds. The yellow Hall of Palaces came into view and he turned toward it. He was met by another guard, who, like the first, wore the gray-and-white uniform of the elite Kremlin Guard.

"Who are you visiting?"

"Minister Yevgenia Perova."

The guard phoned Yevgenia's office. Her secretary gave approval, and the guard asked Victor to walk through a metal detector. He gave Victor a white VISITOR pass, which Victor pinned to his shirt pocket.

The guard said, "Second floor, end of the—"

"I know the way."

But Victor didn't go to Yevgenia's office. Instead, he followed the long hallway past her office, then climbed the twisting Catherine the Great staircase. At the top, he turned left and followed the wide corridor. As he walked, he read the door plates that bore the household names of the members of the Soviet Politburo. He stopped at the last one on the hall:

Podolok, Anatoly Mikhailovich
Party Secretary for Ideology

He went in.

The receptionist regarded Victor distrustfully. "You mean you don't have an appointment?"

"No."

"How did you even get *in* here?" she asked, eyeing the VISITOR pass. "Perhaps I should call security—"

"Comrade Podolok will see me."

"Is that so?"

"I guarantee it."

"Who shall I tell him is here?"

"Donald Mortimer Turnhill."

She got up and, with a quick warning knock, went through the door to Podolok's inner sanctum. She came out a few seconds later.

"You may go in," she said.

Podolok was on his feet looking at Victor with a mixture of alarm and curiosity. He stayed behind his desk, leaning on it for support. Podolok looked so frail that a bad cold might kill him. He was not what Victor had expected from the man he now knew was his mortal enemy.

"Your mother sent you?" asked Podolok.

"Yevgenia doesn't know I'm here."

"You gave a name to my secretary—"

"Donald Turnhill."

Podolok winced. "What do you know of this name?"

Victor told him.

"I assume you can prove this."

"I have his diaries."

Podolok's lip turned up distastefully, and he sat down. He opened a cigarette case on his desk and tapped an imported cigarette against his bony palm. He jammed it into a long, ivory holder and then lit it. He took a deep drag as though it were an asthmatic's inhaler nozzle. Victor remained on his feet.

Victor said, "Before you think about arresting me or turning me over to your hatchet lady, Yevgenia Perova . . ."

Podolok raised his eyebrows at that.

". . . you should know that Turnhill himself requested that his story not be made public. And I have every intention of respecting his wish."

Podolok regarded Victor with new interest. He motioned for Victor to sit down.

"I prefer to stand," Victor said.

"Suit yourself," Podolok shrugged. "So he wrote it all down, did he? Of course he would. Who would have thought that son-of-a-bitch would live all these years?"

"Turnhill wrote that General Vlasov found him after he bailed out of his plane over Czechoslovakia."

Podolok nodded and blew smoke out his nose. "It was chaos, you cannot imagine. General Andrei Vlasov was as charismatic a Russian as you're ever going to meet. That's something they don't tell you in the history books. He recruited me out of a German prison camp, so he meant freedom for me, but there was more to it than that. Vlasov laid it out so clearly—all the blunders Stalin was making, the execution of most of the top officers during the purges, the *tenners* they were handing out just for being captured . . . I mean, a lot of us boys were more afraid of Stalin than Hitler. The most patriotic thing we could do was form a temporary alliance with Hitler—at least, that's the way Vlasov put it. Besides, he assured us the Germans were going to win." Podolok smiled. "Anyway, one day in the fall of '44 Vlasov was moving our regiment west outside Prague: No one trusted us on the Eastern Front. We were humping it through a forest and there he was, this American, his parachute all hung up in a tree like a goddamn kite." Podolok shook his head. "It took us a half-hour to get him down. I should have shot him then."

"But you put him in a German POW camp instead."

Podolok nodded. "That was Vlasov's call. He said the Americans were our friends, even if they were allied with the Red Army, which was supposed to be our enemy. It was crazy. But Vlasov had his own ideas about friends and enemies, as we all know. Anyway, Vlasov asked me to march the American to the nearest POW camp. It took about two days. At the time, it didn't seem a particularly important matter. I rather enjoyed it, actually. He was a nice kid. A bit simple."

"How did you escape? The Americans turned over the Vlasov division to Stalin in 1944. They were executed for treason."

"Like I said, it was chaos. I had deserted General Vlasov a few hours before the Americans got him. So there I was, a Russian, wandering around behind enemy lines. Time was running out for me, I knew. I remembered about Donald Turnhill, and went to Stalag 33. The Russians were just a day away from overtaking it; I could hear their artillery. The commandant had his own worries, so he didn't try to stop me from seeing Turnhill. I pulled a gun on him and confiscated his uniform and his dogtags. I gave him my clothes. When the Russians finally caught up with me, I just pretended to be American. After that it was easy to blend back into a Soviet regiment."

"And you fixed it so Turnhill went to Siberia."

"He was supposed to be executed with the rest of the vlasovites, and to this day I don't know what went wrong. Perhaps the Germans double-crossed me. In any event, there wasn't much doubt about where he would wind up. He was in a German POW camp for Red Army soldiers, and he had my uniform—I knew the Russians wouldn't believe him. They'd think his feeble Russian was some stunt to spare himself a *tenner*. Later, after the war, when there was a big fuss about a missing vlasovite, I got kind of worried. I looked for the American then, but there were too many camps, too many fifty-eighters. Eventually, it all died down. Everyone who knew anything was dead."

"Executed by Stalin. How convenient."

Podolok shrugged.

Victor said, "So you fought beside the Red Army to Berlin and returned to Moscow a decorated war hero."

"I earned those medals."

"You would have a hard time convincing the procurator general about that," said Victor. " 'Vlasovite' means 'scum' on the streets. I hear the drunks in the subway use the word when they talk about rats."

Podolok jammed his cigarette into the ashtray. "What do you want? I assume that's what this is about—blackmail. Like mother, like son."

Victor frowned. "I have the diaries. What has Yevgenia got on you?"

"Bragin's dying confession to your brother. The son-of-a-bitch told him everything."

Victor gasped. That was it! The reason for Anton's incarceration! His brother knew the truth about the stub-nose man. Victor thought about the decision Yevgenia had faced that night in Leningrad—her son's life in exchange for her ministry post—and the choice she had made. The room grew hot, and the walls seemed to press in around him.

Podolok must have read the look on Victor's face. "Your mother signed Anton's commitment order herself. She never hesitated." Podolok sneered. "She's something else, your mother, the polished product of sixty years of communism. The Iron Perova! She's practically an argument against Lenin."

Victor closed his eyes. The betrayal was complete. In setting out to save his brother, Victor had been prepared to confront the rot of his own system. But to find it *within his own family*? It was too much. Yet, realistically, how could his family have escaped cleanly? His mother was a product of communism as much as its emissary. The world had gone gray for Victor, and he could no longer tell the victims from the criminals. Were there no rules?

Suddenly, he thought of something Father Andrei had said. One afternoon several months back, Victor had summoned up the courage to ask the priest about the source of his bewildering self-assurance.

"Is it faith?" Victor asked.

Father Andrei smiled. "Faith in what? Your mother's faith in communism is genuine, but does it bring her peace?" He shook his head, and his deep-set eyes glowed intensely. "You are a scientist, Victor, so you seek certainty. But there is no certainty in the world but the certainty of our own hearts."

Victor wondered what certainty, if any, lay in his own heart. On that day in Father Andrei's study, he had been unprepared to seek the answer. But now, with the truth about his mother laid bare before him, Victor was at last ready to set aside everything he had once believed and peer into the murky confusion of his own heart. It was the most terrifying thing he had ever attempted. At first, he saw nothing, just a muddy cloud like the scene from his nightmares. But then gradually his vision began to clear. His eyes filled with tears at what he saw. Looking back at him were the faces of the people he loved—Anton, Oksana, Grisha . . .

And Katherine.

Victor took a deep breath. Father Andrei was right: It was time to trust his own heart.

Podolok had been watching Victor thoughtfully for signs of weakness. Victor wiped away his tears and met the old eyes steadily.

"First, I want my brother Anton Perov released from Little Rock Special Psychiatric Hospital and flown to the border post on the Norwegian border."

"Norway?" asked Podolok, surprised. "Why there?"

"It's a NATO country. You wouldn't dare fire across the border. And you can get Anton there more easily than anywhere in Eastern Europe."

Podolok nodded.

"Second, I want safe passage to the same border post for myself, Oksana Filipova and her son Grisha. It's a restricted zone, so we'll need special passes."

"Is that all?"

"I want you to contact the Norwegian embassy and tell them to have a physician standing by to treat Anton. You can describe his condition. You know it better than I do."

Podolok's face was placid, impossible to read.

"There are a few other matters," said Victor. "They are small. I will tell them to you at the border."

"And what, may I ask, is the plan?"

"In two days, at precisely five o'clock, your helicopter will land at the border post. You will have Anton with you. Oksana, Grisha and I will be waiting in a jeep. If you touch down one minute before five o'clock the deal is off, and I give the diaries to the KGB. After everyone is across the border, I will give you further instructions."

"And why should I trust you? Once you are all safely in Norway, what guarantee do I have, even if I have the diaries, that you won't reveal everything anyway?"

"You will have a hostage."

"Who?"

"Me. I'm staying in the Soviet Union."

Yevgenia Perova was at her desk when Podolok came through her office door and slipped into her guest chair. She was emotionless as he told her about his visit from Victor.

"I told him to stay out of this," she said softly. She spoke as though some course of action were now ordained.

"You realize that if Anton defects there is nothing I can do to protect you in the Central Committee."

Yevgenia nodded.

"You'll be ruined. For the son of a Central Committee member to defect—"

"I understand," she said irritably. "What did you have in mind?"

"A simple double-cross. We grab the diaries and arrest them on the spot. They chose a poor location. We can control everything."

Yevgenia nodded. "Agreed. But nothing is to happen to Victor, you understand?"

"Belov's team will go up there tomorrow morning to lay the trap. He shouldn't have a problem. After all, it's his old command."

"And you?"

"I'm flying to Little Rock tonight to get Anton. From there, we'll fly to Murmansk. Then on to the border by Navy helicopter."

"I'm going with you."

Podolok blew a gust of air through his nose. "I figured as much."

On the fourth floor of KGB headquarters, the intercom on KGB Director Oleg Shatalin's desk buzzed. He rammed the CALL button.

"I said no phone calls," he barked.

"I'm sorry, comrade director. This is important."

"Who is it?"

"She says her name is Katherine Sears."

49

T h e fifty-two-mile border between Norway and the Soviet Union was bridged at a single point located 130 miles north of the Arctic Circle. The Soviets imaginatively called the point A-1. It was the only place on earth where a person could walk directly from the Soviet Union into a NATO country (excluding the Bering ice bridge, which melts each summer). The nearest village was Nikel, a little, knock-about place for border guards, power station workers, and the occasional sportsman with connections sufficient to wrangle a coveted visa for the heavily patrolled area.

Two days after his meeting with Anatoly Podolok, Victor, Oksana and Grisha arrived by train in Nikel. It was the end of a busy thirty-nine hours.

They had spent the first half-day packing. Oksana filled six enormous canvas bags with a significant portion of her worldly possessions. Victor watched her grimly for a long time. When she put a warped frying pan into Bag Number Four he suggested delicately that perhaps all of these things weren't needed.

"We don't know what they'll have in America," she snapped.

Victor didn't argue. Oksana was leaving her job, her friends, her country and her parents without so much as a good-bye. True, she was to be reunited with her husband, but that was also a source of worry. What kind of shape would Anton be in? He had looked bad when they had seen him through the telescope two months earlier. Since then, his drug therapy had continued. So Victor didn't argue with her about the frying pan, or the plastic ashtray, or even the eleven rolls of toilet paper.

That night they boarded the train to Murmansk. Conversation, in the rare moments when there had been conversation, was about Grisha. What lay ahead of them loomed too monstrous for words. To Victor, it felt as though they were falling. They were in gravity's grip now, and what would happen would happen. He thought a lot about Katherine. He wished she were with him, but he knew she was in good hands with Konstantin Tarasov.

Midway to Murmansk, Victor fell into a peaceful sleep. The dreams of drowning that had haunted him for the past year had ended as abruptly as they had begun. It was as though, having come to terms with what had happened at the river that day in 1960, his unconscious had ended its assault.

He did dream—about Katherine Sears. They were in the bell tower kissing. Only now there was nothing to cut short their embrace, no KGB agents, no snooping Intourist guide, just the two of them, their lips, their breath and their bodies locked together in a kiss that would last a lifetime . . .

He awoke reluctantly. Oksana was shaking him.

"We're here," she said.

Murmansk.

Victor rubbed his eyes and got to his feet. Today was the day.

Their carriage was hitched to the Nikel train, and they began to move again. Until that moment, their journey had been north. Now they were heading west.

Untamed country slipped past the window—dense forests, countless lakes, swamps and so many rivers that it was water, not land, that dominated the landscape. Autumn held on tenuously. In the daytime, a jacket was enough to keep them warm. At night—well, they didn't plan to be there that night.

They came at last to Nikel. Oksana, Grisha and Victor climbed down the ladder from the carriage and a man in a border guard uniform greeted them. He helped Victor retrieve Oksana's bags.

He led them to a jeep with a raised canvas top, spread out a map on the hood and began to show them the way to A-1.

"It's about thirty miles," he said. "The road is treacherous, so take it slowly. If you stop anywhere, whatever you do, don't wander off into the swamp. We've had a lot of rain."

"We won't be stopping," he said.

The man showed Victor everything about the jeep—how to change the tire, use the winch and set the four-wheel drive. When Victor had absorbed all that, the border guard glanced at Oksana and Grisha and said, "I can't say that I approve of you driving there without escort."

"You have your orders," said Victor.

He nodded. "If you get in trouble, there are three checkpoints—" he pointed at the map "—here, here and here."

"How long will it take us to reach A-1?"

"Two hours."

Victor looked at his watch—2:30 P.M. Right on time.

Victor got in behind the wheel. Grisha sat on Oksana's lap in the passenger seat. The little boy was enjoying himself. The train trip, which had been an adventure, was now about to be eclipsed by a jeep ride.

The trip was harrowing. The forest pressed in so tightly against the sides of the narrow road that at times it felt as though two pine walls were joining to squeeze them. They forded a dozen rivers, taking the jeep axle-deep into the fast-moving water. At a particularly large stream, the current lifted the jeep and began to carry it downstream. Fortunately, the river basin rose slightly, and the tires caught the rocky bottom. Later, all four tires became mired in a muddy river bank. Victor looped a wire cable to a tree, and the jeep's winch pulled them out. They went on. Besides the rivers they forded, a dozen other larger rivers were spanned by flat wooden bridges so low they grazed the surface of the water. Many looked unsafe, and Victor got out a few times to inspect them. One bridge looked particularly dilapidated, and Victor instructed Oksana and Grisha to walk across while he carried the bags. He drove the empty jeep to the other side, and they repacked and went on.

All this adversity must have been included in the border guard's estimate of travel time, because exactly two hours after setting out, they pulled up to the final checkpoint, just a mile from A-1. It was 4:30 P.M., September 24.

Victor braked behind the checkpoint's wooden barrier and got out. The sun was low, and the temperature was dropping fast. As he greeted the border guard, his breath was visible in the chill air. The man checked their documents and then poked his head inside the jeep. He made Victor open one of the canvas bags, and he looked through it without much enthusiasm. He used a mirror on a long handle to examine the underside of the jeep.

After several minutes of this, he handed Victor their documents and pointed up the road. "A-1 is just ahead. The road's bad. Be careful."

They went on. The jeep never left second gear. After ten minutes, they crossed a small wooden bridge, came around a corner and there it was.

A-1.

Victor stopped about fifty feet from the fence and turned off the engine. They all looked at it.

In the forty years since A-1 had been built, fewer than fifty people had crossed over the border there, and those were mostly employees of the power station shared by the two countries.

Victor looked at it, and a strange loneliness engulfed him. Here was the edge of the Soviet empire. He felt as though he were peering over the side of a flat earth. As a boy, he had read countless stories portraying the border as a heroic place where brave men kept barbarians at bay. Victor didn't have to look hard to see that there was nothing heroic here.

Two barbed-wire fences stretched in parallel rows separated by about twenty feet of finely groomed sand. Directly in front of them was a simple sliding gate. Beside the gate stood a two-story guard tower topped by an observation post with a searchlight. The whole setup was so simple and obvious that a cattle rancher, given the job of designing border fortifications, could have come up with it. Behind the second gate, a stretch of asphalt drew a line as straight as a ruler through a pine forest. The trees had been cleared for twenty feet on either side of the path so Victor was able to gaze up it as though it were a wide Moscow avenue. The path ended about two hundred yards away at a third fence. A light shone in a hut there. Atop a tall pole, a red flag with a blue-and-white cross waved at them.

Norway.

Victor found the switch for his headlights and flashed them twice. A moment later, the floodlights on the Soviet tower flashed back at him.

"Did you see that?" Grisha asked wide-eyed.

Oksana stroked his head. "Sh, my sweet."

Dusk was falling now. Victor looked at his watch.

"Fifteen minutes," he said. "Everything's ready."

V i c t o r heard the helicopter before he could see it. The *thumpa-thumpa* of its mighty rotors seemed to come from within his rib cage. They all climbed out of the jeep and scanned the sky.

It came over the treetops a few seconds later. It hovered a minute and then descended. A wind storm kicked up around them, and they braced themselves. Grisha, who had been anxiously awaiting the helicopter, now began to cry. Oksana picked him up and talked to him gently.

"It's all right, little angel. Don't be frightened."

The skates touched down about twenty feet away on a grassy landing area. The helicopter's engine fell silent, and the wind from the rotors began to die down. Victor and Oksana started along the path toward the craft.

The door came open and a man in a military fur hat jumped out. A ramp was pushed through the door, and the man helped guide it to the ground. He waved for someone to come down. Anatoly Podolok came down the ramp carefully and turned and waved to someone still inside the craft.

Next came Anton. He was in a wheelchair pushed by a middle-aged woman. Victor caught her profile as she came down the ramp — forward-craning neck; a thin, straight nose; jaw stabbing ahead; hair bun. He grimaced. It was Yevgenia.

Victor said to Oksana, "I'll take Grisha."

Oksana handed over the boy, and they all walked toward Anton.

Anton's eyes stared blankly ahead. The skin on the left side of his face hung loosely over his skull. His mouth was partially open and his head tipped to one side. He looked catatonic.

Oksana knelt before him and took his hands into her own. Yevgenia stood over them, her hands on the grips. Podolok stood beside her.

At first, Oksana didn't say a word. She inspected Anton like a mother cat whose kitten has returned after having wandered off. Anton showed no sign that he knew her. After a minute, she took his face between her hands and kissed his forehead.

"I'm here, my love," she said.

Anton stared through her.

Yevgenia said, "Dr. Lazda says—"

"Shut up!" said Oksana.

Yevgenia's mouth opened with indignation, but she said nothing more.

Oksana stroked Anton's shaved head a minute. Then she put her head in his lap. She might have been crying; Victor couldn't tell.

Victor and Yevgenia stared at each other over top of the scene.

"Hi, Baba," said Grisha.

Yevgenia's face was stone.

"Why is Mommy crying?" Grisha asked.

Oksana lifted her head. "Come here, dear," she said sniffling. "I want you to meet somebody."

Victor put Grisha down and gave him a little push toward his mother. Grisha stepped forward bravely and leaned against Oksana as he faced Anton.

"Grisha, honey," said Oksana. "This is your father."

Grisha looked up at his mother puzzled. Victor could see his little three-year-old gears turning, absorbing this new fact. It was the same expression Grisha made when you laid a new food on his tongue. Grisha dropped his gaze to Anton.

He looked him over a minute. "Why are you in that funny chair, Daddy?"

Anton's eye twitched. It was just a twitch, but Victor saw it clearly.

Victor raised his head again to face his mother. "I thought you would come."

"Of course I came," she said. "You're my son."

"So is he," said Victor, motioning to Anton.

Yevgenia clucked her tongue. "I don't expect you to understand this."

"I understand perfectly, Yevgenia. You and your friends have come to arrest us."

"It didn't have to be this way," said Yevgenia. "I could have helped you if you had let me, if you had just stayed out of it."

"But I was already in it, don't you see? The moment Anton witnessed the shooting, we were all in it—you, me and Anton."

"I'll do everything I can to help you," she said.

"Like Anton?"

"Not like that."

Podolok spoke up. "You're right about one thing, Victor. The deal is off. No one is going to cross the border today. So let's begin with the diaries, shall we? Hand them over."

"I don't have them."

Podolok glared at Victor. He raised his hand as a signal. "Leo!" he called out.

From out of the helicopter, a small man with a finely trimmed beard jumped to the ground. His hands gripped a Kalashnikov machine gun.

Leo Yakunin came quickly toward them and stopped beside Podolok.

"Perhaps you'll give me the diaries now," said Podolok.

"I told you, I don't have them," said Victor.

"Victor, stop this foolishness," said Yevgenia. "Do as he says."

"Where's General Belov?" Leo asked Podolok.

Podolok frowned and looked toward the guard tower. It was dark, a monolithic silhouette against the forest. The sun had set, and the helicopter spotlight provided the only light.

Podolok turned anxiously to Yevgenia. "Where is he?"

She shook her head. "He should be here."

Victor smiled. "Your comrade is indisposed."

"What do you know about it?" snapped Podolok.

Victor turned and nodded at the guard tower. The floodlights snapped on, and instantly they were all bathed in a harsh, white light.

"I want you to meet some friends of mine," said Victor.

They all squinted into the light. Several silhouettes of men came toward them. Podolok put his hand over his eyes. Leo aimed his machine gun uncertainly in their direction. The figures drew nearer and took form.

First to come into view was Konstantin Tarasov. Then Katherine Sears. Then KGB Director Oleg Shatalin. Behind them, five more figures appeared out of the light, as though the light itself were creating people. Four of the men wore border guard uniforms and were armed with machine guns. The fifth figure was being led by them, his hands cuffed behind his back—General Yuri Belov. They stopped a few feet away.

"Comrade director Shatalin," Podolok stammered. "What are you doing here?"

"You are under arrest, comrade secretary," said Shatalin. "And so are you, comrade minister. Now, Leo, drop your weapon. It's over."

Leo stared at Tarasov in disbelief.

"What's the matter, Leo?" Tarasov said cheerily. "Seen a ghost?"

"You . . ."

"Drop your weapon!" said Tarasov.

Leo did.

Tarasov picked up the machine gun and stepped back.

"Whatever these people have told you is a lie," said Podolok. "I've been working to trap them, and now —"

"Tell it to the prosecutor, vlasovite!" said Shatalin.

Podolok paled. For a second, Victor thought the old man was going to have a stroke on the spot.

Suddenly to Victor's right came the sound of movement. He turned. Leo leaped at Grisha, who was still standing beside Anton's wheelchair. He scooped up the boy with his left arm and pressed a pistol to the boy's temple.

Oksana screamed and prepared to lunge for her son, but Leo cocked the pistol. The sound froze her.

"I'll kill the brat!" said Leo. "I swear!"

Grisha squirmed for a moment. Then, feeling the strength of Leo's grip, he gave up. He began to cry.

"Mommy!"

"Put down the gun, Leo," said Tarasov. "There's nowhere to run."

"I want to go across the border," said Leo. "Let me cross, or the brat gets it." He ground the barrel of the pistol into Grisha's temple.

"We can't allow that," said Shatalin. "You must know that."

Victor's eyes caught a small movement beside Leo. In the wheelchair, Anton was stirring. Anton's eyes darted back and forth blinking heavily, like a man coming out of a dream. Their eyes met, and they stared at each other a moment. Victor could see plainly the awareness behind his brother's eyes.

Anton's lips mouthed, "*Shh.*"

Victor looked away. His heart was pounding. He realized Anton was about to try something.

Leo was still talking to Shatalin. "I'm dead if I don't go across. What have I got to lose? And don't get any ideas, Konstantin. I can pump a round into the kid and maybe a couple more before—"

Leo never finished the sentence. Anton leaped out of his chair, and in a flash the two men were on the ground struggling for control of the gun. Grisha rolled free, and Oksana ran to scoop him up. Suddenly, Leo's pistol fired—*crack!*—and Anton collapsed. Oksana screamed. Leo got to his feet. Blood covered his coat. Anton's blood.

Nooooo!

Victor leaped at Leo's pistol hand. Leo easily sidestepped Victor's attack and aimed the gun point blank at Victor. He squeezed the trigger.

At that instant, Yevgenia Perova plowed into Leo's back. His hand was thrown up, and the shot exploded over Victor's head.

Leo went down on his chest, rolled onto his back and aimed his pistol at Yevgenia's chest. He fired. She dropped like a stone.

All at once, Victor, Tarasov and two of the border guards leaped onto Leo. They wrenched the gun from his hand and rolled him over. One of the border guards cuffed him and then dragged him to his feet by his armpits.

Victor and Oksana ran to Anton.

"I'm okay," Anton panted. "It just grazed the arm."

Victor shook his head in wonder. "Well done, brother," he said.

Anton winced and tried to smile.

One of the guards pushed Victor aside. "I'm a medic." He knelt to examine the wound.

Victor ran to Yevgenia. Tarasov and Katherine were already there.

"She's dead," said Tarasov. "Clean shot through the heart."

Victor fell to his knees beside his mother. *Yevgenia!*

Her eyes were closed, and there was no evidence in her face of the violence of her demise. Victor knew her face so well, the squareness of its frame, the delicate skin, and the creases in her forehead earned over decades of service to the communist state. It was strange to just stare at her the way a boy might stare at his mother, memorizing lovingly every pore of her complexion.

"She saved my life," Victor said.

Nobody seemed to know what to say.

In that instant, as Victor knelt over Yevgenia, all the bad receded—the summer of the puppies, her decision to commit Anton to a psychiatric hospital, her interrogation of Katherine Sears—and Victor felt like a boy who had come to his mother's bedside while she lay sleeping. Looking at her face then, he half-expected her to open her eyes and say, "What's wrong, Vitya?" "I had a nightmare, Mama." Then she would raise the blanket, and he would climb into her warm, safe arms. He would be asleep almost before his head touched the pillow.

A lump formed in his throat. She was his mother. And perhaps it was just a son's fancy but, in that moment, it seemed that, in death, her expression held something she had rarely seen in life.

Peace.

"*Do svidaniya, Mama,*" he whispered. *Good-bye, Mother.*

Shatalin came up beside them. "Podolok has disappeared."

Victor snapped from his reverie. "What?" He looked around.

"The border guards figure he ran off into the swamp," said Shatalin. "They're looking for him now."

The medic put a tourniquet on Anton's arm and lifted him back into the wheelchair.

"We have to get him to a hospital," said the medic.

Victor turned to Shatalin. "There's a doctor standing by in Norway," said Victor. "What's it going to be, comrade director?"

Shatalin looked uncertain. He seemed to be weighing his options one more time.

"They fulfilled their part of the bargain," said Tarasov.

"I can't let them just walk out of here," Shatalin said miserably.

"Let me make it easy for you," said Tarasov. "You have two choices. You can murder us all here and take the diaries, or you can go ahead with the deal."

Shatalin's gaze moved over Katherine, Oksana, Victor, Anton and Grisha.

"I am not a murderer," he said as though he wished he were.

One of the border guards came running back. He held Podolok's sable hat in his hand.

"What happened?" Shatalin asked. "Where's the Party secretary?"

"Swamp got him," said the guard, contemplating the hat. "Quicksand."

50

Katherine was still trembling from the shootings, but she was glad to be left alone momentarily with Tarasov. Something was bothering her.

"There's one thing I don't get," she said. "Why would Shatalin honor the agreement? Podolok's dead."

Katherine and Tarasov stood on the road not far from Victor's jeep. The KGB director had gone into the guard tower to phone the Norwegian post to warn them of the coming transfer. Oksana and Victor were in the tower with Anton and the medic. The border guards had Leo and Belov already aboard the helicopter. There was very little time left, and if Katherine was going to be the executor of Tarasov's devil's bargain then she wanted to understand everything about it she could. In a few minutes, the time for answers would pass — perhaps forever.

Tarasov smiled indulgently. "How little you've learned, Katherine. Shatalin is a patriot. He's protecting the motherland from an enormous embarrassment — a vlasovite traitor in the Politburo! Imagine if some historian found out that Thomas Jefferson had secretly conspired with the British during the Revolutionary War. Would you want that to come out, even if it were true?"

"I see your point," said Katherine. "But then why did you need us? You could have gone to him from the beginning."

"No," said Tarasov. "I knew about Podolok — that was in the diaries — and I deduced how Belov got involved. Yevgenia's involvement was a fluke, though I didn't know that until Victor showed me Anton's letter. What prevented me from acting was that I didn't know who my enemy was in the KGB. You helped me with that."

"Me?"

Tarasov nodded. "It was something you said. You told me the Americans disconnected their secured phone line because they figured out it had been tapped by the KGB."

"That's how the KGB knew I was in Ivanovka. And that I was aboard the *Estonia*."

"Aren't you forgetting something? Victor called the Americans *on the same phone line.* Victor told Cameron Abbott he had found Anton in Little Rock. Don't you see? That means the KGB knew about Anton two months ago. If so, why didn't Shatalin grab Anton back then?"

"Why?"

"Because Leo never told him," said Tarasov. "Leo had thrown in with Belov and Podolok."

Tarasov lit a cigarette and blew the smoke out thoughtfully into the frigid air. "Leo was always a good researcher, but his instincts were bad."

Victor strode to where they stood.

"How is Anton?" Katherine asked.

"He'll be okay. But we have to get him to a hospital."

He reached out and took Katherine's hand. Her pulse quickened at his touch. They stood like that a moment, and Tarasov seemed to sense that it was time for him to leave.

"Well, I have to go talk to Shatalin now," he said. "But first, Victor, I've been thinking — we may not be out of trouble yet."

"How so?"

"We never counted on Yevgenia's death. With her dead, the evidence on Podolok will be mailed automatically to the Politburo."

"I wouldn't worry about that," said Victor. His face was grim, and Katherine realized that, in spite of everything, he was grieving over his mother's death.

"Why? I thought she had it set up that way."

"She did. Podolok told me all about it. It was set up as a trust. In the event of her death, the file was to be sent to Anatoly Podolok's most bitter enemy on the Politburo, the man most certain to use the information to destroy him — Oleg Shatalin."

Tarasov laughed. "Now that's justice! Good thing Shatalin didn't know about it: He wouldn't have needed us at all. If you'll both excuse me, there are a couple more conditions I'd like to attach to this deal."

"A couple?" said Victor. "We agreed to just one."

Tarasov grinned and left.

"I wonder what he's up to," said Victor, watching him go.

But Katherine was looking at Victor, her face serious. "Why don't you come with us?"

"To America?" he asked. "I can't. Shatalin needs his hostage. Having me in the U.S.S.R. is the only way he knows none of you will ever talk. If you do, I'm a dead man."

"And if anything happens to you," said Katherine, "I will release the diaries. Yes, I know the deal. It's a stalemate. But that's not why you're staying."

Victor grimaced.

"You don't want to come," she said.

"It would be wrong for me to go."

"How can you say that? After all they've done to you."

"They?" he said sharply. He sighed and shook his head. "You know, Yevgenia wasn't always like she was at the end. I wish you could have seen her before. She really stood for something."

"The wrong thing."

"No," said Victor. "It started out right. She just got in over her head. I know it sounds kind of silly, but that was her biggest problem. She was a peasant, the daughter of a milkmaid-turned-seamstress. She had no education but Soviet propaganda. She built the myth of the Iron Perova, and then she was forced to live inside that suit of armor as though it were her natural skin."

The searchlight from the guard tower swept past them, and, slowly, Katherine's eyes adjusted to the darkness. She raised her head to the sky. The stars shone with such clarity they didn't seem real, like the dome of a planetarium. Victor followed her gaze.

"Quite a sky, yes?" he said.

Katherine nodded.

"This would be a great place for an observatory," Victor said.

"I see the Large Magellanic Cloud," said Katherine, pointing.

Victor nodded.

Katherine asked, "Will we ever finish our survey?"

"I'm afraid my star-gazing days are over, Yekatarina. My work is nearer to earth now."

Tears welled up in her eyes. She didn't know what to say. Victor kept his eyes on the stars as though he were trying to penetrate the mysteries he would now never get to confront.

That reminded Katherine of something. "You know what Vladimir Ryzhkov said to me the day he died?"

A shadow crossed Victor's face at the mention of his old friend. "What?"

"He said he hoped you never got angry at the Soviet government. He said you were perhaps the only person in the world who could bring down the Soviet state with his bare hands."

Victor didn't smile. "That's not what I want."

"What *do* you want?"

"What I want I can't have."

"What's that?"

"You."

Katherine began to cry. He took her in his arms, and they held each other without speaking.

Shatalin came beside them and cleared his throat. "Well, it's all arranged. The

Norwegians have a helicopter and a doctor standing by." He shook his head. "I can't believe I'm doing this."

Victor looked at Katherine and said, "It's time."

Victor left Katherine and went to the guard tower to get Anton, Oksana and Grisha. He found them with the medic, who had just finished bandaging the wound.

A few minutes later, they were all gathered at the gate: Katherine, Oksana, Anton, Grisha and Victor. Tarasov and Shatalin stood a few feet away. They were engrossed in the final terms of the arrangement. Shatalin had a look of disbelief on his face. Victor would have loved to have known what they were talking about. Victor wheeled Anton to the gate and said, "This is where we say good-bye, brother."

Anton looked up from his wheelchair. Anton's left arm was in a sling, and there was blood on his clothing, but there was no arguing that his twin brother had come back from the dark pit into which he had been thrown. Their eyes met. In that instant, Victor felt their childhood bond reforged. In his brother's eyes, Victor could see all the moments, large and small, happy and sad, they had spent together. Yes, even the summer of the puppies. Especially that summer, for in a strange, unlikely way it had propelled them like bullets toward this moment. That summer had encapsulated all the good and all the bad in their lives to reveal a timeless, subterranean nature of people and times, the way smoke reveals invisible air currents in a room.

"You could still walk me to the second gate, if you like," said Anton.

Victor shook his head and motioned toward Katherine. "I'm saving that for someone else." He grinned. "You understand."

Anton smiled and nodded. "Sorry I got you into this, brother. I guess you had to save me again."

"No, Anton. This time you saved me."

The solenoid in A-1's lock clicked, and Katherine Sears nearly jumped: She thought someone was shooting again. One of the border guards slid back the gate and ahead of her stretched a fifty-foot-long path to a second gate in a second fence. Beyond that lay the long walk to the third and final fence on the border with Norway. Two border guards with all of Oksana's bags went through the gate first, followed by Oksana, who was pushing Anton in the wheelchair. Grisha walked alongside his father chattering. Anton listened with a small smile on his lips. Katherine held back with Victor: They were waiting for a signal from Tarasov, who was still with Shatalin.

At last, Shatalin nodded, and Tarasov came over. Tarasov pulled two leather-bound books from his pocket and pressed them into Katherine's hand.

"You know what to do," he said.

Katherine slipped the diaries into her coat pocket, and then offered Tarasov her hand. Tarasov smiled at it, and then raised it to his lips. Then he turned and left.

Katherine watched him go. "He's full of surprises, that one. I can't quite figure him out."

Victor turned to the border guard. "I'm going to walk her to the next gate."

"Okay, but no further. You're in the forbidden zone now."

Victor took Katherine's hand and they went side by side along the path. Their route was bathed in the white glare of the tower's searchlight. Crisp shadows etched the asphalt before them. Outside the boundaries of the light, darkness closed around them like water rushing in behind a passing boat.

Katherine peered south into the darkness. Only a year earlier, Stepan Bragin had been gunned down at a point not far away. She shivered.

"What are you thinking about?" Victor asked.

"Stepan. How he must have felt in those last moments. What about you— what are you thinking?"

"I was remembering that line by Anna Akhmatova you quoted in the bell tower— 'Why does nothing work out for us?' "

"It's not been a normal relationship."

Victor didn't smile. "Do you know how the poem begins?"

She shook her head. He recited:

> We're no good at saying good-bye
> We wander around, shoulders touching.
> It's begun to get dark already,
> You look vacant, I say nothing.

"We'll still get to write," said Katherine.

Victor nodded. That was part of the arrangement. If the letters ever stopped, that was the signal that Shatalin had reneged. Katherine would then pass the diaries to the Politburo member Victor had selected as their best ally against Shatalin. He was part of a new generation of Soviet leaders. His name was Mikhail Gorbachev.

Victor was quiet. "I'll never see you again," he said finally.

"You don't know that," said Katherine.

"Oh, come now, Yekatarina. I'll never get an exit visa, and none of you can ever come back."

"Things might change," said Katherine.

"Not in Russia."

"They could."

They reached the second gate and halted. Victor shot Katherine a sideways grin.

"You're right," he said. "Things could change. But you know, we Russians are not exactly known for our optimism."

Katherine raised her head and laughed. The border guard looked at her as though she had lost her mind. In that grim place, with the floodlights, the machine guns and the barbed wire, her laughter was like an effrontery. It seemed to surprise Victor, too, but he joined in. Perhaps he hadn't expected her to get his little joke, delivered as Russian humor must be delivered: wry, dark and self-critical. But she had gotten it. She was thinking about Sergei Gusin and Maya Timofeyeva and Maxim Izmailov and Vladimir Ryzhkov and every Russian she had ever met who saw nothing in the future but bad, and worse. And so she laughed.

A few minutes later, when Katherine stood in Norway and looked back toward the Soviet Union, it occurred to her that she and Victor hadn't kissed farewell. With the rush to get Anton to a doctor, they had simply forgotten. Or had they? The laugh, she decided, was what they would always have. It was better than a kiss. For those few seconds, she and Victor had stood in a place that was neither East nor West, a place not unlike that band of forbidden zone across which she now looked, and they had shared a laugh.

What the hell, it was a start.

epilogue

July 5, 1991

51

R a i n fell lightly over the manicured grass and solemn headstones of Arlington National Cemetery. A collective hiss rose from the field like whispers of the dead.

In the southern corner of the cemetery, among the mature gravesites of veterans of World War II, one grave stood apart. It was freshly filled and growing muddy under the rainfall. Its plaque was shiny-new and read:

Donald Mortimer Turnhill
February 12, 1923–September 19, 1944

Katherine Sears stood beside the grave. She wore a black dress, a black trench coat and black pumps already soaked through from the long hike across the cemetery. Over her shoulder, she carried a backpack. She looked much as she had that day seven years earlier when she boarded the Aeroflot flight bound for Moscow, though a hint of crow's feet had begun to appear around her eyes, and her hair was cut short, in the style of the day.

Katherine would have liked to have attended the funeral the previous day, the Fourth of July. It was a star-spangled affair with a twenty-one-gun salute and a speech by a congressman. But how could she have explained her presence to the widow and their son, David? Katherine's role in the burial of Donald Turnhill would remain forever a secret.

She had read about the funeral in that morning's newspaper — "Missing WW II Flyer Comes Home." It gave an account of how the remains of a Rochester native had been found six months earlier by a farmer in a Belorussian cabbage field. In the spirit of good relations between friendly nations, the remains were returned to the Americans, over fifty years after his death in the Second World War. Katherine had checked the article's byline — Grayson Hines.

She stood a long time over the grave listening to the rain patter pleasantly on her umbrella. Then a voice came from behind her. It spoke in Russian.

"He's with Nadia now."

Katherine turned. Anton Perov came beside her. Oksana was a step back.

"He's buried in the land of his birth," said Oksana.

Katherine looked down at the grave and nodded. The deal with Shatalin had held up, though no one could have anticipated the way in which the final condition would ultimately be fulfilled. Gorbachev, glasnost, Victor Perov's election to the Supreme Soviet, the end of the Cold War—everything had changed, and so quickly! All Victor had to do to fulfill Stepan Bragin's final vow to Nadia was to compel Shatalin to place the remains in the cabbage field, and then make sure they were found. No one had to know how old Turnhill had been when he died. Why would anyone ask that question? Shatalin, also in the Soviet legislature, had no choice but to agree; he couldn't risk the diaries becoming public. For all his faults, he loved his country too much for that. Once Stepan's remains were found, the new spirit of friendly relations between the U.S. and the U.S.S.R. did the rest.

"Shall we get on with it?" asked Anton.

Katherine set down her backpack and took out a copper bowl and two leather-bound books, the diaries of Stepan Bragin. She put them in the bowl and then doused the books with lighter fluid until they were soaked through. The smell of kerosene stung Katherine's nose in the damp air.

They all stood over the bowl a moment looking down. Katherine was suddenly reluctant to go ahead.

She turned to Anton. "You're the only one who met him. You should do it."

Anton struck a match and dropped it in the bowl. The diaries burst into flame. They watched silently as the memoirs of Donald Mortimer Turnhill were reduced to ashes. It took several minutes, then Katherine dumped the ashes over the grave and put the bowl in her backpack.

It was done.

Oksana asked, "Are you heading straight back to Ithaca?"

"Actually, I thought I might come to New York City with you guys. I'd love to see Sergei—I hear he's in town on business."

"Was," said Anton. "He's gone back to Moscow."

Katherine shook her head in wonder. "He sure gets around."

Anton smiled. "He's a jet-set businessman now. No more black deals in the seat of his taxi."

Oksana said, "He told us he expects to be a dollar-millionaire by the end of August. Apparently, being a ruble-millionaire is nothing to aspire to anymore."

"Why August?" Katherine asked.

"He says there's going to be a coup."

"That's better than any newspaper report to me," said Katherine. "So, what's his latest scam?"

"Scrap metal from decommissioned submarines," said Anton.

Katherine rolled her eyes.

Oksana said, "Why don't you come to New York anyway, Katherine? Let us show you around."

Katherine smiled at that. Anton and Oksana had certainly had their share of difficulties adjusting to life in the United States, yet now they were offering to show *her* around New York. It was a good sign. She looked at them and thought of what an attractive couple they made—Oksana with her round, Slavic face; Anton with his dark hair and brooding, deep-set eyes, and, like his brother, the Iron Perova chin, thrust forward toward a shining future.

"That would be nice."

Katherine's eye caught something in the distance, a figure of a man watching them. Anton and Oksana followed her gaze.

"Who's that?" Oksana asked.

Katherine smiled. "I'll take care of him. You two go ahead."

Anton and Oksana left. Katherine and the man walked toward each other through the stones. At last, the man spoke.

"Dr. Sears!"

"Grayson Hines. Don't you ever quit?"

He grinned. "Nope."

"How did you find me?"

He shrugged. "I called you in Ithaca to get Victor Perov's new telephone number—I wanted a comment on his resignation from the Supreme Soviet. They told me you were in D.C. That seemed too much of a coincidence, so I decided to come down here and cover this Turnhill circus."

"No secrets," said Katherine.

"I'm a reporter. I believe secrets cause cancer. Now, tell me, how are you mixed up in this thing?"

"I gave you my story, Grayson, a long time ago."

"Not all of it."

Katherine shrugged.

Grayson smiled. "At least give me a comment on Victor Perov's resignation from the legislature."

"For the record?"

"Of course."

"It's marvelous."

Grayson groaned. "Oh, *please*. Victor is the man some people rate above Gorbachev in importance to the early days of glasnost. His short campaign as a dissident gave him a moral authority Gorbachev, the communist, will never have."

Katherine smiled. "I've seen your articles, Grayson. You have called him 'Gorbachev's guru,' and 'the conscience of the nation.' "

"Right! And now he says his work is done, and he's leaving politics to go back to *astronomy*? That can't be it."

"He and I have a survey of the Large Magellanic Cloud to complete."

Grayson sighed, exasperated. "Have you heard from him lately?"

"We spoke yesterday."

Grayson's eyes grew eager, and he took out a notebook and pen. "About what?"

Katherine thought about the conversation and grinned. "Put away your pen, Grayson. It wasn't a business call."

Grayson raised his eyebrows. "Oh, *really?*"

"Wipe that look off your face." She laughed. Then she turned and walked away, leaving Grayson Hines alone with a pen in his hand.

Katherine found the package beside her mailbox a few days after she got back from New York. It was a mailing tube postmarked "MOSCOW, RUSSIA."

She carried it inside and set it on the kitchen table. She assumed it was from Victor, but she couldn't imagine what he could be sending. She cut open the end of the tube and pulled out a large topographical map. Clipped to the map was a note from Konstantin Tarasov.

> *Dear Katherine,*
> *I know you've always wondered about the final condition I placed on Oleg Shatalin that night on the border. I thought it was time to finally clear up the mystery. It took him seven years, but the old general came through. See for yourself.*
> *Sincerely, K.V. Tarasov*

Katherine rolled out the map. Across the top it said "Oimyakon Province, Eastern Siberia. Survey Sector 44C-21F."

She studied it a long time. It was impossible to read, all wiggly lines, winding rivers and geographical names in Russian. She couldn't imagine what this had to do with Konstantin Tarasov. Then something caught her eye. A word had been circled along a tiny stretch of river that began on Suntar Ridge, where Stepan and Nadia had built their cabin. It was the name of a river. Katherine read it and laughed.

There on the map was written, "Reka Nadii," Nadia's River.

The River of Hope.